This was going to be a lot harder than he thought.

Why did she have to have eyes that penetrated the very depths of his soul, connecting with that spot he had purposely kept shut off for years?

He broke eye contact. He didn't want her or anyone else invading that private place. Nor did he want her coming home with him.

Think, Haydon! Maybe he could buy her a one-way ticket home and set her up here in a Prosperity Mountain hotel until the next stagecoach.

He scanned the mining town. Several men stood in front of the saloon with their arms crossed and their legs spread, gawking at Miss Devonwood as if they hadn't eaten in days and she were a fresh piece of meat.

His brother should be dealing with this. But with Jess injured, it was up to Haydon to do what he had to do to keep this woman safe.

No gentleman would do anything less. And if Haydon was anything, he prided himself in being a gentleman.

Most of the time anyway.

Debra Ullrick

and

Noelle Marchand

The Unexpected Bride
&
Unlawfully Wedded Bride

HARLEQUIN® LOVE INSPIRED® CLASSICS

ISBN-13: 978-1-335-45463-8

The Unexpected Bride & Unlawfully Wedded Bride

This edition published by arrangement with Love Inspired Books.

www.Harlequin.com

Printed in U.S.A.

CONTENTS

Debra Ullrick is an award-winning author who is happily married to her husband of over thirty-five years. For more than twenty-five years, she and her husband and their only daughter lived and worked on cattle ranches in the Colorado mountains. The last ranch Debra lived on was also where a famous movie star and her screenwriter husband chose to purchase property. She now lives in the flatlands, where she's dealing with cultural whiplash. Debra loves animals, classic cars, mud-bog racing and monster trucks.

Debra loves hearing from her readers. You can contact her through her website, www.debraullrick.com.

Books by Books by Debra Ullrick

Love Inspired Historical

The Unexpected Bride
The Unlikely Wife
Groom Wanted
The Unintended Groom

Visit the Author Profile page at Harlequin.com.

THE UNEXPECTED BRIDE

Debra Ullrick

Blessed is the man that trusteth in the Lord,
and whose hope the Lord is.
—*Jeremiah* 17:7

A ginormous thanks to my dear friends
Staci Stallings, Dennis Bates, Michelle Sutton,
Rose McCauley and Jeanie Smith Cash.
Your endless hours and invaluable input have
taught me so much and helped make this book so
much better. To my wonderful agent Tamela Hancock
Murray and my fabulous editor Emily Rodmell,
thank you for believing in me. To the friendly people
in Moscow, Idaho, who helped with my research,
thank you so much.

And a humongous thanks to my husband, Rick.
Thank you for always being there for me.
You truly are my hero, and I love you very much.

Last, but definitely not least,
to my Lord and Savior Jesus, thank You. You rock!

Chapter One

Paradise Haven, Idaho Territory
1874

If Rainelle Devonwood's mother knew what she was about to do, she would roll over in her grave.

Grave.

That one word ripped at Rainee's heart, but she refused to cry in the presence of the strangers surrounding her. She lowered her head and pressed her fingers over her eyelids in hopes of holding back the flood of tears.

Oh, Mother, you would be astonished to know what I have done. But even you would understand why I did it. If only you and Father were still alive. Then I would still be at home, living without pain and suffering. But, Mother. I had to leave. I just had to.

In the small confines of the dusty stagecoach, only one thing gave Rainee a measure of peace about her drastic decision—her betrothed had assured her he loved the Lord. Otherwise she would have never gone through with her plans to marry a complete stranger.

The uncertainty of what was about to take place, and

the constant cigar smoke from the gentleman sitting across from her, caused her stomach to become unwell. Rainee pressed her hand over her mouth and leaned her head out the window, silently praying the Lord would help her stomach's contents to settle and help to divert her attention elsewhere.

Dust crowded into her nose. *That is not quite what I had in mind, Lord.* She covered her mouth and sneezed. Her eyes started watering from all the dirt particles, but with her stomach still threatening to purge itself, she decided to deal with the discomfort a few moments longer. She blinked away the particles of debris from her eyes as she studied her surroundings.

Rolling green meadows disappeared into the forest at the base of the mountains. Blue skies stretched before her. Several yards away, a rabbit leapt high in the air and landed in the tall bunchgrass. It did the same thing three times. And each time Rainee giggled at its silly antics.

When her stomach stopped churning, she settled back into her seat.

The stagecoach hit a rut, yanking her body sideways and slamming her shoulder into the lady next to her. "I am so sorry, ma'am."

Sleepy eyes glanced at Rainee before sliding shut. How could the woman slumber through so much jostling? Rainee envied her.

Days and days of being jostled about, first on the train when she left Little Rock, Arkansas, and now even more so on the stagecoach heading to the Idaho Territory, were taking its toll on her overtaxed body. Rainee rolled her head from side to side, pressed her palm against her aching side, and shifted in the seat for the twentieth time in the past few minutes.

Horses' pounding hooves, jingling tack and squeaking leather were the only sounds she had heard for miles upon miles until Daniel, the stagecoach assistant, leaned his blond head near the window. "Only a few more minutes, folks, before we arrive at our destination."

A destination Rainee wanted to avoid but knew she could not because her very life and sanity depended on it.

Within minutes, she would soon meet her betrothed.

Her betrothed.

She still could not believe she was about to be married.

To a complete stranger.

But then again, if Haydon Bowen turned out to be even half as nice as his letters had made him sound, with the help of God's grace and a passel of mercy, her life might not end up so dreadful after all. Anything had to be better than her current situation.

Or was it?

A horrid thought fluttered through her mind. What if the man she was about to wed was not the gentleman he had portrayed himself to be?

Merciful heavens, what had she done?

You ordered what?

Haydon Bowen's own words rang through his brain like the continual clang of a church bell. How could Jesse, his own brother, do this to him, knowing he never wanted to marry again? Knowing marriage to his deceased wife had been a disaster. The hour-and-a-half ride from his family's ranch in Paradise Haven to the stagecoach stop in Prosperity Mountain had done little to abate his frustration. Anger over Jesse's latest outlandish scheme clung to him like trail dirt on a sweaty body.

After reining his draft horses to a stop, Haydon pressed his booted foot on the wagon brake. He sat stone still, dreading the task before him, wishing he could forget this whole thing and hightail it back to the ranch. But wishing wasn't going to change a thing. He raised his hat and wiped the sweat off his forehead with his shirt sleeve.

Knowing he couldn't put off the unpleasant mission any longer, he hopped down from the buckboard. As he went to wrap the reins around the brake handle he heard the stern sound of a woman's voice coming from the direction of the stagecoach platform. "Unhand me this instant."

"Aw, I jist wanna little bitty kiss." The man's barely intelligible words slurred together.

Haydon tied off the reins and headed around the corner of the depot to see what was going on. He rounded it just in time to see a petite lady in a frilly lavender dress kick some shoddy-looking man in the shin with the toe of her laced-up boot. It took Haydon so by surprise that he had to stifle a laugh.

"Ouch! Why you little—" Filthy words poured from the scruffy man's mouth. He yanked the woman close to his sweaty, grime-stained body, his face a mere inch from hers.

The woman managed to jerk back and swing her unopened parasol in a wide arc, striking the man's head. That only served to anger him more, and he yanked her close again.

He'd seen enough. Haydon leapt up the wooden step, took five steps to cross it, grabbed the man by the back of his shirt and shoved him away. "You heard the lady. Unhand her. Now!"

The man landed in a crumpled heap, but quicker than the snap of a whip, he darted back and rammed his head into Haydon's gut. All air fled from his lungs. He doubled over and struggled to pull in a breath. His hat slid from his head and onto the ground.

The man punched Haydon's face, causing him to stumble backward. Sharp pain pulled through his nose, and his eyes watered.

His attacker lunged toward him, but Haydon sidestepped him.

The man slammed against the wooden planks face-first.

Haydon jumped on him, yanked his arms behind his back, and pressed his knee between the man's shoulders.

Squirming, the man tried to break free, but Haydon held him in a tight grip.

"Ben! Pack your things and get out of town now!"

Haydon's gaze jumped up to a tall man with a shiny badge splayed against a black leather vest.

"I warned you if you caused any more trouble, I'd run you out of town. I mean to keep my promise. Now get out of here and don't ever show your face around here again."

Haydon stood and hauled the man the sheriff called Ben to his feet. When he released him, the only way to describe what he saw in his beady eyes was evil intent. It tried to curl its way around Haydon, but he shook it off like he would a snake crawling on his hand.

"This won't be the last you'll hear from me," Ben

hissed. He scooped up his sweat-stained hat and slammed it on his greasy head. "You an' yore lady friend'll be sorry you ever messed with me!"

"That's enough!" The sheriff aimed his pistol at Ben's heart and cocked it. "Whether you go peacefully or draped over a saddle makes no difference to me. The choice is yours." Wrinkles gathered around the lawman's narrowed eyes, and his burly mustache buried his lips.

Haydon swung his gaze between the sheriff and Ben, not at all sure that he and the lady weren't about to witness a deadly showdown at point-blank range.

"I'm goin', I'm goin'," Ben spat as he lifted his hands in the air.

The lawman gave a quick jerk of his head and gun, motioning Ben forward. The two of them headed down the boardwalk. Their boots clunked against the wooden planks, and neither of them looked back.

Haydon relaxed his shoulders for a full two seconds, until he remembered the lady. He let out a quick breath and turned toward her. Seeing her stooped over, he snatched up his hat and hurried over to her. "Are you all right, Miss?"

Like a well-trained woman of society, she rose gracefully and faced him. Having grown up with the socially elite, he recognized one when he saw one. And she was definitely one.

"Yes, sir, I am." Her lavender plumed hat tilted back, and she looked up at him. "Thank you for rescuing me."

Haydon's pulse throbbed in his ears and his breath hitched. Staring up at him were the most beautiful brown eyes he had ever seen, soft as a doe's hide. The color reminded Haydon of a whitetail fawn, complete with white specks. Thick but not overly long lashes spread across her eyelids. And that Southern accent. It skipped across his heart before drilling right down into him.

"Merciful heavens. Your nose is bleeding." She opened the little beaded bag hanging from her wrist, pulled out a lace hanky and raised it toward his nose.

He yanked his head back. "Don't soil your hanky." He reached into his inside vest pocket and removed his handkerchief, then pressed it against his nostrils, ignoring the pain the gesture produced. Confident he'd gotten all the blood, he folded his handkerchief and shoved it back into his vest.

"I am so sorry, sir, you were injured on account of me."

"Don't worry about it. I'll be fine."

She studied him for a moment, and he squirmed under her scrutiny. "Would you happen to be Mr. Bowen?" Her drawn out words, mixed with a tremor, snapped Haydon back to reality. No matter how beautiful she was, she was still a woman. The last time he had fallen for a beautiful woman, not only had he ruined her life, but also his.

He slammed his hat onto his head and stepped back. "Yes, ma'am. I'm Haydon Bowen."

She daintily clasped her skirt and curtsied. "It is a pleasure to meet you, sir. I am Rainelle Victoria Devonwood. But please call me Rainee."

He knew his eyes had to be popping out of their sockets, but he couldn't help himself. *This* little beauty placed an advertisement for a husband? Someone who looked like her and bled confidence? His eyes narrowed. What was wrong with her that no one had claimed her for his own? *She's a woman, Haydon. That's reason enough.*

Slanting her pretty little head, she blinked several times before her eyes snapped onto his. Innocence clothed her face, making her even more of a threat.

This was going to be a lot harder than he thought. Why did she have to have eyes that penetrated the very depths of his soul, connecting with that spot he had purposely kept shut off for years?

He broke eye contact with her. He didn't want her or anyone else invading that private place. Nor did he want her coming home with him. *Think, Haydon, think fast.* Maybe he could buy her a one-way ticket home and set her up in a hotel here in Prosperity Mountain until the next stagecoach came around.

He scanned the mining town. Several men stood in front of the saloon with their arms crossed and their legs spread, gawking at Miss Devonwood as if they hadn't eaten in days and she was a fresh piece of meat. Prosperity Mountain was definitely no place to leave a lady without an escort. Women were scarce around these parts, and too many men were less than honorable. From what he had experienced, the place overflowed with raucous silver miners and thieves who wouldn't hesitate to steal a person's silver or something even more valuable—a woman's virtue.

With a sideways glance, he battled with what to do. Frustration toward Jesse for putting him in this mess seeped through his mind again like a deadly poison. His brother should be dealing with this. Not him. But that wasn't going to happen. The sight of Jess unconscious on the floor of the barn slashed through Haydon, and he detested Jess all the more for making him so angry he had lost his composure, and flanked his horse. Haydon knew better than to touch a horse's flank; spurring that tender spot between a horse's ribs and hips was bad enough, and yet he had not only kicked it without meaning to, he had also hit it hard enough that it caused Rebel to rear and knock Jesse unconscious. Haydon still felt badly about that.

With Jess injured, it was now up to Haydon to do what he had to do to keep this woman safe. No gentleman would do anything less. And if Haydon was anything, he prided himself on being a gentleman. Most of the time anyway.

His chest heaved at the idea of being in such close proximity to the flaxen-haired beauty on the long ride back to the ranch. It was the last place he wanted to be. But he would not leave her here, not even to save himself the trouble.

Rainee locked her knees to keep them from giving out. What kind of ruffians filled this desolate land anyway? Why, if Mr. Bowen had not come along when he had, she did not know what might have happened to her. Just thinking about it made her shudder.

As he stared forward, Rainee took the opportunity to study him. Her gaze landed on his arms.

Arms that had easily plucked away her attacker.

Mountainous arms that drew her attention and admiration.

Rainee knew she should look away, knowing if her mother were here, she would reprimand her for her blatant impropriety. But she found she could not help herself. Nor did she want to. The bulges beneath his pale blue shirtsleeves captivated her attention as did the width of his broad shoulders and chest.

Her eyes moved to his firm jaw, and she watched in fascination as the muscle in his jaw worked back and forth. Something about the strength of it set her heart all aflutter.

"Do you need anything before we go, Miss Devonwood?"

She whipped her gaze up to his eyes. Warmth rushed to her cheeks. From the icy tone of his voice, he must have seen her gawking at him.

Perhaps he was agitated because of her blunder in telling him to call her by her Christian name. That was far too forward of her, even if this man was to be her husband. Would she ever learn?

How she despised all those ridiculous rules of etiquette and propriety. Aristocratic rules her British father insisted they follow and her Southern mother had taken pride in enforcing. But, she refused to distress herself further about her social blunder because there was nothing she could do about it now anyway.

"It's a good hour and a half before we get to Paradise Haven. Would you like to get something to eat before we head out?"

Rainee loved the deep sound of his voice. Even though his mannerisms at present were somewhat aloof, some of her doubts about coming here eased. After all, Mr. Bowen had rescued her from that vile man with the overpowering stench and yellow teeth. Not to mention his looks were far superior to those of any man she had ever encountered. Granted, she knew from experience looks could be deceiving, but still, his sapphire eyes and blond hair were quite pleasing to her eyes. In fact, the color reminded her of her father's eyes. Immediately Rainee regretted the comparison. Her heart yearned for her father—to be held in his arms again and to feel the security his protection and love provided.

The back of her eyes stung, but she plucked up her courage, knowing crying would solve nothing.

She forced herself to focus on the gentleman in front of her. "Thank you, but no. I am fine, sir." Even if she had need of anything, it would be far too humiliating to inform him she was penniless because some scoundrel at the last stagecoach stop had stolen her money. Good thing she had already purchased her ticket for the last trek of her journey. Otherwise she shuddered to think what might have become of her.

For the millionth time, Rainee wished she had secured her funds underneath her skirt. Her personal maid and dear friend Jenetta had advised her to do so, but once again Rainee's stubbornness had overruled any such logic.

Many times her father had warned her that her stubbornness would get her into trouble one day. He feared he would not be able to secure a husband for her because of her flawed temperament. Inwardly Rainee sighed. So far, Father was right. Well, that was not entirely accurate. Many a man had pursued her. Not because of any burst of feeling toward her but because of her father's money. Except one man. And she would rather go live with savage Indians than marry him.

Mr. Bowen cleared his throat. She looked up at him.

"That your trunk?"

"Yes." Rainee glanced at the medium-size chest containing everything she owned. With a weighty sigh, she decided to not think about what and whom she had been forced to leave behind. It was all too vexing. And so was this man's aloofness toward her. Gone was the warmness his letters contained. Perhaps his journey had tired him. That she understood. Tiredness had seeped into her bones until every part of her ached with fatigue.

She watched him lift the trunk as if it weighed no more than one of the plumes on her hat. He stepped off the platform and headed around the corner of the stagecoach stop. Rainee followed him, careful to keep her eyes anywhere but on his retreating form. One glimpse of his leg muscles had been enough to make her chastise herself for acting like a wanton woman instead of the lady she had been brought up to be.

Once her belongings were secured on the wagon, he headed to the front of the buckboard where she stood, and he extended his hand.

Rainee glanced at his large palm, admiring the strength of it, then looked up at him. Impatience covered his face. She quickly placed her satchel and parasol on the wagon seat, then settled her hand in his, allowing him to help her onto the wagon. She arranged the bustle of her dress and sat, then snatched her satchel and parasol off of the seat and placed them in her lap. "Thank you, sir."

He responded with a curt nod.

Turning her head away from him, she suppressed the urge to roll her eyes and whistle away the awkwardness. She knew their meeting would be uncomfortable, but she had not anticipated it being quite this bad. Then again, what did she expect? That the moment he laid eyes on her, he would declare his undying love and sweep her off her feet, and they would live happily ever after?

Hah. In a pig's eye. She shuttered at the expression. It must be the length of the trip or the hot sun or the man readying the horses and the wagon—something—because every thought she had was taking her places she did not want to go.

Besides, those kinds of things only happened in the dime novels she and her best friend used to sneak into her room and read. Until the day her mother had discovered them. After a long lecture, she forced Rainee to toss them into the fire. It broke her heart watching the edges curl into black ashes. They were her only reprieve from the stuffy social world she lived in, a world overrun with rules of proper etiquette, rules she had a hard time obeying because they all seemed so meaningless and empty.

The wagon seat dipped, jolting Rainee's mind from past shadows. She looped the handle of her satchel over her wrist and opened her parasol, careful to keep it out of Mr. Bowen's way. Careful to keep herself out of his way as well.

His arm brushed against hers, and his broad shoulders took up a goodly portion of the now cramped seat.

Leather, trail dust, and a scent that reminded her of her father after he had shaved drifted up her nostrils. More reminders of home. A home that no longer existed.

Once again, she could not believe she was about to marry a complete stranger. One *she* had placed an advertisement for. That act alone was scandalous. Claws of dread pierced her insides as she realized once again what she had done. The need for air threatened to swallow her up, but she sat up straighter and fought for every breath. No fainting spell would overtake her. Not this time. Though they had been a problem in the past, she vowed as of this moment she would fight them with all her might.

Mr. Bowen snapped the reins. The wagon lurched forward and Rainee clutched the side of the seat to keep from jostling into him, but her shoulder collided with his anyway, and their eyes connected and held for the briefest of moments.

Long after he turned away, however, the memory of his eyes the color of sparkling sapphires stayed with her. Eyes that were handsome but held no warmth. Only a sort of detachment and something else she could not identify. This was going to be a very long ride indeed.

Haydon couldn't wait to deliver the woman to his brother. This well-bred, beautiful woman sitting next to him was the kind he now avoided like poison ivy because they were shallow and cared about nothing but fancy balls and frippery. Appearance and financial status were everything to them. And he'd had his fill of that type of woman.

"Mr. Bowen."

He wanted to ignore her but his conscience and upbringing wouldn't allow him to be rude. "Yes?" Haydon gave her a quick glance.

"You said in one of your letters you lived in Paradise Haven with your family."

His body tensed. He didn't write those letters, so he had no idea of their contents. No knowledge about what her response had been. What her advertisement was about. Haydon shifted his weight and ran his thumbs over the leather reins.

He looked toward the mountain dotted with several clapboard buildings and mining shafts as he struggled with what to say or do, wishing he could flee into one of those mines and hide out until this whole mess was over and done with.

"Would you mind telling me about them?" Her soft voice was a tad shaky, but her asking spoke of a confidence he couldn't deny.

He let out a breath of relief. At least that he could answer. "My brother Jesse is twenty." He glanced at her, then back at the dirt road. "His wife's name is Hannah. They're expecting their first child in a few months. They have their own place on the ranch. My brother Michael is sixteen. My sister Leah is thirteen and Abby is five. They live in the big house with my mother."

"What about you? Where do you live?" Words poured from her mouth like thick honey. Sweetness and innocence surrounded this woman. This woman he wanted to get away from as quickly as possible, he reminded himself. Even though she seemed harmless enough, he knew just how deceiving appearances could be. His former wife Melanie had taught him that. The dread of going through something like that again twisted his gut tighter than a three-stranded rope.

"I have my own place on the ranch." Concerned she would start asking him more questions, he decided to ask her about her home life instead. He only prayed it wasn't something she had already shared in the letters or her advertisement because then he would have to inform her that he wasn't the one who had sent for her. And he wasn't going to do that. That was Jesse's job. "What part of the South are you from?" he asked, keeping his eyes forward.

* * *

Talons of fear scraped up and down Rainee's body. How did he know she was from the South? She had not told him that in her letters or her advertisement. She had even gone so far as to have one of her friends post her letters and advertisement in Chicago.

What should she tell him? Not one to tell falsehoods, she would have to choose her words carefully. She gathered her courage and forced herself to look at him.

"I'm sorry. Perhaps you aren't from the South. I just assumed with your accent that you were. But then again—" he rubbed his chin "—your mannerisms remind me of some of our neighbors back East. They were British."

Rainee's muscles relaxed.

"My Father was raised in England, and my mother was raised in the South." Before he could ask her any further questions, she plucked up her courage to say what she had wanted to say back at Prosperity Mountain. "Mr. Bowen, I know you must think it quite strange for a woman to post an advertisement in search of a husband. But please believe me when I say I had no other choice."

Her brother had seen to that.

Chapter Two

"Mr. Bowen? I am sorry to disturb you, but could I trouble you to stop? I am in need of a break."

He looked at her flushed face and the damp tendrils of hair clinging to her cheeks. "I'm sorry. I wasn't thinking straight. I should have let you rest a while before we left Prosperity." Remorse for his ungentleman-like manner and his inconsideration doused him with shame.

With her head tilted off to the side, questioning eyes peered out from under the brim of her hat. Sensing it took a lot for her to ask, he wanted to put her at ease. "I could use a break myself. Whoa, Lulu. Whoa, Sally." He pulled on the horses' reins. The tack jingled and the wagon creaked as it came to a stop.

He hopped down and set the brake, then wrapped the reins around it.

The woman beside him rose and closed her parasol, leaving it and her handbag on the seat before moving toward him.

He reached up toward her. When she placed her hands on his shoulders and he sprawled his hands around her small waist, feelings long buried deep inside him poked through the protective wall he'd built around his heart.

He hurried to set her down and once he knew she was stable on her feet, he extradited himself from her as fast as possible.

"Thank you." Her gaze trailed toward a small creek. "Please excuse me."

As much as his gut wanted him to, he couldn't leave her to traverse the rocky ground by herself. Thin rock and rough terrain wouldn't bode well with her fancy dress. Haydon retrieved two canteens from the back of the wagon. "Allow me to help you." Even though he didn't want to touch her again, he slung aside the turbulent feelings raging inside him and clutched her elbow to steady her.

When they reached level ground, ground devoid of rock, he released her elbow. The cluster of pine trees brought a welcoming reprieve from the hot sun.

He filled their canteens with river water and handed her one. She twisted the lid and tilted it up, taking a long drink. His gaze landed on her sleek, graceful neck. She leaned over and refilled her canteen, then dipped her hanky into the tepid water and daintily blotted her face and neck.

What a vision she was. A lady of poise and grace. The epitome of femininity.

Quicker than a flash, an image of Melanie invaded his mind, bringing with it all the bad memories. Memories he'd rather forget.

That Jess, he groaned inwardly. *It's all his fault I'm even thinking about Melanie again. Well, buddy boy, nothing will induce me to get involved with a woman again. Nothing.*

The sooner he got this task over with the better. When he got back to the ranch, he'd hand her over to Jesse to deal with.

To distract himself, he unscrewed the lid on his canteen and pulled in a long drink.

Minutes later, after they'd finished taking their break, he steadied her again until they reached the wagon.

She pointed toward the hillside and asked, "Would you mind if I pick some of those red and yellow flowers to take to your mother?"

Did she have to be so sweet on top of being beautiful? That combination was the worst kind to lure a man in. But he couldn't turn her down. His mother loved flowers and thoughtful gestures like that.

"Sure." He took her canteen and put both of them back into the wagon.

Making sure she didn't slip on the small pile of thin rocks, he held her hand until she stepped over them.

She leaned over and broke the long stem off at the bottom and studied the bloom before she placed the flower under her nose and smiled. "These are quite lovely. What are they?"

"Red columbines. My mother's favorite."

She darted her gaze up at him and her face beamed, even though he had seen her fatigue just moments before.

She started gathering more and stopped only to dab the sweat off her forehead.

Haydon couldn't bear to watch her suffer, so he jumped in and helped her. When they had a nice bouquet, they headed back to the wagon.

He grabbed his canteen and opened it, then retrieved

his handkerchief from his pocket and saturated it with water. “Hand me the flowers.”

She gave them to him, and he wrapped the soaked cloth around the stems. “That will help keep them until we get to the ranch.”

“Thank you.” Her smile lit up her face. She really was sweet.

Not liking that train of thought, he quickly helped her into the wagon, climbed up himself and down the road they went. A road that now seemed longer than it ever had been before. Having her sitting next to him had him squirming like a worm. The sooner he got them to the ranch, the better.

Rainee glanced at the flowers in her lap. It was very thoughtful of him to help her gather them and then help preserve them until she could give them to his mother. Her own mother never tired of getting fresh bouquets of flowers, and Rainee loved seeing her smile. How delightful it was to be able to do something nice for Mr. Bowen’s mother, too.

Soon she would be her mother also.

Her heart smiled with joy.

Rainee cut a sideways glance at him. Whatever it took, no matter how uncomfortable or how hard things became, she would make this situation work. Fear would not dissuade her from doing anything less. Besides, she had no other choice.

When the beatings became more severe, life-threatening even, after months of praying, she and Jenetta had concocted this plan of escape. Good thing their strategy had worked. Because the night she had fled she overheard her brother’s scheme to sell her to their fifty-eight-year-old neighbor—the repulsive Mr. Alexander, or Mr. Gruff as she called him. They were to wed that next day. Just thinking about it made her tremble. That man was cruel to his very soul. Just like her brother, Ferrin.

Thank You, Lord, for guiding my steps and for delivering me from Ferrin's wicked plans. Help me to be a good wife to Mr. Bowen. And if You would be so kind, would You please delay the wedding ceremony to give us a little time to get to know each other before we wed? Thank You.

Rainee hoped God would especially answer her prayer about getting to know each other first because her intended was obviously a man of few words. And even fewer smiles. What if he was cruel like her brother? That thought frightened her. God have mercy on her if she had left one boiling pot for another. Or, she gulped, something worse.

She blocked out the distressing thoughts from her mind and took in the view around her. Several head of magnificent spotted horses grazed in a grassy meadow, which seemed to go on for miles. A frolicking black foal with a white spotted rump bucked and kicked and nuzzled its matching mother. A deep longing to spend time with her mother and to be a carefree child again bled deep into her soul, but self-pity would not change the past. She dragged her slumped shoulders into an upright position, determined to make the best of her new situation.

Farther up the road, she noticed a herd of pigs. She closed her eyes and cringed against the thousands of fingernails scraping their way up her spine. A deathly fear of the four-legged beasts had always plagued her, and she loathed the stench that accompanied them. Her nose wrinkled, and her mouth twitched just thinking about the offensive odor.

To get her mind off of the wretched creatures, she turned her attention onto an amazing cluster of lavender blooms covering the wide-open field. Curiosity got the best of her. "Mr. Bowen?"

He glanced at her, then back at the crusted road. "Yes?"

"Those purple flowers over there…" She pointed toward the field overrun with the fragile flowers. "What are they, please?"

"They're Camas plants."

"Camas?" Rainee tilted her head and shifted her parasol so she could look at him.

"Yes."

"Are the pigs eating them?"

"Yes. They love them." He looked out over the fields. "In fact, the hogs love the Camas bulbs so much the people around here actually call this place Hog Heaven." He glanced at her. "Informally, that is." His masculine lips curved into a smile.

And what a beautiful smile it was. She wished she could see more of them. If only she knew how to make that happen. But at present, that seemed improbable.

"What a dreadful waste of such lovely flowers."

"It's not a waste. The Camas bulbs are the only thing that helps the hogs survive the rough winters here in Paradise Haven. They're about the only animal that can survive the winters here. For now anyway." He glanced at her, then back at the herd of swine. "But, I've heard tell the railroad will be coming through here sometime soon. That'll make it easier to get supplies to feed cattle through the winter so they won't starve."

Just how bad did the winters get here anyway? Although she wanted to ask, she also wanted to know more about the fascinating Camas plant. "Are they only edible to hogs?"

"No, humans can eat them, too."

"Are they native to this area?"

"No. Farmers from back East brought them with them when they moved here." The reins jiggled in his hands as he twisted his head toward her. "I'm sure glad they did."

She wondered why he was glad, but nothing more was said. She also wondered how much farther it would be before they would arrive at his place. Her arms ached from holding her parasol upright, but every time she lowered it, the hot sun burned through the fabric of her jacket.

Minutes later, at the base of a mountain, they rounded a clearing in the trees. A very well-kept, large, two-story clapboard house flanked by long windows with white shutters came into view.

Rocking chairs, small tables and a porch swing sat under a covered porch, making it look quite welcoming. Off to the left of the house, a makeshift scarecrow on a stick watched over a large garden.

Nestled up against the trees set two smaller but generous-size clapboard homes. They, too, had covered porches, a swing, rocking chairs and small tables—and were equally adorable as the larger house.

A young girl with blond braids skipped around the corner of the house. As soon as she spotted them, she hastened their direction. "Haydon! You're back," she hollered and slowed her pace when she neared the horses. "Did you brung me anything?"

Haydon laughed.

Rainee liked the deep rumbling sound.

"You're too spoiled for your own good, Squirt. I hate to disappoint you, but I didn't *bring* you anything. I didn't go to town for supplies."

The little girl scrunched her brows and looked up at Rainee. "Who're you?"

"Abigail. Mind your manners." Mr. Bowen stepped on the brake and tied off the reins before jumping down.

"Sorry." She lowered her head, her long braided pigtails reaching down her green cotton dress.

He ruffled the little girl's hair, then turned and extended his arms toward Rainee. Situating her belongings out of the way, she laid her hands on his shoulders and allowed him to help her down.

The instant her feet touched the ground he removed his hands from her waist and stepped back as if she had bitten him.

"Miss Devonwood." Haydon looked at her, then at the small child. "This is my sister Abby. Abby, this is Miss Rainelle Devonwood."

Rainee smiled down at the girl with the blond hair and sapphire eyes so like her brother's. "It is a pleasure to meet you, Abby." She gave a quick curtsy as was customary back home when greeting someone. "But please, call me Rainee."

"Nice ta meet ya, too, Rainee. I like the way you talk."

"I like the way you talk, too. You have a lovely accent."

"I dun't got no assent."

"Accent," Mr. Bowen corrected her again.

"That's what I said. Assent."

Rainee waited to see if he would correct her again, but he shook his head and mussed her hair once more.

"Haydon. You're mussing my hair." She planted her hands on her waist and narrowed her eyes, but even Rainee could see the smile in the young girl's frown.

"Sorry, Squirt."

"Thas okay." Abby smiled at her brother, then glanced over at Rainee. Her brows curled, and her forehead criss-crossed. "Whach you doin' here?"

"Never you mind, Little Miss Nosey." Haydon tapped his little sister on the nose and winked. "Listen, Squirt, would you do me a favor and run over to Jesse's and ask him to come here?"

Abby bobbed her head and darted off toward Jess's house.

Haydon wasn't sure if his brother was able to be up and about yet, but if he was, then he needed to get his sorry backside out here and deal with this awkward mess.

Without looking at Miss Devonwood, he wondered what he should do or say before his brother got there.

"The place is quite lovely." A whisper would have been louder, but the awe in her voice screamed loud and clear.

Haydon scanned the ranch, trying to see the place through her eyes. He always thought this area was some of the most beautiful country he'd ever seen, but for some odd reason it pleased him that she thought so, too. *Oh-h-h no you don't, buddy. Who cares what she thinks? She's not staying.*

"Who lives in that house?"

He followed her finger. “My brother and his wife.” *The brother that sent for you. But he can tell you that. Not me.*

“And that place?” She pointed to his house.

“That’s mine.” *As in mine alone. As in, not yours and mine.*

She faced the main house. “Then this must be your parents’ home.”

“It’s my mother’s.”

She turned questioning eyes up at him.

Quit looking at me with those beautiful peepers, ma’am. “My father passed away a couple of years ago.”

Sympathy passed through her gaze, and he forced himself to look away. “Oh, my. I am so sorry.” She laid her hand on his arm. Something about her gentle touch sent warmth spreading through his veins.

He stared at the spot where her hand rested. The gesture touched him, but at the same time it sent warning signals flashing through his brain. Her politeness and sweetness were driving him crazy. He dropped his arm to his side, letting her arm slip from his. He didn’t want to feel any kind of a bond to this woman—or any other woman for that matter.

Then he made the mistake of once again looking at her face. Hurt and discomfort gazed back at him. She looked so small and vulnerable. Guilt trailed through him like hungry red ants at a picnic, chewing away at his conscience. His thoughtless gesture had hurt her, and she didn’t deserve the treatment he had dealt her. But then again, he had to protect himself. He needed to harden himself against the emotions she seemed to stir up in him so easily. Emotions he wanted no part of. The sooner Jesse dealt with her, the better. *Just keep telling yourself she's not your problem, Haydon, and you just might survive this situation with your sanity and heart still intact.*

He turned toward Jesse's place, wondering where Abby was and what was taking her so long.

"Excuse me, please?"

As much as he didn't want to, Haydon faced her again. "Yes?"

Her eyes locked on his for the briefest of moments before her lids fluttered, and she looked toward Jesse's house. "Is Abby the only one who does not know why I am here?" She turned those wide innocent fawn eyes up at him again, and his heart lurched.

The last time Haydon saw a look like that was on a puppy he'd owned as a child. That puppy had won his heart and had gotten whatever it wanted. Haydon swallowed hard. *Rainee's not a puppy. She's a woman. And not just any woman. She's the most dangerous kind there is. Sweet and innocent-looking, and beautiful.* "Miss Devonwood, I—"

"Haydon!" Abby's voice carried across the yard.

Haydon wanted to hug his sister for saving him. He spun her direction and watched as she ran toward him.

"Jesse got hurted this mornin' and he can't come."

His heart dropped to his boots. He had hoped Jess would at least feel well enough by the time he got back that he could deal with Miss Devonwood. Now what?

"How come I didn't know he got hurted?"

"Hurt, not hurted," Haydon corrected. "Because you, Mother and Leah were gone all day, remember?"

Abby hiked her little shoulder. "I forgetted."

"I *forgot*."

"Did you forgetted too?" Her round eyes smiled up at him.

"No, I didn't forget. You said… Oh, never mind. Why don't you run along and go play now?"

"Okay." She skipped back toward the corner of the house and disappeared.

Haydon turned toward the sound of Miss Devonwood's twitter.

Her gaze lingered in the direction Abby had gone.

"Just what do you find so amusing, Miss Devonwood?"

Rainee reeled toward him and blinked. Amusement, not anger, fluttered across his handsome face. "Abby is lovely." She stared at the spot where the little girl had disappeared. "To think that precious girl is going to be my sister is so—" Rainee's eyes flew open and hot blood rushed into her cheeks. She pressed her fingertips to her mouth to stifle her gasp.

Merciful heavens! What is wrong with you, Rainelle? Since you got here, he has not mentioned the subject of marriage even once, and here you are talking about Abby being your sister. No wonder Mother had to rebuke you so often. Will you ever learn? She gazed longingly at the forest of trees, wishing she could flee into their thickness and hide away forever.

She turned and retrieved her parasol, handbag and the flowers from the bench seat.

"Haydon. Where have you been all day?"

Rainee whirled toward the big two-story house. A tall, lithe woman strolled toward them and stopped directly in front of her.

The handsome blonde lady with powder-blue eyes

looked up at Haydon and quirked one delicate eyebrow. "Sorry, I didn't know we had company."

"Mother, this is—"

When he stopped speaking, Rainee looked up at him, wondering why he quit talking. Obviously he was not going to say anything more, so Rainee took matters into her own hands. She turned her attention to his mother. "Good afternoon, ma'am." She curtsied. "I am Rainelle Victoria Devonwood."

"Good afternoon, Miss Devonwood. I'm Katherine, Haydon's mother." Katherine looked perplexed as she glanced from Rainee to Haydon and back again.

"It is a pleasure to meet you, Mrs. Bowen."

"Please call me Katherine. We don't stand on ceremony out here. Feel free to address all of us on a first-name basis."

Rainee looked at Mr. Bowen. Mother had always made it clear a man should never call a woman by her given name unless they had known each other for a long time or were courting. Neither one fit this scenario.

His jaw worked back and forth again, but after a few seconds, he glanced at her. "Mother's right. Call me Haydon."

Relief drizzled over her like a warm summer rain. One more detestable rule of etiquette she would not have to follow out here. Mother and Father would not approve of her choice to call someone by their first name, but Rainee loved it. It was much more personable.

"Thank you, Haydon." Using his Christian name felt quite strange and yet lovely at the same time. "Please call me Rainee. I prefer it over Rainelle."

"Rainee," he acknowledged. "Rainelle is a beautiful name, though. I've never heard it before."

Rainee blushed under Haydon's compliment. "My father was British. It was his mother's name." Her gaze lowered and she noticed the flowers in her hands. She extended the bouquet toward his mother. "These are for you, Mrs. Bowen."

"It's Katherine, remember?"

"Yes, ma'am." It would take Rainee a while to get used to addressing an elder by their given name but the very idea brought a smile to her face.

Katherine took the flowers, and her eyes brightened as she smelled each one. "Oh, I love flowers. And these are my favorites. How very thoughtful of you to take the time to pick them for me. Thank you, Rainee." Katherine smiled and again her questioning gaze swung between Rainee and her son.

The joy of the moment evaporated as quickly as it had come. A sinking feeling came over Rainee. Had this man not mentioned her to any of his family? What was going on around here?

Rainee's blood flow slowed way down—either from all the heat she had endured the last several days or the realization no one seemed to know anything about her.

"Don't just stand there, Haydon. Can't you see Rainee isn't feeling well? Help her inside and get her a glass of water."

She wanted to protest, to say she was fine, but she never got the chance. Haydon was at her side, escorting her into the house and onto a comfortable sofa.

"You'd be more at ease, Rainee, if you removed your jacket and hat. May I?"

She nodded.

Haydon helped her out of her traveling jacket and set it on a nearby chair.

She removed the pins from her hat, wondering if she looked a fright.

He took her hat and set it with her jacket. "Would you like me to take your gloves too?" He extended his hand toward her.

She clutched her hands together and squeezed them until her fingers throbbed. "No. No, thank you."

A quick nod her direction, and he left the room. Within minutes he returned with a full glass of water. "Here. Drink this. You'll feel much better."

When she reached for the glass, their fingertips overlapped. A warm tingling sensation started at the tip of her fingers and spread up her arm and into her body, causing her to shiver and very nearly drop the glass.

Haydon yanked his hand back, and she barely kept the glass upright between them. For a brief moment, he stared at her with a look of sheer horror. Then he whirled and disappeared through the doorway as if the house were on fire.

Had he felt what she had? Her heart was still fluttering from that one touch.

If he had, was it a bad thing or a good thing? If his reaction was any indication, it must be quite bad.

Too tired to ponder that, she tipped the water glass to her lips. The tepid water tasted almost sweet. She drank the whole glass of liquid within seconds, even though it was a very unladylike thing to do.

"Feel better?"

Rainee looked over at Katherine, who strolled into the living room and sat in a chair across from her.

"Thank you. Yes," she answered even though she really did not feel better, but she hated any displays of weakness. Yet, sitting here on a comfy sofa, out of the hot sun, her eyelids felt heavy with fatigue. She struggled to keep her tiredness from showing.

An awkward silence filled the room.

Katherine rose. "Would you please excuse me for a moment? And please make yourself at home."

After the woman left, Rainee folded her hands in her lap, not knowing what to do.

Her gaze roamed the living room. On the left of the fireplace were two wine-and-tan-colored wingback chairs. On the right was a matching high-back settee and a tan rocking chair. The wine-and-tan sofa she sat on faced the fireplace. End tables with doilies and oil lamps graced each side of the sofa. The place reminded her of the spacious living room back home. Except this place had Queen Anne–style furniture, and back home the furniture was Chippendale. Sadness crawled inside her, but she shooed it away like an unwanted bug. Dwelling on home would do her no good. No good at all.

Weeks of traveling and being jostled about and the realization no one seemed to know about her had taxed her greatly. Her eyelids were heavy and her stomach was queasy from a lack of food. She really should have eaten something when Haydon had offered. But knowing she was penniless and seeing all those men in Prosperity Mountain leering at her, she just wanted to get away from them as fast as she could.

Her eyes slid shut, and her head bobbed. She sat up straighter, forcing herself to stay awake, when all she really wanted to do was to succumb to sleep and dream about what could have been. Finally she could fight sleep no longer and everything around her faded as she fell into its waiting arms.

Chapter Three

Haydon couldn't get out of the house fast enough as he battled the feelings warring inside him. When Rainee's fingertips touched his, it was as if a bolt of lightning had struck nearby and he felt the effects of it, shocking every part of him. How could a woman, who he'd barely met, affect him so? Whatever the answer, he didn't care. All he knew was he wouldn't allow her or any other woman to penetrate the wall he'd built around his heart.

He glanced toward the house, wondering what was going on in there. Rainee looked so tired, he actually felt sorry for her. He shouldn't have left his mother alone to deal with her, but he had to get away for the sake of his sanity. Besides, why should he feel bad? This whole unbelievable situation was all Jesse's doing. Haydon had nothing to do with it.

Of all the idiotic things his brother had done, this one bested them all. The more Haydon thought about the situation and the sight of that poor exhausted woman sitting on his mother's couch, the more he thought about confronting his brother. He whirled on his heel and headed toward Jesse's house. The brisk walk across the yard felt good and helped relieve some of his aggravation—but not nearly enough. He leapt onto the porch. "Jesse." He banged on the door.

In seconds, the door slung open, and a very pregnant, very perturbed Hannah quickly stepped outside. She jerked her finger to her lips and shushed him. "Haydon Bowen, what is wrong with you? Jesse's sleeping." She closed the door behind her. "Although I'm surprised he can with all that banging you're doing."

That sent Haydon back a piece. "I'm sorry, but he's just going to have to wake up. There are two ladies over there—" he jerked his thumb toward his mother's house "—who need an explanation."

Hannah planted her hands on her hips and glared up at him. "Listen here, Haydon Bowen. I know what Jesse did was wrong. I told him he should have talked to you before answering that woman's advertisement on your behalf. I'm sorry, but you'll just have to deal with it because right now Jesse needs rest. And not you nor anyone else is going to disrupt that. You hear me?" With those words Hannah opened her door and disappeared inside, closing it on him with the softest bang he'd ever not heard.

Haydon raised his hat and ran his hand through his hair. Never before had he seen Miss Timid Hannah act like that. Seeing no other course of action, he stepped off their porch, mumbling, "Must be something about a pregnant woman that makes them cantankerous. It definitely brings out their protective instincts." Haydon slapped his dusty hat against his leg. "Women," he harrumphed, then plopped his hat on his head and strode toward the main house.

He had just finished unloading the last of Rainee's

belongings onto the porch when his mother came out and stepped up next to him. "Haydon. I want to talk to you."

"Not now, Mother." He hoisted his leg up to get into the wagon.

"Oh, no you don't." She grabbed the back of his shirt and tugged him back. "I want to know who that girl is and what she's doing here. And I want to know *now*."

Haydon closed his eyes and blew out a long breath before facing his mother. "You'll have to ask Jesse that question."

"Jesse? What has he got to do with this?"

"Everything," Haydon replied, climbing onto the buckboard. Making sure his mother was at a safe distance, he picked up the reins and tapped the draft horses, Lulu and Sally, on their backs.

By the time he pulled the wagon around to the barn and stepped down, his mother was standing at his side. "Haydon, what's going on?"

He looked down at his mother but offered no answers.

"Where have you been and who is that woman? I will not wait until Jesse gets back from wherever it was he said he had to go today."

"So you don't know about Jesse either?"

"Know what about Jesse?" Her gaze slid toward the direction of Jesse's cabin, then back at him. "I just got home about fifteen minutes before you did and no one was around. Smokey and Michael told me last night they'd be late for dinner. What's going on around here?"

Haydon drew in a long breath. "I'll put the horses up, and then I'll tell you everything, okay?"

"You bet you will. I'll be waiting. Right here." She

sat down on one of the wood-slab benches outside the barn door.

As he tended to the horses, Haydon prayed God would give him the grace to tell his mother all he knew. When he finished, he stepped out of the barn and sat down next to her. He leaned his arms on his knees and clasped his hands together. With his head down, he debated on where to start.

"Well, are you just going to sit there, or are you going to tell me what's going on? And why is your nose so red?"

"Some guy in Prosperity Mountain punched me in the nose."

"What! Why'd he do that?"

"Because I stopped him from assaulting Rainee."

"What do you mean?" Shock rippled through her voice and across her face.

"When I arrived, some ruffian was trying to force his attentions on Rainee. We got into a fight and the sheriff hauled him off."

"That poor girl."

"Poor girl is right." Only she wasn't a girl, she was a woman. With curves in all the right places. A beautiful, feisty woman who brought out his protective instincts. The kind of woman he was a sucker for. *Oh, no, Haydon. Not this time. Just shove any notions about Rainee out of your mind. Don't go getting any ideas where she's concerned. Remember what happened with Melanie.* That was all the reminder he needed. Thoughts of Rainee vanished from his mind.

"Now, I want you to tell me why Rainee is here."

So much for knocking her out of his mind. "Mother,

you know how Jess is always doing stuff without thinking the whole thing through?"

"Yes, but he always means well."

"That might be true, but some of the ridiculous things he's done, he shouldn't have. This is one of them. Jesse answered an advertisement he'd seen…" He rubbed his chin. "I don't know where he saw it. In a newspaper, a magazine or what. But Rainee must have placed an advertisement to find a husband."

His mother's brows rose and her chin lowered. "A husband?"

"Jesse answered her ad and encouraged her to come out here to become…" He swallowed hard before continuing, "my wife."

"Oh, no, he didn't."

"Oh, yes. He did. I don't know what was in the letter or her ad or anything. You'll have to ask Jesse. But judging by our conversation on the way back to the ranch, she believes I'm the one who sent for her."

Mother looked toward the house and shook her head. "That poor, poor girl. I can't believe Jesse would do such a thing. What was he thinking?"

"That's what I asked him. I was going to send her back to wherever she came from, but the stagecoach had already left. It'll be three weeks before it comes through again. I just couldn't leave her alone in Prosperity Mountain to fend for herself." He thought about when he had arrived at the stagecoach stop and saw her bopping and kicking that man in the shins. Maybe they needed protection from her. He smiled. Then again, maybe he did, too.

His mother laid her hand on his leg. "You did the

right thing, son. But why did you go get her if you didn't send for her? Why didn't Jesse go?"

"Because he's laid up. That's why."

"Laid up? What do you mean?"

"He had an accident this morning."

"An accident? Is he okay? What happened?" Although his mother was used to her menfolk getting hurt, it never stopped her from worrying or fretting over them.

"Smokey said he'll be fine." A fresh wave of shame washed over Haydon, even though he was still agitated with his brother. "It was my fault. I got so angry when I found out what he did that I needed to get as far away from him as possible so I could cool down. I decided to go for a long ride. You know, like Father and I used to do."

"I remember." Sadness shadowed her eyes.

"Jess came into the barn right when I was getting ready to leave. I never flank Rebel, but I did. Rebel was so startled he reared and knocked Jesse out."

Her face paled. "You sure he's going to be all right?"

"I'm sure," he said with more confidence than he felt. "I feel terrible about what happened. But to be honest, Mother, I'm still angry with him. He had no right to do that to me or to Rainee."

His mother shook her head. "You're right, he didn't. But unfortunately he did, and now we have to figure out what to do with her."

"We? Oh-h no. Not we. Jesse can figure that one out on his own."

"From what you just told me, Jesse won't be able to do much of anything on his own for a while." She stood, and so did he. "I need to go check on him."

"I wouldn't do that if I were you."

"Why not?"

"Because Hannah said he needed his rest, and she didn't care who it was, she wasn't letting anyone wake him."

"Hannah? Our Hannah said that?"

"Yep. She sure did." They stood there for a second staring at each other before they both shook their heads, chuckling.

His mother's face turned grim. "What am I going to tell that poor young woman?"

"I don't know."

Rainee's eyes fluttered open. She turned her head and started to raise herself, but her body rebelled with each movement. Not one to allow a few aches and weakness of body to stop her, she forced her creaking body into a sitting position, wondering how long she had been asleep.

A young teenage girl with buttery blond hair and powder-blue eyes came drifting into the room. "Hi, I'm Leah. Mother told me to offer you something to eat and drink when you awakened. Would you like some cookies and tea?"

"Tea and cookies sound heavenly. Thank you." Before Rainee had a chance to introduce herself the girl disappeared. Rainee ran her hands over her wrinkled, dirty clothes, but the stubborn creases and dirt would not budge. She was most certainly a mess and not fit to be seen.

Leah returned and set the tray on the end table next to Rainee. She smiled and two dimples accompanied it. "I hope you like them. I made them myself." Leah's look of accomplishment curled Rainee's lips upward.

"I am sure I shall. Thank you." She picked one up, and when she bit into it, a flavorful blend of cinnamon, clove and apple delighted her taste buds.

Leah sat across from her with an expectant look.

Rainee dabbed at the corners of her mouth with the cloth napkin provided her. "One of the best cookies I have ever eaten. You must teach me how to make them." To prove her enjoyment, she devoured another cookie.

"I would love to."

"By the way, I am Rainelle. Rainelle Victoria Devonwood. But please, call me Rainee."

"Nice to meet you, Rainee." Leah chewed on the corner of her bottom lip. "I hope you don't mind me asking, but I saw you with my brother." She squirmed and glanced toward the kitchen. "Are you and he…? You know?" She spiked her shoulder in a quick upward motion. "How do you know Haydon?"

"Leah. That is none of your business." Rainee's gaze swung toward Katherine's voice.

Leah jumped up and lowered her head. "Sorry, Mother." She glanced over at Rainee. "Sorry, Rainee."

"No harm done." She did her best to send Leah a reassuring smile.

The young girl gave a quick nod and then looked at her mother as if she were seeking approval.

"Leah, go see what your sister is up to."

"Yes, Mother." She gave a shy smile Rainee's direction, then quietly left the room.

Katherine sat in the chair Leah had occupied. "Are you feeling better now?" Compassion, so like her own mother's, floated from this woman.

Rainee had to look away. Heartsickness for her

mother consumed her once again. She wondered if she would ever get used to the fact her mother was never coming back. That she would never comfort Rainee or give her words of wisdom again.

She plastered on a smile and faced Katherine. "Yes, ma'am. I am much better. Thank you."

Katherine fidgeted with her hands and darted her gaze out the window, onto her lap, back out the window, until it finally alighted on Rainee. "Rainee, I think there's something you should know."

Rainee braced herself for whatever was coming. From the tone in Katherine's voice, it was not good news.

"Mother, I'll handle this."

Rainee swung her gaze toward Haydon, who stood filling the doorway.

Katherine's chest rose and fell. Her hands quit squirming and finally rested in her lap.

"I'm afraid there's been a huge mistake." Haydon strode over and sat across from her next to Katherine.

"What—what do you mean a mistake?" Rainee felt the blood drain from her face.

"I don't know how to tell you this, so I'm just going to say it. I'm really sorry, but my brother Jesse sent for you, Rainee, not me."

Blinking, Rainee fought not to react. "I—I do not understand." She looked at Katherine, then at Haydon. "You told me Jesse is married."

"He is."

Question after question chased through Rainee's mind about what this all meant. Surely these people were not one of those religious groups who believed it was okay to have several wives. The air in the room thickened. Just what had she gotten herself into? She stared at Haydon, waiting for him to continue, yet dreading it at the same time.

"He sent for you. But not for himself."

Hearing Haydon say that at least put Rainee's fears to rest about the numerous wives, but she still did not have a clue as to what was going on.

"He thought he was doing me a favor. And you." He raked his hand through his hair.

Rainee closed her eyes as disappointment, concern and dread inhabited her body. The cookies in her stomach turned to stone. What would she do now? She did not need him to tell her the rest. She already knew. He did not want her here. Her solution had just evaporated before her very eyes.

Never before had she felt so alone.

Usually when a situation arose, memories of her mother's advice came to her. But not this time. Even her mother's words were as silent as the grave.

Grave. That one word always ripped at Rainee's heart, and this time was no different, but she refused to cry in the presence of these strangers.

"Rainee."

Her eyes drifted toward the woman who emanated compassion.

"Jesse meant well. But my son has a tendency to not think things through before he acts."

"That's for sure." Anger sliced through Haydon's tone. "When he saw your advertisement, he decided to send for you. But unfortunately, he didn't mention it to me or anyone else."

That much was obvious. So now what?

Seeing the lingering question in Katherine's eyes,

Rainee plucked up her courage and looked directly at her. "I know you must think it quite strange a woman would advertise for a husband, but please believe me when I tell you I had to." She glanced at Haydon, then back at Katherine. "You see, my parents died and I…" Her courage vanished. Rainee could not bring herself to share the sordid details of her life with these people. "I just had to."

"I'm so sorry for your loss. If I hadn't had my sons to take care of me when my husband passed away, I'd have probably done the same thing. I think what you did took a lot of courage."

Courage was not what propelled her to write the advertisement. Fear had.

Afraid they would see the moisture forming in her eyes and start asking questions, questions she did not want to answer, Rainee stood and forced one shaky leg in front of the other as she walked to the window.

No one could find out she had a brother back in Little Rock. For she could not risk being sent back. Neither could she risk Ferrin finding her. The only thing that could save her now was to get married right away. And based on what she had just heard, there was not going to be a wedding here in Paradise Haven.

Scenario after scenario about what she could do now ran through Rainee's mind. With each one, the air thickened with fear. The idea of going back home to that monster tied her stomach into knots and breathing became difficult.

With her back to them, the question she hated to ask but knew she must slid past her lips in a choppy rasp, "Where—where does that leave me?" Spots danced before her eyes, and her body swayed, then blackness pulled her into its embrace.

Chapter Four

Haydon leapt to his feet but could not make it to the window fast enough to catch Rainee. Her small body slumped to the floor. Her vulnerability tugged at his heart. The anger and frustration he'd had toward Jesse came back full force.

Willing himself to feel nothing, Haydon slipped his arms under her knees and back and hoisted her up. She didn't budge but hung as limp as Abby's rag doll. She looked helpless, alone and frail. He tucked her closer into his chest. Her vulnerability and the feel of her feminine frame and soft hair draping over his arm touched something deep inside him. Something he never wanted to feel again rose in him. He shoveled away the unwelcome feelings and buried them deep in an unmarked grave.

"Oh, Haydon, that poor girl. Wait until I see Jesse. I am going to give that boy a piece of my mind. What was he thinking?"

That's what Haydon had been trying to figure out, too.

"Take her up to Leah's room and lay her on the extra

bed. I'll get a cool cloth and some water." His mother scampered into the kitchen.

On his way up the steps, he noticed the stains of tears on her cheeks. Protective feelings flooded through him like a massive gulley wash, but he refused to let them take possession. *No! I don't want to feel anything.* However, when he lowered her onto the bed, rather than walking away, he gazed down at her, wondering what would become of her once they sorted the whole muddled issue out.

The stairs creaked. He shook out of the thoughts and strode toward the door. He took the water basin from his mother.

Thinking was dangerous. He held the bowl while his mother dipped a cloth into it and laid it on Rainee's forehead.

The young woman stirred and slowly opened her eyes.

Haydon's breath hitched at the sight of those beautiful fawn-colored eyes—eyes he had avoided the whole way home. Eyes a man could get lost in if he wasn't careful.

Dread and confusion emanated from her.

He hated seeing her like that. His arms ached to wrap her in them and comfort her. To tell her everything would be okay. That he would take care of her and protect her.

What was he thinking?

Fear slugged into him like a fist. He jerked his gaze away and quickly set the basin on the nightstand, sloshing a small amount of water over the side. Without bothering to wipe it up, he spun on his heel and called over his shoulder, "If you need me for anything else, just holler." Haydon skipped steps as he barreled down them. Out the front door and into the fresh air he flew. He refused to give heed to the feelings Rainee aroused in him. Feelings that scared him to death. From now on, the farther he stayed away from her, the better.

Rainee sat up. She would love nothing more than to bury herself with the yellow patchwork quilt underneath her, but that would solve nothing. All her well-laid plans were falling apart around her. She had no money and no place to go. And no future husband.

"Rainee?"

Her vision trailed toward Katherine, who smelled of baked bread and wood smoke.

"I am truly sorry, Mrs. Bowen. I am not normally one given to fainting spells. But this news has come as quite a shock to me. I am at a loss as to what to do next. All I know is, I cannot go back. I simply cannot."

"It's Katherine, and please don't apologize for fainting. I certainly understand. I'd probably faint too under the same circumstances." Katherine sat on the bed next to her and took her hand. "I am more sorry than words can say for what my son did. I want you to know you're welcome to stay here as long as you wish."

Once again, questions chased other questions through Rainee's mind. Should she stay? Should she go? Should she take Katherine up on her offer until she had time to figure out what to do? The way she saw it, she really had no other choice.

She searched the woman's eyes, seeking something. Reassurance perhaps? That all would be well? What she saw was a kind woman offering her compassion and a place to stay. Her chest heaved, expelling some of the tension in her body. "Are you sure you do not mind?"

"I'm positive. Now, why don't I have Haydon bring up your things? I'm sure you'd like to clean up before dinner. I'll heat some water so you can take a bath."

"No, no. Please, do not trouble yourself on my account," Rainee said even though a bath sounded heavenly. She did not want to give this woman any reason to send her back. And while she would not take advantage of Katherine's kind offer and hospitality for long, she was grateful for the time to come up with another plan.

If only her mother's words of wisdom would rise up in her, but they would not because Rainee had never encountered anything like this while her mother was still alive. How could either of them ever have envisioned this? The next-closest thing she had to a mother now was Jenetta. The older woman would know what to do. But she was not here. She was back home in Little Rock with her husband and three children.

Something Jenetta had said popped into her mind. "You hang on to that other Christian gentleman's letter in case thangs don't work out." The other letter. Stems of hope sprouted through the darkness. She did have another option. *Thank You, Lord.*

Having received many responses to her advertisement, she had kept the two most promising letters. One she had responded to, the other, well, his letter was tucked securely in her trunk. Although it saddened her that things did not work out with Haydon, she would write the other man straightaway.

"It's no trouble at all." Katherine's voice snapped her out of her musings. "I'll start heating the water now. As soon as Haydon gets your things up here, you can come down and take a bath." She smiled, stood and turned to leave the room. At the door, she stopped. With her hand still on the knob, she looked back at Rainee. "I really am sorry for what my son did. And I meant what I said about you staying here as long as you like." Katherine's smile seemed to hold a secret. But just what kind of secret Rainee did not know.

"Would you please take Rainee's things up to Leah's room?" Haydon's mother pointed to the trunk he had placed on the porch when they had arrived. "She'll be staying with us."

His eyebrows slammed against the brim of his hat. "What do you mean she's staying with us? For how long?" He could no more hold back the panic from his voice than he could hold back a raging river.

"For as long as she likes."

Haydon recognized that smile. His mother was up to something. Just what, he wasn't sure. But something.

He leaned over and grabbed the handles of Rainee's trunk and hoisted it up. His mother opened the door and motioned him by. "Just what I need," he spoke under his breath as he walked past her.

"She just might be."

Haydon swung around so fast the trunk dropped from his hands and thudded onto his foot. He jerked his foot up, put it down, jerked it up again and put it down, all the while holding back the words he wanted to fling out in anger. Without looking at his mother, he snatched the trunk up again and tromped his way up the stairs.

"Haydon." The sternness in his mother's voice stopped him.

Halfway up the stairs, he balanced the trunk on his knee and turned his head toward his mother.

She shook her finger at him. “You be nice to my guest, and don’t you dare make her feel uncomfortable.”

Make *her* uncomfortable!

“Yes, ma’am,” he said as he turned and trudged up the stairs. This whole stupid mess stuck inside him like an infected splinter.

At Leah’s bedroom door, he stopped and called, “Rainee.” He made every effort possible to keep the irritation from his voice, when what he really wanted to do was take her and her trunk into town and drop her off at Mrs. Swedberg’s boardinghouse. But the older widow woman never had any available rooms. Besides, even if she did, his mother had already made it clear Rainee was her guest now, and that was that.

“Come in,” she said in that sweet Southern drawl of hers that drove clean through every part of him.

“I’m here with your trunk.” He pushed the door all the way open with his back and turned inside. “Where would you like this?” He refused to look over at her. Refused to let her get under his skin any further.

“Over here, please.”

He had no choice but to look now as she pointed to the end of the bed.

His gaze snagged on her hands. She still had on those lacey gloves. Why would she wear such fancy gloves in the house? This wasn’t some fancy ball.

Fancy balls.

Melanie.

Thoughts of his wife were always one careless notion away but exactly what he needed to keep from being drawn in by Rainee. For that, he was almost grateful to the memories. As fast as he could, Haydon set her trunk at the foot of the bed and turned to leave.

"Haydon?"

He looked back at her. "Yes, ma'am?"

"Thank you." She put her head down and played with the tips of her fingers. "I want you to know that as soon as I can, I will be leaving. I am truly sorry for what your brother has put you through."

"Put me through?" Haydon was instantly chagrinned at his uncharitable thoughts. Rainee was the real victim here. "What about what he put you through? You came all this way for nothing. When I think about what you must be feeling right now..." He shook his head. "I still can't believe it. I'm really sorry, Rainee. Truly." He found he meant it. No one deserved to be treated like that.

"It is okay, Haydon. I have a home for now. And one of the other Christian gentlemen who answered my advertisement offered me a home as well, so I am not completely without options."

One of the other gentlemen? How many men had actually responded to her ad? Were there that many desperate men out there?

"I shall contact him as soon as I can send a post off and see if he still wants me."

Haydon's gut twisted into a hard knot. Who was this guy, and would he be good to her? Haydon gave himself a mental tongue lashing. What did he care what happened to her? He didn't want her. What did it matter to him if someone else did? Then he made the mistake of looking into her eyes again. The vulnerability he saw there touched him deeper than he wanted it to. Although he didn't want her, the truth was he hated the thought of this beautiful young woman, who was clothed with despair and innocence, traipsing all over the country to who knows where and into the arms of who knew what kind of man.

Against all rationale and his better judgment, right there, Haydon made up his mind to not let her go. To protect her from undesirables and to provide for her. "Rainee, I—"

"Rainee." Leah burst into the room. "Oh. Hi, Haydon."

He looked at his sister, then back at Rainee, who was gazing up at him with a tilt of her head as if she were waiting for him to continue. "I'll—I'll talk to you later."

She gave a quick nod. "Thank you again, Haydon, for retrieving my trunk." She offered him a sweet smile and to his utter surprise and horror his heart tipped like a schoolboy with a crush.

Chapter Five

Rainee climbed out of the tub and got dressed. Alone in the house and feeling refreshed, she decided to step outside. The late afternoon air surrounded her with warmth. Over by the corral, she noticed some of the spotted horses she had seen on the way here and decided to take a closer look at them.

She stepped up to the corral, and a reddish-colored horse with brown spots came trotting over to her and leaned its head over the fence. "Well, hello there." She ran her gloves over the horse's nose. The horse pressed into her hand and jerked upward. Rainee giggled. "Not only are you lovely, but you are feisty, too."

"And she'll take a chunk out of you if you're not careful."

Rainee swung her gaze toward the barn. Haydon stepped out of the shadow of the stall and into the sunlight of the corral. He came and stood next to the mare and patted the horse's neck. "You behave yourself, Sköldpadda."

The horse stepped back and turned her head into Haydon. He rubbed her cheek and scratched her behind her ears. "You be nice to this lady or no more treats for you, you hear?" Haydon glanced at Rainee but continued to pet the horse.

"Sköldpadda? I have never heard that name before." Rainee tilted her head.

"It's Swedish for a snapping turtle."

"Why did you name your horse after a snapping turtle?" No sooner had the question left her mouth when the horse scuttled back and lunged toward Haydon with its mouth wide open. "Watch out!" Rainee yelled.

Haydon jerked sideways and Rainee watched as he dealt with the horse in the gentlest of manner.

When the horse calmed, Haydon faced Rainee. "Now you know why. Sköldpadda has a good heart and she's a gentle mare, but for some reason I can't seem to break her of this one bad habit." He turned and put his arm around the horse's neck. "You're a good girl, Sköldpadda," he whispered in the horse's ear, but Rainee heard him and admired the gentleness he displayed with the horse.

He never once lost his temper as her brother had so many a time with their horses.

Thoughts of Ferrin and his cruelty sent spasms of pain throughout Rainee's body. *No! I shall not torment myself with thoughts of my brother.* She forced her attention back onto the horse and onto Haydon.

Sköldpadda walked away and joined the other horses at the food trough. Haydon ambled up to the fence and planted one foot on the bottom rail and his arms over the top one.

"What manner of breed are these horses? They are lovely, and I have never seen any spotted horses like these before."

"They're Palouse ponies."

"Palouse?"

Haydon explained their history with such zeal that Rainee got caught up in his excitement. "They're lofty and really active. Plus, they're great for hunting and their stamina is quite impressive." He suddenly stopped and looked at her. "I'm sorry. I've gotten carried away. It's just that I love these animals. They're unlike any other horse breed I've ever been around. Especially Rebel's offspring. If you think these horses are beautiful, you should see Rebel."

"Rebel?" She tilted her head.

"My horse."

"May I see him?"

"Sure. Meet me inside the barn." Haydon headed through the corral and disappeared into the same stall he had come out of.

On the way to the barn, Rainee marveled at the difference between the stoic man who had picked her up from the stagecoach and this zealous, passionate horseman. The two were as different as a bird and a cat.

Haydon met her at the door. "He's in the back." His face glowed with pride.

They headed through the barn. Dust, hay and horse scent swirled around her, tickling her nose with delight.

Out the back door they headed. Behind the barn was a lone stall with a higher fenced corral.

Several yards from the stall, Haydon expelled two short whistle sounds.

A black horse poked its head out of the stall door.

"How you doing, Rebel Boy?" Haydon walked up to him and rubbed the horse on the nose, then patted his cheek.

Rainee stepped up next to Haydon and looked at the horse's shiny coat. She peered into the stall and noticed white spots all over the horse's rump. "Oh, my. What an exquisite animal. God has really outdone Himself on this one. May I pet him?"

Haydon stepped aside and Rainee ran her hand over Rebel's head. "He seems gentle. Did you break him?"

"Yes."

"Do you break all of your horses?"

"Most of them. Jess helps some." He stopped talking and Rainee peered up at him. A shadow covered his face as he looked away. Rainee wondered what was wrong, then realized he had become still when he had mentioned his brother's name. The very one who had sent for her.

"I'm sorry, but it's getting late and I need to finish my chores now."

Rainee knew she had been dismissed. But she understood. Haydon was having a hard time dealing with what his brother had done, and she did not blame him. This most awkward situation vexed her also. To ease his discomfort, she would try and find a new home as soon as possible.

Rainee forced herself not to fidget at the dining room table. Father always hated that sort of improper display, said it showed a lack of confidence and no Devonwood should ever behave in such an unbecoming manner. Because of their wealth and standing in society, they should hold their heads high and have impeccable manners.

As if any of that mattered to Rainee.

She detested all of the snobbery and insincerity that accompanied most people of high rank.

The kitchen door flung open, and in barreled a young man who resembled Haydon in every way, albeit younger and smaller. He stopped short when he saw her, then he hurried around to the opposite side of the table and sat down. His eyes locked onto her. "Who are you? And what are you doing here?"

"Michael!"

Rainee's gaze flew to Haydon seated at the head of the table.

"I'm sorry. I apologize for my brother's rude behavior, Rainee." Haydon turned his attention to his brother and sent several silent but serious messages his direction.

The poor boy's face matched the color of a scarlet ribbon Rainee once had. She longed to ease the young man's embarrassment, but it would be highly improper for her to interfere.

"Rainee, may I present my brother, Michael. And the gentleman sitting next to him is our dear friend, Smokey."

"Ma'am." The man with the gray hair and gentle brown eyes nodded his head once.

"Pleased to meet you, gentlemen." Rainee presented a polite dip of her head to Smokey, then turned her attention to Michael and offered him the same courtesy.

"And of course you've already met Abigail and Leah. Everyone, this is Rainee."

Questioning stares made her want to shrink under the table and disappear out the door.

"Just so you all know, Jesse invited her out for a visit. I do not want anyone in this family embarrassing Rainee again. Is that understood?" His gaze went around the room, holding a moment on each member until they each nodded their assent.

Rainee wanted to hug the man for sparing her any further humiliation. Admiration for his sensitivity sent a strange swirling sensation into her heart.

Confused, questioning gazes fluttered her direction from around the table. She waited for one of them to ask her why she was not eating with Haydon's brother and his wife, but not one person spoke even though she could tell they wanted to. They obviously respected Haydon's authority. And him.

"Let's pray." Everyone bowed their heads as Haydon said a prayer over the food.

Dinner consisted of Swedish elk stew and cornbread. Laughter floated around the table and the lively conversation reminded her of family dinners back home. Only the conversations around her parents' table were much more formal.

Much to her horror, a wide yawn attacked her without warning and escaped before she could catch it. She covered her mouth, but it was really no use. "Merciful heavens. Please forgive me. I did not mean to be rude. I fear I am overtired."

"Of course you are. Traveling has a way of doing that to a person. Why don't you head on up to bed?" Katherine's look of understanding warmed her insides.

"If you do not mind, I think I shall." She started to rise and found Haydon behind her, pulling out her chair.

When she stood, she turned to thank him, and their eyes connected.

The sound of Abby's giggle reached her ears.

Haydon broke eye contact with a frown. Then he

rushed toward the door, snatched his hat off a wooden peg, and disappeared into the night with only a "I'd better check on Rebel" floating out after him.

Rainee stretched her arms above her and allowed her eyes to adjust to the daylight beaming through the windows. The lavender curtains waved in the light breeze. She glanced over at Leah's empty side of the bed and wondered what hour of the day it was.

Weeks on a train and stagecoach had taken their toll on her. Last night, after she had written her letter to Mr. Bettes and snuggled into the soft pillow, her eyes closed and she had fallen into a deep sleep.

She slid her legs out from under the quilt and placed her feet on the cool floor. Her gaze searched the room for a water pitcher and basin to wash her face. In that moment, it was as if someone had doused her head with a pitcher of cold water because once again she was forced to face reality.

Never again would there be water ready for her.

No maid to help button her dresses.

No Jenetta.

Rainee was certain she would either be dead or have gone mad by now had it not been for Jenetta and her kindness.

Jenetta had doctored her wounds, prayed with her and had even gone against Ferrin's orders by continuing to fill Rainee's water basin. In return, Rainee helped Jenetta with the extra chores Ferrin had heaped on her already-long list.

Rainee's chest heaved. She needed to accept the fact this was her new home now. At least temporarily anyway. The burden of being unsettled hung over her like an ominous cloud.

Not knowing what her host expected from her, she decided to make haste and get dressed so she could go downstairs and find out.

Rainee walked to the end of the bed, knelt in front of the trunk and opened it. She pulled out her pale blue day dress and shook it out. Alone in the room, she slipped her gloves and nightgown off, thankful she nor anyone else could see the raised stripes across her back. A painful reminder of where she had come from.

Within minutes she had her corset on. She slid into her bustle gown and made her way to the mirror. In front of the looking glass, she studied herself, admiring the light blue dress with dark blue bows and layers of lace on the skirt, collar and sleeves. Although she preferred a lighter, simpler dress, sometimes she missed wearing such gowns. Since her parents' passing, the only time she had been allowed to wear such finery was when company came. One old man in particular. An old man who made her shudder with repulsion. Rainee hastened to rid her mind of the despicable memories.

She glanced back at her reflection in the mirror. Her hair was in complete disarray.

After she secured her hair in a chignon, she grabbed her fingerless gloves and slipped them on. Flipping her hands over and back, she realized how out of place the lacey gloves looked here. But she had no choice but to wear them. They covered up contemptible, embarrassing scars. Scars she did not want anyone inquiring about.

Rainee opened the bedroom door. Coffee and bacon aromas greeted her, making her stomach rumble. She made her way down the stairs. As she neared the kitchen, her gaze found Haydon, seated at the table with Katherine, each holding a coffee cup, and out of reflex, Rainee ducked back so they would not see her.

"I wish Jesse would mind his own business. He should have never sent for her."

"Give her a chance, Haydon. You've got to let the past go."

Indecision gripped her. She did not know whether to continue forward or to turn around and make her way back up the stairs. Eavesdropping was wrong, but she could not get her feet to move.

Haydon said something, but Rainee could not hear him because his voice was too low.

"Yes, you can. You can't give up."

"I haven't given up, Mother. I keep this place running and even manage to turn over a profit."

"That's not what I meant. And yes, you do keep this place running. You've done an excellent job since your father died. I'm so proud of you, son. You pushed past the grief of losing him and took charge. Now you need to do the same with Melanie's death."

Melanie? Who was Melanie? Rainee wanted to ask, but she did not dare as they would know she was eavesdropping. Guilt took a swipe at her. She should move, should go forward or back, but her feet were not cooperating.

"Mother, we've had this conversation a million times already. It's my fault—"

"It's not your fault."

Rainee wanted to know what was not his fault.

"You remind me of Nora's brother, the one who's

coming to live with her. Nora said he's still stuck in the past. Still hurting. What a tragedy that is."

What in Haydon's past was he stuck in? And why was he like this Nora woman's brother? Had he been responsible for his father's death? Or what? She strained to listen. She wanted to see if her unheard questions would be answered.

"Mother, I know you mean well, and I know what you're trying to do, but you know I plan to never marry again."

Rainee stuffed down the hurt his words inflicted. Although she knew he did not want her, it still brought an ache to her soul. One she could not cast off like she could a piece of unwanted clothing.

She glanced behind her, desperately wanting to dart back up the stairs, but she did not want to risk being heard.

What should she do?

Haydon's words just now, and knowing he was not the one who had sent for her made her extremely uncomfortable, and she did not wish to be around him any longer.

With great care, she turned and made it up three steps before she heard, "Good morning, Rainee."

Rainee closed her eyes and drew in a long breath. Forcing a smile onto her face, she turned and made her way to them. "Good morning, Katherine."

She tried to look natural, not guilty of eavesdropping, wondering if they knew she had. If so, neither said a word.

Out of courtesy, she turned to greet Haydon, but the greeting never left her lips. His appearance was that of a person who had not slept for weeks. Her heart broke for him.

"Can I get you some breakfast?"

Rainee diverted her attention to Katherine. "Yes, that would be lovely, thank you."

Rainee did not know if she would offend her host by offering to help. In the society she came from it would be a huge social gaffe to do so because the wealthy had servants to do that. But Rainee preferred helping—it made her feel useful, instead of like some ornament waiting to be handpicked by an acceptable suitor. Another rigid rule she loathed.

Just because her family had money, she did not believe that she or they were above anyone else. If her father knew she felt that way and had ever caught her helping, he would have been appalled. Back home, even though she had failed miserably, she had always tried to behave in a way befitting their social status. But here, she did not know the proper thing to do.

Should she offer to help, or should she sit down and allow her host to wait on her?

And did she really want to sit at the table with Haydon after overhearing the conversation with his mother?

His eyes that spoke of his confusion and discomfort locked onto hers. Rainee could not blame him for being uncomfortable. After all, this most perplexing situation was no fault of his. But then again, it was no fault of hers either. She thought the man who had sent for her wanted her—otherwise she would have never come.

He broke eye contact, rose and came to where she stood. He pulled the chair out and held it as she sat.

Haydon went back, sat in his chair and became engrossed in his untouched food.

Katherine grabbed a covered plate from the oven. She lifted the towel, revealing a mountain of thick bacon slices, scrambled eggs and biscuits and set them on the table, along with an empty cup. She filled Rainee's cup with steaming coffee and sat in the chair next to her. "Go ahead and eat before it gets cold."

"Yes, ma'am." Rainee nodded, then bowed her head and said a silent prayer. When she opened her eyes, Haydon was staring at her as was Katherine.

"You're a Christian?" Katherine's blue eyes beamed, and wrinkles gathered around her eyes and mouth when she smiled.

"Yes, ma'am. I am."

"Perfect." Katherine clasped her hands.

Perfect for what? Instead of inquiring, she picked up a piece of bacon with her fingers and bit off a piece.

Realizing her gaffe, her gaze flew to Katherine, who appeared as if nothing was amiss. Her mother would have noticed her blunder immediately and given her a lecture on fine table manners. She stopped chewing the piece in her mouth and stared at her plate, missing her mother until her heart bled tears.

"Are you okay?"

Rainee looked over at Haydon. She started to nod her head but then thought better of it when she noticed his genuine concern. "No. Not really. I was thinking about my mother."

"What about your mother?" His gaze never left his plate.

"When I was five, my mother scolded me for eating bacon with my fingers. She insisted I cut it into pieces instead. It took me forever to saw through one of those thick slices. When I had finally managed to do so, my fork slipped across the plate and the bacon went flying. It landed in the flower arrangement in the center of the table."

Haydon and Katherine chuckled. When Rainee looked over at him, his smile dropped with his gaze. Perplexed by his sudden aloofness, Rainee fought to fill the ensuing silence, but she did not know if she should continue. The decision was made for her when Katherine said, "And then what happened?"

"I waited for my mother's rebuke, but it never came. I could tell by her look she wanted to laugh, but with Father in the room, she dared not. Formality was everything to my father, and such things were not acceptable. That was why Mother was such a strict disciplinarian and followed the rules of etiquette. Father demanded it.

"So, Mother showed me how the British use their butter knives to cut their food and gather it onto their fork. After about four or five tries, I finally succeeded in properly cutting the bacon, and my mother's praise was most generous."

Although that precious memory of her mother brought a smile to Rainee's face, it also quenched her appetite.

"How long have your parents been gone?" Katherine asked.

Rainee glanced at her. "Two years." She looked away and stared at nothing in particular. "I now understand what my mother meant."

"What do you mean, what she meant?" Haydon still did not look at her, but instead drank his coffee.

Surprised by his interest, she decided to continue. "Shortly after my grandmother died, I saw my mother sitting in her chair. I knelt beside her and noticed tears in her eyes. I could not imagine what was wrong, so I asked if she was unwell. She assured me she was not ill, but she had been thinking about her mother, and how much she missed her."

The image of her mother dabbing at her eyes with her hanky distressed Rainee further. Perhaps because she knew only too well the cruel pain her mother had suffered.

She could not look at anyone in the room as she relayed the heartfelt words her mother had spoken. "Mother said, 'You know, Rainelle, if I knew my mother was at the end of the earth, I would crawl through thistles and thorns to see her again.' As a child I never really understood because I never really knew my grandmother. But now," she sniffed, "I understand those words only too well. I, too, would crawl through thistles and thorns to see my mother again. I miss her more than words can say."

Tears slipped over her eyelids, and she quickly brushed them away before continuing. "Any time I was sad or hurting, mother would comfort me. We spent many hours going for long walks. Mother would regale me with tales of her childhood. She constantly helped me, protected me and defended me. She always put her family's needs before her own."

With a clatter of his fork, Haydon rose. "I need to get my chores done. Thank you for breakfast, Mother." He gave Rainee a quick nod and headed out the door, and she immediately felt the loss of his presence.

"Your mother sounds like a wonderful person." Katherine's voice snagged her attention away from Haydon's retreating form.

Rainee slid her gaze toward Katherine. "Yes, she was."

"Listen, why don't you eat your breakfast and then go for a nice long walk? It will do you good."

A long walk did sound good. "Thank you. I would like that." She picked up her knife, cut a bite-size piece of bacon and put it in her mouth.

She knew she was about to do something that would not be deemed acceptable back home, but this was not home, and she wanted to help. She finished chewing and swallowed. "Katherine, is there anything you would like me to help with around here? I would love to help you and earn my keep until the stagecoach comes back through." Then what would she do? She had no money in which to purchase a ticket. Those thoughts picked the worst moments to spring their unhappiness on her. She squared her shoulders in the face of them. With God's help, she would figure something out. The Lord did not bring her this far only to abandon her.

"Don't you worry about that. You're my guest."

Her hostess's kind hospitality flooded Rainee. However, she would not trespass on the woman's kindness. When she got back from her walk, she would pitch in and help with chores. "Thank you." Rainee finished her meal, put her plate in the water and headed outside.

Warm sunshine greeted her when she stepped off the porch. She tilted her face toward the sun, relishing the feel of it on her face. For now she was free. And freedom had never felt so good.

Haydon backed Lulu and Sally up to the wagon. He needed to head into town for a few supplies and to think. After hearing Rainee talk about her mother and seeing her tears, he had to get away. He had always been powerless in the face of tears, tears he couldn't dry.

"Mr. Bowen."

He pressed his eyes together before standing and turning around. "Haydon."

She nodded. "Are you going into town, Haydon?"

He went back to strapping the horses. "Yes. Is there something I can get for you?"

"Would you mind if I go along?"

His hands froze mid-air. Yes, he minded. So many emotions were running through his head, he just wanted to get away and think. But seeing her standing there with her hands clutched and her eyes downcast, he knew what how hard it was for her to ask. He would not be rude, no matter how much she reminded him of Melanie, especially dressed in her fancy attire. "Are you sure you're up to traveling so soon?"

"Yes. Yes, I am."

"Very well then. Can you be ready to go in a few minutes? I have a lot to do today."

"Yes. Just let me run in and grab my satchel." She whirled and scurried to the house.

Dear God, give me the grace to get through this with my sanity intact.

By the time he fastened the last strap, Rainee had appeared at the wagon holding her satchel and a letter. He wondered who the letter was to but figured it was her business, not his.

He helped her into the wagon and they headed down the road.

The first mile was filled with a much-needed silence, giving him time to think about his mother's words.

"Haydon."

Holding the reins loosely in his hands, he glanced at her, then back at the road. "Yes."

"Have you always lived here?"

"No. We moved here about four years ago."

"Where did you move from?" She tilted the parasol to her right, and he got a full view of her face.

He turned his attention back to the road. "Back East."

"Where from back East?"

"New York."

"I have never been to New York. They say it is a delight to see. What is it like?"

"Like any other big city."

"Did you enjoy it?"

"Some aspects of it, yes. But mostly no. I like it here much better."

"Why is that?"

"The people here are friendlier, and they're genuine. You can trust them to do what they say they will. It's a nice change from New York."

"Do you regret moving here?"

"Only because I lost my father." An ache for his loss poked into his heart. "I keep thinking if we had not moved to Paradise Haven, he might still be alive. I understand only too well about the thistles and thorns."

She turned almost sideways to look at him, and his heart sped up. "What was your father like?"

Haydon wasn't sure if it was the question, her soft voice or her soft face, but he was having definite problems keeping himself in check. "He was one of the kindest, most generous men you would ever meet. He had a real zest for life and an adventurous spirit. In a lot of ways, I'm just like him." He glanced over at her again. "Well, I used to be anyway."

"It is hard on the oldest son to have a father die. That is for certain."

Haydon yanked his gaze her way, but she had her face forward.

"Back home, there is a young man whose parents passed away. At four and twenty, James knew it was up to him to be strong and to keep his family together. To provide for them. To be their protector. It was quite vexing for James to watch his mother and siblings suffer. His burden was great. And he, too, changed after his father's death. It was as if the real James had been buried with his father."

Rainee's words of understanding tunneled through Haydon with a gentleness he couldn't ignore. No one had ever seemed to understand what he had gone through—and still went through. As the oldest, everything fell on his shoulders. And yet he wasn't complaining. He couldn't. He loved his family. But he could also relate to this James fellow. "I can relate," he whispered, then looked at her.

The softness in her eyes and the compassion on her face encouraged him to continue.

"The first year was the hardest. My heart bled every time I watched or heard my family crying. I wanted to take their pain so they wouldn't have to suffer. But there was no way to do that. And it tore me up inside."

She laid her hand on his arm, and he glanced down at it, feeling it clear to the inner depths of his soul. "Your family seems very well cared for and happy. You have obviously done a splendid job."

Her words were like a healing salve, as was her touch, and he desperately needed them both. "Thank you."

They both fell silent the rest of the way. When they arrived in town, people stared, but no one asked any questions. He helped her down from the wagon and into the general store.

He watched as Rainee headed over to the post office section. She removed a letter from her satchel, handed it to the postmaster along with a coin, then turned and walked over to where he stood. "Well, you will not have to trouble yourself with me for much longer. I sent my post to Mr. Bettes, one of the other gentlemen who answered my advertisement. Soon, I will be gone, and that will be one less burden for you to bear." She smiled at him, but no smile reached his lips.

"Rainee, I—"

"You do not have to say a word, Haydon." She interrupted him, but there was no animosity in her tone. "I want you to know I understand the position you and I have been placed in. You need not feel badly. God will take care of me, of that I am certain."

He nodded through the lump in his throat and pulled his gaze away from her. After he loaded the wagon, they headed out of town.

All the way back to the ranch his heart played tug of war with his mind. He wanted to reassure Rainee she wasn't a burden, but he didn't want to give her the wrong impression. No matter how easy she was to talk to or how sweet she seemed, she was a woman. Personal experience had taught him women caused nothing but heartache. Heartache he could do without.

Back at the ranch, Rainee deposited her satchel in the house. All alone with two hours to go before the noon meal, she decided to take a walk. Her legs were in need of a good stretching.

Her mind replayed the conversations with Haydon on their way to town and back. Haydon was a man who loved his family and would do anything for them. A very tenderhearted man, whose eyes had glistened with unshed tears when he spoke of his father.

It touched her deeply. He was a man who truly cared about people. Here he was, forced into a rather precarious situation with her, and yet he treated her with the utmost kindness and courtesy and protected her despite their highly unusual circumstances.

Haydon was what Ferrin should have been to her.

A guardian. A protector. A provider.

But Ferrin was quite the opposite. Under his care, she struggled daily with hunger, and most of her clothes had become threadbare, except for the few she had hidden away in a trunk. And instead of protecting her, Ferrin had caused her bodily harm many times. That was why she had to flee her once-love-filled home. Homesickness sprinkled over her, but she washed it away. Instead, she determined to enjoy the rest of her day.

On her way to the meadow, she neared one of the smaller houses. A very pregnant woman was standing on the porch, leaning over the railing, shaking out a rug. Or rather the rug was shaking her.

Rainee hiked up her skirt and scurried toward her. "Would you like some help with that?"

The woman stopped and looked at her. "No, but thank you very kindly." She tossed the rug over the porch rail and faced her. "My name is Hannah. Hannah Bowen." She stepped off the porch and extended her hand toward Rainee. "And you're Rainelle."

"Yes, ma'am. I am Rainelle Victoria Devonwood." She returned her handshake, then curtsied. "But please call me Rainee."

Hannah looped her arm through Rainee's and flashed her a mischievous smile. "I have someone who wants to meet you."

Stunned by the woman's fast speech and take-charge manner, all Rainee could do was nod.

Up the steps they went.

They stepped into a very tidy, roomy kitchen. Rainee was surprised to see the cabin was much bigger inside than it looked from the outside. Yellow curtains covered the long windows. A yellow cloth graced the table, and a bowl of fresh fruit had been set in the center of it.

Rainee tried to take in more of the room but was hurried into a bedroom off of the kitchen.

A man with a bandage wrapped around his head lay there with his eyes closed.

Not knowing what to do or say, Rainee waited near the foot of the bed.

"Sweetheart." Hannah touched his arm. "Rainelle is here."

The man bobbled his eyes open. "Rainelle." He started to rise, but pain shrouded his face, and he immediately lay back down. "I'm Jesse." His smile was wobbly and sheepish.

Hannah stepped off to the side of him, and Rainee stepped closer.

"I'm the one who sent for you." He spoke as if every word pained him.

"Yes, I know." She smiled shyly and did a quick curtsy.

"I want to apologize to you for bringing you out here

under false pretenses. But to be perfectly honest with you, when I saw your ad, I prayed long and hard about it." He rolled onto his side and strained toward the glass of water sitting on the nightstand. Hannah snatched it up and held the glass while he took several sips. "Thank you, sweetheart." His eyes and smile spoke of the intense love he had for the woman.

Rainee envied Hannah. What she would give for a man to smile at her like that. To marry a man who truly loved her. She pushed those gloomy thoughts away.

"I would have never sent for you if I hadn't had this peace inside of me." He laid his hand on his chest. "I'm sorry." His Adam's apple slid up and down. "I must have missed God."

Rainee desired to ease his mind straightaway. "There is no need for you to apologize. I prayed about my decision to come here as well. And I, too, had peace. At first I must say I was shocked to discover the truth. But even so, I still believe that God, for whatever reason, led me here."

The wrinkles around his eyes disappeared and his body relaxed. "Thank you, Rainee, for saying that. Now if only Haydon would forgive me," he whispered and then his eyes drifted shut.

Hannah motioned for them to leave the room. "Would you like a cup of tea?"

"That would be lovely. But, please, allow me to get it."

"Don't be silly. I can do it."

Rainee politely led the woman with her bulging stomach over to a chair and after finding all the ingredients, she fixed the tea.

An hour later, after Rainee shook out the remaining

pile of rugs Hannah had by the front door, she headed toward the field, wondering what had happened to Jesse's head.

Ever since the ride into town, Haydon felt scattered. He tried not to think of her, but every step brought a reminder of the situation, which inevitably yanked thoughts of her right back into his mind. Worse, every time he got things in his life and around the ranch under control, Jess and his willfulness did something to throw a kick into the works.

This morning he'd been so frazzled and frustrated when Michael told him Jess wasn't coming out because he still wasn't feeling well, in his haste to get the extra chores done so he could get to town, Haydon had left the corral gate open and the horses had gotten out. Gathering them by himself had cut mightily into his already-long day.

And now Kitty was missing.

If only he hadn't been so thickheaded and allowed his anger at his brother to get the best of him, then Jess wouldn't be laid up and he wouldn't be dealing with Rainee. There she was again, invading his thoughts. He pressed his hand down his face. It was driving him to distraction seeing what Jess's latest antics were costing that poor woman. And himself. Having Rainee around was wreaking havoc in his life. He had enough pressures to deal with—he didn't need to add a woman on top of everything else. "That Jess," he grumbled.

No more dwelling on it, Haydon. You have work to do.

"Here, Kitty." Haydon swung his leg over the saddle and dismounted. "Come here, Kitty." He scanned the trees and field in front of him looking for her, wondering where she was. Usually when he called her she came right away.

"Good afternoon, Haydon."

Haydon spun toward the voice. It was just as he feared. Her. Again. "What are you doing here?" Guilt snapped into him at his lack of keeping the impatience he felt at seeing her from his tone. But he couldn't help himself. He didn't want to be around this woman who stirred his heart and bombarded his thoughts any longer. She was making him senseless.

One look at the hurt expression on her face, and he pushed aside the unwelcome feelings of attraction she aroused in him. Besides, that was no way to treat another human being. His mother's tongue lashing before Rainee had shown up this morning had reminded him of that fact.

Mother said he needed to let go of the past. But he didn't know how to stop blaming himself for Melanie's death.

He sent Rainee what he hoped was his best welcoming smile. "It sure is a nice day for a walk." He hoped his words would put her at ease. Haydon dropped Rebel's reins, knowing the horse would stand there.

"Yes, it is."

"Whatever you do, try to stick to the baseline of the trees. If you do decide to go up into the woods, make sure at all times you can still see the meadow. That way you won't travel so deep you get lost."

"Thank you, Haydon. I shall do that." She looked around as if searching for something. "Yes, well, I will be on my way now. I am quite sorry to have bothered you again. I would not have, but I heard you calling for a kitty." She shrugged. "Well, I had hoped to see it. I love cats."

Before he could correct her, her eyes widened, her face paled and she let out a scream so loud he thought his eardrums had certainly burst.

Chapter Six

Rainee's scream pierced Haydon's eardrums, making him cringe. He whirled to see what had scared ten years off of not only Rainee's life, but his, too. He didn't see anything but his fun-loving pet trotting toward him with her ears flapping and her belly jiggling.

Having thought something or someone might have killed her, relief trotted through him. "Kitty, girl, you're okay."

Kitty leaned into his leg, and Haydon started rubbing her behind the ears.

Movement behind him hooked his attention. He turned just in time to see Rainee slump to the ground.

"Rainee!" He knelt down on one knee next to her collapsed body. "Rainee," he repeated while tilting her face away from the dirt. Kitty sniffed her with her big nose. Haydon placed his hand on her snout and gently pushed her away. "Not now, girl." Kitty pushed back, shoving her way toward the woman's face. Again Haydon forced her back. Kitty placed her head against his hand and moved her backside around in a half circle.

Butting her head, she yanked Haydon's hand off of her nose. Her snout was inches away from Rainee's face.

The woman opened her eyes, and abject horror was the only way to describe what Haydon saw there. She opened her mouth wide, filling her lungs with enough air to be heard clear into Paradise Haven. Haydon braced himself for the piercing scream, but no sound came. Instead her eyes rolled closed, and her head fell limp to the side.

Haydon placed himself between her and Kitty. He scooped Rainee up into his arms and held her, debating whether to take her back to the house or to the river. The river won. It was closer.

Kitty followed closely behind him, oinking the whole way. If Rainee woke up, he didn't want her screaming or fainting again, so as much as Haydon hated doing it, he bent his knee and gave a swift kick to Kitty's rump. The pig squealed, more from shock than pain. She whirled and trotted toward the thick brush. Haydon felt like pond scum for doing that to Kitty, but he had no choice.

He laid Rainee on the grass near the river's edge. He pulled his eyes away from her soft womanly curves, grabbed the clean handkerchief from his pocket and dipped it into the river. He knelt beside her and blotted her forehead. Seeing her so helpless, he fought the emotions rising in him. Haydon had always been a sucker for a woman who needed him to be strong.

Her head swayed from side to side, and her eyes slowly opened.

She bolted upright, clipping his chin with her head in the process.

"What are you doing, woman?" He rubbed his throbbing chin.

"Where is it?" Her wild eyes and hands darted about. Shifting on her rump, using her feet, she scurried to her left, then to her right, before making a complete circle, apparently looking for an unseen threat. "That—that thing."

"What thing?"

"That—that *pig!*" she all but shouted.

"That *pig* has a name. Her name is Kitty."

She blinked and stared at him as if he had lost his mind. Well, one of them had but it wasn't him. "Kitty is a—a pig?"

"Last time I checked she was," he answered with a slow chuckle.

Rainee's eyes narrowed, and she pursed her lips. She shifted her legs off to the side, pushed herself onto one knee and, using her hands for balance, she started to stand.

Haydon leapt up and placed his hand under her elbow to brace her. Touching her was not a good thing. Well, it was, but it wasn't. It made his blood pump faster. But he had no choice. He couldn't very well let her fall again.

"You named your pig Kitty?" She blinked up at him.

"No."

"No? What do you mean 'no'?"

"No. Abby named her Kitty." He moved his gaze away from her, not able to handle how her eyes always seemed to pierce through him. After making sure she was stable, he released her arm to rid himself of the tingling sensation she aroused in him. He could feel her eyes on him even as she brushed the dirt off of her arms and skirt.

"Is there just the one…" she gulped "…pig?" She

said the word “pig” the same way Abby said the word “ghost” when she was scared.

The protective side of him wanted to wrap her in his arms and comfort her like he did Abby, but the way his insides were shaking, his urge to protect her would not be a good thing. “No. Actually, we have fifty sows and three boars.”

“Fif— Fifty!” The whites of her eyes were no longer hidden. “But—but why?”

Did the woman have a stuttering problem or what? “Because,” he drew out, “we raise them. That’s why. Didn’t Jesse tell you?”

Merciful heavens, what had she gotten herself into? “No, Haydon. Jesse did not mention that bit of news. I assure you if he had, I would have never come here. I am terrified of pigs.”

“Why?”

“Why? Because when I was a young girl, I was attacked by one. That is why.” The memory made Rainee’s knees feel as flimsy as a hair ribbon. She searched for something to sit on and noticed a felled log. On shaky legs she took the few steps toward it, tucked her skirt under and lowered herself onto the piece of wood.

Haydon placed his bulky frame next to her. His hard features were softer now.

“What happened?” he asked, sounding like he actually wanted to know.

She brushed the fallen hair from her face. “My parents owned a few head of swine. An acquaintance of mine and I wanted to see the newborn babies up close.” Careful to not mention her brother’s name for fear Haydon would ask where Ferrin was, she chose her words wisely, "I was told by someone it would be fine to pet them, that the sow would not hurt us."

One of Haydon's eyebrows spiked.

"My friend Tamsey and I opened the gate and headed toward the mama sow. The other pigs came toward us and surrounded us. One of them pushed me. When I screamed, they started acting fidgety. We were so frightened. We did not know what to do.

"Everything happened so fast after that, I am not sure what happened next. All I know is the mama sow was charging toward us. We ran toward the gate. Tamsey made it out, and I almost did except I slipped and fell."

"Were you hurt very badly?"

She stared at the crystal-clear water that washed over the rocks and disappeared down the creek. "Yes. The sow kept snapping at my legs, and when I fell trying to get away, she tromped on my hip and thighs until her sharp hooves ripped through my clothing and skin. When I was finally able to roll over, she came after me again, heading right for my face with her mouth wide open. I raised my arms to defend myself, and when I did, my arm brushed against a piece of broken board, so I grabbed it and shoved it into the swine's mouth." Rainee pinched her eyes shut and shuddered at the memory.

When she turned her attention back to Haydon, she squirmed under his intense scrutiny, especially when his gaze landed on her hands. Knowing she could not tell Haydon about her brother and that it was Ferrin who had inflicted the scars on her hands and back and not the pig, and that the only scars the sow had caused were the ones on the back of her legs and hip, her mouth turned dry and swallowing became difficult.

Having secrets was a heavy burden to carry.

In an attempt to stop him from asking questions about her hands, she looked away and quickly added, “My father snatched me out of the pen before that wretched thing inflicted any more harm on me.”

And afterward her father had given Ferrin a beating for telling her it was okay.

Rainee never understood her brother’s hatred toward her, although she had felt it often even before her parents’ deaths. Many times she thought it was because Father doted on her, but there had to be more to it because their father had spent many hours with Ferrin, spoiling him, too.

“Rainee.”

Rainee’s gaze collided with his. “Yes?”

“I hate for you to think all pigs are mean. Granted, they can be when they’re trying to protect their young, but most of the time they’re very loving animals.”

“A pig? A loving animal?” Rainee scrunched her nose. “What a ludicrous notion. Just thinking about them makes me cringe. I have no desire to be anywhere near the little beasts. Ever.”

“Well then, ma’am—” he stood and offered her his hand “—I suggest you stand behind me.”

“Why?” She laid her hand in his abundant one and allowed him to help her up.

“Because.” His chin jerked upward once. “Here comes Abby, and Kitty is hot on her heels.”

Rainee whirled. To her utter horror, that four-legged thing was heading her way. Fear dropped into her stomach like a heavy crumpet. She wanted to flee, but her feet were as transfixed as her mind. Worse, there was nowhere to go.

The closer the curly-tailed beast got to her, the weaker her knees became. "Help me, Jesus," she whispered, gulping down the fear attacking her from all sides.

Haydon stepped between her and the pink animal he called Kitty. "Hi, Abby." He tugged on one of his little sister's pigtails. "What are you up to, Squirt?"

"Just playin' with Kitty."

"So I see." He knelt down. "Hey, Kitty girl."

The pig trotted toward him with her ears flapping like an upset hen. She leaned into his legs. He stumbled but caught himself before the swine toppled him over.

Rainee moved her tongue around to moisten her mouth, but it did no good. Dampness covered the palms of her hands. And air was sorely lacking.

"Hi, Rainee." Abby's sweet voice pulled her gaze away from the frightening creature. One look at her and the little girl's smile vanished. "Hey, you don't look none too good." Abby's eyes narrowed. "You okay?"

"I—I..." She tried to breathe but her tight corset prevented it. The bright outdoors turned into a cloud of hazy black. The only other time she remembered fainting this much was during one of Ferrin's vicious beatings because the pain had become so unbearable her body had succumbed to it with blessed blackness. And that blackness descended upon her now.

Her legs gave way.

In slow motion, she felt herself slipping to the ground, but instead of hitting the rough terrain, her body connected with solid arms before blackness engulfed her in its embrace.

Haydon carried Rainee's limp form back to the house. This was becoming a habit. One he wanted to break. Holding her in his arms affected his heart in a way he didn't need nor want. "Abby, open the door, please."

Abby raced ahead of him and held the door open. The wooden planks creaked as he climbed up the steps and onto the porch. "Mother," he hollered, stepping inside. "Mother!"

His mother bustled into the living room carrying a load of sheets in her arms. One look at Rainee and she thrust the sheets onto the chair and rushed toward the sofa where she propped up a pillow.

Once again, he laid Rainee's small frame on the sofa.

Mother sat next to her and removed her jacket. "What happened?"

"Kitty happened."

Mother's gaze darted up at him. "What do you mean 'Kitty happened'? Did she attack her?" Anger and concern flowed from her voice and eyes.

"No. All it took was one look at Kitty, and she fainted. Twice."

"Twice?" Mother's eyes widened, then narrowed. She looked at Abby, standing beside him. "Abby, grab me a wet cloth." She glanced at Haydon. "I'll call you if I need you."

That was his mother's way of dismissing him.

Even though Haydon saw Rainee as another weak city female, it bothered him she lay there unconscious… again. He hated to leave without knowing if she was all right or not, but he did as his mother bade. With a quick spin on his boot heel, he headed outside. He'd check in on her later.

Leah met him coming in with an empty clothes basket. "Hi, Haydon. What are you doing here? I thought you were checking on the pigs."

"I was. Rainee—" he gave a quick nod of his neck toward the inside of the house "—fainted again."

Leah dropped the basket on the porch, brushed past him and rushed inside. "Mother," she hollered.

"In here."

"Is she okay?" Leah's voice clouded with concern.

"She'll be fine."

Although he was relieved to hear she was fine, he wondered if he ever would be again. How had the little filly gotten under his skin so quickly? And more important, what was he going to do about it?

Chapter Seven

Rainee rolled her head to the side.

"Rainee?"

Hearing Katherine's voice as if she were in a tunnel, Rainee opened her eyes. "What happened?"

"Haydon said you fainted. Don't you remember?"

A floppy-eared, curly-tailed, big-snouted image jumped into her mind. She cringed. "Yes. I remember. How did I get here?" She pressed her fingers to her temples.

"Haydon brung you," Abby piped in.

"Brought you," Katherine corrected.

"That's what I said. Can I go out and play now?"

"May I?"

Abby let out a huff and rolled her eyes. "May I?"

"Yes, you may."

Abby skipped out of the living room and disappeared. What Rainee would give to be carefree like that again. To sit with her mother on the front-porch swing back home and listen while her mother regaled Rainee with stories about her childhood.

"Leah, would you please fix us some tea and bring it in here? And grab some syltkakor cookies, too."

Syltkakor cookies?

"Yes, Mother." She turned but looked back at Rainee. "I'm glad you're okay." Leah smiled and then left the room.

Rainee rose into a sitting position. Her head throbbed.

"The tea will help with your headache." Katherine smiled, but there was uncertainty in it. She stood and moved one of the wingback chairs until it faced Rainee. "Rainee?"

"Yes, ma'am."

"I know this is rather personal, but may I ask you something?"

The thought of Katherine asking a question Rainee had no desire to answer caused her stomach to twist into knots. But if she said no, it would be rude. "Yes, you may." She braced herself for the question.

"Are you wearing a corset?"

The woman was not kidding when she said it was personal. Heat filled Rainee's cheeks.

"I'm sorry if I embarrassed you. Haydon said you fainted because of Kitty, but I also wonder if that corset has something to do with it. They definitely restrict your air flow. This is the country, Rainee. Not the city. Out here, you don't have to wear one if you don't want to. Back home I was always fainting because of mine. Shortly after I moved here and noticed none of the other women wore them, I got rid of mine. The only time I wear one now is when I go to the city. I can't stand the confining things."

Rainee wanted to hug the woman for saying that. Because of Katherine's easy ways and her honesty concerning something as personal as undergarments, Rainee felt at ease to openly share her thoughts. "I, too, cannot stand the vile contraptions. I find them too confining. But my mother always made me wear one.

"I remember on my fourteenth birthday I decided to go without one to see if my mother would even notice." She looked at Katherine and smiled. "She did. And no matter how much I pleaded with her to not make me wear it on my birthday, she would not relent. Told me that properly bred young ladies do not go anywhere without a corset. So even though I despise the wretched things, I wear them out of respect for my mother and her wishes."

"My mother told me the same thing, so I know how you feel. But things are much different out here than they are in the city. It's up to you whether you want to wear one or not. But I must warn you…" Her eyes crinkled with mirth. "There are no fainting couches here."

They shared a laugh.

Every room in Rainee's house back home had a fainting couch. It infuriated her that women were forced to stuff themselves into those things until their bodies actually became deformed and their lungs were deprived of air and proper blood supply, which caused them to faint often.

Rainee thought the person who had come up with all those ridiculous rules of etiquette should have found something better to do with their time. Well, Rainee did. She wanted to walk without being short of breath. And she was tired of almost fainting every time she removed her corset and the blood traveled back into her head. Rainee despised fainting. To her it was a sign of weakness. What must these people think of her for fainting like she had?

If only she had been born a male, then she could wear trousers instead of layers of clothing. And no one would think anything of it if she climbed trees, got dirty, ran up the stairs or fished. Rainee loved to fish.

She placed her hands in her lap, torn between doing what her mother had taught her and the desire to rid herself of the encumbering contraption. She really did not have much of a choice. None of her clothes would fit without the corset.

"If you're worried about your dresses not fitting, Leah and I can help you let them out."

Had the woman read her mind? From the moment Rainee had met her, Rainee felt an immediate kinship with Katherine.

Leah walked into the room with a tray laden with cookies and tea. She set it on the end table, poured three cups of tea and filled three small plates with sandwich-type cookies. The filling reminded Rainee of the jar of red currant she saw sitting on the table. After Leah served her mother and Rainee, she sat on the opposite end of the sofa.

Memories of sharing tea and cake in the parlor with her mother and best friend Tamsey flashed through her mind. But she refused to allow herself to dwell on that memory, knowing it would cause her nothing but great sadness. "Thank you, Leah."

"You're welcome." Leah smiled that beautiful smile of hers, and her eyes sparkled like crystallized ice.

Rainee took a long sip of her drink and daintily set it down before looking toward Katherine. "I am not sure what to do, Katherine. In less than three weeks I will be leaving here. And if I go to the city, it would be improper for me not to wear a corset."

"You're not leaving us, are you, Rainee?" Leah looked horrified, which warmed Rainee's heart even more. Everyone had been so kind to her, making her feel truly welcome.

Too bad Haydon had not been the one to send for her. She would have so loved to be a part of this family, and even more so, Haydon's wife, for there was a gentleness about him she could not deny, in spite of his on-againoff-again aloofness.

And as for them raising pigs, well surely she could help around the house and not be subjected to the curly-tailed terrors. Especially the one Haydon called Kitty. Her body quivered just thinking about the vile creature.

"Are you cold?" Katherine sat her teacup on the saucer.

Rainee shook her head. "No. I was just thinking about—" her nose wrinkled "—Kitty." Her gaze landed on the ceiling, and she blew out a very unladylike breath. "What a name for a pig."

"Abby named her," Leah piped in.

She vaguely remembered Haydon telling her that. Seeing Haydon's strong attachment to his sisters, Rainee understood why he would go along with naming a pig Kitty. She giggled.

"What's so funny?" Katherine asked.

Rainee took another sip of her tea and placed it back on the saucer with a tinkling sound. Mother would have reprimanded her for that one. "When I went for a walk, I heard Haydon saying, 'Here, Kitty.' I went over to where he was and looked around for the cat. Instead I saw a pig charging our direction and screamed." She snickered again. "I am surprised y'all did not hear me."

She looked down at her chest as she fought again to gather in enough air. "You are right, Katherine. This corset has to go." It was clear to her now that being frightened along with not getting enough air had caused her to faint.

Rainee took another sip of her tea. Only this time she gently set the cup down with no tinkling noise. "Perhaps it would be okay to let out a couple of my dresses so I have something comfortable to wear while I am here. But I cannot let them all out as I do not have many dresses anymore. I will need to save some so that I have something presentable to wear when I leave for the city."

"Rainee, you don't have to leave. You're welcome to stay here as long as you like."

Rainee looked at Katherine. "I appreciate your kind offer, but I cannot do that to Haydon. It is obvious he does not want me here. I cannot impose upon your hospitality forever."

Katherine looked her straight in the eyes. "Having you here is no imposition whatsoever. Besides, you never know what God will do. I've seen the way Haydon looks at you. He's scared of you, Rainee. That means he feels something."

Rainee's insides skipped with a flicker of hope.

"I've prayed about it and prayed about it. And I believe God brought you here."

"But you do not even know me."

"That's true. But God does. And I know my Savior's voice." The wrinkles around Katherine's eyes and lips curled. Her look held a secret, but just what kind of secret, Rainee did not know.

* * *

Haydon tried not to think about Rainee, but his worry for her wouldn't leave. He headed up to the house and yelled through the screen door. "Is it okay to come in?"

"It's okay. Come on in," his mother hollered back.

Haydon stepped inside and headed into the living room. His gaze went straight to Rainee, who was sitting up. Relief expanded his chest. "I came to see if you were okay."

But when he got closer to Rainee, he noticed her face was still a bit too pale.

He glanced at his mother and Leah, pointedly feeling the number of people in the room.

His mother glanced around and the opportunity of the situation crossed her face. Haydon knew what was coming next even as his mother stood.

"I think I have some of my old dresses in the attic. Leah, come help me find them."

Haydon gave her a look meant to say he knew exactly what she was doing, and she smiled sweetly back. He watched as they left the room. He turned his attention back to Rainee. A few moments of awkward silence and the room suddenly seemed to be getting smaller.

Not knowing what else to do, he sat across from her and tried not to stare as he assessed for himself that she really was all right.

She cleared her throat. "Would—would you like a cookie? Or some tea perhaps. I—I could get you some." She started to stand but reached for the side of the sofa with a bit of sway to her movement.

Haydon jumped up and steadied her. His whole attention riveted to only her. He helped her onto the sofa and sat down with her. “Rainee, I don’t want any cookies. I came to see if you were all right.”

She stopped and for one second her eyes met his, pulling him into their depths. He found he was unable to move away and that scared him. Yanking reality back to himself, he stood so fast the blood rushed to his head. “Now that I see you’re okay, I need to get back to my chores.” He said the words so fast they almost tripped over each other.

Rainee looked up at him with a slight smirk on her face. “Thank you for checking on me. I am fine, albeit quite embarrassed for my lack of strength.”

“Lack of strength?” The words knocked him over like a team of runaway horses. “Why would you be embarrassed? All of us have weaknesses.”

“Yes, but weakness is all you have seen of me.”

“Nope—that’s not all I’ve seen.”

She quirked her head to the side, the smirk not fully gone. “Really? Well, let us see. First, you had to rescue me from the guy at the stage stop. Then, I nearly fainted when we arrived and you had to help me in. And now, I have fainted again. Not once, but twice. No, make that three times if you count fainting twice within minutes.”

He glanced at her for a moment, trying not to laugh. “Well, I guess you have a point.” For one moment he couldn’t believe he said that until she started laughing and his laughter blended with hers. “But I still don’t see you as weak. It took a lot of courage to travel to a strange place.”

He noticed the appreciative smile in her eyes. “Well, I’d better get back to work. I’m glad you’re feeling better.”

She started to rise, but he motioned for her to remain seated.

He headed for the door and just as he got there, she said, "Be careful of those curly-tailed beasts."

Her laughter followed him out the door.

Rainee was still laughing when Katherine and Leah came into the living room empty-handed.

"It's nice to see you feeling better." Katherine looked lighter and maybe even happier than before. "Now, let's go get you out of that thing and into something more practical and comfortable."

Rainee followed them up the stairs with a lighter, more joyful step than she had felt in two years. Perhaps God was in this after all. That thought brought joy singing through her heart.

Inside Leah's bedroom, without thinking, Rainee removed her gloves.

Leah glanced down and gasped. "What happened to your hands?"

Rainee's gaze flew to Leah. The poor girl stood there staring in utter horror at her hands.

Katherine came from behind Leah, and she too stared at them.

Shame flooded Rainee. She buried them behind her back.

Katherine and Leah's questioning eyes bore through her. She knew she could not hide her hands forever. With a flushed face and trembling insides, she inched them upward for their inspection, trying to feel nothing as the two of them looked on with shock and horror.

Katherine gently took one of Rainee's hands in hers and studied the raised scars. She looked at Rainee with eyes of compassion. "Who did this to you?"

She wanted to tell them they were from the pig attack, but that was an untruth. The pig had not touched her hands, only the back of her leg and her hips. With a heavy sigh, she answered, “My brother—”

“I didn’t know you had a brother,” Leah blurted.

Rainee looked at her and nodded. “I do.”

“Is he—”

“Leah, enough!” Katherine reprimanded her daughter. “Mind your manners.”

“Sorry.” Leah lowered her head.

Katherine’s words reminded her of her own mother. That would have been something Mother would have said. She envied Leah that she still had her mother to correct and love her. Rainee wished her mother were still alive. Homesickness feathered over her as it did so very often.

“Please, go on.”

Rainee lowered her eyes. In a nervous circular motion, she rubbed her fingertips over the welts near her wrists. Rainee looked up at them. “Please, I do not wish to talk about this for it is too painful. And if you would both be so kind, would you please not mention my hands to anyone?”

She looked back and forth between Katherine and Leah, allowing her eyes to plead with them for their total secrecy.

“There is no need for anything we’ve seen or talked about today to leave this room,” Katherine said, more to Leah than anyone else.

“I won’t say a word, Mother.” Leah looked Rainee directly in the eye. “You have my word, Rainee. I promise I won’t say a thing to anyone.”

“And neither will I.” Katherine’s chest heaved. “Now

I understand why such a sweet beautiful woman such as yourself ran away."

Ran away? Oh, no. Her insides flushed with terror. Now that they knew she had run away, would they send her back, regardless of what her brother had done to her? Would they betray her like her Aunt Lena had?

Chapter Eight

The ache in Rainee's stomach disappeared when nothing more was said about her running away. Too bad that had not been the case with her father's sister, Aunt Lena. Before she ran away to Aunt Lena's, she had asked Mr. Pennay, her father's lawyer, if anything was written in the will about Ferrin being her legal guardian, and he had assured her nothing had been.

When Ferrin came for Rainee at Aunt Lena's house, even after she had shown the strict socially proper woman the welts on her back and hands, her aunt still forced her to go back with Ferrin when he lied and said he was indeed her legal guardian. Aunt Lena said it was not proper for her or anyone else to go against a father's wishes, and if he said he was her legal guardian, then he was—pure and simple.

It never ceased to amaze Rainee that, even when a person's life was at risk, people still maintained the rules of propriety. That was just one more reason why she detested those rules.

Today, she had broken two of those rules, and it felt delightful.

After Rainee, Leah and Katherine let out three of Rainee's dresses, they started preparing the evening meal. While Katherine worked on the Lefsa, a traditional Swedish flatbread made from potatoes, Leah helped gather ingredients, peel potatoes and fry the Korv. Korv, Rainee learned, was Swedish for sausage. Rainee baked the pies and made the soup, enjoying every moment of being helpful.

Rainee opened the oven door to remove the pies. Heat drove into her, but with a lighter dress on and no restricting corset, the heat did not bother her like it had back home.

After her parents had died, during the hottest part of the summer, Ferrin had forced her to wear heavy garments with layers upon layers of undergarments. He also had limited her water and food supply to one serving a day, all because he said it gave him great pleasure watching her suffer. Why? She did not know. But suffer she had.

Often, her stomach cramped until she doubled over. Her skin prickled like someone was stabbing it with needles, and her head swam with dizziness.

For fear of getting another beating, she had to force her fatigued body to move.

If it had not been for Jenetta coming to Rainee's aid repeatedly, she would probably be dead by now. But Jenetta had sewn two large pockets into one of her undergarments, big enough to hold a jar of water and some cheese or fruit.

Jenetta's husband, Abram, left a covered bucket of water inside the woodshed, along with a few vegetables he had picked fresh from the garden and managed to sneak inside the shed.

Rainee closed the oven door. The scent of fresh, warm pie crust and sweet huckleberries satiated her nose. With any kind of luck, she would never go hungry or ever endure another vicious beating again—even if she had to move again to Mr. Bettes's.

Katherine hung up her dish towel. "Leah, will you please ring the dinner bell?"

"I will get it." Rainee wiped her hands on her apron and stepped outside.

The breeze penetrated her wine-colored dress, kissing her flesh with its coolness. She patted her damp face with her apron and took a brief moment to enjoy the sensation of freedom the lightweight dress and breezy outdoors created. It was heaven on earth.

She reached up and gave the rope several tugs and winced at the loud clanging noise. Hurrying back inside, she helped put the food onto the table.

The door creaked.

Rainee turned, only to find Haydon standing inside the door, gawking at her.

Her gaze dropped to the floor. After setting down the tray of food, she hugged her waist. All those years of wearing a corset, and she suddenly felt naked without it. Mother's words started to run through her mind as they so often did, but this time she squelched them. Instead she dared a glance at Haydon. Was that approval she saw in his eyes?

Before she had a chance to figure it out, Abby came barreling through the door followed by Michael and Smokey.

Rainee waited for Katherine to reprimand Abby for charging into the house, but the scolding never came. Mother would have made Rainee go back outside and come back in like a suitable young lady, and then she would sit her down to a long lecture on how proper young ladies should act, followed by a tender hug that left no doubt in Rainee's mind about her mother's love.

Everyone sat down at the table and bowed their heads.

"Heavenly Father." Haydon's reverent voice filled the room. "Thank You for what You're doing in our lives and for Your healing power that is at work in Jesse. We thank You for this food and for Your bountiful provision. And, Lord, help us to be a blessing to Rainee."

Rainee kept one eye closed, but the other one snuck a peek at Haydon. Never had she heard such humility or kindness in his voice, especially where she was concerned. In the quietness of her mind, she offered up her own gratitude as everyone said amen. She moved her bowl in front of her. "How is your brother doing, Haydon?"

Sapphire eyes settled on hers. "I don't know. I haven't seen him."

He made a quick glance around the table and then looked down at his soup. Rainee wondered what the sudden change in his disposition was about. Was he still upset with Jesse for bringing her here, or was something else bothering him? She kept her wonderings to herself.

She picked up her spoon, dipped it in her bowl and brought it to her mouth. The thick split-pea and ham soup tasted heavenly. A nice change from the beans and rice Ferrin fed her once a day. If she was lucky.

Smokey cleared his throat. "Jesse's doing a little better today."

"You mean Hannah let you see him?" Leah asked with raised brows. "She wouldn't let me. She said he was sleeping and she would not disturb him. She sure has changed." She laughed. "Hannah's like a protective mama bear watching over her cubs."

Smokey nodded. "Must have something to do with her being in the family way. I pert-near had to beg her to let me check him. And even then she made me promise I'd only stay a minute."

Everyone but Haydon laughed.

Rainee watched as he picked up his spoon and dipped it into the split-pea soup.

"Who knew Hannah could be so feisty?" Smokey commented with a deep rumble in his chest. "Since Jesse's accident, her shyness seems to have fled."

"What happened to Jesse anyway?" Rainee asked.

With a pained expression, Haydon looked at her, then at the rest of his family, then down at his soup. His jaw muscles worked back and forth. Without saying a word, he spooned his soup and ate.

The air thickened with silence.

Rainee scanned the table. Everyone seemed engrossed in the food on their plates. Everyone except Abby. Her bright blue eyes gazed around the table. It was as if she were waiting for someone to say something.

When no one else spoke, Abby did. "Haydon's horse reared and hurted him."

Rainee watched with interest as Haydon's scowling gaze swung toward Abby.

The little girl blinked. Then as fast as she could she wrapped her potato bread around her sausage and took a big bite. Her cheeks bulged like a chipmunk, and she nervously glanced up and down and around the room.

"I think Jesse's just wanting to get out of clipping the newborn piglet's teeth," Leah piped in.

All eyes swerved toward Leah, but no one said anything.

Curiosity and horror got the best of Rainee. "You clip the baby pigs' teeth?"

"Yes." Her gaze transferred to Haydon. "If we don't, when they grow, they can be very dangerous."

"Dangerous." She gulped and worked her tongue around to moisten her suddenly parched mouth. "How dangerous?" She picked up her water glass and took a drink, then rested her hands in her lap and fidgeted with her gloves.

Haydon set the glass he was holding down and locked gazes with her. "Don't worry, Rainee. I won't let anything happen to you."

Haydon broke eye contact and shoved a bite of Korv and Lefsa into his mouth. What he really wanted to do was to remove his boot and give himself a good swift kick in the behind. The last thing he wanted was for her and his family to get the notion he was interested in her.

Their eyes connected for a brief moment before he asked Michael. "Did you get that halter fixed?" He dipped his wrap into his soup and took a bite. When Michael didn't answer, he looked over at him.

Like a lovelorn pup, his brother was staring across the table at Rainee. "Michael!"

His brother jerked his head in his direction, blinking. "What?"

Abby giggled. "Michael's sweet on Rainee. Michael's sweet on Rainee," she singsonged.

Michael's cheeks flamed like a bad sunburn. He dropped his chin.

"Abigail! Stop that!" His mother's stern voice rescued poor Michael.

Haydon watched Rainee's cheeks and neck turn crimson.

"Apologize this instant, Abby," Mother demanded.

"But it's true. Last night I seeded Michael staring at her the whole time we eated. And today, when Rainee was walking, I seeded him hiding in the bushes watching her."

"I was not hiding in the bushes. I heard a scream and went to check it out. When I saw Haydon had it under control and that she was all right, I went back to gathering wood." Michael glared at his sister with narrowed eyes.

"You always stare at her. And I hearded you tell Smokey you thought she was bootiful." She tipped her head, pinched her lips and squinted her eyes. Haydon had seen that look before. Abby was daring Michael to challenge her.

Rainee's cheeks brightened to an even deeper shade of red. Her eyes were downcast, and she shifted in her chair.

"Enough, you two!" Haydon barked.

Abby jumped, and Michael had the decency to look ashamed.

"Can't you see you've made Rainee uncomfortable? You both need to apologize to her this instant."

Abby's lips puckered and tears welled in her in eyes. She dropped her gaze to her lap and sniffled. "Sorry, Rainee."

Haydon glanced at Rainee in time to see her look over at Abby and nod. He glanced at Michael.

"I'm sorry I made you uncomfortable, Rainee." Michael's sheepish grin showed his remorse. "But—" he pressed his shoulders back and puffed his chest out "—I'm not sorry for saying you're beautiful. Because you are." Michael sent Rainee a flirtatious smile and then he shot his older brother a look of direct challenge before his gaze dropped to his soup.

So much for Michael having the decency to be ashamed.

At a complete loss for words, Haydon looked to his mother, who seemed to share his bewilderment.

To take the focus off of Rainee and this whole awkward situation, Haydon shifted his attention toward his sister. "Leah, is that your famous blue-ribbon apple pie I smell?"

"No." She swallowed. "Rainee made it. And it's not apple, it's huckleberry."

So much for getting the focus off of Rainee. His gaze slid her direction.

Her cheeks were as pink as a warm-weather sunset, giving her a wholesome, fresh look. His heart noticed it all.

"You made it?" He didn't mean for his shock to leak through his voice but it did.

"Yes, I did," she answered softly.

Taken aback, Haydon mentally shook his head. At the stagecoach stop when he first laid eyes on Rainee, wearing all the rich city-girl frippery, he instantly thought of Melanie, who thought cooking and cleaning were beneath her. He just assumed the same about Rainee. Had he misjudged her?

Don't let that summer dress and great-smelling pie fool you, Haydon. The Idaho Territory isn't any place for a woman like her. You learned that the hard way.

His gaze slid in his mother's direction. Back home in New York, Mother had been a leader in society. So when Father decided to move out West, Haydon had waited for his mother to protest, but instead, she had readily agreed.

It hadn't taken long for her to adapt to her new surroundings. She was a brave woman with a strong constitution who had survived several harsh winters. Respect and pride for her swelled his chest. He snuck a glance at their guest. Aside from her fainting spells, which he knew happened to the strongest of women, could Rainee be a stronger woman than he gave her credit for?

Not liking where his thoughts were leading, he picked up his spoon and filled his mouth with more of the delicious dinner. "You've outdone yourself on the soup, Mother. This is your best batch ever."

"Mother didn't make it. Rainee did," Leah informed him.

He snapped his head in her direction. "You made this?"

Rainee sat up straight and jutted her chin. "Yes. Yes, I did."

"Rainee can do lots of things," his mother stated, sending Haydon a silent message.

His gaze veered toward Michael, whose admiring gaze clung to Rainee.

Haydon rubbed his neck in frustration. The whole world seemed to have gone crazy with her arrival. What to do about his mother and her not-so-subtle hints was bad enough, but Michael was even worse.

What was he going to do about his little brother and his infatuation with Rainee? As the oldest, Father had left Haydon in charge, so it was up to him to come up with a plan of action to stop his sixteen-year-old brother's boyish passion. And he needed to do it quickly. Not just for Michael's sake. But for hers, and maybe even his.

When Rainee finished helping with the dishes, the Bowens invited her to join in on their family Bible reading.

They all retired into the living room and sat near the fireplace. After Haydon finished reading and praying, Rainee excused herself and stepped outside and off of the porch. The cool air had a penetrating, earthy freshness to it. She headed toward the barn but stopped several yards away from the door and gazed up at the sky. Stars sparkled like sequins on the ballroom gown she had worn at her coming-out party. Just like that dress, they were too numerous to even try to count. But count she would. "One," she whispered. "Two. Three. Four."

"Forget it."

She whirled at the sound of Haydon's voice.

He stood behind her, gazing upward, arms crossed. "You'll never count them all. I've already tried." His gaze alighted on hers. Night shadows fell across his face. And what a handsome face it was.

"There's a bit of nip in the air. I thought you might need this." He draped her wrap securely around her shoulders.

What a sweet man he was to think of her comfort.

A tug on each end of her shawl, and she managed to pull it closer to her. She had not noticed the chill until his warm hands had touched her. “Thank you.” Her heart melted at his thoughtfulness.

“You’re welcome.”

Rainee waited for him to leave, but he did not. He stood there, staring up at the stars.

What an enigma this man had turned out to be. There were times when he was kind to her, times when he barely spoke to her, times when his gaze was soft and others when he looked at her as if he were deathly afraid of her or even outright angry with her.

She could not blame him for his actions or even for his behavior. Though they saddened her, she must not allow the sadness to work its way into her heart. She must accept the fact she had to find another suitable husband. That was best for all involved. Still, this moment, standing here under the stars was not to be wasted, even though it could not last. “Is it always this beautiful out here?”

“Nope. Sometimes it’s even better.”

“Better than this?”

“Doesn’t seem possible, does it?”

“No.”

A comfortable silence stretched between them as they continued to gaze at the sky. This place might be in the middle of nowhere, but it was truly extraordinary.

“Is it always this peaceful?” She had not experienced this kind of serenity in a very long time.

He looked down at her. Their eyes connected, searching and probing and her heart responded with a flip.

He turned his head upward again. “Most of the time.”

Most of the time, as in, before she arrived?

“I never tire of the night sky.” Reverence floated through his voice.

"Nor do I."

"I can't believe God took the trouble to place the stars into various shapes. Like the Big Dipper." He pointed to it, and she followed the direction of his finger until it landed on the pattern of those stars.

"And the Little Dipper," she said. "Slaves used the Little Dipper and the Big Dipper to point to the North Star. They even sang a song about them…'Follow the Drinking Gourd.'"

"I've never heard that before. Did your family have slaves?"

Rainee tensed. If only she could avoid answering everyone's questions about her family until she wed, then she would be free from her brother's controlling clutches. "Before the war my parents had slaves, but they did not treat them cruelly. And after the war ended, they gave them the option to leave or to stay on with a small wage and room and board. How about you? Did you have slaves?"

"No, my parents did not believe in slavery. We had hired servants."

"Is it hard not having servants here?"

"No. Not at all."

"Does your mother mind not having servants to help her?"

"Nope. She loves to cook and clean. She said it's better than sitting around all day doing nothing."

Rainee agreed.

"I've offered to hire her some help many times, but she won't hear of it. It really bothers me watching her work as hard as she does. But she keeps telling me she loves it, and says that if she ever feels it's becoming too much for her she'll let me know so I can hire someone to help her. Speaking of help…" He glanced over at Rainee. "I really appreciate you helping my mother with the baking and cooking. Thank you."

"You are most welcome. I was delighted to do it."

Haydon looked away and the only sounds to be heard were a chorus of frogs and insects. Moments later, Haydon heaved a heavy sigh. "Well, it's getting late and I have to get up early. Let me walk you to the house."

They turned and headed back to the main house.

He opened the door for her.

She slipped past him and then turned. "Good night, Haydon."

"Good night, Rainee."

She closed the door and watched his retreating form until he faded into the darkness beyond, like the moon and stars on a cloud-covered evening. Men were complex creatures. And he was the most complex of all. She had no idea what to expect next with him. In a way that was pleasant and in another way, frightening. Too bad she could not stay long enough to sort it all out.

Chapter Nine

"Now, where is he?" Since his father's death, brother problems seemed to follow Haydon around the ranch like persistent yapping dogs. Between Jess and Micheal, Haydon wondered if he would ever have a moment's peace again.

Haydon checked inside the barn and the woodshed. Chickens flapped their wings, squawking and scattering as he trudged his way through the coop. Inside the filthy pen, the stench assaulted his nose. Frustrated and aggravated the hens and rooster hadn't been fed yet and the eggs hadn't been gathered either, he stomped out of the pen and panned the area for Rainee, knowing Michael would most likely be found in close proximity to her.

Since that night under the stars, he had made it a point to be polite to her, but he had also done his best to avoid her whenever possible. Those few moments felt far too good to him. She radiated a quiet softness by starlight that drew him to her.

Haydon continued looking for his brother and Rainee but didn't see either of them anywhere. He jerked his hat off and raked his fingers through his hair, then slammed his hat back in place. Ever since Rainee's arrival three weeks ago, Michael had slacked on his chores, and the animals were suffering because of it.

Haydon's boots collided with the hard-packed ground as he made his way across the yard. Hearing voices, he thundered around the backside of the house.

Just like he knew it would be, there stood Michael, handing clothespins to Rainee as she hung sheets up on the line strung from one tree to another. His brother could help her, but he couldn't manage to get his own chores finished.

"Michael." He didn't care if anger rolled out of him.

Their laughter and chatter stopped.

"What?" Michael turned disgusted eyes onto Haydon.

Rainee yanked her gaze at him and then at Michael. She put her back to Haydon. Dressed in a light blue dress and matching bonnet, she snatched a sheet from the laundry basket, shook it out and tossed it over the clothesline.

"I need to talk to you."

"Anything you say, you can say here." Michael knew Haydon normally dealt with matters privately so as to not embarrass anyone. Only it wasn't embarrassment reddening Michael's cheeks—it was anger. Shock rippled through Haydon. Michael had never rebelled against his orders before. Father informed his family if anything happened to him Haydon was in charge and they were to do whatever he said. And Michael had… until Rainee showed up.

"Did you forget to feed the chickens and gather the eggs again?"

"Why do I have to do it? Leah can gather the eggs."

Haydon couldn't believe what he had just heard. *Lord, help me out here.* "Because that's your job."

"Not anymore." Michael puffed his chest out and separated his feet.

Rainee snatched up the empty basket and scurried around them. She fled toward the back door without a backward glance. Haydon didn't blame her. This was about to get ugly. He ground his teeth in frustration. Once again he was left to clean up the aftermath of one of Jesse's schemes.

"When was the last time you cleaned the coop?"

"I cleaned it yesterday."

This whole mess was getting worse by the minute. His brother had never been one to lie before, and here Michael was, doing just that. "That coop hasn't been cleaned for quite some time. You need to go do it, and do it right."

Michael didn't move or say a word. He just stared at Haydon as if he didn't care, daring him to call him on his lie.

Haydon opted to try a different tactic. "Michael, Jesse did not invite Rainee here for you to follow around like a lovesick bull. She is a guest in Mother's house and you need to treat her as such."

"I'm not doing anything wrong. I like Rainee." Michael darted a quick glance at Haydon. "And I think she likes me. Besides, you aren't my father. I don't have to do what you say."

Haydon sighed, and his chest constricted. He had wondered when this day would come. *Dear Lord, I'm in way over my head here. Give me wisdom beyond my understanding in how to deal with this.*

"You're right, Michael. I'm not Father, and I wish

he were here to handle this. He would know just what to say to you, and you would do it. But he isn't, and I am." He ran his hand down his face. "I know I can't make you do anything, but I'm asking you to get your chores done to help out around here. I can't run this place without your help. And as for Rainee, you're right. She does like you."

Michael's face brightened.

"But not the way you think. She doesn't look at you the way a woman does when she has romantic feelings for a man."

"What do you mean?"

"Does she look at you with stars in her eyes?"

Michael shook his head.

"Does she touch your arm and smile tenderly at you? Hang on to your every word?"

Michael's gaze dropped to the ground, and he shook his head. "No."

Haydon didn't know what else to say, so he remained quiet.

"Sorry I haven't been doing my chores. I'll go do them now." Michael walked a few steps before he stopped and turned. "Thanks, Haydon. I'm sorry about what I said. You're the closest thing to a father I have. I won't give you a hard time anymore."

"Thanks, Michael. That means a lot to me."

He watched his brother head to the chicken pen. Pride welled in his chest. Today, his brother had taken a step down the path to becoming a man. That thought made him sad and happy at the same time.

Haydon headed toward the barn. Inside, he grabbed the pitchfork and forked hay into the horses' stalls. With each toss, the tension of the morning lifted.

Dust danced at his feet and blades of hay floated like big raindrops from the pitchfork.

One major problem created by Jess's stupidity had been solved. Only one remained—what to do about Rainee. The little woman aroused feelings in him he never wanted to feel again. So before he did anything stupid, like give into those feelings, he wanted her to leave.

But where would she go? Who would take care of her? The guy she had mailed the letter to? Had she heard back from him? Haydon's head started to hurt, and the muscle in his neck ached as the tension returned. None of this was his problem, but he couldn't ignore it. After all, she was a person who needed help. And that he couldn't ignore. He jammed the pitchfork into the hay, trying to take his frustrations out on the dried grass.

"Mornin'."

Haydon's pitchfork hit the top board of the stall with a thud.

"How you doing, Haydon?"

"How do you think I'm doing?" he grunted his reply and stepped over to the next stall. He started tossing hay into it, hoping Jesse would take the hint and leave him alone. But knowing how stubborn his brother could be, he knew that wasn't likely to happen.

"Look. Are you ever going to forgive me? I said I was sorry. What more do you want from me?"

"What more do I want?" Haydon reeled around. "I'll tell you what I want. I want you to take care of the mess your careless thinking created. I want you to get that woman out of here so things can get back to normal. That's what I want."

A loud gasp near the barn door snapped Haydon's attention in that direction.

Rainee stood in the doorway with her hand over her mouth, blinking wide eyes at him. The moment froze around him, and then she whirled and fled from the barn.

"Feel better now?" Jesse shot a look of disdain at Haydon coupled with a quick shake of his head, then bolted after her. "Rainee, wait!"

Haydon closed his eyes and let his head drop backward. He stared at the ceiling as disgust with himself drizzled over him like the particles of swirling barn dust. *"You're a poor excuse of a man."* Melanie's words pierced his soul for the millionth time since she'd first said them. She was right. He was a poor excuse for a man. No real man treated a woman that way even if he thought she was out of earshot.

But then again, he hadn't done it on purpose. How was he supposed to know she was standing there? He hadn't heard her come in. Still, right was right and wrong was wrong. And he was wrong. Although he would love nothing more than to have Jesse deal with this, he knew he needed to go and apologize to her himself. He had been the one who hurt her.

"I'm so sorry, Rainee. I'm sure Haydon didn't mean it."

Without any resistance, Rainee let Jesse guide her toward his house. Sadness pulled her into its embrace, numbing her mind and heart. To actually hear Haydon say he still did not want her here hurt more than it should have.

Though he had already made that perfectly clear,

she had held out hope over the past three weeks, praying that maybe he was starting to change his mind because she had seen the looks he had given her when he thought she was not looking, and she had thought she knew what they meant. Obviously, she was very wrong. It was clear he had not changed his mind about her.

The stairs groaned as they made their way up them. Jesse opened the door for her and she preceded him inside.

Hannah stepped through the bedroom door and her eyes widened. She waddled over to them like a baby duckling hurrying to keep up with her mother. Her gaze slanted between the two of them. "What's the matter?"

"Haydon is what's the matter."

Rainee caught the frustration in Jesse's voice.

"I know he's my brother and all, but sometimes the man needs to think past his own selfishness."

Hannah's forehead wrinkled. "What did he do now?" She placed her arm around Rainee and led her to a simple tan-and-blue Victorian settee.

"I'll get some tea and then leave you two ladies alone."

Rainee did not miss the look of understanding that passed between them.

Hannah reached into the pocket of her dull gray apron and pulled out a clean, folded hanky. She pressed it into Rainee's hand. Rainee wiped her eyes and nose.

"Here you go." Jesse handed them each a cup and saucer filled with a pale yellow brew.

He leaned over and kissed his wife's cheek. When he rose, he looked down at Rainee with compassion. "Don't let what Haydon said get to you, Rainee. I know he didn't mean it. He's not a cruel man. He's just— I'm sorry." He shrugged, then gave a small smile before he stepped outside.

Just what? She wanted to scream at him to complete his sentence. The need to know what Jesse had been about to say pressed in on her, but he obviously did not want to finish whatever it was.

With a weighty sigh of acceptance, she took a sip of the weak tea and set the cup back in the saucer.

"Now tell me, what did Haydon do to upset you?" Hannah's soft brown eyes blinked with concern.

Rainee looked down at her lap and ran her fingers over the hanky, folding and refolding it. "He said he wanted me out of here and for things to be back to normal."

"Well, I never. Wait until I get a hold of that man." Hannah started to rise, but Rainee put her hand on top of her arm.

"Please, Hannah, do not. He is right. I must away. My presence here obviously causes him great distress. And he should not have to feel that way in his own home. Besides, there is another gentleman who answered my advertisement and I—"

Hannah interrupted her. "You're not going anywhere, Rainee. Ever since—" Hannah stopped abruptly. "Never mind that. You can move in here with Jesse and me. If Haydon doesn't like it, well, too bad. This is our ranch, too."

Rainee did not wish to cause any more trouble in this family. She had caused quite enough already.

Her Aunt Lena was right when she did not want to get involved with Rainee's troubles. These people should not have to either. If only she would have thought of that before she had posted the advertisement.

Her heart stung at the thought that she should have just graciously accepted her fate at the hands of her brother and Mr. Alexander. A shudder ran through her spine. At least then, these good people would not be made to suffer as well. "Thank you, Hannah, for your generous offer, but I cannot accept it. I expect a post any day now from Mr. Bettes."

"Mr. Bettes. Who's that?"

"The gentleman I told you about. The other man who responded to my advertisement with whom I felt comfortable contacting. He is a Christian, and he did not sound as terrible as some of them." She shivered at the memory of some of the contemptible letters she had received.

"Rainee, I don't want you to go. I've enjoyed our visits. Besides, I have a feeling about you and Haydon."

The smile came very close to touching her heart. "I, too, have enjoyed our visits, Hannah, but truly, it is clear I must take my leave. I came here to get married. And it is quite obvious that is not going to happen. So I must away as soon as possible. Haydon does not want me here. And I shall not stay where I am not welcome."

Haydon tossed his pitchfork into a pile of loose hay and headed out into the bright sunshine, which was the complete opposite of his mood. He needed to find Rainee and apologize.

When he stepped onto Jesse's porch, through the open window he heard Rainee say she would not stay where she was not welcome. He felt horrible. Without hesitating, he opened the door without knocking. "You don't need to go anywhere, Rainee."

Both of the ladies' attention swiveled to him standing in the doorway.

"Haydon Bowen, how dare you barge in here?" Hannah rose, but he held up his hand to silence her.

"I'm sorry, Hannah. But I—" He glanced over to Rainee, embarrassment shrouded her face.

She immediately looked down at her lap, and remorse for his behavior punched his gut.

"Rainee. Can we talk?"

She raised her head and tilted her chin. "I do not believe there is anything to talk about, sir." She rose with the grace of a queen. "Now, if you will excuse me. I have things I must attend to." She faced Hannah. "Thank you, Hannah, for the tea and for your most gracious offer." Shoulders squared, she glided toward him and brushed his shoulder on the way out the door.

He turned to follow her, but Hannah grabbed the sleeve of his shirt. He looked down at her hand and then at her face.

Fury shot from her big brown eyes. "Don't you dare hurt that woman, Haydon Bowen. You have no idea what she's been through."

He touched the brim of his black hat and slipped out the door and into the fresh air, wondering what Hannah meant by what the woman had been through—cotillions and balls? Yes, they were so very hard on a person.

He spotted Rainee storming her way to his mother's house, and his heart locked on the sight. "Rainee."

She picked up her pace and so did he until he caught up to her. Reaching out, he clutched her by the elbow and turned her, though she spun on her own accord and very nearly took a swing at him in the process.

"Unhand me, please." It was an order—not a suggestion.

"Only if you promise you'll hear me out."

Spunk flashed through her eyes. "There is nothing you could say to me that I would wish to hear. I know how you feel. You have made it perfectly clear, and I am sorry for making your life miserable. You need not trouble yourself anymore about me. I am leaving as soon as I am able to make other arrangements. And the sooner the better. For both of us." With those words, she yanked free of him, hiked up her skirts and closed the distance between her and his mother's house within a matter of seconds.

He should have been happy she was making other arrangements and would be out of their lives soon, but he wasn't. And that bothered him.

Chapter Ten

"Men. Why did You ever create the wretched creatures? What do You have against us women anyway, Lord?" Rainee mumbled as she stomped her way through the kitchen and headed toward the stairway.

"What did you say?"

Rainee stopped and looked over at Katherine sitting in the chair darning a sock.

"Are you all right?" Katherine placed the stocking into the basket at her feet and pointed to the chair near her.

Rainee wanted to keep going, but she refused to be rude to Katherine just because her son was a brute. Plus, she needed to inform Katherine she would be leaving soon. Just how she would finance the trip, she did not know, but she wanted to get as far away from Haydon as possible.

With a heavy sigh, she walked over and sat in the chair next to Katherine. "I want to thank you for everything you have done for me."

"This sounds like goodbye." Worry lines etched Katherine's eyes. "Don't you like it here?"

"I love it here." Rainee nodded and fought back tears. Being around Katherine had made Rainee less lonely for her mother, and she had come to care dearly for this woman. But the reason she had come no longer existed, and she could no longer pretend that it might, nor would she trespass on Katherine's kindness any further.

"Then, why?" Katherine tilted her head, inspecting Rainee. "Does it have anything to do with why you've been crying?"

"How did you know I had been crying?"

"Because your nose is all red and puffy."

Rainee put her head down, but it was too late. Katherine already knew.

"Now, tell me, what has you so upset?"

Not wanting to cause a rift between Katherine and her son, Rainee decided on another tactic. "It has been three weeks since I arrived, and to be honest, there has been no sign of Haydon wanting to marry me. Quite the opposite, actually. So I think it best that I pack my bags and head back to Prosperity Mountain to catch the next stagecoach. If my calculations are correct, it should be arriving in the next day or two."

"But where would you go? Surely not back home to that—"

Rainee knew the words Katherine chose not to speak. That monster, her brother. She took a breath to settle the horror that thoughts of her brother always provoked.

"Rainee." Katherine grabbed her hands. "Why the sudden change? Did something happen to change your mind?"

Reluctantly, Rainee nodded.

"What?"

"I would rather not say. But please believe me when

I say I must go even though I wish to stay. But I simply cannot."

"I won't push you to tell me what has caused you to change your mind, but would you consider staying for my sake?"

"For your sake? I do not understand. How could my staying possibly benefit you?"

"Because, I really enjoy your company, and I've come to love you like one of my own. Besides, I would worry myself to death, wondering if you're okay. Here, I know you will be. Plus, you've been a huge help. But that's not the only reason why I want you to stay," Katherine hastened to add, but Rainee already knew what she had meant. Katherine loved people for who they were, not for what they did for her.

Genuine compassion and love flowed from Katherine to Rainee.

"That is very kind of you, Katherine. I, too, have grown to love all of you. But what about Haydon? I know he does not want me here."

"Did he tell you that?"

Not wanting to be a pot stirrer, Rainee simply said, "Let us just say a woman knows when she is not wanted."

Katherine frowned. "I'm sorry you feel that way. But…" She pressed her finger to her lips. "There are several single men in this county. I'm sure you could have your pick of any one of them. In fact, we're hosting church here tomorrow. You can meet some of them then."

Could this be why God brought her here? Perhaps there would be a kind man among the gentlemen tomorrow who would take her as his bride.

Or perhaps not.

Who would have thought she would have to succumb to marrying a total stranger instead of marrying for love? If only her parents had not died. If only she could wait until she found someone who loved her and she him. But time was not her friend in that regard, so she needed to stop dwelling on the "if onlys" because they did no good whatsoever.

And if Ferrin chose to come after her like he had when she had run away to Aunt Lena's, and if he found her unmarried, he would no doubt use brute force to make her Mr. Alexander's newest wife.

Well, she would do everything in her power to not let that happen and pray that God would give her the strength to do what needed to be done. And He would. After all, God had given her the courage and grace to engage herself to Haydon, who she did not know or love, and she knew He would give her whatever else she needed to survive.

Rainee straightened her slumped shoulders. "I will stay. But only until I find out if another man might consider me or until I hear from Mr. Bettes."

Katherine smiled. "Oh, I'm sure they will." She turned her head toward the living room window. "But I'm even more sure before that happens my son will come to his senses and not let you go to another man."

Rainee was certain she was not meant to hear that last part, but she had. She could only hope and pray Katherine was right and the stubborn man in question would indeed come to his senses.

Later on, before the sun had settled in for the evening, after the dishes were finished and put away, Rainee slipped outside into the warm air. The need to be alone and to think weighed heavily on her because she could not shake Haydon's words from her mind. What had happened to him to make him dislike her so?

"Hello, Rebel."

Inside the barn, Haydon turned his ear toward the sound of Rainee's voice.

"How are you this evening?" she asked his horse.

"I'm fine," Haydon answered.

Rainee whirled in Haydon's direction as he stepped up beside her. Her body stiffened and she turned to leave.

"Don't go, Rainee."

She kept walking.

"Please."

She stopped.

"I'd really like a chance to apologize for my rude behavior and to talk to you."

She faced him. "You do not owe me an apology or anything else, Mr. Bowen. As you are not the one who sent for me, and you have made it perfectly clear you do not want me, I will take my leave as soon as other arrangements can be made. I am not one to burden myself onto another, and it is I who needs to apologize for what my presence here is putting you through."

"Rainee, I can't have you thinking my attitude has anything to do with you. It doesn't. It has everything to do with me. I want you to know you are more than welcome to live here with my family for as long as you like."

She tilted her head in a way he'd come to recognize, questioning him to see if he really meant what he said.

He could only hope he wasn't making a huge mistake with his offer, but right was right and wrong was wrong. And he'd been wrong in his treatment of her—especially these last weeks as he tried to keep his distance. Besides, her staying with them didn't mean he had to marry her.

"Thank you, Haydon."

Hearing her address him as Haydon instead of Mr. Bowen was a good sign, and he felt the relief of it all the way from his head to his toes.

"I appreciate your kind offer. But I have already sent my post to Mr. Bettes, and if he still wants me, I will accept his offer of marriage."

With those words, she headed toward the house. "Good night, Haydon," she tossed over her shoulder.

Sunday morning, Rainee stood at the bedroom window with her hands on the sill and her forehead pressed against the glass. She gazed up at the bright July sun. Today looked to be another scorcher.

Down below she noticed Michael setting up tables. He picked up one end of the long table, and Smokey lifted the other. Michael, such a sweet, sensitive boy, would someday make some woman a fine husband. Just not for her, for he was much too young.

Rainee knew Michael had set his cap for her, but since their encounter with Haydon at the clothesline, she had tried to avoid the boy as much as possible because he was shirking his duties to be in her presence. Still, he seemed to find her wherever she went, and she refused to be rude to him. Guarded, yes. Rude, no. In fact, whenever she was around him, she made sure nothing in her countenance showed anything other than friendship.

It seemed to be working to some degree because Michael's visits had become less frequent and he no longer caressed her with his eyes as he once had. It was if he understood there would never be anything between them.

Haydon stepped into view.

Rainee moved to the side of the window where he could not see her and watched as he hoisted the benches and placed them neatly in rows. How she wished things would work out between them.

He was a gentle man with a caring heart.

A man who loved his family and treated them with the utmost respect.

A man who under unusual circumstances had been polite and courteous to her.

Last night at the dinner table, he had tried to include her in the conversation, but after she had overheard him telling Jesse he wanted her to leave, she had no desire to talk to him. It was such a strange place to be—wanting him to fall in love with her, yet guarding her heart because she knew it would never happen.

So rather than talk to him, she had diverted her attention onto Abby. She loved that little girl as if she were her own sister. Rainee had always wanted a little sister. And if things would have worked out between her and Haydon, she would have had two.

As she continued looking out the window at the handsome man who caused her chest to rise and fall, she whispered, "Lord, Thy will be done." She pushed away from the wall and headed toward the mirror.

Still dressed in her robe, Rainee stood in front of the looking glass contemplating what to do. Since wearing the lightweight dresses without the restricting corset, she never wanted to don that wretched contraption again.

What she did want to do, however, was to take her corset and wrap it around the person's scrawny little neck who had invented it. Did they not know or care how suffocating and stifling the corset and all those layers of clothing were in the scorching heat? And for what? Appearance's sake?

Appearances be hanged. Rainee was sick to death of the whole thing.

Though she loved her father dearly, that was one thing that had always disturbed her about him. Born a British gentleman, position, appearance, and wealth meant everything to him. Since moving to America, however, Mother said he had relaxed some of the stricter parts of his upbringing, but propriety was not one of them.

Rainee scrutinized the articles of clothing she had to choose from. Once again she was faced with the dilemma of what to wear. Her mere wardrobe consisted of four silk gowns and the three dresses Katherine and Leah had helped her let out.

Her mother's words about dressing properly so she did not embarrass her father skimmed through her mind. She did not wish to embarrass the Bowens either, but she did not know what would be considered proper attire for an outdoor church gathering.

Rainee let out a very unladylike snort. She hated having to concern herself with such trivial matters. Sometimes she just wanted to run away and live in the wilds where no one cared about what she wore or how she looked.

A smile graced her lips. The Idaho Territory appeared quite wild to her. And she had run away to it.

She giggled, picturing herself running around in a pair of men's trousers, an oversize shirt and a cowboy hat and boots. She rather liked the visual. It represented a freedom she craved but was likely to never have. In fact, she wondered if she would ever be free from the strict proper upbringing that seemed to haunt her like a ghost no matter where she went.

Unfortunately, clothes were not the only problem weighing heavily on her right now. Today, the Bowen's neighbors would arrive. Just how would they explain her presence at their ranch? How would they introduce her? And what would she say? Her stomach crinkled just thinking about it.

"Rainee." Katherine's voice sounded from the other side of the bedroom door. "May I come in?"

Rainee pulled her robe shut. "Yes."

The door opened and in walked Katherine wearing a pink cotton dress. No ruffles, no frills, no silk and no layers of hot clothing. Just a simple, lightweight garment. The burden of the morning lifted, and the tight scrunches in her stomach relaxed. Perhaps the freedom she craved was within her reach after all.

"I was wondering if you would like me to braid your hair."

Would she ever. "That would be lovely. Thank you."

Katherine's kindness and thoughtfulness never ceased to astonish Rainee.

She grabbed her clothes and slipped behind the makeshift partition. Within minutes she was dressed and feeling carefree and lighter than she had in years. She all but skipped to the dresser and sat down.

Katherine picked up the brush and pulled it gently through Rainee's long hair. Rainee closed her eyes and relished the rare treat of someone else brushing her hair.

Growing up, servants had always styled her hair. And on rare occasions, her mother had. But all that had changed when her parents died and Ferrin had taken over her life. Some of those servants had moved on, and some of them had stayed for Rainee's sake. With her no longer living at her parents' plantation, she wondered if even more of the servants had moved on and what they were doing. Especially Jenetta.

"You have such beautiful hair."

"My mother used to say the same thing every time she brushed my hair, and she would share something with me from her childhood."

"Like what?" The brush stopped mid-air.

"Well, when she was little, Mother had a horse named Beauty whose mane and tail were the same color and thickness as my hair. She loved horses. So did my grandfather. He had taught her everything she knew about them.

"But she had confessed the real reason she loved spending so much time with the horses was because during those times her father would tell her stories about his many business travels. She cherished those times she had been fortunate enough to spend with him. Just like she treasured the time she spent with me, brushing my hair and talking." Rainee could still see her mother's smile as if she were standing here in the room with her. And what a beautiful smile it was.

A smile she would never see again.

"You must miss her terribly."

"Yes. I miss her so much sometimes the pain becomes almost unbearable."

"Oh, Rainee, I shouldn't have asked you to share with me. I can see how much it disturbed you to talk about her."

"Please, do not apologize. While it is difficult to remember those precious times with my mother, for that brief moment it also brings her back to me. So thank you for asking." Rainee looked at Katherine's reflection in the mirror and smiled.

"You're welcome. Any time you want to talk about your mother, I'd love to hear it."

Rainee just might take her up on that offer.

"There. I'm finished." Katherine set the brush down on the vanity.

"Thank you so very much, Katherine. It has been a long time since anyone has brushed my hair for me." She smiled her gratitude.

Katherine lovingly patted her shoulder. "Well, anytime you want it done, you just ask. I love doing it." She moved her hand from Rainee's shoulder. "Shall we go downstairs?" Katherine turned to leave.

Rainee twisted in her chair. "Katherine?"

"Yes?" She stopped.

"I just wondered..." Rainee's gaze dropped.

"Wondered what?"

"People are going to wonder who I am and what I am doing here. And..." She shrugged and glanced up at Katherine.

"You're wondering what we're going to tell them," Katherine finished for her.

"Yes, ma'am. I am." There. She had said it.

Katherine took her hand and pulled her up. She

looped her arm through Rainee's and smiled. "We'll tell them the truth."

Rainee's heart dropped clear to her button-up boots. "The truth?" she squeaked as panic settled inside her. When she had written the advertisement in search of a husband, she had not planned that far ahead. She never thought about what she would say to people when they met her.

Tears battled in the back of her eyes, begging for release for the unfortunate situation she now found herself in. If only her mother and father had not died. Then she would not have to concern herself with such dreadful things. No longer able to hold back her tears, they slipped out and onto her gloved hands.

"Rainee, look at me."

She sniffled, pressed her fist against her mouth and then looked at Katherine.

"The truth we'll be sharing with them is…" Katherine smiled. "That you are my guest."

Rainee let out a short breath.

"No one needs to know otherwise because it isn't anyone else's business why or how you got here. Haydon and I have already discussed it, and we agreed everyone would announce you as my guest. After all, it's the truth. You're my guest for as long as you like." She smiled.

"But what if they ask how you know me?"

Katherine's brows furrowed. She released Rainee's arm and turned puzzled eyes at her. "I'm not sure. Let's go downstairs and see what Haydon thinks."

"But Haydon does not like me. And I know he does not want to be burdened with me."

Katherine laughed.

Rainee did not see anything so funny in what she had just said.

"He likes you, Rainee. He just doesn't want to admit he does. Come here." Again she looped elbows with Rainee and led her over to her bed. Katherine sat down and patted the spot next to her. Rainee sat and faced Katherine.

"I want to tell you something about Haydon and then perhaps you will understand why he acts the way he does. But first, I want you to know why I'm telling you this. For more than a year now I've prayed for God to send Haydon a wife. And then you came along."

Rainee's mouth opened in a very unladylike manner.

"So, we'll just wait and see what God wants on that point."

Not knowing what else to do, Rainee nodded.

"One thing I do know about my son is that he may rebel against something and even refuse to do it, but he's learned the hard way about going against God's will and following his own desires. Now he only wants what God wants for him."

Those words caressed Rainee's heart. She, too, only wanted what God wanted for her. In fact, before she had made her decision to move out here, she had sought the Lord and He had given His approval. Solutions to the obstacles she now faced, therefore, were best left in His hands.

"Haydon would be furious if he knew I was sharing this with you, but I believe it's the right thing to do." Katherine tucked a wayward strand of hair back into place. "Before Haydon moved out West with us, he made sure his wife Melanie approved. She agreed even after he told her they would be moving to a ranch far from town and how harsh it would be. She assured him it would be fine. Melanie loved adventure. Even a dangerous one. That was one of the things that had attracted Haydon to her.

"Anyway, Melanie had this romantic notion about the West. And she wasn't the only one. Many people romanticize it. Haydon warned Melanie a lot of people had lost their lives and their children's lives because of the harshness of this land." Katherine got a faraway look on her face.

Is that what had happened to Katherine's husband?

Shimmering eyes looked back at Rainee. Rainee wanted to wrap her arms around the woman and comfort her. She knew only too well the devastation of losing a loved one.

"Haydon doesn't know I'm aware of how miserable Melanie made him, but I noticed it shortly after they arrived here. Melanie hated living here. She had a hard time dealing with the harsh reality of this place. She despised it even more when she realized she wouldn't be attending any more fancy parties. That there was no place to show off her expensive silk gowns. No more servants to tend to her every whim. And no more extravagant shopping sprees. Haydon had warned her about that, too. But the poor thing just couldn't cope.

"Many times I heard her screaming at Haydon, telling him what a horrible failure he was as a husband and as a man. She would say cruel and hateful things to him. Things a mother couldn't bear to listen to. She told him he was worthless and it was all his fault she was so miserable. Said she would never forgive him for the anguish he was putting her through." Disbelief and heartbreak flittered across Katherine's face.

Horrified, Rainee covered her mouth. How could anyone say such cruel things to another human being? Let alone their own husband?

"Finally, Melanie told Haydon if he really loved her, he would move them back to New York. Haydon promised her he would, but they had to wait until spring because travel was much too dangerous in the winter. But she had no desire to wait. She snuck out during the night, and the next morning Haydon found her battered body at the bottom of a steep hill not too far from here. She had slipped on the rocks and fallen to her death."

Rainee gasped. "Merciful heavens. How dreadful. Poor Haydon."

"He hasn't been the same since. He still blames himself for Melanie's death, and he's built a stronghold around that soft heart of his to keep himself from feeling that hurt again."

Rainee's heart broke for what Haydon had endured. Everything made sense to her now. She even understood why Jesse had sent for her. He just wanted his brother to be happy again. Rainee wanted that, too. Perhaps she could make him happy. After all, not all women were like Melanie.

Rainee was not. She loved helping people, not being helped. Fancy balls and extravagant gowns meant nothing to her. She loved the outdoors and the wide-open spaces. The only thing she did not love was pigs.

Chapter Eleven

Rainee stepped into the living room, and Haydon did his best not to stare at the beautiful woman. He expected to see her dressed in her fancy frippery, but her attire surprised him. The simple yellow dress she wore brought out the gold in her hair and eyes, and her overall appearance was wholesome and not that of a rich socialite.

Something about the way she looked at him caused his breath to hitch. He couldn't say what the look conveyed exactly, but something was definitely different.

"Are we all set up outside?" his mother asked.

He pulled his gaze away from Rainee and looked at her. "Yes. I was just coming to get you two. Shall we?" He offered each of them an arm and tried to ignore the tingling sensation Rainee's touch created.

His mind froze, and the silence in his brain was deafening.

He needed to quit feeling like this, no matter how remarkable Rainee was. But every time he saw her, he liked what he saw more and more, not her outward beauty but her inward beauty. And when she touched him, even as innocent as this was, his feelings became stronger.

His hand itched with the temptation to yank Rainee's arm from his and to flee far away from her while he still could. But he feared it might be too late already and besides, his manners wouldn't allow him to. He corralled his emotions and did what needed to be done—and found he enjoyed doing it far too much.

Outside, under the clear blue sky and warm morning sun, he escorted his mother and Rainee to the rows of flat log benches situated under the morning shade on the east side of the house.

He noticed a small huddle of people off to the side. Jesse and Hannah were among the group, talking to the neighbors. Haydon turned his back on his brother. The last thing he wanted to do was talk to Jess before a church service.

He'd tried to forgive his brother, but every time he got around Rainee, he was reminded again what Jesse had done not only to her but also to him and anger over the situation would settle on him again.

His gaze touched on his mother's for a brief moment. She wasn't pleased or fooled by his actions, but he needed to stay away from his brother for a little while longer. Otherwise he might say or do something he would regret. And he had enough regrets to last him two lifetimes.

Rainee gazed up at him. Her countenance appeared sweeter than it had last night. He couldn't quite read the look in her eyes—nor did he want to—so he broke contact and looked in front of him to where all the neighbors were seated. He was met with glances and stares of curiosity, gaping mouths and whispering.

He glimpsed Rainee's flushed face and wondered again what would drive a beautiful, kind woman to do what she had done. Desperation? Lack of money? What? The more he pondered her reasons for leaving her home and how hard it had to have been for her to place an advertisement, the more his heart softened toward her. It took a brave woman to do what she had done. He admired her for that. She deserved a suitable husband.

Not liking where his thoughts were leading him, he gave himself a mental shake and looked for an empty seat.

Leah and Abby sat with the neighbor's daughters, who were close to their own ages. Michael and Smokey sat at the far end of the back row. Haydon followed Michael's trail of vision to a young blonde beauty talking with Mrs. Swedberg. The girl appeared to be close to Michael's age. Haydon smiled, relieved that his brother had taken their talk to heart and given up his infatuation with Rainee.

He led his mother and Rainee to the only available bench. He stepped back and motioned Rainee forward, but his mother stepped ahead of her and sat down, forcing him to sit beside Rainee. His gut twisted, knowing his mother had done it on purpose.

He sat down on the cramped seat. His leg brushed against Rainee's, and warmth spread down his leg. With one jerk, he moved his leg over as far as he could.

Reverend James walked in front of the makeshift podium and removed his hat. The sunshine blazing down on his head brought out the orange highlights in his copper hair. His green eyes connected with each person. "Thank you all for coming. I look forward to our time together." He smiled. "Today I feel led to teach about the importance of seeking God's will for our lives. Have we become so independent and self-sufficient that we think we don't need our Heavenly Father or His direction? If so, where has that attitude gotten you?"

A deceased wife and nothing but misery. It would have been nice to be able to get clear of those thoughts, but they were chained to Haydon's spirit as surely as if they were physical.

"Whose will do you want in your life—God's or your own?"

Haydon's shoulders dropped. At one time he had longed to do God's will and sought it out on a daily basis. But not once had he sought God's will concerning Melanie.

He had loved Melanie and wanted to marry her, despite the many warnings he'd received from his friends, his father and, if he could bear to admit it, from his Heavenly Father.

He thought back to all the warning signs. Signs he had chosen to ignore. He'd been deceived not only by his own willful stubbornness, but also by his wife and her many charms.

Back East Melanie had attended church regularly. She said and did all the right things. But after they'd married and moved out West, she refused to attend their local meetings. Instead she holed up in their cabin until everyone went home because she refused to socialize with these "backwoods lowlifes," as she called them.

And it had only gotten worse over their short time here. In one of Melanie's fits of displeasure, she mockingly confessed the only reason she had attended church in the first place was to show off her new dresses and to impress everyone with her high social standing. He should have seen that, but he'd been too blinded by what he wanted to see, by what he wanted to be real.

The ultimate blow came when she told him she wasn't a Christian and she didn't believe in God or Christ. She'd faked faith because she knew Haydon wouldn't marry her otherwise.

Haydon's heart ached afresh, knowing Melanie had possibly died not knowing Jesus. He could only hope before she'd drawn her last breath, she had asked Christ into her heart. After all, Melanie had heard the salvation message plenty of times.

The sound of people singing splintered his mind from its painful memories.

Haydon closed his eyes and sang the words that meant so much to him. A few choruses later, his concentration switched to the sweet but slightly out-of-tune voice next to him. Only it wasn't Rainee's off-key singing that had hooked his attention, it was the conviction in her tone. She sang as if the words meant something to her.

He stole a sideways glance, and what he saw mesmerized him—Rainee's face raised toward heaven, shiny drops sliding down her sun-bronzed cheeks and glowing face. Gone was the snobbish image he had engraved in his mind from their first encounter.

Reverend James said the closing prayer. The women excused themselves and started setting out the generous fare.

Haydon stood back and watched Rainee as she jumped right in and helped. She draped tablecloths over the makeshift tables and made several trips to the well, filling bucket after bucket with water and carrying them to the table. She made numerous trips in and out of the house, her arms loaded with homemade desserts.

Melanie would have never done any of that. In fact, Melanie did nothing but read her dime novels, sit in front of a mirror or bark orders at his sisters. When he had found out she had been ordering them about, he had immediately put a stop to it.

Abby's cry snapped his attention in that direction. His little sister was sitting on the ground, looking at her knee, crying loud enough to alert everyone within a 30-mile radius to her plight. He started toward her but stopped when he saw Rainee hurrying toward Abby. Haydon watched as she dropped to her knees in front of the child, never once giving heed to what the dirt was doing to her dress.

"What happened, Abby?" The kindness and genuine compassion in her voice touched a chord deep inside him. A chord he would rather not have strummed.

"I hurted my knee," Abby cried.

"Oh, sweetie. I am so sorry. Come. We will make it feel all better." She scooped Abby up and carried her into the house.

Minutes later, they stepped outside together. Abby held Rainee's hand, smiling and skipping happily at her side.

Haydon picked up another bench and carried it over to one of the tables, eyeing his neighbors as they too watched Rainee's every move. They had to be wondering who this woman was. So far, his mother had offered no other information other than her name. It wouldn't be long, though, before someone asked how she came to be here.

From yards away, Haydon's gaze zoned in on

nineteen-year-old Jake Lure strutting up to Rainee like a bull on the hunt. Haydon dropped one end of the bench. It thudded as it hit the ground.

Abby pulled away and ran toward her friends.

Jake cocked his shoulders back and tipped his nose up higher than normal. He reached for Rainee's hand and kissed it.

Her cheeks suddenly reddened. To make things worse, within seconds, forty-five-year-old Norwegian widower Tom Elder, seventeen-year-old John Smitty, and twenty-three-year-old Peter James, Reverend James' brother, each took turns introducing themselves and kissing her hand. Each tried to outdo the other. They reminded Haydon of a bunch of young bucks trying to claim their territory. It would have been funny if he could have allowed himself to laugh about it, but his protective side had already kicked in.

He wanted to forget moving benches and go stand next to Rainee's side to keep the predators away.

But what gave him the right to do so?

Her new admirers were only doing what he refused to do.

Rainee looked around until her gaze touched his.

His heart did an upward kick like a frisky colt on a brisk spring day. The quiet desperation in her fawn-colored eyes pled with him to rescue her. And rescue her he would. After all, a promise was a promise, and he had promised the Lord and himself that he would watch over her today. Even so, he would have done it without a promise, knowing how desperate men out West were for womenfolk.

Haydon finished setting the bench down and strode over to where she stood. He extended a hand to each of the men. "Hello, gentlemen." They each shook his hand but never took their eyes off of Rainee. He couldn't really blame them. She was a very beautiful woman. A woman who was under his care for the time being. "The ladies have the food ready now if you'd like to grab yourselves a plate."

"Miss Devonwood, would you do me the honor of joining me?" Tom bent his elbow and offered her his arm.

John stepped in front of Tom. "I'd be mighty honored iffen you'd join me, Miss Devonwood."

"She's eating with me." Jake grabbed Rainee's arm and yanked her to his side.

This whole thing was getting out of hand. He needed to do something and fast. Haydon stepped up along the other side of her. "Sorry, gentlemen." He eyed each one with a warning glance. "Rainelle is with me." The second those words left his mouth, his gut cringed. Where did that come from? Couldn't he have said something else?

She looked up at him. Her smile of approval warmed his soul. Even though it felt hypocritical, he knew he had done the right thing. He tucked her hand through his arm, and the sudden fluttering of his heart made him even more confused about what the right thing was.

As he led her to the food tables, the men's stares bore through him like railroad spikes. No doubt, the men believed he was staking his claim on her. Well, let them think what they wanted. His only intention was to watch over her while she was a guest in his mother's home. *Just keep telling yourself that, Haydon, and you just might believe it yourself pretty soon.*

Then, a few steps forward, he realized his mistake.

The perfect resolution to the mess Jess had gotten him into might very well be standing in the food line. If she married one of his neighbors, he would be free of his burden.

Burden.

But was she really a burden? Or was he scared to death she wasn't?

Since her arrival, she had helped his mother and sister prepare meals, bake bread and desserts, weed the garden, scrub the kitchen floor, clean the house, wash clothes and do any other chore that needed done.

He liked that about her. She was at home being one of them. More important, when he was honest with himself, he realized he liked her. He always had. In fact, the word like was starting to feel too tame.

Reverend James's message trailed through his mind. The point here wasn't whether or not she was a burden. But what did God want him to do? Determination rose in Haydon. He needed to find out just what God's will was in this situation. This time he needed to know before he let his feelings take over.

While Rainee gathered a small amount of food onto her plate, Haydon filled his with fried fish, quail, a thick slice of ham, morel mushrooms, potatoes boiled with dill, a slab of butter to eat with his potatoes and Lefsa.

She grabbed two tin cups and dipped them into one of the buckets of water and handed one to him.

"Thank you."

"You are welcome." There was that smile again. The one that could turn a man's head and heart into mush, including his. He mentally shook himself.

Drinks and plates in hand, he led her to an empty table. At least it was empty—until Rainee sat. Then her group of admirerers barreled to their table and sat across from her.

Guess they didn't think he was staking his claim on her after all. Haydon sighed inwardly and lowered himself next to her. His shoulder brushed hers. Their gazes connected. Her eyes sparkled and she smiled that sweet smile of hers. Haydon's heart melted like sugar in a cup of soothing hot tea, and his lips curled upward.

She looked away, and he heard her suck in a sharp breath.

Wondering what was the matter, he followed her gaze. Locked in one of the pens, Kitty's little beady eyes looked directly at them through the slats in the fence. The sow dropped her nose to the ground and started scooping up the dirt under the bottom fence rail. After several scoops, she looked through the slats again. Then repeated the process.

He laid his hand on Rainee's arm and leaned over to whisper in her ear. "Kitty can't get out. I promise."

She looked at him, unconvinced. "Why—why is she penned up so close to the house?"

Kitty wasn't all that close, but he'd let that part of the question go. To Rainee, having the pig anywhere within eyesight would be too close. Once again he whispered in her ear to protect her from any kind of embarrassment she might encounter in front of his neighbors. "If I didn't pen her, she would be joining us in the yard like she often does. I locked her up this morning because I didn't want her frightening you again."

"That is so sweet of you, Haydon. Thank you. You will never know how truly grateful I am for your thoughtfulness." She glanced toward the pen again and back at him. "Are—are you sure she cannot get out?"

"I'm sure. Don't let her digging get to you. She'd have to dig a huge hole before she could slide her fat belly under the fence. You're perfectly safe. Trust me."

Could she? Could she trust him when he didn't even trust himself anymore?

She nodded and then picked up her drinking cup.

"So, tell me, miss." Tom shoved a huge chunk of ham into his mouth. "How do you know the Bowens?"

Haydon's insides stilled and his smile vanished.

Chapter Twelve

Sunday evening, after everyone had gone to bed, Rainee draped her shawl around her shoulders and headed downstairs. She stepped out onto the porch to think things through and to pray for guidance about her situation. She tucked her robe around her and lowered herself onto the porch swing. Using the balls of her feet, she put the front porch swing in motion.

Stars glistened like precious gems in the endless inky sky, and a chorus of frogs filled the silence. Rainee leaned back in the swing and closed her eyes, sighing, relieved this day was over.

Sitting at the table with all those men at lunch asking her how she knew the Bowens had been quite daunting. She had been prepared to answer anyone if they asked why she was there but not how she knew them. Why, if Haydon had not spoken up when he had, diverting their attention away from the topic, Rainee shuddered to think what would have transpired.

Because of her love for the Bowens, she had prayed fervently the night before the church service that God would work everything out and spare them any humiliation her being there might cause.

God, in His tender mercy, had once again answered her prayers. Even when Katherine had introduced Rainee to her neighbors as her guest, the questions lingered in their eyes, but none put a voice to their curiosity, much to Rainee's relief.

Rainee smiled as contentment wrapped itself around her. Though she had only been here a few weeks, she felt at home because of the kindness of these people. Especially Haydon, who kept her in a constant state of confusion. He wanted her to leave, then he protected her from the onslaught of male neighbors. Somehow he had even managed to keep the conversation off of her and onto other things.

Against her better judgment, she admired everything about him. How he protected and took care of not just his family, but her, too.

His obvious love for the Lord.

His kindness and compassion toward his neighbors.

His deep love for his family. Well, except Jesse, perhaps. She noticed he avoided him.

She also admired his physical attributes.

Eyes the color of sapphire gems.

Teeth as white as freshly fallen snow.

Hair the color of winter wheat.

Strength in his masculine jaw.

And muscular arms Rainee longed to feel, to see if they were as solid as they appeared.

Rainee's cheeks heated at that thought. If Mother knew she was thinking about a man's muscles, she would surely give Rainee a tongue lashing. Before her mother's words had a chance to formulate in her mind,

Rainee blocked them. Proper or not, she found she did not want to stop thinking about him. He represented everything she desired in a man.

Gentle yet strong.

Kind but bold.

Sure and steadfast.

A man who under all that gruff exterior had a heart as big as the Idaho Territory. A man she now greatly esteemed, perhaps even loved.

A conversation she and her mother had shared about that very thing strolled through her mind.

"Mother, how will I know when I am in love?" Rainee had asked.

Her mother had stopped working on her tapestry and gazed at Rainee. She wove her needle through the fabric and rested her hands in her lap. "Trust me, Rainelle, you will know."

"But how?"

Mother rang the bell and asked for tea. "The day I met your father, I knew he was the one for me."

"How did you know?" Rainee had asked again.

With a smile, she looked at Rainee. "The truth is, the moment I laid eyes on him, I knew."

"You knew that fast?" That idea completely astonished Rainee.

"Yes." Her mother straightened and gave Rainee a stern look. "It does not happen that way for everyone," Mother had cautioned her, then relaxed her austere facial expression. "But it did for me."

"Did Father return your affection?"

Mother's sweet laughter had filled the room. "No. He told me he did not even notice me as more than a businessman's daughter until one day when I was gathering roses for the table. I was so engrossed in their beauty and lovely scent I did not hear your father approach. When he said my name, I whirled so fast, I tripped over my flower basket and landed on my backside. Your father said when he offered me a hand to help me up, the second our hands made contact he felt a strange, unexplainable attachment to me.

"When I stood, he kept hold of my hand. Our eyes connected and held. And it was as if we were the only two people in the world." When she looked at Rainee, her eyes had sparkled with love for her husband. Rainee hoped and prayed she would someday know the special kind of love her parents had for each other.

"Before I knew what was happening, he had taken me in his arms and kissed me. That very same day he asked Daddy if he could marry me." Stars had filled her mother's eyes.

They had silently finished their tea, each lost in their own thoughts. She and her mother shared many precious moments like that. How she longed to hear even just one more tale of her mother's life.

After reliving that memory, Rainee opened her eyes and sucked in a sharp breath. There, standing with his arms and ankles crossed, resting against the porch post was Haydon, staring at her. "When—when did you get here?"

"A few minutes ago. Sorry. I didn't mean to frighten you or disrupt your thoughts. You looked like you were a million miles away." He uncrossed his ankles and arms and walked toward her. "May I?" He pointed at the swing.

Rainee could not find her voice, so she nodded and moved over as close to her side of the swing as possible. But even that was not far enough because his broad shoulders covered a major portion of the swing. Rainee found the open space and endless sky did not appear so vast anymore. In fact, it seemed to be crowding in on her closer and closer.

Soap and peppermint filled her senses.

"Would you like a piece?"

"What?" She blinked. "A piece of what?"

"Of peppermint." He reached inside his leather vest pocket and pulled out a small pouch and opened it.

It had been a long time since Rainee had enjoyed any peppermint. She reached inside the bag and removed one stick. "Thank you." She bit off a piece.

Eyes closed, she savored the feel of the hard candy in her mouth and the clean fresh sensation. She opened her eyes and found Haydon watching her. Embarrassment flooded into her cheeks. "I—I am sorry. It has been years since I have had peppermint. Mother used to buy it all the time."

Haydon broke off a section of candy before he closed the bag and slipped it back into his vest pocket. "Did your mother give you candy often?"

Rainee wrapped her hand around the rope holding the swing. She planted her feet firmly and gave the swing a shove, repeating the process until Haydon finally slowed it down. "Mother always made sure we had special treats. And my father often had candy shipped over from England. He wanted us to know the delicacies and delights of his country, too. I sure miss them."

"I miss my father, too."

Rainee swung her gaze his way. Astonishment trickled through her. She could not believe once again Haydon was opening up to her. She only prayed he would continue.

* * *

Haydon stared into the darkness, amazed he was sitting out here on the porch with Rainee. For a man who was trying to avoid her, he wasn't doing a very good job of it.

"Tell me about your father. What was he like?"

He barely heard her request. He glanced over at her silhouette. She wasn't looking at him but straight ahead. An air of serenity radiated from her, a serenity he had never felt around a woman before.

"My father was a kind, caring, generous man. He loved us all so much. It was my father's dream to move out West. He said he might have been born a city boy, but he belonged out here. I feel the same way. He was never comfortable with city life, and neither was I.

"My father detested all the hypocrisy of his acquaintances and how they flaunted their wealth with extravagant parties instead of helping those less fortunate. Out here, he loved the freedom to be himself. Loved the outdoors.

"He and I used to go for long rides and talk about what we could do to build up the ranch. To make it a better place to raise a family. This place has so much lumber, and the volcanic ash soil is so rich you can grow just about anything.

"He had such great plans for this place, but he didn't get to enjoy it for very long. Two and a half years after we moved here, a tree fell on him and crushed his chest." Haydon pressed his eyes shut to blot out the horrific memory.

"I am so sorry." She gently laid her hand on his arm.

He glanced down where her gloved hand rested, then up at her.

She plucked her hand from his arm, and he immediately felt a sense of loss.

"Thank you," Haydon whispered.

Rainee nodded. From what little he could see in the dark, compassion was the only thing he noticed on her sweet face.

"How did your parents die?"

In the shadow he saw her chest rise and fall. "My family and I attended a neighborhood ball. Mother, Father and a few other guests were standing under a second-story balcony. No one knew it would not hold the weight of so many guests." Her voice hitched. "It collapsed, killing six people, including my parents."

Losing a parent was a terrible thing to endure. And she had lost both of hers at the same time. In that instant, his heart softened toward her another notch. "I'm sorry for your loss, Rainee."

Though darkness surrounded them, he saw the stars reflecting from her glistening eyes. He couldn't turn away from them, and as he looked into those eyes, he didn't want to. Rainee surrendered all fears in a soft gentle glance that begged him to do the same thing. For one tingly moment, he did, and they shared a breath. He broke eye contact, blinked to regain control and asked, "Do you have any other family?"

Rainee stopped rocking. She knew she could not avoid his questions forever, but she could control what information he did receive. "Yes."

"And they wouldn't let you stay with them?"

"My aunt Lena died three months back."

"I see. I'm sorry, Rainee."

She picked her gaze up and studied his profile. Boldness overtook her. It was not her place, but she wanted to know just the same. “Jesse sure looked miserable today. He and Hannah went home early.”

Haydon pushed with his feet, setting the swing into a rocking motion. “Well, that’s not my problem. He should’ve left well enough alone.”

“With me.” Her gaze slipped out into the darkness. His silence gave her the answer she already knew. “I understand how you feel, but Jesse meant well even if he did not go about it the right way.”

“I don’t recall asking for your opinion.” At his bluntness, she whirled her head toward him and squared her shoulders.

“No, you did not, but I am going to give it anyway. Family is extremely important. And even when they do vexing things to us, things that are hard to forgive, refusing to forgive hurts not just them, but us also. I am truly sorry my being here has caused a rift between you two,” she said with a softer tone. Their eyes, shadowed by the darkness, locked. “Will you at least consider forgiving Jesse?”

“You don’t give up easily, do you?”

“No. I do not.”

When he nodded, there was almost a laugh attached to it. “I’ll think about it.”

For a long moment, that seemed to be the end of the conversation, and Rainee would not have been surprised to see him stand up and leave.

“Rainee?”

She swallowed back the apprehension that rose in her throat at the soft hopefulness in his voice. “Yes?”

“Would you like to go for a horseback ride tomorrow and see the rest of the ranch?”

Rainee's mouth fell open. It was a very unladylike thing to do, but she could not help it. Of all the things she thought he might ask, that was not one of them.

Through the darkness, she tilted her head and tried to study his face but could not see it well enough to judge his expression.

Why would a man who made it clear he wanted her to go back home protect her from his neighbors, sit and visit with her and then invite her to go for a ride? Whatever his reasons were, they did not matter. She wanted to spend more time with him, to get to know him better. And this was her chance to do so. "I would love to."

Haydon rose and faced her. "I'll have Mother pack us a picnic lunch then."

"No need to bother her. I can do that." She stood. "When would you like to leave?"

"After I finish my chores."

Rainee tilted her head and placed her finger against her lips, then smiled sassily. "Kitty will not be there, will she?"

Haydon laughed. Rainee loved the deep rumbling sound.

"Only if you want her to be." The teasing in his voice caused Rainee's lips to tip upward.

He walked down the porch steps. "See you tomorrow, Rainee. Good night." Off into the darkness he went, heading toward his house.

In the secret garden of her soul, hope sent up a new shoot. She could scarcely contain her excitement at the idea of spending more time with Haydon. Tomorrow seemed as far away as the stars.

Chapter Thirteen

No matter how hard Rainee tried, sleep eluded her. Thoughts of spending the day with Haydon kept her tossing and turning. Finally, she gave up, got dressed and went downstairs.

She grabbed a couple of oil lanterns and lit them and then put on a pot of coffee. She could do this. Katherine had taught her well. "Let me see. Katherine said she wanted to have ham steaks, fried potatoes and Swedish pancakes. I think she called them plättar or something like that," she whispered to the empty room.

Arranging wood and kindling into the stove, she got the fire started and decided she would make the pancakes first.

She grabbed a bowl, the lingonberry sauce and several of the ingredients she needed from off the shelf. She cracked three eggs into the bowl and whipped them until they were nice and thick. Just like Katherine had shown her. Next, she stirred in the milk, flour, sugar and salt, and mixed until it was smooth before covering the bowl with a towel.

Humming while she added a small amount of batter

onto the hot buttered pan, she spread the batter until it was thin. When it turned a light brown on the bottom, she turned it over. Moisture beaded her forehead, so she used her apron to blot it away.

She retrieved a baking sheet and placed a clean towel on it, then added the finished plättar on top of the towel. She repeated this process until the batter disappeared. The last one, however, did not make it onto the towel or into the oven to stay warm.

Rainee looked around, smiling, feeling like a child sneaking a licorice stick. She laid it on a plate, spooned melted butter over it, sprinkled it with sugar and rolled it up. Then she added a dollop of lingonberry sauce on the side, dipped the pancake into the sauce and bit into the thin, sweet pastry. The first bite melted in her mouth. Sugar and butter ran down her chin. The texture of the treat reminded her of the crepes their French cook used to make back home.

"Couldn't wait, huh?"

Rainee whirled at the sound of Haydon's humor-filled voice.

Her cheeks, already hot from the stove, heated even more. She swallowed the last bite. It was so large she had a hard time getting it to go down. "What are you doing here so early?"

"I could ask you the same thing." He walked over to where she stood by the stove.

Rainee put her head down. "I could not sleep." She looked up at him. "You?"

He shrugged. "I have a lot of chores to do before our ride, so I thought I'd get an early start."

Rainee tilted her head. "So what are you doing here?"

"I came to see if there was anything to eat before heading down to the barn."

"I just finished a batch of crepes. Well, Frenchie, our cook called them crepes anyway." Realizing the blunder she made about mentioning her life back home, she rushed on, "Katherine says y'all call them 'plättar.' She taught me how to make them, so I thought I would get an early start on breakfast."

She pivoted her back on him and reached for a coffee cup before filling him a cup of the hot brew and handing it to him. "Would you like some crepes? I mean, plättars?"

"Looks like you've already had some." He pointed to her mouth and humor curled his lips and sniggered through his words.

At this rate, if her cheeks got any hotter, they were certain to burst into flames. "I did." A twitter of a giggle followed. She sighed and wiped her mouth off with her apron. "Caught in the act again. I never was very good at being sneaky." She turned and retrieved a cup of coffee for herself. "I always told on myself when I did something wrong. Well, most of the time anyway. Mother called it 'bearing harmful witness.'"

"What do you mean, 'most of the time'?"

"On occasion I opted not to tell Mother."

"Why's that?"

Merciful heavens, the man has beautiful eyes. "Because I knew if I did, a certain hour-long lecture would follow." Rainee took a sip of her coffee. The bitter taste slid down her throat. Truth be known, she preferred tea, even at breakfast.

"Ah, I see. I know that only too well. At one time, my father was a stickler like that also. I sat down to many a lecture when I was younger. I used to dread them. And now, I would give anything to hear one of them." Sadness crossed his face.

"I, too, would give anything to hear one. To hear my mother's voice again. To see her face just one more time." Not liking the uncomfortable gloominess that had rested upon them, she wanted to lighten the mood. "Mother always said she lectured me because she loved me. Said if she did not love me, she would not even bother. I must have been the most loved person in the entire universe."

"Me, too."

They both laughed.

"Now, how about some breakfast?" She set her cup down and reached for the potatoes.

"No time for potatoes. The plättars will do just fine."

"At least allow me to fry you a slice of ham." She motioned for him to be seated before she sliced off two thick chunks of ham and tossed them into the cast-iron skillet. While they cooked, she placed in front of him dishes, silverware, plättars, bread, a small bowl of melted butter and the lingonberry sauce, then added the fried ham onto his mounding plate.

"These are delicious, Rainee," he said around the large bite in his mouth.

Rainee's heart skipped with happiness. She watched as he devoured one crepe after another. If he kept this up, she would have to make another batch, and she would do it with pleasure.

"Aren't you going to have any?" He sliced off a massive chunk of ham and shoved it into his mouth.

Rainee marveled, wondering where he put all of that food. "No. I am going to start tending to the potatoes.

It will not be long before everyone else arrives. I want to surprise your mother and have breakfast all ready."

His eyes sparkled as if she had pleased him with her comment. Rainee turned to the task of peeling and dicing the potatoes. Minutes later, she heard the chair scrape against the floor. She glanced in his direction.

Haydon headed toward her, carrying his empty dishes. She wiped her hands off on the apron and hurried over to him. "Here. Give them to me."

He handed them to her. "Thank you, Rainee, for breakfast."

She glanced up at him. "You are most welcome."

He stood there for a moment, looking as if he wanted to say something, but instead he turned on his heel and headed out the door, taking a portion of Rainee's heart with him. She could hardly wait for their ride.

After everyone had their breakfast and the dishes were finished and put away, Rainee packed a light lunch. The thought of spending more time with Haydon sent excitement coursing through every inch of her. Rainee raised her skirt and ran up the stairs.

She scurried inside Leah's room and donned her brown riding habit. She stepped in front of the looking glass and tucked in the wayward strands of her flaxen hair, grabbed her hat with the feather plume and tied the ribbon under her chin. It would have to do. If she had her way, she would put on a pair of man's breeches and a cowboy hat, but it was not to be.

With a smile on her face and her heart feeling lighter than it had in so very long, she floated down the stairs, grabbed their picnic lunch and headed outside.

* * *

Haydon scanned the barnyard and saw Jesse out by the woodshed. Rainee's words about forgiveness swam through his head. He started to head toward his brother, but when he glanced toward his mother's house, he stopped.

The sight of Rainee in her fancy riding habit brought back painful memories of the last time he'd watched Melanie leave on horseback wearing a similar outfit. At the time Haydon didn't know his wife was heading out to meet her lover. When he discovered her affair, the man fled the county. Melanie blamed Haydon for her actions, saying if he wasn't such a horrible husband, she would have never been tempted. Even now his blood boiled thinking about how innocent she had always acted, when all the while she was a vixen.

"Good morning, Haydon." Rainee's gaze traveled upward toward the sky and then back at him. "It looks to be a lovely day." A smile graced her face.

"Is it?"

Her smile vanished. "Is something wrong?" She tilted her head, looking innocent. But Haydon knew better. Women like her were anything but innocent.

Judge not, lest you be judged. The Bible verse poured through his spirit, searing his conscience.

You're right, God. I need to stop judging Rainee and comparing her to Melanie.

"Did you change your mind?" Turbulence filled her eyes and remorse flashed through him like a bolt of lightning.

He wanted to say yes, he had changed his mind, and flee, but his desire to replace the hurt he had caused her with his attitude wouldn't let him. "No. I didn't change my mind." This time he held his frustration back.

He reached for the sack she held. "I'm sorry I haven't gotten the horses saddled yet. I had to finish fixing a few broken boards on the corral." He motioned for her to follow him to the barn.

She stepped up alongside him. The feather in her hat flopped in tune to her steps. "I can saddle my own horse. Just show me which one it is and what saddle you want me to use, and I can take care of it."

"You? You're going to saddle your own horse?"

"Yes, me." She peered sideways and stopped. "I have been doing it for years. And if my mother had known, I would have been sat down to yet another one of her lectures on etiquette. I mean, really…" She huffed and planted her hands on her small waist.

"Young ladies are quite capable of saddling their own horses. But because someone decided it was not proper for a woman to saddle a horse, or to run up the stairs, or to use a fork instead of her fingers or wear those dreaded binding cors—" Her words suddenly stopped, her eyes widened and her mouth plunged open. "Merciful heavens. I—I…." Her hand flew to her mouth, and her eyes blinked rapidly. "I am so sorry," she stammered. Her cheeks dusted scarlet.

Haydon threw back his head and laughed as relief poured over and through him. Never before had he heard a woman speak such things with such passion. Except for his mother. Mother loathed and rebelled against all the rules of society, too. His laughter deepened until his gaze landed on Rainee's scowling face. His laughter evaporated like morning dew kissed by the heat of the sun.

She pierced him with her pursed lips and narrowed eyes. "Are you laughing at me, sir?" Because of her pronounced Southern accent, the word "sir" sounded like more like "sah." The grit in her voice and her feisty attitude fished another chuckle out of him.

Haydon held up his hand in surrender. "I'm sorry, okay?" But he really wasn't. "But look at you." He eyed her up and down before his gaze landed once again on her disapproving face.

She bent over at the waist and scrutinized her body. Narrow eyes and scrunched up lips met him. She stared at him as if he had lost his mind. "There is nothing wrong with my appearance, mister." Again he wanted to chuckle, but this time it was how she said "mister." It sounded more like "mistah." He kind of liked when she got all fiery. He loved her accent and could listen to it for hours.

He corralled the laughter rolling around inside long enough to speak. "You're dressed as if we were going to a social outing and yet you're willing to saddle your own horse. And from what you just told me, you don't much appreciate the rules of etiquette either. You are a mystery, Rainelle Devonwood, that's for sure." He smiled, feeling the happiness clear to his bones. "Come on then. Let's get started." He closed the distance between them, placed his hand at her elbow and led her toward the barn.

"What did you mean I do not appreciate the rules of etiquette *either?* Do you know someone else who feels a strong aversion to them as I do?"

"Yes. My mother."

"Your mother?" Tilting her head back, her wide eyes looked up at him from under the broad brim of her hat.

Again Haydon chuckled. It felt good to laugh again. "Yes." He stopped at the barn door, tugged it open and motioned for her to precede him. They stepped inside and let their eyes adjust to the dim interior before he set the food bag down on a bench inside the door.

Rainee faced him. "Katherine mentioned a couple of social rules that she no longer abided by, but I had no idea she felt as strongly about them as I do. Are you teasing me?" The look she gave him was incredulous and suspicious.

"Nope." He walked past her, grabbed a couple of halters off of a wooden peg from inside the tack room and headed toward the stalls. "She never let on she felt that way until we moved out West."

Rainee stepped up beside him and reached for one of the halters.

Haydon tightened his hold.

"I want to help. Please?" Seeing her sincerity, he handed her a halter.

"You take Raven." He pointed toward the stall that held his most gentle mare.

He watched her open the stall door and shut it behind her. She coaxed the Palouse pony to her. And with expertise she slipped the halter on the black horse with the white spotted rump and led it out of the stall.

Haydon haltered Rebel. When he stepped inside the barn, he saw Miss Piggy heading his way. "Well, hello there, Miss Piggy."

Rainee whirled around and jumped back. Raven balked, but the pint-size woman kept the horse under control. Her eyes darted wildly about the barn. "Where—where is the pig?" She pressed her back against the horse.

Haydon laughed again. "*Miss Piggy* isn't a pig."

Rainee's brows darted heavenward as if being held at gunpoint. "What is it then?"

With his back to Rainee, he squatted down and scratched Miss Piggy behind the ears. He picked up the gray-and-white cat and hugged the feline to his chest. He turned and faced Rainee. "*This* is Miss Piggy."

"*That* is Miss Piggy?" Her eyes danced with surprise. "You have a cat named Miss Piggy?" Her head weaved back and forth and the feather on her hat waved. "Wait." She stopped shaking her head. "Let me guess? Abby named her, right?"

"Nope. I did."

Her hand shot to the side of her face. "Very strange. Very strange indeed." She stepped in front of him. "May I hold her, please?"

"Sure." He handed the fluffy ball of fur to her.

She held the cat close and stroked its fur. "What a sweet little thing you are." She rubbed her nose against the cat's.

Haydon couldn't believe he was standing there wishing it was him she was lavishing her affection on and rubbing noses with.

After a couple of minutes, Miss Piggy squirmed. "You want down, sweet thing? Okay." She lowered the pet to the ground. Her gaze followed the feline, who was strutting toward the barn door with her tail held high. "Goodbye, Miss Piggy."

Rainee tugged on the horse's lead rope and started walking away. "A cat named Miss Piggy, a pig named Kitty and a horse named after a snapping turtle. I suppose if you had a dog you would name it Fishy, or Moosey or Miss Cowey?" Dust swirled at her feet as she continued walking.

"Actually, we had a dog named Mule, but it died."

Rainee stopped and her spine stiffened, but she did not look back at him. Seconds later, she led Raven toward the tack room. "I had to ask," she muttered, but Haydon heard her.

Again she surprised him by refusing the side saddle and opted for a regular saddle instead. He glanced at her dress. Just how would she accomplish that feat?

From the corner of his eye, he watched with admiration as she brushed and saddled the mare.

A new respect for the tiny woman dusted over him. Maybe God knew what He was doing after all. He chuckled inwardly. Of course God knew exactly what He was doing.

"Do you not just love the smell of horses?" she asked, raising her pert nose in the air and sniffing.

Haydon drew in a long whiff. Horse, hay, dust, leather and a hint of manure filled his nostrils. "Sometimes." He could do without the dung smell. But he wouldn't tell her that. He'd never known a woman to admit liking the scent of horses.

Haydon tied the bag of food onto the back of his saddle, adding some string and a few homemade hooks. "Well, let's go." They headed out of the barn, leading the horses into the warm morning sunshine.

Before he had a chance to help Rainee onto her horse, she placed her left foot into the stirrup and swung her right leg over the saddle. Haydon's eyes all but popped out of their sockets. This woman was something else. *What* yet he didn't rightly know. But he was actually looking forward to finding out.

Atop the horse, Rainee glanced over at Haydon. The whites of his eyes were showing. She followed his gaze to her split skirt. What would Mother do if she could see her now? Rainee abhorred riding sidesaddle and hated straddling a horse in a dress. So, she had asked Jenetta to make this split skirt for her.

The first time she had put it on, her mother had come close to having a fit of apoplexy and made her take it off straightaway. She had not worn the dress since. Until today. She hoped out here it was okay to wear such a garment. Judging from the shock trailing across Haydon's face, perhaps it was not.

"I—I am sorry if my skirt offends you. I shall go and change." She started to dismount.

"No, no. It's fine." He captured her gaze. "You're really something. Ya know that?"

Rainee situated herself back onto the saddle. Was being something good or bad? She dared not ask.

He swung his bulky frame into the saddle and headed around the barn.

Nudging Raven forward, Rainee caught up to him. "Haydon?"

Leather creaked as he shifted in his saddle toward her. "Yes?"

"Are we going to be around any pigs today? I mean, you are not going to introduce me to any more animals with weird names, are you?"

His crooked grin sent a thousand tiny fingers tickling her insides.

"We will have to ride through some in order for you to see the whole ranch. But you'll be on horseback, so don't worry, okay?"

Not okay, but Rainee nodded anyway. She refused to let anything stop her from enjoying this outing or from getting to know him better. Not even the dreaded curly-tailed beasts.

As far as the eye could see, rolling hills of wheat decorated the landscape. They rode their horses up the mountain and wove their way through spruce trees, fir trees and several species of pine trees. But the most fascinating of them all was the huge grove of giant cedar trees. Rainee felt like a speck of volcanic ash next to them.

Along the way, Haydon waited while she stopped to gather wild strawberries to have with their lunch.

They continued riding around and down through the woods. Rainee heard the faint sound of running water.

Within minutes a small river came into view. It was not much of a river compared to those back home, but it mattered not because the surrounding area was exquisite. "Does this river have a name?" Rainee asked.

"The Palouse."

"What an odd name for a river."

"Don't forget the horse you're riding is a Palouse."

Rainee reached down and patted the horse's neck. "She sure is a nice mare. You did an amazing job breaking her. Raven is so calm and easy to handle."

Raven?

"Wait." She reined her horse to a stop, and he stopped alongside her. "I cannot believe it."

"Believe what?"

"Raven is a bird."

"No, she isn't. She's a horse." The smirk on his face had humor written all over it.

"How did I not catch that before?" She shook her head, and he laughed. "I shudder to think what you will name your children." Realizing what she had just said, she nudged her horse forward to hide her embarrassment.

Two hours later, Rainee was ready to take a break and eat their noon meal.

Haydon must have felt the same way because he followed the Palouse River until he came to a nice clearing.

Rainee swung her leg over to dismount, but sturdy hands circled her waist and lowered her to the ground. When Haydon let go, she turned and faced him. "Thank you."

"You're welcome." His gaze traveled over her face for a moment.

Under his intense scrutiny, she held her breath, watching, wondering what he was thinking. His eyes eased toward her mouth and stayed there. Hopes of him kissing her stayed hidden inside her heart.

All of a sudden he whirled and strode toward his horse.

Perhaps she had not hidden her desire so well after all and had frightened him off. With a one-shoulder hike, she hurried to remove her hat. By the time she finished and had it tied to the saddle horn, Haydon had their bag of food.

Rainee made haste toward him. "Here, let me get that."

He glanced at her, then nodded. Gathering their horses' reins, he led them to the river. Both horses dipped their heads and drank.

Rainee removed the tablecloth and spread it out in the shade of a cottonwood tree. She knelt down and placed the ham, rye bread slices, jam-filled shortbread cookies, strawberries and water on the cloth.

Something blue caught her eye. A gorgeous bluebird perched on a low branch descended on an insect, then flew off. Birds were such fascinating creatures. Always happy. Always flitting about. And free. Something she envied. She wondered if she would ever feel truly free as long as the threat of her brother finding her still lingered.

Haydon tied the horses to a tree and came and sat opposite her.

"Did you see that magnificent bird?" Rainee pointed toward the bush it had evacuated.

He followed her gaze. "No."

"It was the prettiest color of blue I have ever seen." She pointed toward a bush. "That woody-looking plant with the red berries on it, what is it, please?"

"It's a kinnikinnick bush."

"Are the berries edible?"

"They are. Bears love them."

"Bears?" She glanced all around, up into the trees, then back at him. "Do you have bears here?"

Broken shafts of light seeped through the trees and danced across his handsome profile. "Don't worry, they won't bother you."

She took that as a yes and hoped he was right. Seeing a bear did not appeal to her. She placed a thick slice of ham between two slices of buttered rye bread and handed it to him before fixing one for herself.

They bowed their heads.

"Father, thank You for Your bountifulness, and for this beautiful land. Bless this food and bless this time Rainee and I spend together. In Jesus' name. Amen."

"Amen," she echoed.

As they ate their sandwiches, she listened to the water lapping over the rocks and the birds singing in the surrounding trees. Serenity rolled over her like the water rolling over the riverbed rocks. This place was delightful. A place she could stay at forever. *Oh, Lord, let it be so.*

He picked up his canteen of water, unscrewed the lid and took a long drink.

Rainee watched his neck as he swallowed and marveled at the strength it possessed.

She reached for her own canteen and strained to loosen the lid.

"Here, let me get that."

She handed it to him and watched as he opened it with ease before handing it back to her. "Thank you."

"You're welcome." He popped the last of his sandwich into his mouth. "Rainelle is such a beautiful name. I'm curious." He leaned forward. "Why do you prefer Rainee over Rainelle?"

"Because Rainelle sounds too stuffy. Too sophisticated. But Rainelle is better than Sissy."

"Sissy? Who called you Sissy?"

"My brother. He used that name to taunt me. To dare me to do things he knew I was not supposed to do. And because I despised his teasing, I usually gave in to his dares. Which usually led to another lecture," she twittered.

She tilted her canteen up to her lips, took a sip and dabbed her mouth with her riding gloves. Not very ladylike, but she did not care. "Sometimes his challenges were quite dangerous."

"What kinds of dangerous things did he dare you to do?"

Rainee thought about it for a moment. "To ride Maggie, for one. I was not allowed to ride newly purchased horses. Father feared I would get hurt, so he had Jimmy, the stable boy, ride them until they were gentle enough for me to ride. The second day we had Maggie my brother dared me to ride the mare, but he failed to tell me no one had ridden her before and that she was only saddle- and bridle-broke."

"So what happened?" He removed his hat and laid it beside him. His blond hair reminded her of the petals of Arkansas tickseed flowers or the color of the yellow-breasted chat bird she had seen back home. He leaned his back against a tree, crossed his ankles and joined his hands behind his head.

"After he saddled and bridled Maggie, he led her out of the stall and around the barn. My brother was no dunce. That side of the barn was out of my parents' view." She picked up a twig and started snapping it into tiny pieces. "He held the mare while I put my foot in the stirrup and climbed aboard. The horse stayed still. It was when he let go of her that she took off at a dead run, bucking all the way."

He removed his hands from the back of his head and sat up straight. "What did you do?"

"I was able to hang on until we got to the river. As soon as the horse got to the riverbank, she stopped and whirled sideways. I lost my grip and flew face-first into the river. I do not think I have ever seen my father so vexed."

"Did you get hurt?"

"Only my pride." She raised her canteen to her mouth and drank freely.

"How old were you then?"

"Sixteen."

"Where's your brother now?"

To avoid his question, she took another long pull of water and took her time replacing the cap.

Once the lid was secured on her canteen, she set it down and looked around, stalling for time. "I am so glad you found a spot without any pigs." She looked back at him. "Thank you for that."

"You're welcome."

Rainee handed him three cookies. He popped a whole one into his mouth. And what a well-formed mouth it was. Her gaze trailed up his face until it landed on his sapphire-blue eyes. Eyes that were staring at her. Eyes that had caught her studying his lips. She dropped her head and quickly snatched up a cookie and bit off a piece, looking everywhere but at him.

"You never answered me. Where is your brother now? Is he still alive?"

Cookie crumbs sucked down her windpipe. She covered her mouth as she struggled to free her lungs, but it was either cookies in or cookies out, and she was not sure which would be worse.

Haydon flew toward her, patted her back and handed her his open canteen. "Take this." He knelt on one knee beside her.

Rainee put the canteen to her lips and took several sips before handing it back to him. "Thank you, Haydon," she rasped.

She coughed again, her mind a swirling mess about how she would answer his question without giving anything of her past away.

His masculine nearness overpowered her senses. Sensations she never knew existed. Horse, leather, fresh air, male scent emanated from him.

Their eyes collided for the briefest of moments before Haydon turned his gaze away and shifted his body sideways.

"Rainee."

Please do not ask me again about my brother. Please. Her eyes followed him as he stood.

He leaned over, grabbed his hat and set it on his head before looking down at her. "I brought you out here today for a reason." The serious look on his face caused her stomach to churn like a strong undercurrent in a rushing river. Was he going to send her home? She would not go. She would run away first. Her heart stopped beating as she waited for him to speak.

He raised his hat, raked his fingers through his damp hair and rubbed the back of his neck. Playing with the brim of his hat, his gaze shifted from her to the hard ground beneath him.

Whatever he wanted to say was sure giving him a bad case of the nerves. And her, too. She brushed the crumbs off her skirt and stood. "What is it?" She braced herself for the answer.

He stepped closer.

Her breath caught.

"After Reverend James' sermon Sunday, I've been doing some serious praying."

Something moved behind him. She looked beyond him to see what had snagged her attention.

Her eyes widened.

"And I want to—"

"Oh, no. Not again," Rainee screeched.

Chapter Fourteen

Haydon's heart kicked like a bucking horse and his ears ached from Rainee's high-pitched scream. He whirled around to see what had caused her distress and turned her face as pale as his grandmother's dusting powder.

Kitty was trotting toward them. Her pink ears flopped and her belly jiggled as Kitty called with her little throaty grunt.

Before Kitty had a chance to get any closer, Haydon hurried to the pig and stopped her.

Over his shoulder he said, "It's okay, Rainee. Kitty won't hurt you." He knelt by the pig's side. "Kitty, you naughty girl, are you following me?" He looked back at Rainee, who had climbed atop a fallen log and looked ready to bolt through the brush at the slightest move of his beloved pet.

He hated seeing her so frightened. Wanting to ease her fears, and knowing Kitty wouldn't hurt a soul, he rubbed behind the sow's ears with one hand and extended his other toward Rainee. "Come here, Rainee. I want to show you that Kitty won't hurt you."

Her mouth opened, but no words came forth. Her head jerked back and forth, but her fear-stained eyes never left Kitty. Seeing her frightened face tore at his heartstrings.

Lord, please don't let her faint again. Haydon looked at Kitty, who leaned into him so hard she almost pushed him over. *You're not making this easy, Kitty.* "Trust me, Rainee," he coaxed, trying to keep his balance from the two-hundred-plus-pound pig bearing her full weight against him.

His gaze trailed to Rainee's rigid body and pallid face. Softly and calmly he continued, "I promise you won't get hurt."

For a brief moment her gaze darted to him before landing back on the swine. "I—I cannot." Her voice quavered.

"Yes, you can. I'll help you." He could tell she wanted to, but her fear kept her feet planted yards away from him. Like an infected splinter under the skin, it irritated Haydon what someone had done to her, making her so fearful of these playful creatures. Sure, they could be mean when it came to protecting their babies, but otherwise they were fun-loving animals. He waved her toward him. "C'mon on, Rainee. I know you don't trust Kitty, but you can trust me, can't you?"

Her eyes bounced back and forth between him and the pig. A battle was definitely going on inside that pretty little head of hers.

"I trust you. But I am not sure I trust her." She pointed at Kitty. "Are—are you sure it is safe?"

"I'm sure. I wouldn't ask you to come here otherwise." Haydon shifted his weight onto his other leg and waved her forward.

Her chest expanded. She stepped off the log and took one tiny step forward and stopped.

"It's okay," he encouraged again.

She took another small step forward.

He nodded his approval.

Then another.

"That a girl. You're doing great. Keep coming."

Five more steps and she was standing beside him, on the opposite side of Kitty.

"Squat down here."

She looked back and forth between him and Kitty, shaking her head. "I—I cannot do this."

"Yes, you can. I'll help you. Give me your hand." He used the same gentle voice with her that he used while breaking a young filly. He stood and extended his free hand toward her while keeping his other hand on Kitty.

Inching her hand toward his, she laid her fingers in his palm. He gently tugged her forward, and with his hand on top of hers, he placed her hand behind Kitty's ears.

With a muffled whimper, she jerked back.

Keeping his hand on hers, Haydon patiently and tenderly placed her hand there again and rubbed. Contented, Kitty stood still. After a few moments, Haydon eased his hand from Rainee's and grinned when she continued the rubbing motion, never taking her eyes off of the pig.

Stepping back a foot he watched them.

Kitty sidestepped closer to Rainee and closed her eyes. Soft grunts emerged from the friendly sow. She leaned into Rainee.

Rainee gasped, jerked her hand back and fixed questioning eyes on Haydon.

"It's okay," he whispered. "You're doing great." He stepped next to her.

Her lips quivered as they edged upward in a tremulous smile. She nodded with short jerks. Her chest heaved, and then with trepidation in her eyes she placed her hand back on Kitty.

One minute turned into another, until finally Kitty opened her eyes and straightened.

Rainee's hand fell away.

The pig glanced up at Rainee. Her snout moved in a sniffing motion, almost as if to say thanks. Kitty waddled off to a muddy spot where she scooped at the mud with her round nose before lying down.

"Oh, my."

Haydon glanced toward the sound of Rainee's soft voice. Seeing her wide eyes replaced with wonder caused his chest to swell with pride. She had taken her first step in casting down her fear of pigs. "Now that wasn't so bad, was it?"

Rainee stopped watching Kitty and looked up at him. Gone was the fear, replaced with relief. "No. Not at all. I never knew pigs could be so friendly."

"They can be. I think Kitty is friendlier than most because when she was born we had to bottle-feed her to keep her alive. Abby and I took on that chore together. After Kitty was able to eat on her own, she spent more time with us than with the rest of the herd. That silly little pig followed us everywhere." He chuckled. "Still does. I'm surprised you've only seen her near the house one day since you've been here. Then again, knowing how afraid you are of pigs, maybe God kept her away." He could feel the mirth dancing in his eyes.

Rainee laughed, then headed to the river and stood at the bank.

Haydon grabbed the string and hooks he'd brought with him and stood beside her. She looked so beautiful and serene. His affections toward her were growing, along with the urge to pull her into his arms. It was getting harder and harder to not give into the desire to kiss her. He needed to get his mind off of that before he gave into his yearnings. "Do you mind if I do some fishing while we're here? I'd like to take back a mess for dinner."

"No, not at all." She clasped her hands in front of her and dipped her chin. "Do you mind if I join you?"

One eyebrow hiked upward. The woman fished too? What else did she do?

"I know it is not proper for young ladies to fish, but I do so enjoy it."

Again he wanted to kiss her. Just to be close to her. This woman was lovely inside and out. He realized how wrong he had been to compare her to Melanie. Melanie would have never saddled a horse, gone for a horseback ride, taken a picnic in the wilds as she called it, touched a pig, fished or anything else other than attend parties with high-society folks and complain about everything else.

Feeling lighter than he had in years, Haydon couldn't wait to finish their talk. But right now it would have to wait. If this woman wanted to fish, then fish they would.

"You caught the fish?" The look of incredulity lit up Michael's face as he stared at Rainee in awe. Rainee was glad Michael and she were friends. He had even apologized to her for his earlier behavior.

"She sure did." Haydon's smile contained his promise to her that he wouldn't tell anyone she had taken the fish off the hooks and had cleaned them, too.

A silent thank-you passed between them.

Once again she was thankful her mother had not witnessed her not only going fishing but cleaning them, too. Mother would have fainted straightaway.

Haydon poked a piece of fried trout into his mouth and ate it. "You did an amazing job of frying them, too." Admiration showed in his eyes.

"Thank you," she said, feeling the blush clear to her toes. "But I had help. Leah and—"

"Me," Abby cut in, pointing her thumb at herself.

Rainee shifted in her seat and faced Abby, sitting next to her.

"Me helped, too." The little girl's face beamed with pride as she pointed to herself again.

"I helped," her mother corrected.

"Nuh-uh, Mother," Abby said, shaking her head. "You didn't help. Just me and Leah did."

"I know I didn't help. It isn't 'me helped.' It's 'I helped.'"

"Huh?" Abby wrinkled her little pixie nose. "But you didn't help."

"Oh, never mind." Katherine scooped a spoonful of fried potatoes into her mouth.

Rainee kept her laughter inside. She loved this wonderful family. She cut a glance at Haydon. She loved him, too. That thought scared her half to death.

While he had been very attentive to her today, he still had not given her any indication that his feelings toward her had changed. When she had first arrived at the ranch, she had overheard Katherine telling him to be nice to her. So she was not sure if that was all he was doing or if maybe he had begun to consider her as a bride.

Not liking how the uncertainty made her feel, she focused on Abby and smiled. "I do not know how we would have finished frying all these fish if it were not for you, Abby."

The little girl wiggled in her chair, sitting up taller.

After everyone finished eating, Rainee rose and put water on the stove. While it heated, she shooed everyone away and gathered the dishes from the table.

"I'm not leaving you to do the dishes by yourself." Bags hung under Katherine's eyes. And her face was devoid of its usual color. She was either unwell or in need of rest. Whatever the case, Rainee would not let her help. "I want to do them. Please."

Katherine studied her face. "Are you sure?"

"Yes, I am sure."

"Well, okay. But Leah can stay and help you."

Leah picked up her plate and leaned over to pick up another.

"Leah, you would not be offended if I want to be alone, would you? I love doing dishes."

Leah looked at her as if she had gone daft. Rainee giggled. "I know, I know. I am quite strange. But truly, I enjoy doing them. It gives me time to think."

Leah turned toward Katherine. "Mother?" Her blue eyes lit up with anticipation.

Katherine shrugged. "What can I say? If Rainee wants to do dishes, then we'll let her. Besides, we have a basketful of mending that needs taking care of."

Leah nodded. "I'd rather do mending than dishes any ole day." Smiles flitted through her words. "Thank you, Rainee." Leah's face brightened. Her waist-long blond braid swished like a horse's tail as she sashayed into the living room.

Katherine's steps were slow as she too headed toward the living room. Rainee frowned. She quickly snatched up the dishes from the table. She wanted to hurry and get the dishes done so she could help Katherine with the mending. Katherine's pale face bothered Rainee.

"Lord," Rainee whispered as she picked up a pot holder with her lacey-gloved hand and dumped the water into the sink. "I am worried about Katherine. She seems quite unwell. Either that, or something is really bothering her. Whatever it is, Lord, would you please tend to her needs and heal whatever is ailing her? Thank you, Jesus."

"Amen."

Rainee whirled at the sound of Haydon's voice behind her. When he had walked up, she did not know, but his nearness stole her breath and caused her heart to beat faster.

"That's so sweet of you to pray for my mother."

Her eyes collided with his, and she found she could not pull her gaze away, and it appeared he could not either.

"I've never met a woman like you before, Rainee," he whispered.

His eyelids lowered to her mouth. His lips parted and a cloud of peppermint circled the air.

Neither moved.

Rainee's eyelids lowered. She could feel his presence closing the distance between them.

A warm, calloused finger touched under her chin

and tugged it upward. Lips, both soft and slightly dry touched hers.

She locked her knees to keep them from buckling. Delight swept through in shivering waves.

Haydon jerked back. "I'm sorry, Rainee. I—" He took a step back and ran his hand through his thick hair. "I don't know what came over me. Forgive me." With that he whirled and fled, the screen door shutting behind him.

Rainee reached behind her, feeling and searching for something to grasp on to for support because her knees were too weak to hold her upright. She leaned against the sink. Closing her eyes, she touched her lips where the peppermint still lingered. That man could kiss. Of course, she had nothing to compare it to, but she did not need to or want to either.

"Are you okay?" Katherine asked softly.

Rainee's eyes flew open. She pushed away from the sink, praying her legs would hold her. "I—I am fine."

Katherine looked at her and then at the door Haydon had just exited. A knowing smile graced her lips. "I'm sure you are." A twinkle lit the woman's eyes.

Heat flooded through Rainee and onto her cheeks. She did not want to discuss that kiss with Katherine or anyone else. She just wanted to keep reliving it. Better yet, she wanted Haydon to keep kissing her so she did not have to relive the memory of it alone.

Katherine giggled. "That good, huh?"

What? Rainee could not believe Katherine would comment about the kiss she and Haydon had shared. The woman was the man's mother, after all. Reeling with shock, Rainee needed to distract the attention off of her, so she planted her hands on her hips. "And what pray tell are you doing in here? You are supposed to be sitting down and resting. I mean, mending."

"I just came for a cup of tea. Is there any hot water left?"

Rainee grabbed a cup and saucer off the shelf and started to fix the tea.

"I can do that."

Rainee stopped and faced Katherine. "Please. Let me." After the tea was fixed, she sat down beside her. "Are you unwell, Katherine?" Rainee searched her eyes.

Katherine drew in a deep breath, glanced into the living room, then back at Rainee. "Just lonely." Katherine picked up her cup and took a sip. "I try not to dwell on it, but since my husband died, the isolation is almost unbearable. While Mr. Bowen was alive, I didn't mind living out here. But now..." She shrugged.

Compassion and empathy for the woman drizzled over Rainee.

Rainee had been under the impression that Katherine was extremely happy living out West. That she loved living where she was free from the strict rules of etiquette and high-society snobbery. She also believed the two of them were a lot alike, but perhaps she had been mistaken because Rainee would rather be lonely and isolated then have to revert back to the rules she abhorred.

"You're probably wondering why I shared this with you."

Rainee nodded.

Katherine laid her hand on top of Rainee's. "You might be young enough to be my daughter, but we share a common bond."

Rainee could not imagine what that was.

"I can never go home again either."

Rainee blinked. "What—what do you mean you can never go home again?" All sorts of scenarios ran through Rainee's mind. But rather than let her thoughts run wild, she patiently waited for Katherine's answer.

Katherine took a long sip of her tea, then set the cup on the table. "At seventeen, I ran away from home and eloped with Haydon's father."

Rainee's mouth formed a wide O.

"My father was a very abusive man, Rainee. Not just physically but mentally as well."

Her heart went out to Katherine. For she knew only too well the cruelty of abuse.

She clasped the woman's hands and cradled them with her own. She wished she could remove her lacy gloves, but she feared someone other than Leah and Katherine would see her scars, so she kept them on.

"To everyone else Father appeared to be a loving husband and father. But to my sisters, my mother and me, he was evil personified. We all have the scars to prove it."

"You have scars, too?" Rainee blurted without thinking. She wanted to scan Katherine's arms, neck and any other skin showing, but she forced her eyes to remain on Katherine so as to not make her uncomfortable.

"Yes, I do."

Rainee wanted to ask where, but she did not, and Katherine did not offer the information.

"Before my father had a chance to follow through with his plan, Sylva, my personal maid, came to us in the middle of the night to tell us she had overheard my father talking to some man in his study. I knew my father was a vicious man, but I never knew the true depth of his maliciousness until that night." She looked at Rainee, then her gaze dropped to her lap. "Father had hired a man to kill my soon-to-be husband and to make it look like an accident."

Rainee tried to stifle a gasp but failed. She squeezed Katherine's hand, and Katherine returned the gesture, holding on so tight Rainee's hand began to tingle.

"He wanted my husband dead so he could take back control of my life. My father was foolish enough to believe I would let him have control of not only my life again, but all my husband's assets as well. That same night we fled to New York. Years later, we moved out here, and I haven't seen any of my family since."

Now it all made sense why God had led her to this particular place and why Katherine had been so kind to her from the very beginning. Katherine understood exactly how she felt.

Rainee hoped and prayed she would never have to leave Haydon or this wonderful family she had grown extremely fond of.

But how could she stay when she needed to get married? Getting married was her ticket out from under Ferrin's care, and Haydon's intentions on that account were confusing at best.

Then she remembered Haydon's kiss. Did his sweet kiss mean he had feelings for her? Hope peaked into her soul, making it soar as high as the night stars.

Chapter Fifteen

Haydon scrambled to the barn, saddled Rebel and raced into the woods. When he reached the river, he dismounted and lowered himself onto a large boulder near the water.

The full moon threaded silver-and-black ripples over the riverbed rocks, and the trees cast their lots over him.

He closed his eyes and allowed the lulling sound of the water to calm his racing heart. How could one barn-raising kiss have such a powerful effect on him? It was wrong of him to kiss her, but when she closed her eyes, it was as if his lips were drawn toward hers beyond all reasoning.

Chills spread through his whole body when their mouths had connected. "Lord, I didn't want to have feelings for her, but I do. Now what?"

What had he been thinking by inviting her to see the ranch, knowing that against his will his affection toward her had already been escalating? He couldn't help but notice her actions over the past few weeks.

Couldn't help but notice *her.*

Her kindness, her willingness to help do anything,

her beauty inside and out and the feisty spirit she displayed so often had knocked a gaping hole in the wall he had built around his heart.

And he didn't want that wall to crumble.

His heart yanked him in several directions.

"Lord, I don't want to love anyone. It hurts too bad. I can't bear the idea of failing again or hurting another human being, including myself. Once was devastating enough. I'm so confused."

Fear wrapped around his heart and squeezed until he could hardly breathe. "I can't handle this. Being with her is out of the question."

"You betcha it is!"

Haydon whirled toward the sound of the voice. His leg slipped on the slick rock. Pain shot through his hands and knees as they collided with the hard ground. He scrambled to stand but froze when the cold barrel of a gun pressed against his right temple.

"Stay right where you are."

That voice. He had heard it somewhere before. From the corner of his eye, he spotted a worn-out boot. If he spun just right, he could knock the man's leg out from underneath him and grab his gun.

The gun cocked.

Haydon froze. He didn't dare move.

While Rainee finished up the morning dishes, she gazed out the kitchen window above the sink, wondering again why Haydon had not come to breakfast.

Michael waved at her from the wagon as he and Smokey wheeled by the house, heading toward town. She raised her wet hand and wiggled her fingers in a wave. Water ran down her arm. She plunged her hands back into the dishwater and glanced out the window again, hoping to get a glimpse of Haydon. She scanned the yard, and her gaze stopped at Jesse's house. Jesse was standing on his porch, with his arms wrapped around Hannah, kissing her. Rainee knew she should look away, but the sweet, tender sight mesmerized her. Envy wrapped around her like a choking vine.

"Well, I'm off to Nora's," Katherine said from behind her.

Rainee whirled with a jump.

"Sorry, I didn't mean to scare you. I'm leaving now. Today's the day I will meet Mr. Svenska." Katherine's eyes sparkled.

"Who is Mr. Svenska?" Rainee dried her bare hands on a towel.

"Nora's brother."

"Oh. And pray tell, how old is this Mr. Svenska?"

"Fifty-three." A knowing smile passed between them before Katherine hugged her.

"Have fun."

"Oh, I will. You, too." Katherine turned and gathered the gift basket she had prepared for Nora from off the kitchen table.

Leah strode into the room and pulled Rainee into a quick hug. It felt good to be hugged by those she cared about. "Seems like we don't ever get to talk much anymore. I'm either at my friends' quilting or helping Mrs. Bengtsson with her twins. They're sure cute. I'm going to hate it when Mrs. Bengtsson gets better and doesn't need me anymore."

"Leah!"

They both jerked their heads that way.

Leah giggled. "I see how that must have sounded,

Mother, but that's not what I meant. Of course, I want her to get well, but I just meant I will miss the twins."

The wrinkles around Katherine's eyes relaxed and she nodded in understanding.

"I'll see you later, Rainee." Leah and Rainee smiled at each other before Leah picked up her bundle from off of the table and headed out the door.

Abby darted into the kitchen from outside and barreled into Rainee's leg, knocking her into the sink. Her tiny arms flew around Rainee's hips.

"Abigail!" Katherine shook her head and Abby's wide-eyed gaze darted toward her mother. "I really did raise my children better than this, honest. Sorry, Rainee."

"Do not be sorry, Katherine. You did a fine job of raising your children." *Especially a certain handsome man.*

Abby sent Katherine a smile that said, "See there is nothing wrong with me," then she looked up at Rainee. "See ya later, Rainee. I love you."

Rainee's heart melted. This sweet little girl, who Rainee adored, loved her. "I love you too, Abby." She leaned down and pulled Abby into her arms, careful to keep her scarred hands hidden. When everyone except Katherine and Leah had left the house that morning, Rainee had taken a chance and removed her gloves and laid them next to the sink. She eyed them now, wishing she had them on.

Abby gave her another hard squeeze around the neck and skipped outdoors again before Rainee finished standing.

Katherine studied her. "You sure you don't want to go with us?"

"I am sure. But thank you for asking."

"Oh, and don't worry about Haydon not showing up for breakfast. With him not working yesterday, he said he had a lot of chores to catch up on."

Rainee nodded even though Katherine's words did nothing to reassure her.

"A lot of times Haydon gets up early and, after he finishes his chores, he'll go for a long ride. Especially if he has a lot on his mind." Katherine sent her a knowing glance. "I'm praying things work out between you and Haydon. After that kiss last night, I'd say it's only a matter of time." With a wink, Katherine flew out the door, chuckling all the way.

Rainee stared after Haydon's mother. If she did not close her mouth soon, a fly would surely land inside it. Rainee clamped her lips together.

She watched as Katherine, Leah and Abby squashed themselves into the buggy to go visit their neighbors as they had done a couple times since she had been there. Rainee thought it sweet of them to invite her along, but she did not feel up to being very social today because she could not shake the uneasiness dwelling inside her. Haydon not showing up for breakfast snatched any hopes she had of staying here.

Had he regretted kissing her?

And had his regret kept him away?

Katherine believed things would work out between them. But she surely must be mistaken.

With a weighty sigh and a heavy heart, Rainee washed the last pan, dried all the dishes and put them away, and tidied up the rest of the kitchen. She stood back and surveyed her work. Seeing the kitchen sparkling clean was so rewarding. She removed her apron and hung it on the hook by the door.

The warm sunshine beckoned her. A walk would do her good and give her a chance to pray.

In case Haydon showed up and wondered where she was, she grabbed Abby's slate and a piece of chalk and scribbled a note indicating she was going for a walk. She tugged her gloves on, placed apples, biscuits, left-over bacon, and a canteen of sweetened tea in a sack and headed outside.

"Good morning, Rainee," Hannah hollered and waved.

She did not feel like talking to anyone, but she would not be rude to her dear friend either, so she walked over to Hannah's house. "Good morning, Hannah." She looked around the area. "Where is Jesse?"

"He's doing his morning chores and Haydon's, too. I sure worry about him sometimes. I know he's doing better and you can't keep a man down, but I sure wish he would have given himself more time to heal. But no, within three days he was outside working again. Of course, I forbid him to do a lot of heavy work. But he never listens to me. You know how men are."

She sure did know how men were. "Wait. Did you say that Jesse was doing *Haydon's* chores?"

"Yes. Why?"

So, Haydon did not stay away from breakfast because of chores. That unsettled feeling she had earlier escalated. She needed someone to talk to about her concerns. A friend she could confide in. And Hannah had turned out to be that person. "Do you mind if I sit down?"

"No, of course not. Would you like some tea?"

"No, thank you." She lowered herself onto the swing, stabilized the food sack on her lap and turned her face toward Hannah.

"What's wrong, Rainee?"

Rainee looked around to make sure they were alone. Of course they were alone. Everyone had gone except Jesse, and he was away doing chores. "Please keep this between us, okay?"

Hannah nodded. Fine strands of red hair outlined her face, and her brown eyes studied Rainee, waiting.

"Yesterday Haydon and I went for a ride."

"Yes, I know."

"You do?"

Hannah giggled. "I saw you two ride out together."

Rainee smiled. Nothing got past Hannah. She placed her hands on top of the food sack and pulled and tugged at the palm of her lacy glove as she relayed everything that had happened up until the kiss. "And then he kissed me."

"He kissed you?" Hannah's eyes lit up. "Oh, Rainee, I'm so happy for you."

"I would be happy for me too, if after he had kissed me he had not apologized and run off. I have not seen the man since."

"Rainee." Hannah took her hands into hers. "Trust me when I say that Haydon has feelings for you, but he's scared. I can't say anything more than that. It's not my place. But things will work out. Have faith."

It was faith that had brought her to this strange land to marry a perfect stranger. And it was faith that had kept her alive. Hannah was right. She needed to have faith that God would work everything out. No wonder the Bible said to encourage one another daily. Even though she knew God would work things out according to His perfect will and His timing, she still needed to be reminded of it on a daily basis.

"Rainee. Haydon has only kissed two women in his life. And you're one of them. The other—" Hannah stopped and tucked her bottom lip with her teeth.

The other he married, Rainee mentally finished Hannah's sentence for her. She could only dream that he would marry her, too. Their shared kiss had scarce given her hope that perhaps there might be a future for them after all. Time would tell.

"I've said enough already." Hannah let go of Rainee's hands.

Although she was disappointed Hannah had not continued, she felt a measure of relief at Hannah's revelation. That alone reignited the spark of hope she had yesterday. And she could not very well ask Hannah to say more. After all, Hannah was not aware that Rainee knew about Melanie. Katherine had told her about Haydon's wife in the strictest of confidence, and Rainee would not break her word. "Thank you, Hannah."

"You're welcome." A smile of understanding passed between them.

Rainee clutched the sack of food and stood. "I need to go for a walk, to think and to pray. Please, do not get up. I will talk to you later." She headed down the porch steps and turned to wave at Hannah.

Unable to shake the nagging feeling that something was wrong with Haydon, she headed toward the barn to see if he was there. Instead, she found Jesse.

"Good morning."

Jesse turned and a hint of a smile wafted through his eyes. "Morning." He went back to scooping the hay.

"Have you seen Haydon?"

"Um. No. I haven't."

Rainee stared at Jesse for a long moment, sensing something was not quite right. "All right. If you do see him, would you please tell him I am looking for him?"

"Okay."

She turned and had almost reached the outer sunshine when his voice stopped her.

"Rainee."

When she turned, she knew it was serious. He came toward her, head down, boots sliding on the dusty barn floor. Stopping only two feet from her, he removed a crumpled envelope from his pocket and held it out to her.

"I should have given this to you when I picked it up last week." His gaze was only on the letter and never lifted to hers. "I'm sorry."

His hand came up, offering the envelope to her.

Rainee stared at it, perplexed as to its meaning. Then she glimpsed the name on it. Bettes. Her breath caught. With shaking fingers, she took it from him. "Thank you, Jesse."

He nodded. "I better get back to work."

Taking the letter that could change her life, she walked out and into the grassland covered with those beautiful purple flowers Haydon called camas plants.

She should look at it. Yet she could not bring herself to. What did she want it to say? If Mr. Bettes was sending for her, she could easily be gone from here tomorrow. Rainee followed along the edge of the field near the tree line. Seeing the pigs grazing in the distance, her pulse quickened but she kept her wits about her. She increased her pace, keeping her eyes on the swine, hoping and praying that Kitty or any of the other pigs would not spot her and follow her. She may have petted Kitty, but she still was not over her fear.

She spotted the trail Haydon had shown her and tucked the letter into her pocket. It could wait. She headed up into the trees until she reached the Palouse River. Along the way, Rainee stopped to sniff the white blooms on several of the syringa bushes. A divine citrus smell tickled her nose. She watched and listened to the bees buzzing around the flowers, fascinated that they enjoyed the flowers as much as she did.

Rainee followed the riverbank. Water lapped over the smooth rocks on the bottom of the river, and sunlight glinted off the small caps of the water, glimmering like diamonds. She smiled. How could she be so fortunate as to have come to such a beautiful country? And could she now leave it behind if God beckoned her forth from it?

Ahead she saw a thick grove of trees and brush, and for a moment, she wondered how far she had come. Was she even on the Bowen's property anymore? She panned the area in search of something familiar. She smiled when she found it. Twigs snapped under her feet as she hurried toward the special place she and Haydon had shared the picnic together.

Haydon? Why did his name bring such a jangling in her spirit? After all, it was silly of her to worry about him. He was a man who could handle himself, but still, the unsettled feeling in her stomach said all was not right with him. She hoped during her walk she would run into him, but so far she had not seen any sign of him.

Her throat felt scratchy and her mouth was as dry as

the hard-crusted ground beneath her. She reached for her canteen and tilted it to pull in a long drink, enjoying the sweet taste and the feel of the liquid as it glided down her throat.

She heard something in the distance and stopped to listen.

A harsh male voice carried its way through the trees, but she could not make out what he was saying. Her skin prickled. Whoever belonged to that ill-tempered voice was not someone Rainee wanted to meet.

She made haste in screwing the lid back on the canteen, shoved it in the food sack and looked around for a place to hide. Trees rustled as she buried herself into their thickness and stopped.

"You'll never get away with it."

That sounded like Haydon talking. She moved closer toward the angry voices.

"That's what you think. I'm here ta do a job and I aim ta do it right."

Raucous laughter followed. She steeled herself. Now was not the time to lose her nerve. Easing her way through the thick brush heading toward a cluster of cottonwood trees, she could hear the voices more clearly.

She froze, knowing if she got any closer they would surely see or hear her. Her gaze trailed up a large cottonwood tree and then down to her skirt. A plan formulated in her mind. If she thought about it, she might talk herself out of the crazy idea, so she started acting on it. Making haste, she pulled the back of her skirt between her legs and tucked it securely into the waistband as she had done long before she became a lady.

Placing her foot carefully and securely, Rainee climbed up the tree, like she had so many times before. Unbeknownst to her mother, when Rainee was a little girl, she had mastered the art of climbing trees in dresses. She could scale them as quietly as a cat sneaking up on its prey. Good thing Mother could not see her now. She would be appalled.

No time to think about or concern herself with propriety now.

Rainee lowered herself onto her stomach, and like a caterpillar, she inched her way out onto a sturdy limb. She scanned the area until she spotted Haydon propped against a tree in a small clearing near the river. His legs were stretched before him, tied with a rope. And from what Rainee could see, his hands were bound behind his back.

Who would do this to him? And why?

Rainee held her breath as she looked for the person responsible. When he finally came into view, she could not see his face because of his hat.

Something seemed vaguely familiar about the man's stance and clothing.

Her mind scrambled to figure out where she might have seen him before.

She sucked in a breath and quickly pressed her mouth against her arm lest he hear her.

It was that ruffian from the stagecoach stop.

The very one who had accosted her.

The man she had hoped she would never see again. The man the sheriff called Ben. Just the thought of how he treated her sent a wave of shivers throughout her body.

She shifted her head, trying to get a better view of the layout. A flash of silver reflected off the gun in his hand, and that gun was pointed at Haydon.

Her heart slid into her toes. Surely he did not plan on using that thing on Haydon. Then she remembered Ben saying they would be sorry they ever messed with him. She closed her eyes for a brief moment as she realized he had followed through with his threat that it would not be the last they would see of him. She had to do something to keep him from carrying out the rest of his threat.

From the way he had treated her and Haydon at the stagecoach stop, she knew Haydon's life was in danger. Somehow she needed to come up with a plan to help Haydon escape. But what could she possibly do? Her first thought was to run back to the house and get help, but by the time she made it to Jesse's and back, the man might kill Haydon. That thought brought a rush of boldness descending on her. She would not let that happen.

Chapter Sixteen

Lying motionless on the limb, watching and praying for the right time to make a move, Rainee forced herself to stay calm. With each minute that stretched by, her hope of setting Haydon free slipped further away.

But she was not about to give up. She watched patiently until the man grabbed his canteen and headed toward the water.

Now was her chance.

Careful not to make a sound, Rainee wormed her way back down the limb and tree trunk. Hunched over, she wove her way to the tree where Haydon sat.

Ben turned his head in her direction as if he had heard something.

Rainee dropped to the ground and flattened herself in the tall grasses behind a bush. She could still see him, but she prayed he could not see her. When he turned back around and squatted to fill his drinking vessel, Rainee dug her elbows into the ground and inch by inch she wiggled forward until she came to the base of the tree.

The tall grass concealed her as she peeked around

the side of the tree, the side away from the man's view, to make sure the coast was clear. "Psssttt, Haydon," she whispered as loud as she dared, without letting her nerves come out through her voice.

Haydon's shoulders stiffened, but he did not move his head.

She glanced at the river where Haydon's kidnapper was still crouched. It looked like he was having trouble removing the lid from his canteen. Good, she hoped the thing was screwed on tight. "Do not move while I untie your hands," she whispered again. Only this time she was unable to keep the quavering from her voice.

He gave a quick nod.

Rainee tugged and pulled at the knot but it would not budge. Ben had tied it tight. As fast as her fingers would move, she continued working at loosening the knot, while her eyes vacillated between the rope and the gunman.

Ben started to rise just as Rainee freed the last knot. She quickly worked her way back through the brush.

Several yards away, she hid behind a thick bush, keeping her eyes fixed on Haydon.

Ben glanced over his shoulder at Haydon. With his back still facing Haydon, Ben tipped his canteen and took a long drink.

Quietly Haydon hunched over and stretched his arms toward his feet. His large hands tugged at the rope binding his ankles together.

Crouched like a lioness ready to pounce and forcing air in and out of her lungs as quietly as possible, Rainee watched and waited for Haydon to make his move. Her blood pumped through her ears so hard and fast she thought they might burst at any moment now.

Behind her, a twig snapped.

Rainee darted her neck around and frantically searched for the source of the noise.

If she thought her heart was pounding hard before, it was nothing compared to what it was doing now. Her instinct was to flee, but the last thing she wanted was to reveal her whereabouts in case she had to run back to the ranch for help.

She scoured the ground searching for something to use as a weapon. A broken tree branch would work. Quietly she picked out a sturdy one.

Armed and ready, she watched, waiting to see what would emerge.

A pig's head came into view.

A scream hitched into Rainee's throat but it did not escape.

She watched in horror as the pig, which she now recognized as Kitty, trotted toward Haydon grunting, oblivious to the danger that lay ahead.

Ben whirled.

His canteen flew from his hand and hit the ground with a watery tin echo.

He fumbled to free the gun from his holster.

Rainee's hand flew to her mouth, and she bit into her flesh to keep from screaming out.

Quick as a gunfighter's bullet, Haydon leapt up, tackled Ben to the ground, and knocked his gun a good six feet away from them.

Between the leaves of the thick bush, Rainee struggled to see what was going on, but she could no longer see the two men.

Not knowing what was happening, she could no

longer stand it. Without thinking things through, she rushed through the bushes.

Branches scraped at her face.

She ignored them and the pain they brought and continued to plunge forward.

Spotting the gun, she kept her gaze locked on it as she rushed to it and snatched it up.

Fists hitting flesh echoed in her ears.

Haydon and Ben rolled over and over.

"Stop! Or I'll shoot!" she yelled with more confidence than she felt. Her knees were seconds away from buckling, though her hand held steady as she aimed the gun at Ben's head.

Ben froze. His sinister dark eyes turned on her, burning right through her. She wanted to toss the gun aside and run, but Haydon's life depended on her remaining brave. That was all it took. Her courage rose to the occasion.

With a quick jerk of the gun to let him know she was in charge and that she meant business, she stared Ben down.

Haydon jumped up, jerked Ben up by his vest and shoved him the opposite direction from Rainee.

Arms thrashing, Ben tumbled backward. He tripped and fell over Kitty.

Kitty squealed and ran toward Haydon, who had moved next to Rainee.

Before Rainee had a chance to react to her fear of the pig, Haydon spoke, "Don't let her frighten you, Rainee. Keep the gun on Ben, while I tie him up."

Rainee pressed her shoulders back and pointed the weapon at Ben. Her hands clutched the gun so tight her fingertips turned white.

Haydon tied Ben up.

"You dirty—" Ben stopped and glared at Haydon. Vile laughter poured from his tobacco-stained mouth. "Purty bad ya weren't man enough ta save yourself. A woman had ta do it fer ya."

"Shut your mouth," Haydon growled.

"Wassa matter, the truth hurt?" Ben sneered.

Rainee wanted to whack the man over the head with the handle of the gun for talking to Haydon like that. But the risk of Ben possibly taking it from her gave her the ammunition she needed to fight against the urge.

Haydon jerked the rope tight.

Ben flinched. "Watch it, you—" His evil gaze slithered from Haydon to Rainee. "C'mon, sweetheart. Why don't ya rid yerself of this loser?" Ben jerked his head once toward Haydon. "And hook up with a real man." Lust-filled eyes raked over her body.

To stop Ben from leering at her, she wanted to hide behind Haydon, but she refused to give Ben that satisfaction.

"I told you to be quiet," Haydon hissed again.

Along with the cringing going on inside her, the urge to beat him with the butt of the gun grew stronger.

"What'd ya want with a man who cain't even save hisself? He hassa have a woman do it fer him. I'm twice the man he'll ev'r be."

Rainee had heard enough. Beating him with the gun would not be enough to satisfy her anger at him for kidnapping and insulting Haydon. Shooting him, now that just might work. She stepped closer and aimed the gun at Ben's heart. "There is only one *real* man here. And it is not you. Now, silence your mouth, or I will pull this trigger." She cocked the gun.

* * *

Hearing the gun cock, Haydon swung his gaze toward Rainee. Fire flashed from her eyes. A jolt of shock rushed through Haydon's body. The woman meant business. Before she did something foolish, Haydon jerked the last knot tight and rose from his squatting position. He laid his hand on top of hers. Resting his finger between the hammer and the cylinder, he took the gun away and pointed it away from them. With his thumb firmly on the hammer, he pulled his finger out and put the hammer back into its resting spot.

He pointed the weapon at Ben, but his eyes strayed to Rainee.

With narrowed eyes and pursed lips, she glared down at Ben.

For a little bitty thing she sure was feisty. Haydon had never met a woman like her: sassy, intelligent, kind, compassionate and brave. Even her deep-seated fear of pigs hadn't stopped her from doing what needed to be done. His deep respect for this woman opened his heart up to feel again.

From the corner of his eyes, Haydon glimpsed movement.

Ben was rocking on his backside, struggling to get lose.

"Sit still!" Haydon ordered. "Or I'll let her have the gun again."

Ben squirmed, and a hint of fear flashed across his face.

Haydon had to keep himself from laughing. He would no more give Rainee the gun back than he would return the weapon to Ben.

"Rainee." Haydon looked at her and stopped. His

gaze trailed down her arm. He shook his head and chuckled.

Rainee looked up at him like he had gone plum loco. "What is so funny?"

He gave a quick nod toward her hand.

Rainee followed his gaze, and her hand froze. Kitty was leaning against her leg, an inch away from Rainee's fingers. He waited for Rainee to scream or faint, or both. Instead, she hiked a shoulder, dropped to her knees and threw her arms around the sow's neck. "Good girl, Kitty. Who knows what would have happened to Haydon if you had not shown up," she cooed and gave the swine's ears a good rubdown.

Haydon ran his hand over his whiskered chin. If he himself hadn't witnessed Rainee showing the pig affection, he would have never believed it. Her concern for him had annihilated her fear of pigs. Not only that, with her skirt tucked into her waistband, she had tossed aside all the rules of propriety to save his life. His insides felt as warm as the noonday sun. In that instant, he decided he would not let her leave, and he would do whatever it took to win her heart. She may have come here to marry him out of convenience, but now he hoped she would marry him out of love.

Before he could put his plan into action, however, he needed to take care of the no-good scoundrel on the ground in front of him.

"Rainee, can you untie the horses and bring them here?"

She removed her hand from Kitty. "Sorry, Kitty, I have to stop. Haydon needs me." She stood and started to swipe the dirt from her skirt. Her hands froze midair. She whirled around and when she turned back her cheeks were the color of ripe apples, her skirt no longer tucked in at the waist.

She looked so cute standing there that all he wanted to do was pull her into his arms and give her a big hug and maybe even steal a kiss or two. But now was not the time. He needed to get Ben safely tucked behind bars first. Maybe later. No, *definitely* later.

Haydon smiled and winked at her.

She blinked as if in shock. "I—I will be—" She hiked up her skirt and darted toward the horses, taking his heart with her.

A thousand winking eyelashes fluttered through Rainee's stomach. How could one smile and wink affect her so? For one second she thought she might faint straightaway. Instead, she bolted toward the horses, only slowing when she neared them. While untying them, she drew in a few steadying breaths before she led the animals over to Haydon.

Her gaze caught his. There was something soft and caring in his eyes. Something that hadn't been there before. Gone was the aloofness. And gone was her heart. It now belonged to him.

"Here, hold this, but don't do anything crazy," Haydon said, handing Rainee the gun. Their fingers touched. Warmth spread through her. "Keep it pointed at him."

Rainee said not a word for fear her words would come out raspy. Instead, she gave Haydon a quick nod, took the gun from him and aimed it at Ben.

Haydon led Ben's horse next to him and jerked him up by the ropes. Ben twisted and tossed out obscenities.

Rainee narrowed her eyes and shook the gun at him.

"If I were you, sir, I would be still and hush your foul mouth before I decide to pull this trigger."

He stopped fighting and glared at Rainee. "You wouldn't dare."

With Haydon standing behind Ben, a surge of boldness possessed her. "Try me." She sent him her cold, crazed-woman stare. The one she had practiced in the mirror. The look she had used to run off unwelcome suitors who only wanted her for her father's money.

As she continued giving Ben that cold, hard stare, shaking the gun wildly at him, Ben glanced between her and Haydon, who stared at her as if he too wondered if she would do it.

Ben's shoulders slumped and his steely gaze turned to that of a whipped puppy. She found no pleasure in making a man feel like that, but at the same time, she did find it came in quite handy when a man tended to get rough or forceful with her.

Haydon tied the horse to a tree. He wrapped his arms around Ben's legs, squatted and hoisted him up and over the saddle.

"This saddle horn is killin' my side." Ben kicked and squirmed until his body slipped from the horse and landed on the ground with a thud.

"You should have thought about that before you decided to hold me at gunpoint." Haydon yanked him up and slung him over the saddle again.

Ben's belly slapped against the saddle. "Watch it. You dirty, no-good—" He went on and on, swearing until Rainee could stand it no longer. She wanted desperately to press her hands over her ears.

Haydon walked around to the other side of Ben's horse, shoved his hand inside the man's filthy pocket and pulled out a stained handkerchief. Rainee wrinkled her nose at the disgusting sight. Repulsion wrinkled Haydon's face, too. He tossed the vile thing into the river and pulled a clean bandanna out of his own pocket.

Ben continued his tirade until Haydon shoved the bandanna in the man's mouth and tied it behind his head. Even gagged Ben continued on, but at least the insulting words were muffled.

Haydon looked as relieved as she felt.

With the same rope Ben had used on him, Haydon tied Ben's hands and legs together under the horse's belly.

Haydon took the gun from her and tucked it into his belt.

After untying Ben's horse, he handed Rainee the reins. He grabbed Rebel's from her and tossed the leather straps over the horse's neck. He swung into the saddle and reached his hand toward her. Rainee handed him the reins to Ben's horse. He kicked his left foot out of the stirrup and with his free hand motioned for her to join him.

She hesitated, wondering how she could manage mounting the horse in her dress with Haydon in the saddle. She looked down at her dress and then up at him.

"Head over to that rock." Haydon jerked his head toward a large stone.

Rainee walked over to the boulder and climbed on it with as much grace as she could muster.

Leading Ben's horse, Haydon maneuvered Rebel as close to the rock as he could.

Rainee yearned to pull her skirt between her legs and tuck it at her waist again, but she did not want to embarrass herself further. Sometimes being a woman living in an age where certain things were forbidden vexed her greatly. But other times, she discovered being a woman held certain advantages.

Haydon cleared his throat.

She swung her leg over Rebel's back. The horse shifted. Rainee threw her arms around Haydon's waist. He clutched them and secured her behind him.

She glanced at her arms, still clinging to Haydon's waist. She yanked her body away from his, but Haydon's voice stopped her. "Stay." He turned his face toward her. Their gazes collided. "I like having your arms around me." His voice did not sound the same. It had a low, broken timbre to it.

With their searching gazes still joined, Rainee realized that her mother was right when she said Rainee would know when she was in love because true love now kissed Rainee's heart. She smiled shyly at Haydon and wondered if her eyes revealed her true feelings. Did he feel the same way she did, or were the feelings hers alone?

His blue-eyed gaze softened before drifting toward her mouth.

Rainee looked at his.

Haydon leaned his face closer to hers, and his eyes drifted shut, and hers did as well. Their lips met, and a shudder ran through her.

Good thing Ben could not see them.

She lost herself in the exquisiteness of Haydon's tender caresses. His soft lips continued to hold hers captive.

Rainee concentrated on the feel of Haydon's mouth against hers. This kiss was every bit, if not sweeter than, the one they shared in the kitchen. She wanted this moment to last forever, but Haydon pulled back. A sigh of disappointment escaped her.

"Rainee, I—"

Ben's mumbling stopped Haydon's words.

He closed his eyes, and his chest heaved. He shifted in the saddle and reined the horses toward home.

Home. It had a nice ring to it.

She secured her arms around Haydon's waist and pressed her head against his back. Would she finally be able to call this place home?

Chapter Seventeen

"Weren't you scared?" Leah's wide eyes followed Rainee's every move as the two of them sat on the bigger house's front porch drinking a spot of tea with Katherine and Hannah.

"Only after I thought about what I had done." She giggled. "The more I think about it, the more I realize it probably was not the wisest thing to do. But at the time my concern was for Haydon."

"I could have never done something that brave." Leah's admiration poured through the tone of her voice.

Rainee caught sight of Abby down the way, carrying a bucket of water and heading toward Kitty. That sweet little beast had followed Rainee and Haydon back to the house. She smiled, then looked back at Leah.

"Ki-i-ty, you gotted me wet. Stop it." Abby stood there with one hand on her hip and shaking a finger at Kitty with her other. "Hold still or I'll shoo you outta here." Abby raised the third pail of water and dumped it over Kitty's head.

Kitty squealed and shook her head.

Rainee actually felt sorry for the little creature as

mud ran down her sides, over her face and into her eyes. Kitty scrubbed her face against Abby's skirt, knocking Abby onto her backside. Abby jumped up and gave the pig another good scolding, while all of them sat laughing until their eyes were damp.

Rainee marveled at how fond she had grown of that curly-tailed animal. Although she was not completely over her fear of pigs, she was getting used to Kitty.

"Well, I need to get back to the house and put my feet up. They're swollen again." Hannah rose, and Rainee noticed her protruding stomach was getting rounder with each passing day.

"Leah, if you're going to the Bengtsson's you'd better leave now so you'll be back before dark."

"Yes, Mother." Leah rose from the swing she and Rainee occupied. She looked down at Rainee. "Thanks for saving my brother today. I don't know what we would do without him." She leaned over and gave Rainee a big hug and a kiss on her cheek before she rushed to the barn to retrieve her saddled horse.

Katherine looked out toward the yard and Rainee's gaze followed her. Kitty waddled next to Abby as the little girl headed into the field covered with camas flowers, and small puffs of dust swirled behind Leah's horse as she cantered down the road.

"Thank you again, Rainee. I shudder to think what would have happened to my son if you hadn't shown up when you did."

They both stood, and Katherine hugged her. A hug so like her own mother's that Rainee had to cast aside the melancholy that tried to force its way inside her.

Rainee helped hitch the horse and buggy and watched as Katherine, too, headed down the road to check on an elderly neighbor. She headed back to the porch and sat down, waiting and watching for Haydon to return from taking Ben in to town, which was silly because he said it would be late.

Tired of sitting, she paced the length of the porch, pondering what to do to make the time go by faster. It was then that she remembered the letter, tucked in her pocket, waiting for the chance to be read. After the events of the afternoon, Rainee was not at all sure she could even read its contents, and yet, she knew she must.

She slipped the envelope out and with shaking fingers tore it open. The letter was handwritten and only two sentences long:

> *Dear Miss Devonwood, It is with my sincerest regret that I must inform you I am no longer searching for a bride...*

That was all she read. The rest scattered into the joy of knowing it meant she was to be with Haydon. She refolded the letter and tucked it once again into her pocket. Life suddenly felt immensely livable again.

After pulling in a long breath of relief, she contemplated what to do next. It was too early to start preparations for the evening meal, and with everyone gone and all the chores finished, Rainee decided to go for a walk. She left a note on Abby's slate again in case anyone wondered where she had gone.

She made her way through the pine and cottonwood trees and up the rocky soil. She stopped to admire a cluster of flowers growing amid the craggy rocks. Tiny white flowers with pink centers surrounded a darker pink center. The dark green leaves with white tips reminded her of the shape of pine cones.

After a long stroll, she walked toward the road so she could watch for Haydon. She wondered how she would tell him the news and if he would think it as wonderful as she did.

Billowing dust clouds on the road caught her attention. She stepped over a felled tree and hastened toward the road, anxious to see Haydon again. But as she got closer, she realized the dust was not from Haydon but from two men on horseback.

She ducked behind a large cottonwood tree and strained to see if she recognized the men. The branches made it difficult to get a clear picture of them. Wanting to see better but not wanting to give her position away, she rose on her toes and shifted right, then left, but she still could not tell who they were.

Something about them, though, filled her spirit with dread.

Rainee dropped to the ground and crawled to some bushes nearer the road. Pine needles pricked her hands and knees, but she kept going. She had to see who those men were because even at a distance, there was something vaguely familiar about them.

At the base of the bush, she spread the branches far enough to peer through them while keeping her position hidden. Her gaze zeroed in on the riders until she could finally make out their features. She released the branches. They fell back into place with a slap. *Dear God. No. No. This cannot be happening. Not now.* Rainee struggled to draw a breath. "Not him. Please, not him."

Getting them back into view, on her hands and knees

Rainee crept backward until her back collided with a tree. She hurried around the base of it and stood. With her palms flattened against the trunk, she forced air into her lungs. The giant black dots dancing before her eyes faded, and she could once again see clearly.

Running through the woods with a dress would make getting away in a hurry difficult. She reached down and pulled the back of her skirt through her legs, tucked it into her waistband and darted into the thick wooded area, running as fast as her short legs would carry her.

Several yards into the forest, she stopped and glanced behind her to make sure no one was following her. Through a haze of sheer fright, shadows danced behind her in the shape of men. She whirled and fled as if her life depended on it because if her brother caught her, it would.

Panting from exertion and fear, Rainee continued running, fighting branches and dodging rocks as she darted her way through the trees and bushes.

The toe of her shoe hooked on something. She plunged toward the hard ground. Her hand shot out to break her fall, but it slipped on the floor of pine needles. Her face collided with a large tree root, sending a surge of pain through her cheek.

Although dazed, Rainee managed to scramble into a sitting position. She plucked the pine needles out of her hand, arm and knees—the pain from each one battling with the fear for her attention. When she finished, she touched the tender spot on her face and looked at her hand.

Blood stained her white lacey gloves. Her stomach churned, and the black spots returned, but there was no time to dwell on that now. Once again she pulled in large gulps of air until the spots slipped away.

She had to escape. Pushing to her feet, her first few steps were shaky, but before long she took off running again. She pushed her body to its limits. Because she would rather die in the wilderness or be eaten by a wild animal than have them find her.

Having dropped Ben off at the sheriff's in Paradise Haven, Haydon knew home was only minutes away. He couldn't wait to see Rainee. He pictured her holding a gun on Ben and chuckled. *That woman has spunk, Lord, and she's gutsier than any female I ever encountered.*

He nudged Rebel into a canter and reined his horse around the row of trees and into the ranch yard.

Abby ran toward him. "Haydon!"

Before Rebel came to a stop, Haydon swung his leg over the saddle and planted his feet on the ground. "What's wrong, Squirt?" He squatted eye level with Abby.

"She's gone."

"Who's gone?"

"Rainee." Abby sniffed and ran the back of her sleeve across her wet nose.

"What do you mean, Rainee's gone?" He scooped Abby into his arms and carried her toward the house. Dread plunged into his gut as all sorts of scenarios ran through his mind.

He ran up the porch steps and flung the screen door open. When he stepped inside, his instincts went on full alert. Inside the kitchen were two well-dressed strangers sitting at his mother's table.

Haydon's gaze flew from the two men to his mother.

Her skin was pale. She was wringing her hands, and his mother never did that.

He whispered in Abby's ear as he let her down slowly. "Go find Jess and tell him to come here right away."

Abby glanced at the two strangers and nodded. She bolted from the house, letting the screen door slam behind her.

Thank God he had grabbed his gun and strapped it around his waist before he had taken Ben to the sheriff. Knowing it was within reach, Haydon strode toward the men. "Afternoon, gentlemen." He extended his hand toward the elderly man, who in return gave him a limp handshake. He stuck his hand out toward the younger man, who kept his hand at his side and looked Haydon up and down. Dark features perfectly matched the black hair and mustache.

Haydon refused to be intimidated by the rude man. "What can I do for you?" He looked the younger man directly in the eye.

"You have something that belongs to us." The bitterness in the man's tone snaked around Haydon's spine.

Haydon squared his shoulders against the man in the expensive black suit. "And what would that be?" He never took his eyes off of the stranger.

The man stepped closer to Haydon, a sneer on his lips. "Do not play games with me. You know exactly what I am talking about." The man had a good four inches on him, but Haydon was acutely aware that what he lacked in height he had always made up for in strength and agility.

Haydon took a step closer and put his hands on his hips. "I don't have a clue what you're talking about.

Now, if you want to tell me just what it is you think I have of yours, I'll be happy to return it."

"Stop playing ignorant. The name is Ferrin Xavier Devonwood. And we—" he glanced at the older pot-bellied gentleman with disdain and then back at Haydon "—came to take my sister Rainelle back home in time for her wedding."

His sister?

Her wedding?

Fury and frustration slid down over his spirit. Rainee was engaged? Haydon's lungs ceased to draw air, but he refused to let the man see just how hard his words struck him. How could he have been so stupid to trust another woman? A woman betrothed to another. A woman he had gone and fallen in love with.

He should've learned this lesson the first time around with Melanie. A trip to the woodshed to beat himself black and blue for giving his heart to yet another deceptive woman was in order. But first things first. If these men wanted her, they could have her. And he would help them find her.

Rainee forced her body through the woods. Her muscles rebelled, her stomach ached from hunger and her cotton mouth begged for water. She glanced around, trying to get her bearings. The trails Haydon had shown her were nowhere in sight. She had probably long since passed them. Her heart fell to the rocky soil. She was lost. Lost without food and without water. The sun was dipping low into the western sky. Night would be here in no time.

Out of hope and mind-numbingly tired, she dropped to her knees, raised her head toward the color-tinted sky and cried out, "Lord, I am so frightened. I do not know where I am. Please, Lord, if You would be so kind, show me the way to the Palouse River. Keep me safe and give me the grace and strength I need to keep going, for I cannot go back home, Lord. I cannot." She placed her face in her hands and wept.

Rainee thought about her parents and the secure life she had when they were alive. "Oh, Mother. I need you." She sniffed and wiped her eyes. "I wish you were here. You and Father. Everything is falling apart around me, and I do not know what to do." Craving the love and security her parents had provided for her, she wrapped her arms around herself, longing to feel her parents' arms around her, telling her everything would be okay.

Again she was reminded that those things were long gone. They had been replaced with a life of uncertainty and worry, and not even the Bowens could help her now. Her arm crunched against something in her pocket. The letter. Even that possibility for escape had been closed. Tears burned the backs of her eyes, but she refused to cry.

She had to face the fact she was on her own. She willed her fighting spirit to rise to the occasion. Glancing toward the heavens, Rainee let out a hard breath, raised her voice, and declared, "I might be exhausted, and I might be alone. But I shall never give up. Never." Although it took great effort, she rose and forced one trembling foot in front of the other, stumbling her way deeper into the trees.

Minutes turned to hours as Rainee searched for anything familiar. Every tree and every spot looked the same as the last. "Lord, You said You would never leave me nor forsake me. I am in great distress here and in need of guidance. Where are You, God?" She stopped at a tree and listened, but the only sounds she heard were the whispering breeze rustling through the tree branches and the twittering of birds as they sang their happy melodies.

If only she had wings like those birds. She would fly far away. Someplace where no one could ever find her. Someplace safe and warm. Haydon's arms came to mind. She felt secure and safe in his embrace. But they would never offer her comfort or security because she would never see him again.

Rainee sat on a felled log and removed her shoes. Angry red blisters covered the heels of her feet. She gently rubbed at the soreness, trying to soothe them, but nothing helped.

She rolled her neck in a circle. Her muscles cried out with want of rest. But she had to force her body farther. She rose, wincing with pain.

Each step she took was pure torment, but she knew she had to keep going, to put as much distance between her and the Bowen's ranch as possible.

Where she would go, she did not know. All she knew was she had to keep going—even though she knew beyond any doubt there was no place out of Ferrin's reach. He had proved that.

Chapter Eighteen

Still dealing with the shock of Rainee's betrothal and betrayal, Haydon gathered his wits about him and turned to his mother. "Did Rainee say where she was going?"

"She—she left a note saying she was going for a walk, and I haven't seen her since." With dread-filled eyes, Mother looked at him, then at the two men.

"Are you trying to pull a fast one on us?" The one who'd said he was Rainee's brother, Ferrin, glared at Haydon's mother.

Her face turned a blotchy white.

How dare these men come into his mother's home and frighten her. Haydon placed himself between her and the men. "No one is trying to pull anything. You heard my mother. Rainee went for a walk and hasn't gotten back yet." He passed a warning glare at each of the two men.

"Liar!" Ferrin flicked a small derringer out of his pocket, cocked it and aimed it at Haydon.

The door swung open.

Jesse, Smokey and Michael barreled into the room, guns aimed at the two men.

Ferrin whirled. His gun fired.

Michael clutched his arm, and his pistol clambered onto the floor.

Seeing an opportunity, Haydon rammed Ferrin with his body, sending them both crashing to the ground. Ferrin's gun flew from his hand and slid across the floor. The older man rushed toward the derringer and stooped to pick it up.

"Touch that gun and you're a dead man." Smokey's voice held the authority of one who meant what he said.

The man froze, then rose slowly with his hands raised in front of him.

With Smokey's gun aimed at the older man and Jesse's aimed at Ferrin, Haydon jumped up, plucked Ferrin to his feet and twisted the man's arms behind his back.

A quick glance at Michael told Haydon he was okay.

Ferrin yanked one arm free.

Haydon snatched the man's arm back and tightened his hold. "I suggest you stand still if you want to live to see another day," he ground out before reverting his attention to his youngest brother. "Michael, you okay?"

"I'm fine." Michael lifted his hand off of his arm. A large patch of blood soiled his shirt sleeve.

Their mother scurried over to Michael's side. She ripped open his sleeve and examined his wound.

Knowing Michael was in good hands, Haydon aimed his attention back onto the two men. He shoved Ferrin forward and pushed him onto a nearby kitchen chair. "Move and you're dead." Haydon turned to do the same to the older man, but before he got a chance to say anything, the wide-eyed man plopped his portly frame down.

"Look, I didn't come here to cause any trouble. Only to get what is rightfully mine." The gray-haired man's trembling words drew out slow and long.

"What do you mean 'what's rightfully yours'?" Haydon asked, his eyes narrowing on the man.

"Rainelle. I own her. Paid Ferrin a handsome price for her, too. She's mine."

Disgust roiled through Haydon's gut. He couldn't believe what he was hearing. Did this man just say he had bought and paid for Rainee as if she were some animal sold at a livestock shipyard? He bore down on his teeth as anger pressed in on him. He turned and glared at Ferrin.

Ferrin smugly crossed his arms over his chest, and a smirk of satisfaction covered his face.

Haydon wanted to beat that haughty grin right off of his face. What kind of brute was this man anyway?

No wonder Rainee had placed an advertisement looking for a husband. Realization kicked him in the head as the full weight of the situation came rushing in on him. Rainee was running away from this no-good scoundrel of a brother. Haydon wondered what else she had suffered at this gutter rat's hands. He had to find her. To do whatever he could to protect her and keep her safe from these two lowlifes.

Haydon grabbed a length of rope from a peg by the kitchen door, cut it in four pieces and tied the men up. He stopped by his mother. "How is he?" He kept his voice low.

"The bullet just grazed the skin," Mother whispered. "We'll bandage it up. He'll be okay." The color had returned to her cheeks and the wrinkles around her eyes disappeared. Having cleaned the flesh wound already, she tore strips of cloth to bandage Michael's injury.

Haydon looked at Michael, then at Jesse. They could handle these two men. The two of them were each as strong as a draft horse.

"Michael?"

"Yeah?"

"Do you think you and Jesse can take these two to Sheriff Klokk and tell him what's going on while Smokey and I go look for Rainee?"

Michael skimmed his gaze over his arm, then turned a scathing glare toward the two men. "You bet we can." At that moment, Michael no longer looked like a sixteen-year-old boy but a mature man. It was one more step on his path. If only their father could see him now. He would be so proud. Haydon sure was.

He squeezed Michael's shoulder, then strode across the room to Jesse, who kept his gun trained on the two men.

"Jesse, you up for taking these two to the sheriff?"

Jess gave a quick nod, never taking his eyes or his gun off the two men.

Haydon turned. "Smokey, I want you to come with me. If anyone can find Rainee, you can."

"Yes, sir, boss." Smokey handed his gun off to Michael.

Haydon shook his head at Smokey, but now was not the time to correct the older man about calling him boss. They had to find Rainee. And fast.

When she had finally found the river, Rainee followed it until the sun dipped behind the mountain and an evening chill replaced it. Her stomach ached with hunger, and every inch of her body cried out from fatigue. She walked to the edge of the river and dropped down on her knees. Cupping her hands, she scooped the cool water up and drank freely before sitting back on her feet and perusing the area.

Moonlight reflected in the ripples in the water along with the shadows of trees and rocks that seemed to come to life in the slow current. An eeriness settled in around her. Rainee kept looking over her shoulders, even when she sat down to rest.

Her body trembled at the thought of being alone in a strange place, in the dark, without food or warm clothing or anything else. Except wild beasts. Both animal and human. Farther travel at this late hour was not wise. All that remained now was to wait until morning came and hope and pray that no one found her in the meantime.

Exposed by the openness of the riverbank, one could find her easily. That thought terrified her. Not only did she fear Ferrin, but there were other dangers lurking in the darkened wilderness. Were there wild savages nearby? She had heard tell of them from travelers back home. Fear squeezed the breath from her lungs. She hopped up, stumbling and fumbling as she scurried back into the safety of the trees.

With only the moonlight to guide her, Rainee searched for a spot where no one would see her. Each step she took made her legs threaten to dump her to the hard ground.

"God, help me find a spot." No sooner had the words left her mouth than her gaze snagged on a small opening between a boulder and bush. She dropped to her hands and knees and burrowed herself into it.

She wrapped her arms around her knees, hugged them tight against her chest and rocked herself gently.

Her thoughts placed her in another time and another place—a situation similar to the one she now found herself in.

Shortly after her parents had died, when the beatings had started, Rainee found she could no longer tolerate the painful abuse so she had run away, but she had not gotten far before Ferrin and his men had found her. Her brother threw her into the woodshed with no food and very little water for three days.

If it had not been for Jenetta slipping her tiny scraps of food through the knothole, she did not know what would have become of her. Jenetta had also sneaked out during the night and slept outside the shed, singing Rainee to sleep. Many times, the poor woman tried to break the lock so she could provide Rainee with adequate food and water, but she was unable to do much more than make noise.

Spiders and bugs had crawled on Rainee's arms and legs until Rainee thought she would go mad. The sensation that insects were crawling on her even now felt so real Rainee swiped at her arms and legs, brushing away the invisible bugs.

Jenetta's words drifted through her mind. "Honey, child, don't you be frettin' nun. Jist think of dem bugs as God's creatures. Dey won't bodder you none. Besides, ole Jenetta, she done threatened dem and dey knows better den ta hurt you." If only Jenetta were here now. If only her mother were here now.

Rainee had never felt so alone or so frightened in her life. She looked over her right shoulder and then her left. She looked behind her, beside her and in front of her. With each turn her fear escalated. Did snakes or any other unwanted creatures share her tiny quarters? The very idea made her tremble. The thought of the bears Haydon had mentioned drifted into her mind and held there.

Rainee hugged her knees again, only tighter. She rocked harder, fighting the tears coated with fear, but she could not beat them. They slipped over her eyelashes and ran down her cheeks, stinging the open scratches on her face. She blotted the moisture away as best as she could, but it did not take the sting away. Mother used to wipe Rainee's tears and fears away. "Oh, Mother. I wish you were here." She sniffed. "I need you so desperately."

As if her mother were right there, her words drifted through Rainee's mind. "Anytime something causes you to be afraid, all you have to do is call on the name of the Lord and He will help you. He will never leave you nor forsake you. He lives inside you and is only a whisper away."

If she ever needed the Lord, now was that time. She closed her eyes and bowed her head. "God, I am so very frightened. Mother always said You would comfort me and give me peace. And she was right. You always have. Thank You for reminding me that I can come to You when I need help. Wrap Your loving arms around me and hold me close." A clear image of a painting she had in her bedroom back in Arkansas popped into her mind.

The little blonde girl in the picture was sitting on Jesus's lap. His large hand held the girl's head against his chest, and his other arm encircled her. It was a picture of serenity, of the Lord's protection. Of His comfort. Of the safety of His arms. A measure of peace enveloped her like a comforting hug. "Thank you. I needed that."

Dampness seeped through her dress, sending chills rushing through her body. She rubbed her arms, trying to warm them and trying desperately to ignore the hunger pains gnawing at her stomach.

Somewhere, not very far away, a twig snapped.

Rainee's attention whirled toward the sound. Her body cemented statue-still.

God, please do not let it be them. I cannot go back there.

Only with her eyes did she search for the source of the noise. Through the distorted shadows of the trees an outline of an animal appeared.

Rainee pressed her teeth into her hand to stifle her scream. Pain sliced through her thumb. Her wide eyes followed the animal heading toward her.

A pig stepped into view.

Rainee did not know whether to be relieved or more frightened until she remembered Kitty and how gentle and loving the little beast was and how Haydon had said a pig would not bother her.

When it neared, her breath caught.

The swine stuck her head in between the gap of the bush and the rock. "Kitty?" she whispered, recognizing the chunk missing from the bottom of the sow's left ear. Rainee let out a long whoosh, and the fear went with it. "I never thought I would say this, but am I glad to see you." Who would have thought that she, Rainelle Victoria Devonwood, would be relieved upon seeing a pig?

With her nose in the air, Kitty sniffed and pushed her way into the thick brush. The small space had just gotten smaller. But Rainee did not mind. She would gladly share her space with Kitty.

Kitty sat on her rump in front of her. Rainee patted her head and rubbed her behind the ears. Pig odor filled the small space, but Rainee did not care. She felt somewhat more secure with the creature here. With each rub, the tightness in Rainee's muscles loosened, and she found herself relaxing little by little, until her body shook with another chill. Rainee stopped scratching Kitty behind the ears and curled into a ball, hoping to get warm.

Her stomach cramped. At this moment, even bark sounded good. Thoughts of wild strawberries made it ache worse. But she did not see any along the way, so she would have to suffer through the pangs.

The dankness soaked into her bones. Her whole body trembled. Kitty flopped on her side in front of her. Heat drifted from the sow and seeped into Rainee's body.

The warmer Rainee got, the heavier her eyelids became until she could no longer hold them open.

Through the haze of slumber, Rainee heard a noise. Her eyes darted open.

Darkness surrounded her.

She tilted her head, straining to listen. Her ears honed in on muffled voices somewhere in the distance.

She flounced into a sitting position, kicking Kitty in the process.

Kitty squealed and bolted upright, sniffing the air. Squeezing her rotund body through the opening, the pig waddled away until Rainee could no longer make out her shadow as Kitty disappeared into the darkness.

The voices neared.

Rainee pressed her back against the rock, wishing it would crack open and ingest her into its crevice.

Her overwhelming fear and shallow breaths strangled her.

She prayed Kitty's squeal had not captured the attention of whoever was out there and that she was far enough in the thick bushes that whoever was there could not see her.

Without Kitty's body heat, she started shivering again. She longed to rub her arms in hopes of getting her circulation going, but she did not, for fear the movement would draw attention to her whereabouts.

A horse snorted.

Rainee froze.

Leather creaked.

Male voices echoed through the trees, but she could not make out what they were saying. She had a sick feeling those voices belonged to her brother and Mr. Gruff. *Dear God, please do not let my brother find me.*

Time crawled at a turtle's pace.

Again leather creaked, but this time the sound was closer.

Pine needles crunched under the weight of someone's boots as they neared.

Kitty and two pairs of legs stopped in front of her hiding spot.

Rainee swallowed the cry welling up inside her.

Then a man knelt in front of the opening.

Rainee scarcely drew breath and remained stock still.

The bushes parted. Leaves rustled and branches crunched. The urge to bolt shot through her like the blast of a cannon, but her body would not move, and there was nowhere to go.

On hands and knees, the man crawled through the small opening.

Rainee screamed, but she would not give up without a fight. A strength she never knew she had visited her at that moment. She raised her legs and kicked wildly at the intruder. Strong hands clasped her feet, rendering her powerless.

Her hands took up the battle.

In vain she struggled to free herself, but no matter how hard she tried, she could not break his hold on her. "Let go of me, Ferrin. I would rather die than go back with you. I will not marry him and you cannot make me. I refuse to be sold off like a piece of merchandise."

"Rainee. Rainee, it's okay. It's me, Haydon."

Rainee stopped struggling. "Haydon?" Through moisture-filled eyes she saw the blurred image of him hovering before her in the darkness. "Is—is it really you?"

"Yes, it's really me." He released her legs.

Rainee lunged forward, throwing herself against Haydon. His arms wrapped around her and pulled her against him.

Pools of tears pocketed her eyes and sobs tore from her.

Haydon rubbed her back. "It's okay. You're safe now."

Rainee wrenched away and shook her head venomously. "No! It is not okay. It will never be okay again," she cried before melting into the haven of his sturdy arms. Ferrin had found her. She would have to leave the man she loved. Because his life was now in danger, too. Ferrin would stop at nothing to get his way.

Haydon held Rainee's trembling form close to him. He needed the connection to her. Almost losing her had frightened him half to death. When he had first discovered she was betrothed, he had been angry until he learned the truth. Now, Haydon refused to let those infidels take her. "Come on. Let's get you out of here and get you warm."

She nodded against his chest and slid from his arms. He crawled out and held the bushes back while she climbed out.

"It's too late to try to get back to the house. We'll have to camp out here."

Her chin shot upward. "I—I cannot sleep out here alone with you. It—it is not proper," she said through chattering teeth as she wrapped her arms around herself. That was one rule of propriety she would never break.

Haydon removed his jacket and held it out as she slipped her arms through the sleeves. She wrapped her arms around herself and closed her eyes as if relishing the heat his jacket provided.

"We're not alone, Rainee."

She glanced at Kitty and looked up at him like he had slipped a few knots.

He smiled. "Smokey's here, too."

Smokey stepped out of the shadows. "Miss." He gave a quick nod.

"Smokey, why don't you…"

"Get some wood for a fire. I'm already on it, boss."

"And quit calling me boss," he spoke to Smokey's retreating shadow.

Haydon placed his arm around Rainee's shoulder and led her to an opening near the river. Reluctantly he let her go to roll a log over for her to sit on.

She clutched his jacket tighter. In the light of the moon, her lost, sad eyes pecked at his heart. Haydon wanted to pull her into his arms again and make her forget all of her troubles.

"Sit down. I'll be right back."

"Where—where you going?"

He wrapped his arms around her and pulled her close. His lips pressed against her hair and he kissed her there. "It's okay, sweetheart, I'm not leaving. I need to get a blanket from my horse. I'll be right back."

A moment and she nodded her head against his chest.

He didn't want to let her go, but he helped her sit down and then walked over to his horse. After securing Rebel to a tree branch near the river, he untied the blanket from his saddle and reached inside the saddlebag and pulled out the sack his mother had given him before he'd headed out the door.

Smokey was arranging the wood he had gathered into a pile.

Haydon unrolled the blanket and draped it over Rainee's legs, then sat next to her.

The small fire started to crack and pop. Within minutes it grew stronger and warmer, filling the air with smoke, pine and heat.

"I'm going to gather more firewood."

Haydon nodded at Smokey, then reverted his attention back to Rainee. Shadows from the fire danced across her face.

"Here." Haydon handed her the bag of food. "You need to get something in your belly."

Rainee took the sack from him and wrenched it open. She dove her hand into the bag. Her actions reminded him of Abby at Christmastime. His little sister couldn't wait to open her Christmas stocking. When Abby finally received permission, she dove into it and yanked the items out as fast as her little hands would let her.

That's what Rainee was doing now. Only this wasn't a happy occasion like Christmas.

She yanked out the sandwich and removed the cloth around it. In one bite, a huge portion of the sandwich disappeared. Rainee's cheeks swelled like a chipmunk's. She tore off another large portion and then another until the sandwich disappeared.

Haydon watched her devour the sandwich like a starving animal, and the sight tore at his heart.

Without saying a word, she rammed her hand into the sack again and plucked out an apple. She opened her mouth wide and bit into it, closing her eyes as she chewed. Within minutes it too vanished.

All of a sudden, she froze and turned wide eyes up at him. "Merciful heavens," she spoke through the last bite of apple. "Where are my manners?" She quickly turned away.

Haydon reached over and gently pulled her chin toward him. Yellow-orange, fiery shadows pranced across her face. Her eyes refused to look up at him. "Rainee." He tilted her chin up. "It's okay. I won't tell anyone." Humor threaded his voice.

Her gaze flew to his, and he smiled. After a single moment, her lips tilted upward as well. Haydon stared at her lips, and then his eyes traveled to hers.

She blinked, and her gaze dropped to his mouth.

Haydon leaned slowly toward her and gently nudged her chin closer to him. Her soft skin under his fingers was intoxicating.

Her eyes slid shut, and their lips connected. Rainee's parted lips tasted like sweet apples. His mouth caressed hers and she returned his kiss with a sweet, innocent passion.

All the popping and cracking coming from the fire didn't even come close to all the sizzling and popping going on inside him.

Suddenly she pulled back and scooted away from him.

Why did that always feel like such a rip to his soul? "What's the matter?"

"I am sorry, but I cannot do this. As much as I want to, I just cannot." She shook her head.

"Do what? Kiss me?" He searched her eyes as if they held the answer, but all he saw was fear and pain. He reached for her hand, noticing the lacey gloves she always had on. The question of why she always wore them drifted over him. Another time he would ask. Right now he wanted, no needed, the connection to her again. He reached for her hands, but she tucked them under the blanket. Disappointment drifted over him like the smoke from the fire.

"There is something you need to know. And once you hear it, you will be sorry you ever kissed me."

Chapter Nineteen

Her heart had never hurt this badly before. Rainee stared into Haydon's bewildered face. He deserved to know the truth. And once he heard it, she feared he would no longer want anything to do with her.

"Haydon, I—I..." She drew in a long breath for courage and shifted her body toward his. "Remember when I first came here, and I told you to trust me that I had no choice but to place an advertisement? You need to know the real reason why I left and the truth about my family."

"I know what you're going to tell me, Rainee."

"You—you do?" She swallowed hard and stared at him. How could he possibly know?

"Yes. You placed the advertisement looking for a husband so you wouldn't have to marry that old man your brother sold you to like some worthless animal." His words spewed bitterness.

Rainee sucked in a sharp breath and slammed her hand against her chest. *Dear God, no. Ferrin must be at Haydon's ranch.* She swallowed the lock of air lodged in her throat. "Where—where is Ferrin now?" Her heart slowed to a crawl while she waited for his answer.

"He's in jail. Right where he should be."

Ferrin? In jail? She gulped. All sorts of scenarios dashed through her mind about what Ferrin must have done to land in jail. Each idea increased the dread inside her. "What happened?"

Haydon relayed what had transpired and how Ferrin had pulled a gun on them. Knowing what evil her brother was capable of, relief rained over her that no one had been seriously hurt. Or worse, killed.

"I am so sorry, Haydon." Her eyes met his. "I never meant for your family to get involved in my family's problems. I thought I had done a secure job of covering all my tracks so that he would never find me. I should have known better. When Ferrin sets his mind to something, he will do whatever it takes to achieve it. And right now, he is determined I shall marry Mr. Alexander." She shuddered at the very idea.

Haydon took her hands in his.

She stared down at their hands, relishing the strength and feel of his even through her lacey gloves. Her heart ached for what could never be.

"Rainee, you don't have to marry him. He can't make you."

"Yes, he can, Mr. Bowen. For he is cruel to his very soul, and he will stop at nothing to get his way. And there is nothing you, nor I nor anyone else can do about it." Her body had the scars to prove it.

So it was back to being called Mr. Bowen again. That didn't bode well.

She removed her hand from his.

He wanted to snatch it back, but he controlled the urge.

What did she mean there wasn't anything anyone could do about it? The Civil War had ended the sale of one human being to another. "Of course you have a choice." His gaze sought hers. "You can stay and marry me."

Her eyes widened. "Marry you? But I thought you did not want to marry again."

"I didn't. Then I met you."

She faced the fire. The light from the flames danced across her lovely face, accentuating the glistening trail of tears trickling down her cheeks. Haydon slid his arm around her shoulders. He tucked her under his arm and pressed her head against his chest.

Smokey tossed a few more logs onto the fire. A look of compassion passed between the two men. Smokey jerked his head toward the bushes, a signal that he would give them some privacy. Haydon mouthed his thank you and Smokey slipped into the thick brush.

He positioned Rainee so he could see her face. Her eyes were downcast.

Haydon thumbed the tears from each cheek, then lifted her chin toward him.

With her eyes still closed, Haydon lowered his head, inching his lips toward hers. When their mouths touched, Rainee clutched a fistful of his shirt with one hand. They clung to each other. Their hearts beat as one as their kiss deepened. Salty tears trickled over his lips. Whether they were hers or his, he didn't know.

He wanted to pull her close, but the way they were seated made that impossible. Instead, he allowed his lips alone to get closer to her.

When his need to show her how much he loved her increased, he released her mouth and once again snuggled the side of her face against his chest. "Rainee. What would I do without you?" He struggled to calm his erratic breathing and noticed she was doing the same. They held each other tight for a long time.

Smokey slipped from the shadows, carrying a bedroll.

He tossed several more logs onto the fire. Haydon shifted Rainee until he could see her face. A yellow-and-orange glow danced across her lovely features. Her eyes searched his with a yearning he could not describe. He wanted to kiss her again. To hold her forever. To shield her from the beast that waited to take her from him.

He pressed his lips against her forehead, lingering for several moments before he reluctantly withdrew his arms from around her. It was time to get some rest. "We'll talk more in the morning."

After helping her get situated by the fire, he lay opposite to her and watched her until she fell asleep.

As he drifted off to sleep, he determined that no matter how long it took, he would find a way to stop her brother from marrying her off to that old man. He had to. His heart depended on it.

Hours later, daylight filtered through Haydon's eyelids. He slowly opened his eyes to greet another sunny day. He scratched his neck and yawned, then looked toward Rainee.

The blanket she had used lay neatly folded on the ground.

Haydon sat up and scanned the area.

Smokey stepped into the clearing and headed toward him. "Miss Devonwood is gone again, boss."

He closed his eyes, then slipped his boots on and stood. "Where'd she go?"

"Her tracks lead that way." Smokey pointed down the river. "I'm sorry I didn't hear her leave. I must have been more tired than I thought."

"Well, I did. I heard her moving about earlier, but I thought she was just going to relieve herself." Haydon snatched his hat up and plopped it on his head. "Listen, I don't want Mother worrying about us, so will you head back to the ranch and tell her what's happened? I'll go look for Rainee."

"Yes, sir, boss." Smokey bent down and hoisted his saddle over his shoulder.

"Smokey."

The older man faced him. "Yes, boss."

"Please stop calling me boss and sir. You're family, remember?"

Smokey just smiled and then proceeded to saddle his horse.

After Haydon snuffed out the fire, he hauled his saddle over his shoulder and saddled his horse. "God, please help me find Rainee, and keep her safe until I do." A sigh squeezed out of his heart and past his lips.

"Amen," Smokey added.

Rainee glanced over her shoulder before she stopped and leaned her back against a tree to catch her breath. Having traveled so far and so fast yesterday, every muscle in her body ached, and the blisters on her feet screamed with pain. She had no idea where she was or how far she had gone.

Last night, her fears of what Ferrin might do to the Bowens if she did not leave them had kept her from a good night's sleep. After all, he had already shot one of them. Worse was the understanding her brother had found her even though she and Jenetta had been so careful. On her journey here, she had even disguised herself as an old woman and had worn several other disguises to keep Ferrin off of her trail. Only at the last stage stop had she changed into her own clothing because she did not want to meet Haydon looking like a haggard old woman.

She still could not believe he had actually mentioned marrying her. It was the one thing she had wanted to hear since her arrival. But she knew that marrying him would put his life into jeopardy, and she could not stand to be the one putting a target on his back. He didn't understand what Ferrin was capable of. She pressed her lips together and sniffed. Choppy, short breaths were all she could manage as she silently cried, stumbling through the underbrush.

She had to keep going. The idea of being at her brother and Mr. Alexander's mercy was all the incentive she needed to force her body into submission.

Broken tree limbs crunched under her feet and the sound of water rolling over the river rocks echoed in her ears.

Coming around a bend in the river, Rainee stopped. In the distance, Indian men, women and children milled about. Knots of terror twisted in Rainee's stomach. She had heard stories about the savage Indians out West and how they brutally murdered and scalped white people. She touched her blond hair and fingered a loose strand. The spotted mule deer jerky she had eaten before her escape churned in her stomach. She pressed her hand against her mouth, gulping down her fear.

On unstable legs, Rainee backed up, then whirled, smacking hard into a wall of flesh. The pulse in her neck matched the rapid drumbeat coming from the Indians' campsite. She opened her mouth to scream but stopped when her trail of vision landed on Haydon.

"Rainee, why did you leave?"

She pressed her hand against her heart, willing it to calm down. Ignoring his question, she asked, "What—what are you doing here?"

"I came to take you home."

Rainee swung her head back and forth. "No! It is too great of a risk." She pointed toward the Indians. "I would rather be taken captive by those—those savages than go back and be forced into marrying that ogre."

Haydon threw his head back and laughed.

Rainee frowned. When he continued laughing, she slammed her hands on her waist and glared up at him. "And, pray tell, just what is so funny about that?"

"Those savages, as you call them, Rainee, are Nez Perce Indians. They're friendly."

"Well then, all the better for me. I shall go live with them."

"And just how will you communicate with them? Do you speak their language?" Humor waltzed through his eyes.

Glad he was finding this whole situation so funny, she planted her hands on her hips. The idea of going back and being forced to marry a man she did not love… a man old enough to be her grandfather…a man who was every bit as cruel as her brother was, there was nothing funny in that.

She whirled, placing her back to him. She did not know any Indian language. That fact caused her spirit to deflate. Now what would she do? Every time she ran, Haydon followed her, determined to take her back. She could not let that happen. Not with the threat of Ferrin nearby. No jail cell would hold him. That she was certain of.

"Rainee." Haydon's hands rested on her shoulders. He circled her until she faced him. He clasped her hands in his. "Trust me. I meant what I said last night about you marrying me. And I promise I won't let him harm you or force you into marrying that man. Let's go back to the ranch and—"

"No!" Rainee ripped her hands from his, and one of her lacey gloves came off in the process. Her eyes widened in horror. She slammed her gloved hand on top of her naked one to cover the hideous scars.

Horrified by what he had seen in that one, short flash, Haydon gawked at the raised scars trailing up and down Rainee's hand and wrist, which he could still see although she tried mightily to cover them. Concern and compassion drove through him as he gently raised her hand off the one she covered. His stomach churned at the sight of the raised scars marring her small hand.

She yanked her hand back, and with shaky fingers she snatched the glove from him and rammed her hand into it.

"Rainee." He wanted to see her, but she turned from him. Red flooded her cheeks, and she slid her hands behind her back. "How did you get those scars?"

Rainee chewed on her lip.

Haydon waited for her to answer, but anger at the one who had done that to her boiled within him.

Finally, she whispered something, but he didn't hear what she'd said. "What did you say?"

"Ferrin." This time she spoke a little louder.

His fist clenched at his side and his blood ran hot. That man was even worse than Haydon had imagined. If Ferrin thought Haydon would let him anywhere near Rainee, the thug was sorely mistaken.

In that second, he made up his mind to marry her as soon as possible. She may have come here to marry him out of convenience, but someday he hoped that convenience would turn to love. One thing was for sure, he vowed he would not fail her like he had Melanie. Haydon extended his hand toward her. "Come on." Contempt for her brother spewed through his voice.

Rainee jerked her head up and looked at him. "I am so sorry, Haydon. I know my hands are hideous," she blurted. "I never meant for you or anyone else to see them. But you jerked my hand so quickly the glove came off, and I could not get them hidden fast enough. I know they are grotesque. The ones on my back are even worse."

She was talking so fast Haydon had a hard time keeping up with her.

"My Aunt Lena was right. She said no one would ever want me because of them, but I—" Tears glistened in her eyes, and her shoulders rose and fell as the words died away.

Haydon stood there speechless. She actually thought he was offended by the scars and that no one would want her? And what did she mean by the ones on her back? Just how many beatings had she endured? He reached for her, but she stepped backward and bumped into a tree.

"I am so sorry. I should have never come here." Faster than a bolt of lightning, she shifted past him and took off running.

"Rainee, wait!" He bolted after her, barely dodging the branches. When he caught up to her, he captured her by the elbow and turned her toward him.

Tears streamed down her cheeks. "Let me go," she said through gasps of air. She tried to jerk free, but Haydon clutched her forearms. "You are better off if I leave."

At that moment he could only be ashamed of his previous behavior toward her. All he had thought about was himself and what he wanted. He never once cared about why she had written the advertisement. Or why Jesse had responded to it.

Wanting to shield her from everything she had ever been through, he wrapped her in his arms, pressed her head against his chest and her body against his and cradled her.

Moisture from her eyes seeped through his shirt.

"Rainee, I'm so sorry."

Her body trembled and sobs racked her small frame.

"I'm not offended by your scars. I'm angry at Ferrin for doing this to you." Enraged was more like it. Any man who would hurt a woman like that, let alone his own sister, deserved to hang from the nearest tree.

"Then—then they do not bother you?" She pulled back enough to look into his face. The pain he saw there, mixed with a smudge of relief tore at his soul.

"No, sweetheart, they don't." He reached for her hands and tugged on her gloves, pulling them off.

Rainee blinked several times as she watched him remove her gloves. With the lightest touch, he ran his thumbs over the raised scars that covered her hands and wrists. His heart was weeping hard for her and what she had endured.

Rainee's eyelids dropped. She stood there like a frightened fawn ready to bolt but knowing there was no place to run.

Haydon struggled to keep back the tears burning the back of his eyes. He raised her hands and gently pressed his lips on them, kissing them. His tears dropped onto her marred flesh. "I'm so sorry, Rainee." His voice quavered. He kissed her hands again and again. "I'm so sorry for what you've had to endure." With each touch of his lips against her hands another tear fell. He pressed her tear-covered hands against his wet cheeks and cradled them there.

He heard her short intakes of breath and her silent cries. He tilted her chin upward and gazed down at her. His heart ached with the desire to comfort her, to hold her, to kiss away the uncertainty in her eyes. Haydon cupped her face with his hands and allowed the love and compassion he had for her to rain through his eyes without shame or restraint. He leaned his head down, and tenderly touched his lips to hers.

He raised his head and locked gazes with her. "I promise you, Rainee, that man will never hurt you again. You and I are getting married. Today."

Chapter Twenty

Still dazed at Haydon's second mention of them getting married, Rainee brightened but dimmed just as quickly. Her gaze fell along with her heart. She had never met a more tender, loving man in her life. "We need to talk." The huskiness in her voice matched Haydon's. She led him over to a large tree stump. She sat down, and Haydon lowered his bulky frame beside her and faced her.

Wishing she could blot away the confusion from his face, Rainee drew in a long breath to settle the words inside her. What she had to say was breaking her heart, but she wanted to do right by Haydon, so she reached down and pulled out the words buried inside her. "When I first came here, I was in desperate need to get away from Ferrin. No, let me back up a bit. I had already written to you—to Jesse—because of the severe beatings, but then I overheard Ferrin telling Mr. Alexander he had just bought himself a wife and how he would have his hands full with me. I quickly found Jenetta and told her. She and I packed a few things in the dead of the night, and I left. I stayed with a friend in Chicago until plans were made for my trip out here.

"But when I got here and discovered it was not you who had sent for me and that you did not wish to marry me, I panicked. I was so afraid Ferrin would somehow find me before we married that all I thought about was trying to figure out a way to get you to marry me." Her eyes snagged on his. "But since then, I have gotten to know you, and you are a very kind, caring person, Haydon Bowen."

He smiled.

"And that is why I cannot marry you."

His smile faded and his forehead wrinkled. "I don't understand."

"I cannot in good conscience marry you just to relieve myself of my family's burdens. Nor can I marry you knowing you never wanted to wed again, let alone marry someone you do not love. I cannot. No. I will not do that to you."

"You wouldn't be doing anything *to* me. You'd be doing it *for* me."

She tilted her head sideways. "Excuse me?"

Haydon reached for her hands. "I meant what I said last night. I *want* to marry you, Rainee. Not because I feel like I have to. Actually, my motive is a rather selfish one. Because you see, I do love you. And I can only hope that in time you can come to love me, too."

Hope ignited within her as she searched his eyes for the truth. Tenderness and love mirrored through his eyes and into hers. "Oh, Haydon. I already love you. I have for a long time. You are everything I want in a man. And much much more. But before I answer you, I do have one more thing that concerns me. It is the reason why I fled this morning."

Puzzlement darted across his face and landed in his eyes. "What's that?"

"I fear my staying here will…*has* already put your family in danger. You have seen what my brother is capable of. He does not like to lose. He and Mr. Alexander are very powerful and controlling men who will stop at nothing to eliminate anything or anyone who gets in their way. If Ferrin struck a bargain with Mr. Alexander, neither will stop until they get what they came for."

"You," Haydon interjected.

Rainee nodded.

"Well, sweetheart, if that's all that's stopping you from saying yes, then we have a wedding to plan. I have dealt with worse men than your brother. My brothers and I, and Smokey, are more than able to protect ourselves and our families from the likes of Ferrin. We've done it before, and we'll do it again. I won't lose you. And I know Mother and my family will agree. There is no way any of us will let you go. We all love you too much. So what do you say? Will you marry me?"

Rainee searched his eyes, seeing he meant every word he said. She dipped her head coyly and responded the only way she properly could. "Why, Mister Bowen," she drawled, "I thought you would never ask a third time…." She laughed, then frowned. "But are you sure that is what you want?"

In one swift motion, Haydon rose, pulled her into his arms and kissed her. When their lips parted, he whispered, "Does that answer your question?"

His lips found hers again. The intensity and love behind his kiss melted any remaining doubts Rainee had about his love for her.

With her heart racing like the wind, she pulled back

and slowly stepped out of his arms. "So, now what?" she asked, her voice rasped with love.

He gathered her hand in his and led her toward Rebel. "We have a wedding to plan. So let's head back to the ranch."

As they mounted the horse, sitting in front of Haydon, Rainee silently prayed, *God, please work everything out for Haydon and I to wed before Ferrin can stop us.*

Haydon reached around her, pulling her against his chest. She loved the feel of his arms around her. Loved the security they offered. She sighed. She may as well enjoy it while it lasted. For as soon as they reached the ranch, she was certain it would all come to an end. Ferrin would find a way to get to her before they could wed.

"Rainee." Haydon's breath tickled her ear. "You said the scars on your back are worse. What happened? Whatever possessed him to treat his own sister like that?"

Rainee licked her lips and swallowed. "Ferrin said I was in need of discipline because I was spoiled. Said I needed to be taught a lesson. So he put me to work. When something was not done to his satisfaction, I was punished. Ferrin would whip my hands for each watermark I left on the dishes or silver.

"I also had to haul wood to the firebox. It was backbreaking work, and we had servants to do it, but he informed me I was no longer a member of *his* household but a paid slave whose wages were a roof over my head and food.

"He forced the servants to pile wood in my arms until it reached my nose. If I dropped any on the way to the house, Ferrin would rip the back of my dress open and give me a lash for every piece I dropped." The memory of his beatings tore at her heart and mind, reopening cavernous wounds like the leather strip that had torn her flesh. She felt the pain of those beatings as if they had happened yesterday instead of months ago, but she refused to shed any more tears over them.

"Several times the beatings were so severe, I blacked out. It was as if he were punishing me for something more than watermarks and dropped wood. Ferrin said it was for my own good. That he needed to break my wild spirit. But as you have daily proof, you can see he did not break my spirit." She chuckled, but no humor accompanied it.

"If I ever get my hands on that man, I'll—" Haydon's chest vibrated with his throaty groan.

"If you put your hands to him that would make you like him. And you are nothing like him."

"It still makes me livid to think about what he did to you."

"It makes me sad." She shifted in the saddle. "I do not wish to talk about this anymore."

"I didn't think about how difficult it would be for you to relive what he did. I'm sorry. I should have never asked."

She laid her hand on his arm and patted it. "You have nothing to be sorry for." She tilted her head up at him, and he kissed her cheek.

They dismounted near the river to fill their canteens and to allow Rebel to get a drink.

"Rainee." Haydon took her hands in his. "I've been thinking. You've shared your past with me. Before we get married, it's only fair that I tell you something as well. And after hearing it, I can only hope and pray you'll still want to marry me."

"Nothing you could tell me would make me not marry you."

"I hope so."

He prayed God would help him to tell her all, no matter how ugly the truth was. "In Jesse's letter, did he tell you I was married before and that it's my fault my wife died?"

"No. He did not. But I cannot imagine it is your fault that she is dead."

"It is. Even though Melanie was warned ahead of time what it would be like and how hard it would be out here, she still agreed to move. And was even looking forward to it. When the reality of this land hit her, she ended up hating it and resenting me for bringing her here. I should have noticed all the signs sooner. But I didn't. I failed my wife, Rainee. I failed her in every way. And because of that failure, she ended up having an affair."

He turned, not able to bear looking at her, as he told her the awful truth, and he debated whether to take her back now and forget about marrying her or to continue. He decided he had to take the risk. He loved her too much. Plus she may as well hear all of the ugly, sordid details.

He faced her.

"The night she died, we got into a big argument. She said she wanted to go back East. I promised her that as soon as traveling weather permitted I would take her back. She said she wouldn't wait. She would leave right away with or without me. I forbade her to go, ordered her to wait. I should have never done that, knowing that as soon as I told Melanie she couldn't do something, she would do it out of pure spite."

He rubbed the back of his neck. "She left during the night on foot and I found her body the next morning at the base of a hill wrapped around a tree. I could see the trail of broken branches down the hill where she'd fallen." He shook his head. "I should have guarded my words more carefully."

Rainee laid her hand on his arm. "There is no way you could have foreseen her leaving, Haydon. What woman in her right mind would leave in the middle of the night out in this wilderness territory?"

He wanted to mention that she had, but he didn't. She was right. Most women wouldn't. And yet…

"If I hadn't gotten so angry and hadn't slept in the barn that night, I could have prevented her death. I would have heard her leave. I knew better. It's as if I killed her myself. I drove her away by being such a lousy husband. I'm so afraid I'll do the same to you. I failed her and I've already failed you. Last night I didn't even know you'd left. You could have fallen or been attacked by a wild animal." As if a rain cloud had burst open, tears poured from his eyes and drizzled down his face.

Instantly, Rainee's arms were around him, pulling him close and cradling him. He clung to her, pulling the love she offered into his soul.

"You are no more to blame for Melanie's death than I. Do you not see she made a choice to leave? As did I. Haydon, my love, you cannot stop people from making wrong choices. It is impossible for you to be with someone every second of the day and night. We all make choices every day. And we have to live with the consequences of those choices whether they be good or bad. Sometimes the consequences of our actions hurt the ones we love. Melanie's spitefulness and poor choice caused her death—you didn't."

Her words poured warm honey over his soul. She was right. Melanie did have a choice. For the first time since his wife's death, he found a glimpse of forgiveness for himself, knowing eventually Melanie would have left whether or not he was there.

He pulled back and looked into Rainee's eyes. "Thank you, Rainee. I've carried this guilt around for so long. The Lord told me I needed to forgive myself and to tear down the wall I'd built around my heart, to be open to love again. I'm not sure I could have done that without you, but now I'm so glad I did. I love you, Rainee." His lips parted and covered hers in one of the sweetest kisses he'd ever given and received. The weight of the past disappeared with his sigh of contentment.

When their lips parted, Rainee's eyes were shining. "There is just one more little thing." She reached into her pocket and brought out a yellowed piece of parchment.

Haydon's heart hitched when he saw the name scrawled there. Bettes. He looked at her, willing her not to say what he was afraid she might.

Her gaze stayed on the letter. "Jesse gave this to me yesterday. I do not know how long he had it in his possession." She laughed. "You never know with Jesse."

The center of Haydon's heart began to pang painfully. He saw nothing funny in this news.

Then her eyes captured his again, and there was mirth in them. "It appears in my absence Mr. Bettes found himself another bride. He said he has no use for my services."

The relief came out in a whoop as Haydon scooped her up and twirled her around. "Rainelle Victoria Devonwood, I do believe that's the best news I've heard in years."

She smiled as she lowered her lips to his. "I was hoping you would say that."

The closer they got to the ranch, the more a nervous fluttering filled Rainee's stomach. Thoughts of seeing either of the two men still sent chills of dread up and down her spine. She tucked herself farther into Haydon's chest, wanting to disappear into him.

As she and Haydon rounded the trees heading to the ranch, Rainee started trembling.

Haydon tightened his hold. "You have nothing to be afraid of, Rainee. I'll take care of you."

Rainee wanted to believe him, wanted it to be so regardless of the fantasy she had allowed to take root in her heart, but knowing her brother's determination, along with his uncanny knack of twisting things and making people believe the worst of lies, it would not surprise her if he and Mr. Alexander were at the ranch waiting.

The house came into view. Rainee expected to see Ferrin's horse along with the sheriff's. Instead, she saw Katherine leap from the porch swing and race toward them.

Haydon slid from his horse and reached up to help Rainee down.

The moment Rainee's feet touched the ground Katherine grabbed her and threw her arms around her.

"Rainee, I'm so glad you're okay." She pulled back. "I've been so worried about you." She hugged Rainee again.

"I am so sorry I caused you concern, but I just had—"

"There's no need to explain. None at all." Katherine jerked back and clasped Rainee by the elbows. "You're here now. And there is no way that you are *ever* going back to that—that man again."

"That's right, Mother. Because—" Haydon joined his hands with Rainee's and flashed a luminescent smile her direction "—Rainee and I are getting married."

Katherine's gaze whipped to Haydon, then back at Rainee. She grabbed Rainee in an exuberant hug. "I knew God was in this." His mother released her and turned to collect Haydon in her arms. "Congratulations, son. I'm so happy, I could just cry." She pulled back. Squaring her shoulders, she ran her hands over her skirt and patted her hair. "Yes, well. It looks like we have a wedding to plan, now don't we?"

"We sure do." Haydon faced Rainee. "I'll need to send someone to get the reverend so we can get married right away. We can have a proper reception later on. Would that be all right with you?"

Before she had a chance to respond, Katherine blurted, "Surely we have time to make Rainee a dress and invite all our friends and neighbors, don't we?" Disbelief and disappointment flitted across Katherine's face.

"No, Mother. We don't want to take any chances."

"Katherine, I am sorry it has to be this way, but if we make haste and get married, then Ferrin will have to accept that I am legally wed to another. If we do not,

I fear he will do something drastic, and I cannot marry that evil man, for he is far worse than my brother."

"Worse than your brother? In what way?" Katherine asked.

She raised her hands and showed them to Haydon and Katherine. "These are nothing compared to what Mr. Alexander did to his wife. At least I am still alive. I cannot say the same for the first Mrs. Alexander."

"Mrs. Alexander? What about her?" Haydon frowned.

"She died two years ago at her husband's hands. No one ever proved it, but Mother believed it to be so because Mrs. Alexander had confided to her the brutality of her husband. Mother offered her sanctuary in our home, but Mrs. Alexander feared what would happen to us if she accepted, so she refused Mother's help. Shortly after Mrs. Alexander shared her fears with Mother, the poor woman was found at the bottom of her stairs with a broken neck and bruises on her body."

Katherine gasped. "Oh, how awful."

"Mr. Alexander claimed her shoe had caught the hem of her dress. Mother wanted to tell the sheriff of her beliefs, but Father said they had no proof, so she needed to remain silent and that God would vindicate Mrs. Alexander's death. As you see, the man my brother sold me to has likely gotten away with murder."

"It's even worse than I imagined." Katherine looked up at Haydon with concern and determination.

Just thinking about her brother gave Rainee a case of the nerves. She scanned the area.

"What are you looking for?" Haydon asked.

She gazed up at him. "Ferrin."

"Ferrin? He's in jail."

"He very well may be, but you do not know my brother and what he is capable of." Rainee closed her eyes and swallowed the lump of dread before she captured Haydon's eyes again.

"There's no way I'm letting that man take you anywhere." Haydon spoke confidently, but Rainee knew even his confidence would not keep her safe if Ferrin was released from jail.

Rainee's breath hitched when Michael came around the corner. Before she saw his face, for a moment she feared it might be Ferrin.

Haydon put his arm securely around her shoulders. "Michael. I need you to run an errand for me."

"Sure. What do you need?"

"Rainee and I are getting married."

Michael's eyes brightened. "That's great. Congratulations."

"I need you to fetch Reverend James for me."

"Now?"

"Yes, now."

"Why the rush?"

"It's a long story, Michael. I don't have time to explain it. Will you run and get him for me?"

"Well, I would, but he's not here."

"What do you mean he's not here?"

Rainee's heart hitched in her throat. She wanted to know the answer to that question, too.

"When I went to town the other day, I ran into Reverend James. He said he had some business to attend to, something about a close relative who passed away and left everything to him. Anyway, he said he'd probably be back for our next gathering here in two weeks. I'm sorry, I forgot to tell you."

Rainee's stomach plummeted. Exhausted from running and all the emotional ups and downs of the day bore down on her. She needed to sit. She walked over to a handmade bench near the barn door and plopped down. The shade gave her a nice reprieve from the hot August sun.

Katherine joined her on the bench.

"Now what?" Rainee asked.

"Don't worry." Katherine patted her knee. "Haydon will think of something."

Rainee stared at Haydon as he talked with Michael. Moment after moment slipped by, and to Rainee, each moment felt like an eternity.

Michael nodded then headed back around the barn and out of sight.

"What if you, Leah and Rainee hid out for two weeks?" Katherine suggested when Haydon walked up to them. "You could head over to The Eye of the Needle at *Coeur d'Alene*. There's a lot of narrow passages in those mountains where you could hide out. It would take weeks for Ferrin to find her there."

"That's a good idea, Mother, but I don't know how long Ferrin will be in jail, and from what Rainee said about her brother, I won't risk leaving you for two weeks and risk him coming back and hurting you."

"Smokey and Jesse will be here."

"They won't be near the house. They have to get the wheat in and take care of the hogs. No, I think it best if I send Smokey into town. I sent Michael to tell him to run in and talk to Sheriff Klokk to see how long Ferrin will be in jail and what can be done. After all, he did shoot Michael. That's attempted murder. Charges could be brought against him."

If only they *could* leave until Reverend James arrived, but Rainee knew Haydon was right. Leaving his mother and sisters unguarded would not be safe or wise. Nor would she ask him to do such a thing. Ferrin was too crafty a man. He could talk or manipulate his way out of any kind of trouble. She had seen him do it often enough. To keep this family from any further danger, there was only one solution. "Perhaps it would be best for everyone if I just took my leave."

In the blink of an eye, Haydon squatted in front of her and laid his hand on her arm. "No, it would not be best for everyone, and I know it would not be best for me."

"Or me," Katherine added.

"I love you, Rainee. And I will not lose you. Please don't do anything foolish and run off again. Promise me you won't." His eyes frantically searched hers.

Rainee knew he was remembering his wife and what happened to her when she had fled. As badly as she wanted to protect them all, she would not do that to him. She had been foolish enough to try it before. "I promise."

Relief pressed through his eyes. "Good." He stood and gazed down at her. "You look exhausted, sweetheart. Why don't you go inside now and get some rest?"

She nodded. "Yes. I am quite done in for, actually, and a nap sounds lovely. Thank you." She only hoped and prayed she would be able to sleep.

Haydon extended his hand to help her up. Before letting her go, his gaze bore into her. "Remember, you promised."

She held his gaze. "Yes, I did. So, please, do not

make yourself anxious. I will not do anything foolish. I gave you my word, and I shall keep to it."

He nodded and gave her a quick peck on her cheek. "I need to go take care of Rebel. But I'll be back."

"Come on, Rainee." Katherine stood and looped arms with her. "I'll walk with you."

At the house, Katherine opened the door, and Rainee stepped inside the kitchen.

Leah turned from stirring a pot at the stove. "Rainee!" Leah wiped her hands on her apron and ran toward her, throwing her arms around her friend. "I'm so glad you're safe. I was so worried about you."

"Rainee!" A sleep-rumpled Abby barreled into her, nearly knocking her and Leah over. "I'm so glad those bad men didn't finded you."

Rainee knelt down, scooped Abby into her arms and hugged her. Soon, if everything worked out, this little girl would be her sister.

The next morning, Rainee woke up refreshed. Realizing the lateness of the hour, she made haste in getting dressed and heading downstairs. Haydon was the only one sitting at the table, and he had a coffee cup in front of him.

He stood when she entered, and she could not help but notice the relief on his face. He probably feared in spite of her promise that she would run away again. She did not blame him because she had not given him reason to trust her in that area yet.

He rose and gave her a kiss on her cheek. "Morning, sweetheart. Sleep well?"

"I did. Thank you. Where is everyone?"

"Michael and Jesse are out in the field. Smokey's

finishing up a few chores before he heads in to talk to Sheriff Klokk, and Mother, Leah and Abby are out seeing the new baby kittens."

"Kittens?"

"Miss Piggy had kittens last night."

She did not even know the cat was expecting little ones. "I want to see them. Will you take me to them?"

"Mother left you a plate of food in the oven. Don't you want to eat first?"

"No. I want to see the babies first."

Haydon stood, chuckling. "You're as bad as Abby. She couldn't wait to see them either."

Rainee grinned. "No, I am as good as Abby."

He shook his head. "I give up."

They stepped out onto the porch. As they headed out to the barn, a chill settled over her.

She stopped, shivering in the warm morning sun. "Can you wait a moment? I need my wrap." She whirled, gathered her skirt and ran toward the house.

Near the back door of the house, she found her wrap hanging on a hook. When she reached for it, something covered her head and a hand slammed against her mouth, preventing her from screaming. She was suddenly yanked backward and her body slammed against a solid form.

Smothered by fear and the lack of air, Rainee jolted right and left. Her legs shot out, trying to connect with her kidnapper's legs. Someone grabbed her ankles in a strong grip, and she was powerless to move them. She twisted with all the strength she possessed, trying to break free, but the lack of air pressed the darkness in around her.

Chapter Twenty-One

Haydon walked into the barn. His mother and sisters were huddled over the kittens making a big to-do over them. "Well, is Miss Piggy letting you see them?"

Katherine stood and Leah and Abby squatted closer together. His mother looked around him. "Where's Rainee?"

"She ran back to the house to get her wrap. She should be along any minute now." He walked over to where Miss Piggy was and leaned over to count the kittens. Two white, three gray-and-white, and one black.

He stood and glanced toward the barn door. It shouldn't be taking her that long to get her wrap. His gut told him something wasn't right. "I'll be right back."

Dashing out of the barn, he scanned the area all the way until he ran up the porch stairs and into the house. "Rainee." He glanced around. When she didn't answer, he headed to the back porch where she kept her wrap. The door was standing wide open, and Rainee's wrap was lying half-inside and half-outside.

Haydon quickly stepped out of view of the door and

went to the closest window. Careful to stay out of sight, he peered out.

His breath snagged. Two men were carrying Rainee between them. A sack covered her head, and she was twisting, squirming and kicking. Haydon immediately recognized Ferrin's expensive suit.

He needed to do something and fast. Neither man appeared to have a weapon on them. And Haydon didn't see any on their saddles either.

He ran to the front door, grabbed the rifle hanging above the door and headed toward the back porch, loading the gun along the way.

He made sure neither of the men were looking before he slipped out the back door and hurried behind the woodshed. He peered around the building, and his breathing stopped. Rainee was no longer moving; her body hung limp as a rope.

Time was running out.

Their backs were turned to him as they prepared to load her onto one of the horses.

Now was his chance.

Haydon stepped out from behind the outbuilding and cocked his rifle. "Put her down now, or I'll shoot!"

The old man dropped her legs and threw his hands in the air.

Ferrin yanked Rainee up against his chest. Her arms and legs flopped around like those of a rag doll.

Rainee's brother faced Haydon, his face filled with arrogance and spite. "Go ahead and shoot. But before you do, I'll snap her neck in two." He wrapped one arm around her neck.

"I wouldn't do that if I was you."

Haydon's gaze swung toward the sound of the voice.

Sheriff Klokk and five men stepped out of the trees with their rifles aimed at the two men.

Crazed fear flashed through Ferrin's eyes.

Sheriff Klokk pressed the tip of the rifle into Ferrin's back. "Let her go now, or you're a dead man."

Ferrin closed his eyes, then slung Rainee away from him, slamming her body onto the hard earth.

Anger blurred Haydon's vision. He rushed to Rainee and dropped to his knees beside her. He untied the knot holding the sack in place over her head and gently removed it. He placed his hands under her arm and back and pulled her into a sitting position. Her head swayed, hair going in all directions, and her arms hung wilted at her sides. "Come on, sweetheart, stay with me. Breathe."

Rainee moaned and coughed. Her hazy eyes rolled open. "Haydon?" she rasped. "What—what happened?"

"Your brother's what happened."

"What do you mean?"

"He tried to kidnap you."

Rainee stirred and glanced toward Ferrin. Never had Haydon seen such hatred and evil in a man's face.

"Is she all right?" the sheriff asked.

Haydon nodded.

Sheriff Klokk yanked Ferrin by the arm and handed him over to his deputy several yards away, then he strode toward Haydon.

"How did they get away?" Haydon glanced up at the sheriff.

Klokk raised his hat and swiped his sleeve across the moisture on his forehead. "I reckon when they realized they wouldn't be getting out of jail until the circuit judge came through, they hit my deputy over the head. When he came to, he told me what had happened. I knew just where to look for them because of Ben."

"Ben?" Haydon stopped. "What does he have to do with this?"

"Well, the way Ben tells it is, Devonwood here—" he yanked his chin once toward Ferrin "—heard about Ben's run-in with his sister in Prosperity Mountain. Ben's buddy told him where they could find him. Devonwood paid the guy to take him to Ben and then he hired Ben to find Miss Devonwood and bring her to him. Apparently Ben ran into you first and he figured he'd get even with you for getting him tossed out of town. But then Miss Devonwood rescued you, and, well, I guess you know the rest. Ben was so mad he didn't get paid that he spilled the beans on these two and told me where they were headed. Looks like it's a good thing we got here when we did."

With Haydon's aid, Rainee stood on shaking legs and looked her brother in the eye. "I do not understand, Ferrin. Why do you, my own brother, hate me so much?"

"I am *not* your brother." He spat on the ground.

"What—what do you mean?"

"I mean," he sneered, "you and I are related in name only. I was adopted."

Rainee could not believe what she was hearing. Never had she even suspected such a thing. "That—that cannot be true."

He snorted. "Well, it is. I overhead Father and Mother talking about how after years of trying to have a baby, how blessed they were to have adopted me from the orphanage. And how shortly afterward Mother discovered she was with child. That child was you."

A million centipede legs crawled up and down her spine as Ferrin stared at her with scorn and hate.

"Father favored you even in the end."

"That is not true. Mother and Father treated us equally."

"For once, you are quite right." He snorted. "Even in death they treated us equally." He laughed a laugh of the devil, and a mocking look of derision covered his face.

Nothing he said was making any sense. In fact, the more he talked the more confused she became. "I do not understand."

"Of course you do not. Do you want to know the real reason why I despise you?"

Did she? Could she handle the truth? She searched her heart for the answer and decided it would be better knowing than always wondering. She braced herself for the truth. "Yes, I want to know."

"The day Mr. Pennay came to the house to draw up Father's will, I snuck through the secret passageway and listened to their conversation. Most fathers leave everything to their son, but not ours. No. He could not leave out his precious Rainee." He said her name with such spite, it slithered over her ears like a slimy serpent. "The more I listened to him, the madder I became. Father stipulated that upon their death half of Father's estate went to you, and you would have equal say in running it. That meant everything I did I would have to come to you for your approval. Whoever heard of a man having to get a woman's approval? He showed his favoritism of you right up to the end."

"I had no idea."

"Of course you did not. Why do you think I encouraged you to stay home from the reading of the will? I am no dunce."

"I thought you were protecting me. I trusted you. You made me believe Father had left nothing to me. Not even a dowry." She pressed her eyes shut as the pain of his lies and vicious beatings sliced her heart and soul in slow painful shreds. If only she would have thought to ask Mr. Pennay to reveal everything in her father's will when she contacted him about whether or not Ferrin was her legal guardian. But she had not. Her mind was too filled with fear and thoughts of running away. "To think I stayed there and bore your constant abuse when I could have taken my leave at any time."

"Pretty clever of me, don't you think?"

Rainee's heart crushed under the weight of his words. For it was all true. She had not imagined it. He really did hate her that much. "It all makes sense now. When we were younger, you were nice to me and then all of a sudden you started doing things to bring me harm. I now understand why you beat me. Why you ran off every suitor. You knew if I got married I would discover the truth about my inheritance. It had nothing to do with watermarks or dropping wood. You wished me dead." She leaned into Haydon as the truth of her words sunk in.

Ferrin sneered at her. "You are not as ignorant as I thought. And you are a whole lot tougher than I gave you credit for. That was my first mistake. My second was coming after you. But then again, I could not risk you coming back for your inheritance, now could I?" There was no remorse in his voice. Nothing but coldness. A coldness that chilled Rainee to the bone.

"You were finally rid of me, Ferrin. So why did you bother to come looking for me?"

"If it were not for old man Alexander here, I would not have bothered. I would have told the lawyer you were dead and then your part of the inheritance would have been mine. But Alexander threatened to kill me if I did not give him what was rightfully his."

"I paid you a small fortune, Devonwood," Mr. Alexander butted in. "I just knew you were pulling a fast one on me when you told me Rainelle was gone. Threatening you was the only way I could think of to get you to give me what was rightfully mine. I would have never followed through with my threat." Mr. Alexander's jowls wiggled with the fast movement of his head as his gaze darted between Ferrin and the sheriff.

"Do you expect me to believe that?" Ferrin looked at Rainee. "We both know the old man is capable of murder, do we not?" Ferrin sneered the look of Satan himself first at her and then at Mr. Alexander, who said nothing to deny it.

"I've heard enough," Sheriff Klokk interjected.

"As have I." She looked Ferrin in the eye. "I am sorry for you, Ferrin. But no matter what you have done to me, you will always be my brother and I shall always love you."

For a brief moment, his face softened, then just as quickly it turned to stone. "As far as I am concerned, I do not have a sister. I am still an orphan. I have no one in the world but myself." Hatred filled every word. He diverted his attention away from her.

Having scarce drawn breath the whole time, she filled her lungs and slowly exhaled. "I am so sorry you feel that way, Ferrin." She turned away from her brother and faced the sheriff. "What will happen to him?"

"Well, after the judge gets here, I reckon he'll hold a trial. I can almost guarantee he'll send these two away for quite some time."

Rainee nodded her ascent.

The lawmen handcuffed the two men and none-too-gently hoisted them onto the horses.

Haydon wrapped his arm around her. "Come on. Let's get you out of here." He led her toward the house.

Leah, Abby and Katherine were standing in front of the window, their anxious faces peering through the glass.

They disappeared and within seconds all three of them darted out the back door and took turns hugging Rainee and telling her how much they loved her. Their love warmed her.

Rainee looked back at her brother. The cold look he sent her saddened her.

As they led him and Mr. Alexander away, she faced Haydon, who looked down at her with concern.

He brushed at her hair, which had come down in all the ruckus. She did not bother to straighten it. Even her mother would understand why. His hands slid down her shoulders to her arms. "I'm so sorry, Rainee." He pressed her head into his chest. His lips covered hers, smothering her with even more warmth.

When the kiss ended, Rainee drew back and looked Haydon in the eye. "Haydon, I must go away."

He jerked back. Rainee staggered but his strong arms steadied her. "What do you mean you have to leave?"

Abby threw her little arms around Rainee's legs and hugged her tight. "I don't want you ta go."

"Me either," Leah and Katherine said in unison.

Rainee picked Abby up and held her. "No, no, it is not what y'all think. You are not getting rid of me that easily." She looked at their shocked faces and smiled. "I shall only be gone a short time."

"Yay!" Abby gave Rainee's neck a tight squeeze, then squirmed until Rainee set her down. Off the little girl scampered, disappearing around the corner of the house.

"We need to follow Abby's example and leave you two alone." Katherine smiled, hooked her arm through Leah's, and the two of them walked away.

"You're not going back to…" Haydon frowned. "Just where are you from, anyway?"

She smiled. "Little Rock, Arkansas."

"Well, you're not going back there without me."

She tilted her chin sideways and frowned. "How did you know where I was going?"

"Well, I figured with Ferrin in jail, you would want to go back to make sure your parents' place is being taken care of."

Stunned by his perception, she only nodded.

"Why don't we get married first and we'll both go? I'd love to see where you grew up."

"What a delightful idea. I would love to show you my family's plantation. It is quite lovely." They smiled into each other's eyes.

Haydon bent and his mouth covered hers in a long lingering kiss, melting her heart into a liquid pool of love. With his lips still against hers, he whispered,

"Rainelle Victoria Devonwood, you'd better get busy planning that wedding. And the sooner the better."

Rainee giggled under the light pressure of his lips and silently agreed.

Epilogue

Before Rainee had left Little Rock, she and Jenetta had hidden her mother's beautiful silk wedding gown, long white gloves, single-strand necklace with matching earrings and one other precious treasure in her trunk, her mother's wedding ring. Soon to be hers.

Mother would not be here today to witness her marriage, but wearing her dress would help Rainee feel as if she were.

Sitting in front of Leah's bedroom mirror, Rainee watched Katherine remove the last cloth strip from her hair.

"Oh, Rainee, you look so beautiful." With her hands on Rainee's arms Katherine locked gazes with her in the mirror. "My dear, I know I can never take the place of your mother. No one can. But I want you to know I love you like a daughter, and I would be honored if you would call me Mother."

"You mean that?" Rainee swallowed the tears clogging her throat.

"Of course I do."

Rainee's heart could scarcely contain one more exciting thing. But contain it, it must. For she had something even more exciting awaiting her—a compassionate, loving, handsome mail-order groom.

After a bath and a shave, Haydon dressed. The formal black jacket and pants looked out of place in the rugged Idaho Territory, but he wanted Rainee to have the wedding she deserved. Although she cared nothing about the high-society frippery, he knew this one time she would appreciate it.

On the way to the backyard where the guests were already gathering, he met Jesse.

His brother whistled. "Don't you look nice?" Jess fell in step with him.

"So do you." Haydon glanced at Jesse's scar. Even though he'd asked Jess's forgiveness, every time he saw it remorse and shame for his stubborn selfishness knifed his spirit. He turned, stopping them both.

"Something wrong?"

"Nothing's wrong. I just wanted to thank you for sending for Rainee. If you hadn't, I wouldn't be getting married today. Thanks, Jess." He grabbed his brother in a bear hug.

"You're welcome. Now let me go. I have a special job to perform, and I don't want to be late. I'm giving the bride away, remember?"

Rainee slowly descended the stairs like a proper young lady, knowing her mother would be so proud.

At the bottom step, Jesse reached for her hand and looped her arm through his. "You ready?"

She nodded. "Jess. Thank you for answering my advertisement. If you had not, I would have never met Haydon."

Jesse chuckled. "I heard those same words from Haydon a few minutes ago." He patted her hand. "You're welcome."

She looked at her mother's long white gloves and marveled at how they covered her hideous scars. Scars that were a sign of what God's great mercy had delivered her from.

"Now, let's go get you two hitched," Jesse said.

Outside, Rainee's gaze locked on Haydon already standing by the preacher.

She and Jesse strolled down the aisle between the rows of benches, smiling. Her smile grew as she gazed on Katherine, Leah, Abby, Hannah and her newborn baby Tomas, Michael and Smokey. When they reached Haydon, Jesse handed her over to him and with a wink whispered, "Here's your order."

"Best one I ever got too," Haydon whispered for her ears only.

Her heart and lips grinned.

"Dearly Beloved, we are gathered together to join this man and this woman in the bonds of holy matrimony. If there be any just cause why these two should not be joined, speak now or forever hold your peace."

A loud grunt came from the barn area. Rainee's gaze swung that way. A hearty laugh rose from her. Good thing Mother was not here to witness it. But then again, even Mother might laugh at the sight before Rainee.

Ears flapping like an upset hen, Kitty headed straight for them at a fast trot.

Michael and Smokey leapt up and tried heading her off, but Kitty dodged them, racing around the festivities until the sweet little beast ended up at Rainee's side. Without touching Rainee's gown, Kitty sat, ooooing with contentment.

Laughter filled the ranch yard.

Rainee looked at Haydon and laughed.

His mouth hung open, his eyes were fixed on the pig and he was shaking his head.

He looked at Rainee. "Sorry about that, sweetheart."

Her shrug was accompanied by another laugh. "Do not be sorry. Kitty is family, and now she is an honorary bridesmaid." She winked at Haydon, then faced the preacher. "Please continue, Pastor James. Kitty has no objections and neither do I."

* * * * *

Noelle Marchand is a native Houstonian living out her childhood dream of being a writer. She graduated summa cum laude from Houston Baptist University in 2012, earning a bachelor's degree in mass communications and speech communications. She loves exploring new books and new cities. When she's not scribbling out her latest manuscript, you may find her pursuing one of her other passions—music, dance, history and classic movies.

Books by Noelle Marchand

Love Inspired Historical

Bachelor List Matches

The Texan's Inherited Family
The Texan's Courtship Lessons
The Texan's Engagement Agreement

Unlawfully Wedded Bride
The Runaway Bride
A Texas-Made Match

Visit the Author Profile page at Harlequin.com.

UNLAWFULLY WEDDED BRIDE

Noelle Marchand

The just shall live by his faith.
—*Habakkuk* 2:4

To God for completing this good work in me.

Acknowledgments

Thanks to my family for fostering a spirit of creativity. Special thanks to Mom for being my first and most avid reader. To my sister, for believing I actually could write a novel, thus allowing me to believe it, too. Thanks to the Butterfly Sisterhood for being you and allowing me to be me.

God bless you, Elizabeth Mazer, for all of your encouragement, advice, patience and expertise! I am so proud of what we accomplished together.

Prologue

August 1877
Peppin, Texas

"We ordered a husband for you."

At the sound of her little brother's voice, Kate O'Brien's finger froze on its trek down the page of her financial ledger. Her gaze shot to the kitchen doorway where twelve-year-old Sean stood next to their ten-year-old sister, Ellie. She met their serious stares blankly. Surely, she'd heard wrong. "I'm sorry. You did what?"

Sean exchanged a look with Ellie, then met Kate's gaze before carefully repeating himself. Kate's heart began to beat faster in her chest. She placed the ledger on the kitchen table and tried to swallow the sense of foreboding that skittered down her backbone. "What exactly does that mean?"

"Something wonderful," Ellie exclaimed with a smile before slipping into a chair across from Kate. "I heard Mr. Johansen talking about mail-order brides at his mercantile. I knew that was what we needed so we put an advertisement for a mail-order groom in a few newspapers."

She glanced from Ellie to Sean, hoping for some indication that they were joking. They both looked perfectly serious.

"We received a lot of responses," Sean said as he pulled a small pack of letters from behind his back and placed it on the table in front of her. She spared the packet a brief glance before meeting her little brother's sincere green eyes. "One response was special. We knew he was perfect for us so we wrote back."

"Oh, Sean," she breathed in dismay.

His gaze faltered for an instant before he continued. "I knew he wouldn't respond if we told him we were children so we just told him all about you and took a few passages from Ma and Pa's love letters to make it sound more grown-up."

Her heart froze in her chest. "You forged letters from me? That's against the law."

His eyes widened and he shook his head adamantly. "We didn't forge letters. We just never said which Miss O'Brien was doing the writing."

"Why did you do this?"

"We wanted to help," he insisted quietly.

She widened her eyes imploringly. "How does this help?"

"You do a lot, Kate," Sean said. "We don't always say thank you for it, but when we stop to think about it we know."

"I do what has to be done."

He nodded. "That's just it. Ma's and Pa's deaths were just as hard on you as they were on us but you were strong. You had to be. We wanted you to have someone who would do for you what you do for us."

Kate was astounded at the maturity in his voice but still shook her head in disbelief at their actions. "I appreciate that, Sean, but what you two did was wrong."

Ellie leaned forward earnestly. "We knew what you needed and that you would never get it for yourself. You're too shy around handsome men."

She gaped at her younger sister. "Oh, Ellie, really."

"Well, it's true," the girl declared obstinately. "You never let men court you. It's all that awful Mr. Stolvins's fault. Ever since he—"

"Ellie, bringing *that* man into this conversation *really* isn't going to help you."

Ellie allowed her words to stumble to a halt then lifted her brows archly. "It's true and you know it. Besides, you need someone to take care of you."

Kate slammed the ledger shut. "I do not."

"You do so, but you won't admit it," Ellie said firmly. Her small fist pounded on the table. "That's why we had to act."

Kate crossed her arms. "You were trying to marry me off without my consent."

"I know," Ellie said then lifted her chin nobly as tears gleamed in her large green eyes. "We couldn't because you have to sign a silly paper."

Kate's eyes widened. A dry laugh spilled from her lips. "Well, thank the Lord for that."

"It isn't funny," Ellie said as large tears began to roll down her cheeks. She pulled a folded-up paper from the pocket of her skirt and held it toward Kate. "Please, Kate. You just have to sign it."

"No."

"At least, read the letters," Sean urged pleadingly. "Give the man a chance."

"Absolutely not." She pushed the letters away from her as though they might bite her.

Ellie pulled the letters to her chest. The effect of her glare was slightly ruined by a large hiccup. "He's wonderful. His name—"

Kate silenced Ellie with a look. "I don't want to know anything about that man. I've heard enough from both of you on this subject. I've made my decision and the answer is no."

Sean shook his head. "You're making a mistake."

"If I am then it's my mistake to make." She pinned them both with a stare. "I don't want to hear that you two have been writing to this man again. Ever. Do you understand me?"

"Kate," Sean protested.

She cut him off with a shake of her head. "Both of you go to bed. I'll figure out a more suitable punishment for you when my head stops spinning."

Ellie met her gaze defiantly then threw the folded paper on the table before rushing from the room. Sean pulled in a deep breath. He picked up the paper and smoothed it out carefully. Meeting Kate's gaze patiently, he slid the paper across the table until it rested in front of her. With that silent urge for her to think about it, he calmly left the room.

"I don't have time for this," she muttered as she shook her head. She had more important things to think about, like how she was going to save her family's farm. She opened the ledger and continued to search the farm's financial records for some indication the situation wasn't as bad as she feared. Hours passed and she kept coming back to the same conclusion.

Somewhere between buying food for her family and the livestock, the mortgage payments would have to be made. That meant she wouldn't be able to pay the wheat harvesters, which in turn meant she wouldn't be able to sell her wheat. Without selling the wheat, she wouldn't be able to make the other mortgage payments. It was a dizzying cycle with dangerous implications.

If something didn't change soon, they were going to lose the farm. She braced her elbows on the table, then covered her face with her hands. She heaved out a quiet sigh. "Lord, what do I do?"

She'd applied for a short-term loan at the town's only bank and had been denied almost immediately. The banker, Mr. Wilkins, had kindly informed her it would not be in the best interest of either party to enter into another loan agreement when the farm was heading toward foreclosure. She'd put her pride aside long enough to ask if there was anything at all that would make him change his mind. He'd said the only way he would consider giving her a loan was if she married. A single woman in her position would have little success paying back the loan. However, if she had a husband the situation would be entirely different. Since she didn't, he couldn't help her.

Her breath stilled in her throat. Her gaze slid from the mess of papers in front of her to the official-looking document across the table. The bold font read Absentee Affidavit. The only way she could get a loan was to find a husband. Suddenly one was literally at her fingertips. Was it pure coincidence or was it something more?

She set the paper on the ledger in front of her. All

she had to do was sign it and she could save the farm. She swallowed. She toyed with the pen, then pulled it carefully from the bottle of ink. Impulsively she set it against the paper. It only took a minute for her to fill in the little information that was required. She signed her name with a desperate flourish, then shoved the pen back into the bottle of ink.

Staring at her signature, dread settled in her stomach. She couldn't do it. The farm was her parents' heritage, yet she could only imagine how appalled they would be if they knew she'd given up her entire future to keep it. She let out a deep sigh, then set the paper as far away from her as possible. *I am not that desperate, but I am not giving up. There is another way. There has to be. Perhaps if I spoke to Mr. Wilkins one more time...*

Exhaustion pulled at her senses. She'd take a moment to rest her eyes, then clean up the mess she'd made and go to bed. Someone called her name and she jerked her head up. Sean stood at the end of the table watching her in concern.

"I'm awake." She pushed her hair away from her face. "What are you doing up? It must be late."

"It's almost midnight. I couldn't sleep." He settled into the chair opposite her.

She closed her drowsy eyes and leaned back in her chair. "You worry too much."

She heard the smile in his voice as he responded. "I promise not to worry anymore."

"Good."

"I know what Ellie and I did was wrong, but I think you made the right decision about everything in the end."

It took a moment for her sleep-fogged mind to catch

up. When it did, she felt relief fill her being. She forced her eyes open. “Good. I’m glad you think so.”

His gaze flickered to the table then back up to meet hers. “Do you want me to take care of this for you?”

“Would you? That would be wonderful.” She glanced at the table strewn with papers and shook her head. “If you could just stack the papers for me, I’ll put them away in the morning.”

“Sure,” he agreed.

She carefully pushed back from the chair then reached out to touch his dark blond hair as she passed. “Good night, Sean.”

Satisfaction filled his voice. “Good night.”

Chapter One

Three weeks later

Kate felt Ellie's side of the bed dip, then rise. She listened to her sister's small feet pad against the wooden floor of the farmhouse loft. She turned on her side to watch Ellie drag a chair to the window. The soft blue light of morning spilled through the glass as Ellie pushed back the curtains for a better view. Kate sighed then sat up in sleepy curiosity. "What are you doing?"

"I can see the road from here," Ellie said, then jumped down from the chair with a decided thump. She ran to kneel in front of the bed and lifted her sparkling green eyes to meet Kate's. "Do you have a feeling that today will be a very special day?"

"No, not particularly," she said. Seeing Ellie's crestfallen expression, she amended, "I suppose that every day can be a very special day if we let it."

Ellie gave her a half smile seemingly more out of politeness than anything else. Kate hid her bemusement as she turned away from Ellie and quickly dressed. Her siblings seemed to have made a concerted effort to behave since she'd managed to stop their plan to marry her off. While she was relieved to see such an improvement in their behavior, she found it unnerving. How could they possibly not be up to something?

Kate smoothed her hair into an upturned twist as she watched her sister suspiciously. The girl had gone back to her post at the window. "Are you looking for something, Ellie?"

"Hmm? Oh, no," she said absently.

"Then please get ready for school."

"Yes, Kate."

Sean and Ellie stepped into the kitchen just as she set the food on the table. Kate packed their lunch pails and set them in the usual place, then turned to survey their progress and was satisfied to find them nearly done eating. "Do you both have your slates and your homework?"

"Yes." They answered as they deposited their empty plates in the sink.

"Don't lollygag on the way or you'll be late again," she warned, then sank into an empty chair and sent them a smile. "Be good and have fun."

Sean grabbed the lunch pails and slates before hurrying out of the kitchen. Ellie began to follow him then paused to look at Kate. She met the girl's measuring stare. "Yes, Ellie?"

"Are you going to wear that the rest of the day?"

She looked down at her serviceable blue dress. "Why? Is something wrong with it?"

Ellie stepped farther into the room. "Wouldn't it be nice to get dressed up this once?"

"I'll be doing the wash all day. Why would I dress up for that?" she asked in confusion.

Ellie shrugged. "If someone stopped by, you would want to look presentable. Don't you think—"

Sean appeared at the door and frowned at Ellie. "Let's go. We're going to be late."

Ellie nodded then sent Kate a hopeful smile. "Perhaps just your hair—"

"Bye, Kate." Sean grabbed Ellie's arm and pulled her toward the door. As they left Kate heard him whisper, "What are you trying to do, anyway?"

The door slammed shut behind them leaving Kate in perplexed silence. She shook her head in frustration even as her lips curved in an amused smile. It looked like things were finally back to normal. She grabbed a biscuit for breakfast, then went about the chores with her usual determination.

She gathered their laundry and carried the large basket through the forest to the small creek that ran through the property. She washed clothes until her fingers became wrinkled from the cool water, then took a break to let the sun warm her freezing hands. She carefully stretched the kinks from her back. The waterfall that pooled into the small creek provided a drumming rhythm that lulled her senses into disarming relaxation.

A gunshot reverberated through the still morning air. Kate started, then spun toward the sound. Stunned, it took her a moment to realize she was staring into the forest toward her family's farm. She picked up her skirts and ran. She dashed through the trees, her bare feet creating a quick rhythm on the path she'd traveled only an hour ago.

The edge of her petticoat caught on a fallen branch but she refused to slow down as she neared the large clearing where her father had built their farm. The curious sound of masculine voices made her pause. She cautiously moved around the side of the barn toward them. The voices grew louder. With one last step, she cleared the barn and found herself in the middle of a standoff.

Kate froze. Her gaze traveled from the tall cowboy on her left whose gun was drawn toward the house, to the young man standing just outside her doorway. He was struggling to keep his grip on his pistol and control the haphazard pile of possessions in his arms. She narrowed her eyes as she recognized the items, then gasped as realization tumbled over her. She stepped forward. "What do you think you're doing with my things? Put those down!"

He jumped and turned to stare at her with panic in his gaze.

Her eyes widened as she realized he was just a boy. She lifted her chin and her tone turned imperious. "I said, put those down. Just you wait until—"

A wild shot flew from the boy's gun.

She jumped, then stared at him in surprise.

"Get down!" The deep unyielding command from the cowboy made her obey without question. Another shot broke out, this time from her side.

"Of all the foolish things to do…" The cowboy let out a volley of shots. The boy ran for the horse waiting in the barnyard and somehow managed to mount with his armful of goods.

A shot from beside her sent the boy's hat flying from his head. Kate caught her breath then pushed the man's gun away from its target. "Don't do that. You'll hit him!"

She watched as his aggravation seemed to flare along

with the golden ring outlining his deep brown eyes. “Woman, don’t touch my gun.”

She gasped at his harsh tone. “I was trying to keep you from killing a child!”

“If I had meant to hit him, I would have.” He stood then caught her elbow to help her to her feet. “As it is, he got away with my horse.”

“Not to mention his life,” she delivered testily.

He frowned at her.

She glared back.

His frown slipped, then pulled into an amused half smile. “I wondered if you’d have a temper to match your hair.”

She let out a confused breath, then caught an escaping lock of her rich strawberry-blond hair and vainly tried to tuck it into place. “What do you mean?”

“Not a thing I didn’t say,” he said seriously, but his eyes held hers teasingly.

Kate found herself momentarily distracted by him as she suddenly became aware of his strong yet dangerously handsome features. She took a small step back, feeling a telltale warmth spill across her cheeks. He eyed her for a long moment, then gave his gun a small spin before tucking it safely into the holster. He tipped his Stetson to introduce himself, “I’m Nathan Rutledge.”

She lifted her chin. “Miss O’Brien.”

“Rutledge,” he reminded with a nod.

Didn’t he just say that? she wondered. “Yes, I know.”

Unnerved by the friendly grin her statement caused, Kate glanced away. “Thank you for your help. Unfortunately he still got away with everything.”

“Oh, he hasn’t gotten away with anything yet.”

She glanced up to survey the determined glint in his eye. "You're going after him."

"Of course I am," he said. "Delilah's been with me more than three years. I'm not letting some little thief get away with a horse of that stock."

"Delilah?" she asked, unsuccessfully denying her curiosity.

The man nodded. "Yes. Delilah."

Uncomfortable with his warm gaze, she glanced down at her dress. "That's an interesting name for a horse."

"One of a kind," he admitted.

Kate frowned.

He stepped closer.

Surprised, she looked up and couldn't seem to look away. She closed her eyes against the searching, his and her own. *What is going on here? This is not normal. No one should have this sort of rapport with a total stranger. I may spend most of my time alone on the farm when Sean and Ellie are in school, but I can't be that lonely. Can I?*

"Kate," he said, and her eyes flew open at the sound of her name. Snapped from whatever spell held her, she lifted her chin and stared at him. She hadn't given him her Christian name. Perhaps she'd met him before and forgotten? She allowed her gaze to sweep from his dark brown eyes and past his blue checkered shirt. His dark gray pants fit loosely against his long legs, and the dark metal of his gun rested against his thigh while his low-slung gun belt stretched across his hips. Meeting his gaze, she shook her head. If she'd met him, she would have remembered.

She opened her mouth to question him but he was

already speaking. "I have to go after him. May I use your horse?"

She managed to nod, then watched him hurry toward the barn. A few minutes later, he reappeared on her horse and went in pursuit of the thief without a backward glance. Kate watched him disappear into the distance and vainly tried to sort out what just happened.

An hour later, back on Delilah and with the thief secured on Kate's horse, Nathan Rutledge rode down Main Street, noting the curious stares from the citizens of Peppin, Texas. He had been on the receiving end of a town's stares before, only they hadn't been so friendly. But this was his new beginning—the fresh start he'd prayed for. He tipped his hat toward the young women who watched him shyly, then nodded at the older man sitting on the feed store steps.

The man narrowed his eyes suspiciously, then sat up in his chair to spit a stream of brown chewing tobacco juice on the ground in Nathan's direction. He smiled wryly. Now, that was more like what he was used to. He was ready to put that life behind him as sure as he was breathing.

A "howdy" broke into his thoughts. He glanced down to find a man with graying hair and a belly that overlapped his belt watching him suspiciously.

"Can I help you with something?" the man asked.

Nathan eyed the star on the man's chest and nodded. "I'm looking for the sheriff. Is that you?"

The man gave a single nod. "That's me."

He dismounted. Tipping his hat back, he nodded toward the person who had really been drawing all the attention. The young thief sent him scathing glares from where he sat with his hands bound and tied to the saddle horn of Kate's horse. "I found him trying to steal from the O'Brien place this morning. He took off with my horse when I tried to stop him. He's just a boy so I'm not sure what's to be done about it."

The sheriff's suspicious gaze went from him to the boy and back again as the man obviously tried to discern who was guilty of what crime. "Is that so? What were you doing out at the O'Brien's in the first place?"

"With all due respect, sir, I reckon that's my business." He wasn't sure how much Kate had told the town about him, but he wasn't about to announce his presence to strangers without even a proper first meeting with the woman.

The sheriff's eyes narrowed for a moment. Nathan held the man's gaze, looking him straight in the eye without shifting or backing down. Finally, the sheriff nodded. "Let's get him down from there and we'll sort all this out."

Nathan cut the boy free, then waited for him to slide off the horse. The boy looked as if he might try to bolt but the sheriff put a hand on his shoulder and steered him toward the jail. Though his stomach tightened in dread, Nathan had no choice but to follow. The sheriff directed the boy to a chair in front of the desk, then sat across from him.

Nathan's gaze nonchalantly surveyed the walls of the office until he found the "wanted" posters. He was relieved when only the grizzled faces of strangers stared back at him. Movement to his right caught his eye. He nodded at the young-looking deputy who rose from that side of the room to watch the proceedings curiously.

"This man says you tried to steal from the O'Brien

place. What do you have to say about that?" the sheriff asked.

The boy glared at them defiantly. "I gave it all back. Let me go!"

The sheriff sighed. "You know I can't do that. Are your parents around here?"

"No."

"Who's taking care of you?"

"I am."

The sheriff grunted. "Deputy Stone, take him in the back for now."

"What's going to happen to him?" Nathan asked after the boy was led away.

"I don't rightly know. He isn't from around here and it doesn't look like he has any family." The sheriff eyed him carefully. "You aren't from around here, either, are you?"

Nathan tensed but played it off with a shrug and an easy smile. "You can tell that easy?"

"You sure don't look familiar. In a town this small, that's clue enough." The sheriff narrowed his gaze. "I guess I won't get a chance to know you much if you're just passing through."

"I guess not," he said, hearing the sheriff's message clearly. He'd just been told to get his business done and move on. Apparently, Peppin didn't tolerate strangers coming through and causing trouble. Nathan wasn't looking to cause trouble and he certainly wasn't planning to leave Peppin anytime soon. He had too much to stick around for, like that red-headed woman he'd promised to return to. When he stepped outside, Delilah's whinny was just the distraction he needed after visiting the jail. He stepped close to the large black mare to tenderly stroke her nose.

"You knew I'd come for you, didn't you, girl?"

She blew out a puff of air onto his hand. Then with a final wary glance toward the town jail, he stepped into the saddle and turned the mare toward the O'Brien place.

Kate leaned on the kitchen table with her elbow while she placed her chin in her palm. As she turned the next page of the family Bible, she realized she'd barely skimmed the past few verses. Dissatisfied, she closed the large book and sank despondently into the chair. She had already finished the laundry. Most of their clothes were flapping in the wind outside while she waited inside for the stranger to return. *If* he returned.

She was beginning to wonder if the whole thing had just been a big ruse between the pair of strangers. They were probably both thieves. Now not only had she lost a number of her family's few valuable possessions but she'd also lost Pa's horse. She groaned. What had made her think she could trust that man?

The sound of horse hooves in the barnyard drew her gaze toward the kitchen doorway. Rising from her chair, she hurried to the living room window to peer out. The stranger rode into the barnyard on his large black horse with her bay trailing after it. Relief poured from her lips in a heavy sigh.

Her relief did not change the resolve that filled her being. She was going to get some answers from this man. Her determination did not fade as she opened the door and marched toward the barn. It did not falter when she caught up to him or while she watched him loop the horses' reins around his hands to walk them into the barn. It was only when his friendly gaze met hers that it wavered.

"I found him, but he can't be more than fourteen," he said as they stepped into the relative coolness of the barn. "The sheriff isn't sure what to do with him. He isn't from around here and doesn't claim to have any family."

Take your time, she reminded herself as he guided the horses to their stalls. She waited as he removed the saddle from her horse to place it back where it belonged. He repeated the process with the reins and bridle, then glanced up questioningly. She opened her mouth to speak but he was already asking, "Where's the brush?"

She blinked. "It's on the shelf near the bridles. I'll get it."

She moved toward the hooks, then glanced up at the shelf trying to see over its edge. Her father had been much taller than her and, as a result, everything was nearly out of her reach. It took a moment for her to spot it. "There it is."

"I see it," Nathan said at the same time.

Her hand reached it a moment before his did. She stilled as his hand covered hers. She pulled the brush down half expecting him to release it, half hoping he wouldn't. He didn't. She turned toward him and slowly glanced up past his blue checkered shirt to his face. His gaze solemnly slipped over her features. She swallowed. "There's something I have to ask you."

His gaze met hers.

She lifted her chin. "Who are you and why are you here?"

He frowned and released her hand. "What do you mean, who am I?"

"While we're at it, how do you know my name?"

"Why shouldn't I know your name? I am Nathan Rutledge and you are Kate—"

"O'Brien," she finished. "Yes, I know that."

"Rutledge," he reminded.

"What?"

"Rutledge."

"Why do you keep saying that?"

"Because your name used to be—" He paused and looked at her for a second. "You mean to tell me that you, Kathleen 'O'Brien,' have never even heard my name before today?"

"That's exactly what I mean."

He began to speak, then shook his head and strode over to where his saddlebag rested near Delilah's stall. "I suppose you'd better have a look at this."

She took the piece of paper he extended to her. She glanced up as she unfolded it. "What is this?"

"It's our marriage certificate," he replied quietly.

"What?" Her gaze held his before she stared down at the certificate. "You don't mean—"

"I mean," he interrupted with quiet authority, "that you, Kate O'Brien Rutledge, are my wife."

Chapter Two

"I don't understand how you could marry me without my consent," Kate said as she handed him a glass of water, then settled onto the dark green settee in the living room a few minutes later.

He sat at the other end of the settee, then turned toward her. "What are you talking about? You signed the affidavit."

"I signed it but I never intended to send it," she admitted.

A confused frown marred his face. "I don't understand."

She bit her lip. "Mr. Rutledge, I'm afraid my family owes you an apology."

"An apology?"

She pulled in a deep breath. "Let me explain how this started."

She watched a myriad of emotions flit across his face as she carefully explained what her siblings had done. Shock, confusion and disappointment battled for dominance before a bemused, disbelieving smile settled upon his lips. Once she finished, his gaze strayed to the saddle bag he'd set on the low walnut table in front of them. "So your little brother and sister are the ones who wrote the letters."

"I'm afraid so."

He watched her carefully. "Were they also the ones who sent the affidavit?"

"They must have because I certainly didn't."

He nodded, then looked as though he didn't know what else to say. An uncomfortable silence filled the living room. What was she supposed to do now? She shrugged. "You're welcome to stay and help me sort this out when they get home."

"Thank you."

Silence again. She glanced around the room for something to do and her gaze landed on his saddle bag. Meeting his gaze, she asked, "Is there any chance I could see one of those letters?"

"Of course," he said, then pulled out several letters from the saddlebag and handed them to her.

She looked at the curved letters written in a formal script. "This isn't Ellie's handwriting."

"Then whose is it?"

"It looks like Ms. Lettie's. She must have helped them." The young widow would do whatever she could to support Kate and her family. Still, if not for seeing her familiar handwriting, Kate would never have suspected the woman of doing anything this drastic.

She continued to read the contents of a letter and frowned. "This is something I told Ellie about Ma's wedding dress. It was destroyed in a fire when I was eight. Nothing was left but—"

"A small strip of the Irish lace that trimmed the hem of the dress," he continued. "Your mother brought it with you on your journey here from Illinois and just a week before she died she sewed it into your own wedding dress. You keep it in your small wooden hope chest."

"Yes, that's right," she said quietly. "That was all—"

"In the letter?" he asked. "Yes, it was all there."

Her eyes narrowed as she softly queried, "What else was written in there?"

"Oh, just the generalities."

"Such as?"

He grinned. "Such as your name, birth date and other general information."

Her lips curved into a slightly amused smile. "How helpful."

"I thought so."

"Right," she breathed, looking at the letter in her hand, realizing this man whom she knew nothing about could probably recite her entire life story. "You know so much about me yet I know nothing about you."

"You could ask," he said with an inviting lift of his brow.

Curiosity begged to accept his invitation but wouldn't it be best to let the man remain a mystery? The more she knew, the harder it would be to forget this ever happened. She planned to do that as sure as she planned to send him away. Until then, there was only one thing she really wanted to know. "Why would you even agree to something like this in the first place?"

Nathan should have known that would be the first question she asked. "I explained the best I could in the letters but I guess you didn't read those, did you?"

She shook her head.

He was quiet for a long moment as he searched for the right words. Finally, he asked, "Have you ever felt like God took your plans for the future, crumpled them up in his hands and scattered the pieces?

"That's what happened to me," he said gravely. "Then I saw the advertisement. I scoffed at it at first, don't get me wrong. Still, try as I might, I couldn't get it out of my head. I finally just broke down and wrote to you. I didn't expect anything to come of it, but you responded and the more I learned about you the more I felt God leading me to continue."

Her blue eyes filled with doubt and skepticism. "Then why didn't you just try to meet me first? All of this could have been avoided."

He shrugged. "The letters insisted on a proxy marriage. They said you wanted to cause as little disruption to the farm and your family as possible. I'm not saying it didn't seem a little odd but at that point I believed God wanted me to do it. I wasn't about to go against that."

She smiled sympathetically then lifted her shoulders in a shrug. "We all make mistakes. I've certainly made my share. Thankfully, this shouldn't be too hard to fix."

"I never said I was mistaken."

Her eyes lit with surprise. "Oh." Her gaze faltered for a moment then shot toward the large window. "I think I hear the barn door."

As she went to the window, he carefully refolded the letter she'd read, then slid it back into his saddle bag with the rest of them. He was in trouble if Kate's last statement was a hint of what was to come.

He'd questioned his sanity for taking on a proxy bride but that advertisement had sparked more hope in him than he'd had in a long time. He hadn't fooled himself into thinking their marriage was a love match. That would surely have been impossible. He had hoped that within a relatively short time that would change. Now, if he wasn't careful, it would all slip through his fingers.

Suddenly Kate turned with a frown marring her delicate features. "They're here."

Kate forced herself to sit calmly on the settee as she waited for her siblings to come inside. She couldn't stop herself from peeking at the man sitting next to her. He nearly caught her sideways glance so she pulled her eyes away to let them land on the front door.

"Kate, calm down. We'll figure this out." His deep voice startled her but she covered her reaction to it.

"I know. It's just—"

Childish voices approached. The wooden door creaked open and Ellie appeared. Kate watched as the girl's gaze skimmed deliberately over her before moving on to the stranger. "Oh, Mr. Rutledge, I see you've made it. That's wonderful!"

Sean entered the room but paused at the doorway to cautiously take in the scene before him. Ellie glanced at her brother, seemingly for support, then smiled brightly. "What's for supper?"

Kate glanced at Nathan hoping to convey a message and he seemed to receive it for they both sat in silence. The silence drew all eyes to her. Once she had her siblings' attention she quietly commanded, "Sean, Ellie, sit down."

They moved to their seats, placing their lunch pails and slates on the side table. Neither would meet her gaze. Sean stared at the floor while Ellie looked off into a corner.

"Explain this," she commanded with a sweeping gesture toward Nathan.

Sean finally met her gaze. "It all started out as a misunderstanding. I thought you changed your mind when I saw the filled-out form. I asked if you wanted me to take care of it. You said yes. I mailed it the next morning before school. I didn't realize you just wanted me to stack those papers until much later."

She groaned. "Why didn't you tell me?"

"You told us never to mention it again," Ellie reminded, giving Kate a pointed look.

"I also told you not to send him any more letters."

"We didn't," Sean interjected. "We just sent that paper. He sent something telling us when he was coming. That was all."

She glanced up to find Ellie surveying her carefully. Her sister shot a glance at Nathan. "Did she try the ring?"

He lifted his eyebrows as an amused smile teased his mouth. "Somehow we haven't quite gotten to that part."

"That's too bad. Do you still think it will fit?"

He discreetly glanced at her ring finger. "It probably would."

Ellie nodded. "Can I see it?"

"May I," Kate automatically corrected, then frowned. "Ellie, don't you think there are more important things to discuss?"

"I was wondering." Ellie glanced between them. "Did you fall in love at first sight like Jacob and Rachel did in the Bible?"

Kate's mouth fell open. "Ellie, that's enough! This is serious. You've tampered not only with two people's lives but also with one man's emotions. He came all the way from who knows where—"

"Noches, Texas," he supplied.

"He shows up and defends me and our house, all the while thinking I'm his wife. A wife created by a ten- and a twelve-year-old."

Sean lifted his hand to speak. "Remember we just told him about you. We didn't make you up."

"And we didn't do it on purpose," Ellie interjected, then blushed. "Well, not this time."

Ignoring those statements, Kate continued firmly, "I want you to apologize to Mr. Rutledge for lying and interfering in his life before doing the same to me."

They looked properly ashamed, and humbly apologized before they went outside for their evening chores. Kate rose to heat up the food for supper. The clamor of the pans hitting the stove seemed jarring in the silence. Clearing her throat, Kate apologized, "Mr. Rutledge, I don't know what to say."

"It's Nathan," he said, his voice sounding closer than she anticipated.

She turned to look up into his dark brown eyes and persisted. "Mr. Rut—"

He smiled knowingly, then shook his head. "Nathan."

Frowning, she yielded. "Nathan, I guess the only way to get out of this would be to get an annulment."

He leaned back against the table. "Should we want to get out of it?"

"Of course we should." Her eyes widened. "Why? Don't you?"

His gaze slid thoughtfully over her face. "I don't know."

She placed her hands on her hips. "How can you not know? It's the only sensible thing to do."

"Sensible to me is this. You need a husband, I need a wife, and we're already married. Why not stay that way?"

She laughed. "You can't mean that."

His jaw tightened. "Just why can't I?"

"Because..." She wavered and he seemed to sense it. Why couldn't she stay married to him? It was too dangerous. He was too dangerous. She wasn't ready. She'd never even met him before today. It simply wasn't plausible. Yet she looked into his eyes and reason began to melt, along with her resistance.

"We can make this work," Nathan insisted. "I'm already fond of you and I have nowhere else to go."

She slowly shook her head. "I won't do this. It isn't fair to expect me to honor a commitment I never made."

He stepped closer. "You were willing to honor that commitment when you signed the affidavit."

"That was different."

"How?"

She bit her lip then admitted, "I needed a loan from the bank. The banker said he would only give it to me if I was married."

His gaze filled with a concern that strengthened into compassion. "I'm sorry to hear that."

"I never intended to send the affidavit because I decided to look for some other way—any other way. I pleaded with Mr. Wilkins to let me postpone the payments until after harvest. He agreed, with the understanding that if I don't make a payment after the harvest, the farm will immediately go into foreclosure. I planted more wheat than usual so I'm sure the harvest will be enough to keep the farm safe."

"In other words, you don't need me anymore and you'll risk everything you own to keep it that way." He paused, looking at her searchingly. "Why put yourself through that when it would be so much easier to go through with your original plan?"

She stiffened. "You're right. I don't need you. I have a plan and it's going to work. It may be hard, but I'm going to make it the same way I have for two years. That means without you or any other man getting in the way."

"So that's it? I sold my property back in Noches because you said you wanted the children to grow up here. All of that was for nothing?"

"I'm sorry, but I hope you realize that I never said any such thing."

"No, I guess you didn't." He took his Stetson from the table. Holding it in his hands, he nodded. "Sorry for the trouble, Ms. O'Brien. You'll get your annulment. I'll make sure of it."

Nathan slid the bridle onto Delilah's head, then glanced at the two children who watched him in disappointment.

"You're leaving," Sean said, more as a statement than a question.

"I'm afraid so."

The boy looked down. "You aren't coming back."

"I doubt it."

Ellie climbed onto the short wall that sectioned off Delilah's stall to stare at him with imploring green eyes. "Why don't you win her back?"

"You can't win something back you never had, Ellie."

She crossed her arms. "You didn't even try."

He *had* tried but Kate wasn't willing to do the same. If Ellie thought he was the problem, then so be it. He'd caused enough strife in his own family to know better than to start it in someone else's. Besides, Kate was probably right. He'd thought God was leading him to a new life, but this seemed to be just as much of a mistake as everything else he'd done lately—everything he was trying so desperately to forget.

He did his best not to let Ellie's glower bother him as he finished saddling his mare. He led Delilah from her stall. The children followed him in silence until Sean asked, "What are you going to do now?"

He glanced back and was surprised to see deep concern in the boy's eyes. Ellie seemed to have lost most of her defiance, because while her chin still tilted upward, her eyes looked suspiciously moist. He realized that even though he was nothing more than a stranger to Kate, her siblings probably felt they knew him well. In truth, they probably knew him better than anyone else in his life right now.

Impulsively he knelt to put himself on their level. "Hey, I hope you two aren't worrying about me. I'll figure something out. I always do."

Ellie's chin quivered. "We want you to stay."

"I know you do." He guessed he didn't have to tell them that things didn't always turn out the way you wanted. He figured they'd been through enough in their short lives to know that better than most. "I'm sorry I can't do that, but you two have each other and Kate. You'll be all right. Just remember to mind your sister. No more of this kind of stuff, you hear?"

They both nodded.

He stood and didn't bother to knock the dust from his britches before he swung onto Delilah. He glanced down to offer the pair parting smiles. "Goodbye, now."

A few minutes later he turned Delilah so that he could get one last look at the O'Brien's farm. The children had gone inside, so all he could see was the house and its fields. He swallowed against the unexpected emotion in his throat. He'd failed just like he always did when it came to chasing down his dream.

Hadn't his Pa told him this would happen? He tried to push away the memory of his father's parting words. He heard them anyway. "You're going to fail. You're going to come crawling back. Stay at the ranch and take your place like your brother. This is where you're supposed to be."

Turning Delilah back toward the main road, he urged her into a canter. It looked like his Pa had been right about him all along. It had just taken him five years to figure it out.

Kate swayed in her seat as the wagon jolted over a bump on the road to town the next morning. They were nearly to Peppin before anyone dared to bring up the subject foremost on their minds.

"I think you should ask him to come back," Ellie said, over the groaning wagon wheels.

"I'm sure I know what you think, Ellie." Kate's grip tightened on the reigns. "I've already made my decision."

"I liked him," Sean said.

"So did I," Ellie chimed in with a slight lift of her chin. "Didn't you like him, Kate?"

"I'm sure he's a nice man." She was sure because

she'd seen the way he'd knelt in the dirty barnyard to talk to her siblings before he left. The sight had touched her more than she cared to admit.

"And handsome?"

Kate glanced at her sister in interest. "Since when do you care about handsome?"

"I don't." Ellie recoiled then sent Sean a mischievous glance. "That's just what Lorelei Wilkins always says about Sean."

"Really?" Kate asked as Sean's face lit up like a red beacon.

"It is not," he protested.

"It is, too. I heard her at recess. She told all the girls how much you like her and how you'll get married one day."

"That's just because she's a dumb girl."

Kate arched a brow. "I hope you didn't tell her that."

"No, but I'd sure like to," Sean growled.

"I'm sure you would. Don't worry, Sean. She'll move on soon enough. In the meantime, try not to let it bother you."

He looked over at her. "I thought we were talking about you, Kate."

She feigned disinterest. "Not anymore."

He frowned as he surveyed the row of businesses on either side of Main Street. "Are you really going to get a whatever-it's-called?"

"An annulment? Yes. That's why I'm driving you to town to today."

That put a damper on the conversation until the children jumped off the wagon and called goodbye as they headed to the schoolhouse. Kate pulled the horses to a stop across the street from the town's small courthouse.

She stared at the gray wooden building and frowned. *Exactly how does one get an annulment?*

She didn't know but she was certainly going to find out. Filled with resolve, she discreetly swung her legs over the side of the wagon and hopped down. Her forward momentum suddenly stopped when her dress caught on the wagon wheel and caused her to stumble. She managed to catch her balance just as she heard shouts sound farther down Main Street. Curious to step over and see what the commotion was about, she worked to release her skirt from the splintery clutches of the wagon's axle. She pulled at the dark green fabric until she heard the sound of pounding hooves and a wild neigh behind her.

She glanced up to find a startled horse and struggling rider almost upon her. The man on the horse looked down. She took in the detail of his eyes widening before he yelled, "Get out the way!"

She gasped, then suddenly a strong arm snaked around her waist and she was slammed against the wood of the wagon. The force of a hard body pressing against her own knocked the wind out of her. Her breath came in ragged gasps. She heard the horse scream and a loud thump, then found herself struggling to hold up a limp and heavy body. Losing the battle, she sank to the ground along with the man.

She glanced up in time to see the terrified horse give one last turn and a swift kick in the air before galloping away, its rider also thrown to the ground. Her gaze flew back to the man whose body pinned her arm to the ground beneath him. Her sharp gasp rent the air as she looked into the handsome features of Nathan Rutledge.

She was close enough to see the golden flecks lighting his mahogany eyes when they fluttered open. He murmured her name, then his eyes drifted shut. His face went pale. She stared at him in disbelief. Surely he wasn't dead!

She cradled his head in her hand, then pulled her arm from beneath him to place her other hand over his heart. Though she couldn't feel its beat, she detected the slight rise and fall of his chest. Kate heard someone calling for help and realized it was her own strangled voice. Then arms were pulling her away and setting her aside as Doc Williams attended to Nathan.

She stared at the pale face and large form of the man sprawled in the middle of the street. A comforting arm came around her. She clasped her hands beneath her chin. Feeling something wet on them, she looked at her hands to see one mottled with blood. She stared at the traces, realizing it was Nathan's. Her body went cold and she began to tremble. Everything flashed black for a moment.

A voice she absently identified as Mrs. Greene's chided, "Now, don't you swoon, child. We already have one out let's not have another."

Gathering her courage Kate locked her knees, forcing the darkness away by the sheer power of her will. Then she fainted.

Chapter Three

Kate pulled in a cleansing breath as she stood at the window in Doc's waiting room. Her nose twitched as she remembered awakening to the acrid scent of smelling salts ten minutes ago. She heard gasps sound behind her. She whirled to find the sheriff and Mrs. Greene staring at her in astonishment. She looked from their faces to Ms. Lettie's pleased one and groaned. She never should have whispered the truth about Nathan's identity to the woman after waking up. "Oh, Ms. Lettie, you told them, didn't you?"

Ms. Lettie's eyes widened. "Don't tell me you wanted to keep the marriage a secret."

Mrs. Greene frowned. "You mean to tell me Kate is really married to that man?"

"I suppose I shouldn't have told you anything, but yes, she is."

"Goodness," the other woman breathed, placing a dainty hand over her heart.

Sheriff Hawkins frowned. "Wait just a minute. He acted like he was just passing through. Why didn't he tell me you two were married?"

"He is just passing through," Kate said, smoothing her green dress calmly. "And we're not staying married for long. Mr. Rutledge and I are getting an annulment."

Ms. Lettie gasped. "You're getting an annulment? Kate, whatever for?"

"Surely you didn't expect me to agree to this crazy scheme?"

"Why not? The man is nice, he's a Christian and he's half in love with you already," Ms. Lettie stated.

"He's a stranger! Even if he was completely in love with me, it wouldn't change anything. I don't need a husband. We are getting an annulment," she said with determination as she leaned her shoulder against the window sill.

"No. She's right, Lettie," Mrs. Greene said. "She's trying protect herself from getting hurt, as well she should. We all know what happened with that Stolvins fellow down at the saloon."

Kate glanced out the window hoping to hide the flush spreading across her cheeks. "That was before he sold the hotel to open the saloon."

"To think, he tried to convince you to marry him even after you found out he was only after the pittance your parents left. I'm sure he broke your heart straight to pieces."

"Hardly," she breathed in disdain. Perhaps it was a little true, but she'd never let on; especially not to Mrs. Greene. She lifted her chin and met the woman's prying gaze. "That was a long time ago."

The woman arched her brow. "Andrew Stolvins doesn't seem to think so."

"I'm sure I don't care what he thinks, but that has nothing to do with me getting an annulment."

"I was only complimenting you on keeping a level head in the matter." Mrs. Greene lifted a hand as though to ward off Kate's anger. "Really, you're a nice enough girl, I suppose, but your siblings are a handful. Especially Ellie. Why, every time I'm around that girl, she causes trouble. Sometimes I wonder if she does it specifically to annoy me. You can't really believe the man would stay once he's met them." She shook her head. "Why frankly, I don't think you'll ever be able to marry."

Kate's breath caught at the woman's rudeness. Her temper rose with the color in her cheeks but Ms. Lettie came to her defense. "Amelia, that's a horrible thing to say!"

"We've all thought it, haven't we?"

"No, we haven't," Sheriff Hawkins said.

"Certainly, we have. The girl is no great beauty and has a temper hotter than the Fourth of July. To make matters worse, she's saddled with two young children who aren't even her own. Why, her chances are slim to say the least. Now that she is married, it's really no great surprise to me that her husband is eager to leave."

Kate lifted her chin defiantly. "I'm the one who wanted the annulment. Not him. He wanted to stay."

"But he wouldn't stay long."

She shook her head incredulously. "How can you know that?"

"I know you and your family," Mrs. Greene said with a nod.

Kate felt her temper soar. "Please, don't talk about my family."

"Don't get angry, child. I'm agreeing with you.

You're doing the wise thing and it's better now than when an annulment isn't possible."

"Mrs. Greene, I could keep that man as long as I want," she said with more confidence than she felt. "The problem is I don't want him."

Mrs. Greene stood. "I saw that man and he's too much for you. Now, my Emily would be a right fine match for him in looks and temperament."

"Good. She can have him. Though there might be a small problem in the fact that he's still married to *me*."

"As you've said, that will soon be rectified."

"Kate, give the man a chance," Ms. Lettie insisted.

"I am not going to discuss this."

Doc Williams appeared at the door and cleared his throat loudly. "Kate, I need you to come with me."

Grateful for the interruption, she immediately stood to follow him but glanced back at the others with a beseeching look. "Please, don't tell anyone else about the marriage. He'll be gone soon and I'd rather not have everyone know."

Mrs. Greene nodded staunchly. "I wouldn't say a word about it. It certainly wouldn't do Emily any favors for everyone to know."

Somewhat comforted by their agreement, she followed Doc to Nathan's room. She stepped inside and immediately noticed Nathan's prone body stretching from one end of the bed to the other. He was still pale, though some color was beginning to return to his face.

"I think he'll be fine if we can bring him back to consciousness," Doc Williams said.

She frowned slightly. "We? But what can I do?"

"I'm hoping the sound of your voice might bring him back."

She looked at him in suspicion. “Why should it?”

“You’re the only one he knows in town—the only voice that will sound familiar. And even though he’s not awake, you’re probably in his thoughts. He was hurt protecting you.”

Kate stiffened. “That isn’t my fault. I could have taken care of myself.”

Doc sighed. “Kate, I didn’t agree with what Lettie was planning at first but she convinced me it was the best thing for you.” He shook his head. “I know you can take care of yourself. We all do. But you shouldn’t always have to. That’s what marriage is for.”

Kate sent him a knowing look. “Speaking of marriage, when are you going to get around to popping the question to Ms. Lettie? You’ve been courting over a year now. I’d say it’s about time.”

“I’ve been busy.” Kate knew that was the truth. Doc Williams had devoted himself to their town since his arrival fifteen years before. But now that the man had entered his forties, everyone was ready to see him nicely settled.

“She could help you with that. She is an expert in natural remedies and would be a good nurse.”

He frowned at her, though his eyes continued to twinkle. “I doubt even Lettie could find a natural remedy for busyness.”

“I didn’t mean—”

“You meant to distract me, but it won’t work.” He ignored her exasperated protest, to continue, “My marital status is not what matters at the moment. What matters is that however you became this man’s wife, you are exactly that—his wife. Regardless of what happens in the future, he needs you right now.”

Kate bit her lip as she gazed back at the doctor, then with a sigh she relented. "What do you want me to do?"

Doc smiled. "Just call to him, talk to him, anything for him to hear the sound of your voice."

Kate looked at Nathan a moment then moved to the side of the bed. "Nathan."

He didn't respond.

"Nathan." Her heart jumped. Did his eyelid twitch just the littlest bit? She glanced at the doctor who nodded encouragingly. She frowned thoughtfully. *If the doctor thinks there is a chance he might regain consciousness, then shouldn't I give it a real try?*

Wishing she knew his middle name, she commanded in a stern voice, "Nathan Rutledge, open your eyes this minute!"

She narrowed her eyes. Did he blink or had she?

Determined, she sank to her knees beside his bed. An idea hit her and she reached for Nathan's hand, feeling the rough calluses on his hard palm. She glanced at Doc Williams. He was watching her intently if not with some amusement. Glancing back to Nathan, she called in a helpless voice, "Nathan, save me. Oh, save me, Nathan."

His eyelashes drifted upward then closed again.

She looked at the doctor triumphantly. He smiled in return. Kate looked toward the closed door before lending an air of desperation to her voice. "Nathan, please help me. Help me, Nathan."

Caught in the throes of her theatrics, she threw her head back dramatically before dropping it on the bed beside his pillow. She let out a puff of air. There. She'd given it all she had and the man still wouldn't come out of his state. No one could say she hadn't tried. Now maybe she could leave.

Kate leaned back onto her heels to look at Doc Williams. "Doc, I really don't think this is going to work. Have you tried the smelling salts they used on me? I—"

She paused realizing the large hand in hers was squeezing back. Her eyes widened as she slowly turned to meet Nathan's gaze. Eyes more golden than brown stared back at her as his dark brows lowered into a frown. His voice was strong and clear as he responded to her cries for help. "You said you didn't want me, so why are you in my bedroom?"

She gasped, pulling her hands from his grasp.

He wasn't finished. "And what do you need saving from this time? Honestly, I can't seem to turn around without having to get you out of trouble."

"Never mind," she said as her gaze darted to the doctor whose lip twitched with suppressed laughter.

"Where am I?" he asked as he tried to sit up.

Doc stepped forward. "No sudden movements. That's good. Lie back down. Now, tell me. Does your head hurt?"

Nathan grunted. "Yeah, it hurts."

Kate slowly edged toward the door.

"How would you rate the pain?"

"Bad enough."

"That's to be expected since you were—" the doctor faltered as though trying to find the right words "—hit in the head by a horse about twenty minutes ago."

Nathan looked at the doctor in surprise. "I've been out for twenty minutes?"

More than ready to leave, Kate used their distraction to sneak quietly out the door.

* * *

Nathan's head pounded like the ground after a stampede. Actually, he felt as if *he'd* been the ground during a stampede, which wasn't too far from the truth. He'd never felt as much panic as when he'd seen that horse barreling toward Kate. Thankfully, that panic had turned into action so he'd been able to keep Kate from getting injured.

Where did Kate go? he wondered, glancing toward the door. It sure had been nice to wake up finding his hand in hers with her wide blue eyes watching him in astonishment. He frowned. Why was it that he always ended up snapping at the woman?

His mother would be ashamed. Snapping at a person was never allowed no matter how irritable, tired or in pain someone was. Heaven forbid if that snapping was directed at the more delicate one of Adam's ribs.

He wished the doctor would stop asking annoying questions and let him go. He'd only been awake a few minutes and he already had cabin fever.

The distinguished-looking doctor broke into his thought. "I'd like to observe you for a few days before I let you go."

Nathan grimaced. "Do you have to?"

The doctor frowned thoughtfully. "Well, you certainly can't be alone—someone will need to keep an eye on your condition. But I suppose I could tell Kate what signs to look for regarding the concussion."

Nathan waited as hope began to rise within him. Surely Kate wouldn't mind letting him stay in the barn a few days. The barn would be a much better place to rest than this tiny room in the doctor's house where he'd be poked and prodded and bored. The farm would have something for him to do. He might have to sneak around to do it but there would be something, anyway.

Doc nodded at some unsaid thought. "I just might let you go with Kate. I'll write down some instructions for caring for the wounds you have on your back and head. Make sure you show them to Kate. You'll need her help to change the dressing."

He frowned. "What type of wound did you say I have on my back?"

Doc didn't look up from his tablet and continued to write as he said, "You have some heavy bruising and a laceration. I think the hoof must have scraped you on the way down. The cut is long but thin. I think it will heal without stitches, but you'll have to be careful."

Doc ripped the page from the tablet and handed it to Nathan. "Make sure you change the dressing every day. I'll give you something to ward off infection but it won't be effective unless you keep everything clean."

"I'll be careful," Nathan promised as he tucked the paper into his right pocket. Now he only had to pray Kate would be like the Lord and extend mercy to help him in his time of need.

Two hours later Kate paused in the entrance of the barn, watching in disbelief as Nathan raked a pile of new hay into the stalls. "What do you think you're doing?"

He froze, then looked up guiltily. "The stalls needed fresh hay and I was in the barn anyway…"

She took the rake from him. Holding it in front of her threateningly, she said, "You are supposed to be resting not pushing hay around my barn."

"Yes, but—"

"Doc Williams gave me orders and I mean to follow them even if you won't."

He carefully took the rake from her as though afraid she'd wield it against him. Then leaning on it, he gave her a smooth half smile and drawled, "You get the prettiest little lilt of an accent when you're angry. Irish, isn't it?"

Kate narrowed her eyes. "Your charm doesn't work on me, Nathan Rutledge, so you'd better get into the house before I resort to speaking Gaelic."

"Yes, ma'am." He tipped his Stetson with a rakish grin and started toward the house, then turned to face her with a curious glint in his eye. "Did you tell Doc we were married?"

"Actually, we aren't really—" She stopped when he lifted a knowing brow. Instead, she settled for, "Ms. Lettie told him."

"Ah," he said as though enlightened. "Don't think you're stuck with me forever. When I get a chance, I'll head back into town and see about the annulment."

"Good." She watched him exit the barn and go inside the house, and shook her head. "He's an interesting man that Nathan Rutledge."

She looked to Delilah for support but the horse only stared at her. "You're sort of an odd one yourself but that goes back to him. Why would anyone name a perfectly good horse Delilah? Esther I might understand, but Delilah?" Kate extended her hand to Delilah slowly and attempted to stroke the horse's nose. The horse lowered her head. Her large nostrils flared, then she sneezed directly into Kate's hands.

"Oh, gross." Kate grimaced as she stared down at her slimy palm.

"Isn't that Mr. Rutledge's horse?" a voice chirped from behind her. She whirled to find her brother and sister watching her curiously. Her clean hand covered her heart. "You scared me half to death."

Sean spoke again. "Well, isn't it his horse?"

Kate looked away from their hope-filled eyes. "Yes. It's his horse."

Ellie stepped forward. "So he's staying?"

"No, he isn't staying. Well, he is," she amended. "But only for a short time. He was injured by a runaway horse so Doc asked me to keep an eye on him for a few days."

Sean grinned. "So he's here."

Kate nodded. "He's inside."

They whooped and took off running toward the house. Leaving her calling to the empty barn, "He won't stay long."

Kate could hardly keep up with the flow of conversation during dinner. Sean and Ellie were coming up with question after question about what it was like to be a cowboy. Nathan didn't seem to mind but his answers were becoming slower and his eyes seemed to hold the pain he disguised in his face. At the moment, he was smiling. "Of course I'll teach you to lasso."

Kate raised a hand to silence the celebration. "I hate to ruin your fun, but Nathan needs some rest. He's tired and I'm sure he's in pain. Why don't you two finish eating while I show him to the barn?"

Neither Ellie nor Sean protested, but instead looked at their newfound hero with concern. Kate lit a candle as the two said good-night to Nathan, who then stepped outside. She waited for the door to close behind them before apologizing, "I still don't feel right about you sleeping in the barn. What if you start feeling worse?"

"I'll be fine," he returned optimistically. "I've gotten over worse injuries than this."

At the barn, she turned to light a lantern hanging there. "I left a few blankets out here earlier for you. Is there anything else you need?"

He was quiet for a moment and she turned to find him staring thoughtfully at his boots with his right hand in his pocket.

"Nathan, are you all right?"

"I was thinking." He glanced up and shrugged. "I've bothered you enough. I don't need anything else."

"I'll have to bother you for a moment. Doc told me to check your eyes before you went to sleep," she explained.

He nodded and seemed amused though Kate couldn't fathom why. She simply ignored him and did as Doc had instructed her. She lifted the lantern so that it was near his eye level, then raised its wick until it was very bright. She waited as he tipped his chin down to give her a clear view of his eyes while she stared at what Doc Williams called his pupils.

They quickly grew smaller as the bright candlelight reached them. Finally, she lowered the wick to a small flame and watched his pupils widen slightly. She couldn't help noticing that he had beautiful eyes. They were coffee brown but tinged with gold with a slight ring of gold encircling his pupil. She took a quick step back.

Thankfully, he couldn't know that she'd gotten distracted by something as basic as his eyes' color. "They seem normal. How do you feel? Do you have a headache? Do you feel as though you're going to throw up or anything?"

He frowned. "I have a slight headache but my stomach is fine."

"Are you dizzy?"

"No."

She looked down. "Don't you think you should sleep inside for just this one night?"

"Kate, I'll be fine."

She frowned. "Well, if you're sure."

He nodded. "I'm sure. Thank you, Kate."

"Good night, then," she said, already stepping backward to leave.

"Good night," he returned sincerely.

She took another step backward, almost reluctant to pull from his warm gaze before she turned away. Reaching the door, she paused to glance over her shoulder at him. He smiled gently. Her lips tipped into an answering smile before she stepped into the warm night air.

She hadn't known he was coming, she hadn't wanted him to stay but somehow, oddly, it was nice to have him there.

Chapter Four

The stalks of wheat seemed to whisper to each other about the stranger she led through the paths of their uniformed rows. Kate tucked an escaping tendril behind her ear, then turned to look for Nathan. Why he cared to tour a farm he wouldn't stay at for more than a few days was beyond her.

Apparently he found it fascinating because he'd been lagging behind since they'd started. Every time she turned around he'd stopped to look at something new. If he didn't hurry up she'd be late starting lunch, which would probably put her behind on the chores for the rest of the day.

She spotted him a few yards away kneeling in the dirt to get a better look at the wheat head in his hand. She smiled at the confused frown that marred his face. "You really don't know much about wheat, do you?"

He glanced up, then slowly rose to his feet as though the movement pained him. No doubt that was a result of him throwing himself in front of the horse to save her. Maybe she should cut him some slack. She glanced up at the sky to gauge the sun and realized it was still before noon. She had more time than she thought.

"I grew up on a cattle ranch in Oklahoma so wheat and I haven't been much more than nodding neighbors," he said as stepped up beside her.

She glanced at him in surprise. "You're from Oklahoma?"

"I guess you thought I was from Texas." At her nod, he grinned. "I'll take that as a compliment. But yes, I grew up in Rutledge, Oklahoma, with an older brother and three younger sisters."

She stopped walking and turned to him with a suspicious smile. "Wait. You grew up in Rutledge. Does that mean your family owned the town?"

"That means my pa owned the land the town was built on. He was a cattle baron and he wasn't much interested in running a town." He took off his Stetson and fiddled with its brim. "He wasn't especially interested in anything else, either."

"I'm sorry," she said softly.

"For what?"

"You said 'he was.' I guess that means he passed away."

His confused frown lifted into an amused smile. "I should have said 'is.' He isn't dead. At least, he wasn't the last I heard."

"It sounds like it's been a while since then," she said as they continued walking toward the end of the field.

He put his Stetson back on. "My folks weren't pleased when I left for Texas to become a cowboy. I haven't heard much from them since then."

"That has to be hard."

He shrugged away her concern. "A man can get used

to almost anything, given the chance. It helped being on the trail. You get so caught up in being busy that it's easy to forget how alone you are."

"So that's what you did before you came here? You were a cowboy?"

He shrugged. "Nothing else worked out."

He was intentionally being vague and she knew it. She figured since he was living on her farm, she had a right to a real answer. "What didn't work out?"

He was quiet for a long moment, then turned to meet her gaze. "I met two brothers while I was on the trail. We became really good friends and decided to start a horse ranch. I was in charge of training the horses. I loved it. I thought I'd found my calling. Things were great for a while, then they turned bad—real bad. We lost the ranch. There's nothing left of it now."

She bit her lip. "That's what you meant about God scattering your plans to the wind, isn't it?"

"Pretty much."

"What happened to your friends?"

He frowned then tugged his Stetson farther down. "One of them died. The other one didn't end up being such a good friend after all."

"I'm sorry to hear that," she offered softly.

He gave a short nod in acknowledgment of her sympathy. "That's why your advertisement seemed Heaven-sent. I wanted a new life and there it was."

"You thought it was God's will."

"Yes, I did," he said, then shot her a half smile. "But, as you said earlier, I guess I was wrong."

She glanced at the fields thoughtfully. "You know, I can't hear the words 'God's will' without thinking about my parents' deaths."

"Why?"

"After they died, I can't tell you the number of people who tried to comfort me by saying that. 'It's God's will.' It became almost more of a cliché than 'He needed them in Heaven.'" She swallowed, then shook her head. "I remember thinking if that was God's will then I didn't want it."

"You were grieving," he reminded gently. "People think all sorts of things they don't mean when they're grieving."

Yes, but I meant it. She pulled her gaze from the field to meet his. The sympathy there unnerved her. What had she been thinking? She'd told a stranger more than she told her close friends. There was aura of warmth about Nathan that made it easy to talk to him.

It was like the feeling she'd had when they first met: an implicit knowing. It hadn't made sense then. Now she knew it stemmed from the information he'd received through the letters. He knew enough about her without her confiding even more.

They were both quiet for a while, then Nathan tilted his head to gesture toward the field. "How do you normally bring in the harvest? I guess it's nothing like herding cattle."

She smiled. "Probably not. The harvesters are coming in about a month. They have a big machine that goes through the field and cuts the wheat. After that they use another machine to separate the wheat from the hay. They'll take fifteen percent of our wheat as payment."

Nathan glanced at her in surprise. "They take fifteen percent of a crop this small? That seems like a lot."

Kate frowned at him. "First of all, this isn't a small crop. It's even larger than the one I planted last year.

Secondly, there isn't much I can do about the cost of the combine unless I want to use a scythe. It would take much longer for me to do it that way by myself. I wouldn't get it to the market on schedule."

"I see your point."

She glanced up at the sky, realizing she'd gotten distracted. "Speaking of time, I'd better get back to my chores."

"Can I help?"

"You can rest or go explore the farm by yourself." He looked frustrated by her statement but she pinned him with a look. "No working. Doctor's orders, remember?"

He caught her arm before she could turn away. "Before you leave, you should know I'm planning to go to town tomorrow to find out what needs to be done for the annulment. You might want to come with me in case there's something that can be done right away."

"That sounds fine. I have some supplies to pick up from the mercantile anyway. You can take care of the paperwork. Just come get me when I'm needed, and we might be able to finish this matter then and there." Strangely enough, she couldn't make herself smile at the thought.

As she walked away from him she realized she'd taken a dangerous step by finding out so much more about Nathan. He wasn't a stranger anymore. He was a man she could sympathize with. He had feelings, hopes and dreams that deserved respect. She was going to crush one of those dreams when she signed that annulment, but it couldn't be helped. She'd forget about the man she'd known for a few days. He'd forget about her and move on just as easily. That's all there was to it.

* * *

Nathan hit his Stetson against his leg impatiently, then leaned against the wall of the cramped waiting room of the only courthouse in a fifty-mile radius, fidgeting uncomfortably as the cut on his back started to itch. He hoped that meant it had already scarred over but he couldn't be entirely sure since he couldn't actually see the wound.

The note Doc had given him said to change the dressing every day but he hadn't done that because he couldn't reach it. He knew he was supposed to ask for Kate's help but he couldn't get himself to ask. He'd be long gone in a few hours anyway so it hardly mattered now.

He'd considered getting a job in Peppin, but that would mean seeing Kate and knowing she thought of him as nothing more than a mistake. Perhaps he should contact Davis Reynolds. The Rutledge and Reynolds families had been neighbors in Oklahoma. The Reynolds main crop had been cattle but they'd also maintained a beautiful herd of horses. As a teenager, Nathan had sneaked away to the Reynolds' farm to watch the ranch hands work with the horses. Eventually, Davis had recognized his passion, taken Nathan under his wing and taught Nathan everything he knew about raising horses.

Nathan's father had never gotten along with Davis and was chagrined to watch the man encourage what he called Nathan's goofing off. He'd begun to restrict Nathan's freedom more and more. The less freedom he had, the more he'd yearned for it. He dreamed of wandering the open plains as a cowboy. He'd longed for the chance to combine the skills he'd developed with horses with the knowledge that had been drilled into him about cattle.

When the Reynolds family had sold their ranch and decided to move to Texas, Nathan traveled with them. They parted ways not long after passing the state line. Davis made Nathan promise to send word if he ever needed anything. Now it looked as though he needed a new future—again. He'd be willing to settle for a new job.

He looked up as a small man with spectacles perched on the end of his nose stepped into the waiting room. "Who's next?"

"I am," Nathan said. He walked into the office to find shelves of books lined the wall while a large mahogany desk stood in the middle of the floor.

"Sit right down there," the man said before sitting behind the desk. "What can I help you with?"

Nathan sat, placing his hat on his knee. "I'd like to receive an—" His throat closed as he tried to get the word out. Clearing his throat, he tried again, "I'd like to find out how to receive an annul—annulment."

The man sat up in his chair. "Do you mean a marriage annulment?"

Nathan's affirmation was low.

The man took off his spectacles to clean them on his shirt. "Well, how about that? I don't remember the last time someone asked for one of those."

Nathan shifted his hat to his other knee.

Placing his spectacles back on his nose, the man peered over them. "I sure hope you aren't leaving some little lady high and dry."

He smiled ruefully. "No, it's kind of the opposite."

The man laughed in an almost cackling sort of way. "Well, how about that? Run you off, did she?"

He cleared his throat nervously. "Well, not exactly."

"I wouldn't take that from my little woman," the man said between laughs, then, taking a gasping breath, continued. "You shouldn't give up on one of those little spitfires. I've heard tell they're mighty fun to tame."

Nathan shifted in his chair, causing his hat to fall to the ground. He picked it up and placed it back on his knee. "So do you think you can give me one?"

"One what? Annulment?"

He began to grow impatient. *Isn't that what this whole conversation is about?* "Yes, an annulment."

The man removed his spectacles to wipe away his tears of laughter. "No. I don't think I can."

Nathan shot to his feet, then wished he hadn't when a searing pain ran across his back. Had he just broken the cut open? "What do you mean you can't? Why can't you?"

"Sit down, sit down. No use getting all excited about it."

Eyes narrowed, he carefully sat in the chair, ignoring the pain.

"I told you it's been a while since we've had to give one."

"Yes."

"Well, I've plumb forgot how it's done."

Nathan looked at him incredulously. "You've what?"

The man shrugged carelessly. "I can't remember for the life of me."

"But you're a judge. You can't forget things like that," Nathan protested.

"I'm no judge. I'm just his assistant." The man leaned

forward conspiratorially. "I mostly hand out forms and tell folks to come back later."

"His assistant?"

"I declare, there's an echo in here."

"If you're his assistant then where's the judge?"

"He's seeing to a case north of here, then he'll visit his family near Abilene. He has a pretty little daughter who had twins, can you imagine? Then his older son settled about ten miles from there—"

Nathan held up his hand to still the flow of words. "So how do I get my annulment?"

"Well, I don't rightly know. You see, even if I could trouble myself to remember how to do it, I'm pretty sure I wouldn't be able to make it legal. I suppose the only thing you can do is wait for Judge Hendricks."

"How long will that be?"

"Not sure."

"Any guesses?"

"I'd say about a month. He may decide to go an extra thirty miles and see his cousin. Then you're looking at two months, easy."

Nathan's jaw slackened. "Two months?"

"Maybe more. You see, there is always a chance someone else will call for a judge. There aren't many in these parts so he does a lot of traveling."

Nathan sighed. "So no one really knows when the man will be back."

"Oh, I know he'll come back. I just don't know when."

"That's what I just s—never mind. I don't suppose there a chance another judge might travel this way?"

The man paused thoughtfully, then shook his head

adamantly. "Probably not, seeing as this town has a judge."

Nathan frowned as he stood. "I guess you're right. I have no choice but to wait."

"It was a pleasure doing business with you." The man shook his hand.

Nathan walked out the door, barely hearing the small man call out, "Who's next?"

What was he going to do? Two months. Two long months!

After Kate's refusal he'd been able to put aside… well, to put aside Kate. After all, this was just one part in a long string of things that had gone terribly wrong. He'd dusted himself off from the latest fall in the dirt, literally; he fingered the sore spot on his head, and he'd told himself he'd just have to find something else.

For two whole months he would be reminded of everything that he'd thought he'd have. Every time he looked into Kate's eyes he'd have to remind himself that there must be something better or brighter waiting for him. There must be some reason that yet another dream, another hope had been deferred and had become only that—a dream.

"Rutledge, wait!"

Nathan paused and turned to find the sheriff hurrying toward him as fast as he could amble. "Sheriff Hawkins," he acknowledged in greeting.

"Rutledge, I have an idea," the man said eagerly. "Come with me."

The sheriff turned and headed toward the jail. *Not again,* Nathan thought as he followed the sheriff into the stone building. Upon entering it, his gaze was immediately drawn to the jail cells in the back of the room.

He swallowed, then quickly glanced away. His eyes landed on the little thief from a few days ago, prompting a wry smile. It was almost as though the child had never moved because he sat in the same off-to-the-side chair. He still wore the same sullen look of disinterest that unsuccessfully hid his obvious curiosity about what was going on around him.

The sheriff sank into the wooden chair behind the desk and motioned Nathan to sit down. "I've been bringing the boy here during the day and home with me at night but it unnerves the missus some. I was thinking on what I could do for the boy and it hit me."

Nathan waited as the sheriff let the tension build.

"You and Kate should take the boy."

"What?" Nathan exclaimed.

"You and Kate should take the boy. He could work in the fields and sleep in the barn with you. You two would only have to feed him and steer him in the right direction."

Nathan stared at the sheriff in disbelief. "We can't do that."

"Why not?"

Nathan glanced at the boy, who tried not to appear to be listening to the conversation. "It just isn't right. The boy should have a home if he doesn't already. Surely someone will want to take him in."

"Yes, but not everyone would be a good influence on the boy. He's been a thief and a drifter. All I'm asking is that you let him work as payment for the things he tried to steal. It will be a good lesson for him."

Nathan leaned across the desk to speak in a low tone. "If he's a thief, wouldn't he be a bad influence on Sean and Ellie?"

"No, those kids are strong. Their ma raised them right. Look at it this way, the O'Briens will be three good influences. Wouldn't three good influences cancel out one bad one?"

Nathan sat back in his chair, wincing just a tad when his back made contact with the wood. *If the boy and I harvested half of the field, Kate wouldn't have to pay fifteen percent off that. That would be a fair amount of money saved. The boy needs someone to turn his life around. Who knows why he's on his own?*

Nathan glanced at the boy, who'd dropped all pretenses and was eagerly listening to the conversation about his future. He couldn't be more than a year or two older than Sean. But by God's grace, life could have dealt him such a blow.

Nathan looked at the sheriff, who waited tensely for an answer. *Two months,* Nathan reminded himself. *All I can offer is two months,* and no more. Nathan's voice was low, hopefully too low for the boy to hear, as he said, "If Kate and I take him in, it can't be forever, understand?"

"Of course," the sheriff complied. "I'm just asking you to show him how to do good, honest work. Give him some sort of skill so he'll have something to fall back on other than stealing."

"And you'll look for a real family for the boy?"

"Yes."

Nathan blew air past his lips then shook his head before he stood. "I'll try to convince Kate but if she says no..." He shook his head again.

"I understand," Sheriff Hawkins said, rising quickly to shake his hand. "Thank you."

Nathan strode toward the door then turned to look

at the boy still watching from his seat. "What's your name?"

"Lawson," he responded clearly.

"Lawson what?"

The boy's hazel eyes watched him carefully. "It's just Lawson."

Nathan looked at him for a moment, then nodded. "I'll see what I can do."

Chapter Five

Kate carefully took inventory of the small pile of goods Mr. Johansen deposited on the counter. Something was missing. She checked her copy of the list. "Were you out of corn meal, Mr. Johansen?"

"No, I gave it—" The tall Norwegian lowered his thick blond eyebrows as he surveyed the counter. A grin bursted across his face. "I lost it. I will find it. When I come back, I will count the eggs you brought for me. I will be back in half a minute. Do not leave."

"Yes, sir. I'll be right here," she said then smiled when the man was quickly distracted by another customer. It looked like this was going to take a while. She placed her elbows on the counter and rested her chin on her hand as she watched Mr. Johansen conclude his business with the other customer and turn toward his storage room.

She wished the smell of those lemon drops behind the counter wasn't so strong and tempting. Her stomach let out a small rumble, reminding her she hadn't eaten since early that morning. Suddenly a tanned arm came to rest next to hers on the wooden counter. She tensed as a too-familiar voice called, "Johansen, grab me a few packs of that tobacco while you're back there."

Mr. Johansen glanced over and paused. His gaze bounced warily between Kate and the man beside her before he nodded. "I'll be right back."

Kate straightened and slid farther away from the man, hoping he'd take the hint. He didn't. "Kate O'Brien, why do you have to go around looking so pretty?"

She kept her gaze trained on her egg basket. "Andrew Stolvins, why don't you find some nice girl to settle down with and leave me alone?"

"How can I think about another girl when you're around?" He leaned sideways onto the counter to get a better look at her.

She dodged the hand that reached toward her, then turned to pin him with a cold gaze. "Don't."

He stared at her with predatory green eyes. "You're going to have to start being nice to me again."

He looked entirely too satisfied with himself. She narrowed her eyes. "What are you talking about?"

"It's amazing what you can find out in a small town if you ask the right questions," he said nonchalantly. "For instance, I heard your financial problems are so bad that you're going to lose the farm if this harvest isn't enough to stop the foreclosure."

"That's none of your business."

"I made it my business." He smiled smugly. "You see, I just bought the wheat combine and thresher from Mr. Fulsome. If you want your wheat harvested, you'll have to go through me now. I'm raising the rate three percent on each farm. I know you can't afford that so I'm willing to negotiate. What are you willing to bargain?"

Her fingers clenched the handle of the basket tightly. “I’m not bargaining with you. I’ll pay the same rate as everyone else.”

“How do you plan to pay me? You don’t expect me to accept these, do you?” He chuckled, then snatched one of her precious eggs from the basket. He held one in the air to inspect it. “They look like they’re worth a pretty penny but appearances are deceiving, aren’t they?”

“Put it back.”

He tossed it back and forth between his hands but his gaze never left Kate’s eyes. “What’s it going to be, Kate?”

The egg slipped from his clumsy grasp. Kate gasped and reached out for it but Nathan appeared from behind her to beat her to it. The egg landed safely in his cupped palm. He stepped between them to carefully deposit the egg in the basket, then turned to face Andrew Stolvins. “Is there a problem here?”

Andrew glared up at Nathan. “This doesn’t involve you.”

“If it involves Kate, it involves me.”

Andrew shifted to stare over Nathan’s shoulder at Kate. “Is that how it is now?”

Nathan answered for her. “That’s how it is. From now on, you’ll leave her alone. Is that clear?”

A tense moment passed in silence before Mr. Johansen emerged from the back room. The store owner apologized for taking so long. Andrew grabbed his tobacco and left. Kate let out a sigh of relief. Mr. Johansen looked perplexed but shrugged. “I guess I will add that to his account.”

Kate waited while Mr. Johansen totaled her order, then applied the credit for the eggs. She paid him for the rest and was finally ready to go. Once Nathan had her purchases settled into the back of the wagon he turned to meet her gaze seriously. "Do you want to tell me what just happened in there?"

"I'd rather hear what happened at the courthouse."

He nodded. "That's fair enough. You can tell me about that fellow and I'll tell you about the judge while we eat lunch at the café."

"I'm not paying for lunch at the café when I have food at home." She covered her stomach as it growled in protest. It would take at least another half hour to get home and it was already long past one.

Nathan grinned. "It's my treat. I may not be a cattle baron but I can afford to pay for one meal in the café while I'm here."

She didn't like the idea of him paying for her but perhaps this was his farewell lunch. He'd order the food, tell her what he'd learned, they'd sign the paper he must have folded away somewhere and finish the meal. He'd make a quick exit. It would be amiable and painless. They'd go their separate ways, which was exactly what she needed.

At first Nathan did exactly as she'd planned. He ordered. After that he didn't seem inclined to talk about his meeting right away. Instead, he asked about the man in the store. Kate sent him a quelling look. "First tell me what happened at the courthouse."

He shook his head. "I'd rather wait until we get our food so we won't be overheard."

"Oh," she breathed, then took a sip of her water. She didn't need privacy for her explanation. The whole town knew the story he wanted to hear. "That was Andrew

Stolvins. He courted me for a while two years ago, after my parents died."

Nathan's brows rose with interest. "He doesn't seem like the kind of man you'd want as a suitor."

"He was new in town. I was young and vulnerable. Andrew seemed like a nice, stable young man, so when he asked to court me I said yes." She shrugged. "Like you, I was convinced I was following God's will. For the first time in the six months since my parents' deaths, I was hopeful. I thought my life was finally turning around."

Nathan's gaze filled with concern. "That isn't what happened, is it?"

She shook her head. "I found out that Andrew wasn't the man I thought he was. Or, rather, Sean and Ellie spied on him enough to find out the truth. Andrew didn't want me. He wanted my inheritance."

She paused as their food arrived and waited until the waiter left, to continue. "When I found out, I broke off our relationship. It's lucky for him that I did, since my inheritance was hardly anything more than an expensive mortgage on the farm."

Nathan pulled the napkin away from his cutlery. "Why is he bothering you if you didn't have what he was really after?"

"My siblings weren't shy in telling the town what type of man Andrew really was. It hurt his reputation but it hurt his pride more. He's gone out of his way to make my life difficult since then."

"That's what I walked in on." He glanced around the café with a frown. "Why doesn't anyone stand up to this man and make him leave you alone?"

"I can handle Andrew Stolvins just like I handle everything else—on my own."

He looked at her carefully then gave a slow nod. "I think I understand."

"Good." She took in a deep breath then smiled. "Now, let's say grace, then you can tell me what happened at the courthouse."

"It seems we have run across a slight…problem," he said a few moments later.

"What kind of a problem?" she asked suspiciously.

He glanced around at the busy café. The room was loud and everyone seemed too involved in their own conversations to listen in on theirs, but he inclined his head to speak lowly. "Kate, we can't get an annulment. At least we can't for a month or two or even longer."

She stared at him in confusion. "What do you mean we can't? Why not?"

"There's no one to perform it."

"But didn't the judge—"

"He isn't here."

"I know that, but he left Mr. Potters in charge. Surely Mr. Potters can help us."

Nathan shook his head, stating dryly, "He doesn't remember how."

"I should have known," she said with a moan, then bit her lip thoughtfully as she searched for some other option. Unable to think of anything, she asked, "What do we do?"

He swallowed a piece of his chicken pot pie and shrugged. "We wait."

She pushed her green beans around on the plate, knowing he was right. "What will people think? I don't want to tell everyone we're married—it'll just make talk when you leave. But if you stay at the farm, there are sure to be questions."

"We'll tell them I'm your hired hand, but I agree. We need a chaperone."

"Where would we find a chaperone?"

"In jail."

She froze as he continued eating. "What?"

"Do you remember the little thief from a few days ago?"

"You mean the one who made off with your horse?"

"Yes, unless you know of a different one," he said with a grin. "The sheriff doesn't know what to do with him so he asked if we would consider taking him in."

"We can't! I feel for the child but I can hardly manage my brother and sister. How can I take on another child?"

"Sheriff Hawkins just wants to have him work a bit for us as a form of restitution. I was thinking, if the boy and I took on part of the harvesting, you wouldn't have to pay the harvesters for that part of the field. That would mean you get to keep more of your money."

She shook her head. "I can't let you do that."

"I'm not afraid of hard work and the boy needs a roof over his head and a new start. It'll be good for him to put in an honest day's labor."

"I couldn't just make the boy work. I would need to feed him, clothe him and get him into school. He'll have spiritual and emotional needs."

"You won't have to do it on your own. I'll take responsibility for him. He could live with me in that abandoned cabin not far from the farm. I'll pay room and board for us both."

"Well…" she wavered. How could she turn the needy boy away? What if no one else would take him in?

"I told the sheriff we couldn't take him in forever and he agreed to keep looking for a more permanent option. Besides, I'll be leaving in a few months. The boy should have a family by then."

"Fine. You convinced me." She pulled in a deep breath. "Now we'll just have to convince Ellie and Sean."

Nathan tugged his Stetson a bit farther down on his head as if that would shield him from the boy's wary stare. It didn't. He leaned back against the wood behind him and crossed his arms as he snuck a glance at the boy sitting in the back of the wagon. The boy's gaze shot away from him toward the schoolhouse where Kate talked with Sean and Ellie. Sean glanced at the wagon, then nodded soberly. Ellie crossed her arms looking less than convinced at whatever Kate was saying.

"Who are you?"

Nathan tipped his hat to look at Lawson. From the way the boy was staring at the schoolhouse, it appeared as though he hadn't even spoken. Nathan felt the hair rise on the back of his neck. "I'm Nathaniel Rutledge, but I go mostly by Nathan. You're Lawson, right?"

Lawson gave a stiff nod.

"Well, it's a pleasure to meet you, Lawson." He smiled wryly. "I mean without also meeting your friends, Smith and Wesson."

The boy didn't respond.

Nathan allowed the conversation to fall into silence for a few moments, then he couldn't help but ask, "How long have you been on your own, Lawson?"

"It's been two or three years the best I can figure."

Two or three years ago the boy would have been ten

or twelve. That was certainly no age to be forced to fend for himself. "That must have been mighty hard."

Nathan glanced at him to find the boy looking in the opposite direction, seemingly intent on studying their surroundings. Nathan cleared his throat. "Do you know where we're going?"

"We're going back to the farm where you shot at me."

He raised his brow. "I shot at you? I remember you did a fair share of shooting yourself."

Lawson looked at him with a frown. "You hit my hat and busted a hole clean through it."

Though he inwardly smiled at Lawson's first real display of emotion, Nathan frowned back at him. "You stole my horse. I think we're square."

"You got it back, didn't you? 'Sides I didn't shoot him," Lawson grumbled.

"Good thing you didn't, either," he said dryly.

Lawson turned indignant. "I wouldn't shoot a horse, mister. My ma taught me right from wrong."

"I suppose that's why you went around stealing, too."

"Better stealing than begging," he said. There was a short silence before the boy spoke again. "Since you killed my hat I think you ought to give me yours. That would make it an even trade."

Nathan chuckled, then pulled the article more firmly onto his head. "No."

Lawson frowned, then looked past Nathan to where Kate was still talking with her siblings. Ellie shrugged and gave a long-suffering sigh. Kate turned to send them a victorious smile.

"Who are they?"

Nathan tensed in surprise, then turned to find Lawson sitting much closer than he had been earlier. "The young lady is Kate O' Brien. You have her to thank for letting you stay at the farm. The other two are her little brother and sister."

"Are you two sweethearts?"

He watched Lawson curiously. "Not quite. Why?"

The boy shrugged. "You've been watching her the whole time."

"I was not."

Again, the boy shrugged then settled farther away. Kate led her siblings toward the wagon and introduced them to Lawson. For a moment everyone under the age of fifteen stared at each other. Sean broke the uncertain silence with a friendly grin. "I won a new marble today. Do you want to see it?"

Lawson nodded hesitantly. Sean lifted Ellie into the back of the wagon, then climbed in after her. Ellie frowned. "You didn't show me the marble when I asked earlier."

"You know I couldn't take it out in class. I'll show it to you now." Sean settled next to Lawson and pulled Ellie down beside him.

Kate smiled as she stepped up beside him to whisper, "I'd say that went pretty well."

"Ellie didn't seem to like the idea."

She rolled her eyes. "It wasn't personal against Lawson. She just didn't want to add another boy. She said we're overrun with them now."

He laughed. After helping her into the wagon, he started down the road to what would be his temporary home. But only for the next two months, he reminded himself. This home, this growing family was only his for the next two months. He couldn't let himself get too attached, or it would hurt to leave them behind.

He ignored the sinking feeling in his gut that told him it was already too late.

The first few stars began to twinkle in the huge Texas sky as Nathan and Lawson made the short walk to the cabin that evening. Lawson trudged beside Nathan with his head down. Occasionally he'd glance up at the woods around them and each time his face seemed to grow more troubled. "Is something on your mind, Lawson?"

The boy ducked his head again. "I was just thinking."

"About what?" Nathan prompted when it became obvious the boy wasn't going to continue without some prodding.

Lawson glanced up to survey him with a measuring stare. "How did you end up here?"

Nathan smiled wryly. "That's a pretty complicated story. It all started when I saw this advertisement in the paper—"

"No, I didn't mean here as in 'this place.' I just meant..." Lawson's words stumbled to a halt. His gaze searched the forest as if the words he needed were written in the trees. Finally he turned back to Nathan. "I've never had this before."

Nathan had never felt more confused. "Had what? Supper?"

"Yes. I've never had supper in a house with people who acted like I mattered." Lawson rubbed the furrows in his brow. "I don't usually talk to people much, but I don't know how long I'll be here and I need you to tell me something."

"I'm listening," Nathan said quietly.

"I don't know much about who you are to that family. Maybe you're just a hired hand, but you fit, Nathan. You fit it there with them and I want to know how you did it." Lawson swallowed, then continued urgently, "I want to know what made you the kind of man who can fit in a family."

Nathan met Lawson's gaze for a long moment, then he turned to look at the farmhouse. Light danced cheerily out the windows. The house looked worn in a lived-in sort of way that made it feel like a home. A home he'd thought would be his. Lawson thought he fit there. He didn't, but telling Lawson that wouldn't really answer the question so he said the one thing that came to his mind.

"Choices." He turned back to Lawson with a helpless shrug. "I guess somewhere along the way, I made enough good choices to cancel out the bad ones."

"What kind of good choices did you make?"

"I decided not to let the mistakes I've made in the past define who I am in the present. I decided to be honorable even when those around me aren't." Nathan paused. He wondered if he should continue but Lawson's rapt attention urged him onward. He wondered if this was the first time anyone had told the boy that he could decide what kind of life he wanted to lead. Perhaps the Lord had arranged everything just to bring them to this moment. "I decided to admit that I wasn't a good man."

Lawson's rapt expression turned into pure shock. "You aren't?"

He shook his head. "We all fall short of being completely good. It's when we admit that we aren't good enough by ourselves that we can finally make the best choice of all."

"What's that?"

"We can choose to let God cleanse us of our sins by simply asking Him to do it. As soon as we allow that to happen, He makes us good and fits us into His family, joined together by faith. It's just like how members of the same family have the same blood. The same spirit that would be in you is in everyone else who has ever believed. I believe, so if you decided to do the same then that would make us brothers, in a way. Does that make sense?"

"Yeah, it does. I guess it's something to think about."

Lawson began walking away, so Nathan figured their discussion was over. Once they reached the cabin, Nathan hung his Stetson on the bed post and sat on the lone chair in the cabin to take off his boots. "That was a pretty deep discussion when I don't even know your last name," he said teasingly.

Lawson scrubbed his face, neck and arms with water from the pitcher and bowl, then blotted his face on his shirt before he deigned to respond. "My parents moved to Nebrasky Territory when I was little. Ma said it'd be best if I didn't come because she'd rather see me gone than bleeding from a beating. That's why, as far as I'm concerned, I don't have a last name."

It seemed wrong to delve into platitudes after all the things the boy must have been through so Nathan simply said, "Fair enough."

"What about you? I bet your family was nothing like mine."

"I came from a loving family, but we had our own problems."

"What kind of problems?"

Nathan placed his boots by the side of the bed then

admitted, "My pa cut me off not long after I left home. I haven't heard from my family since then."

Lawson frowned. "Why did he cut you off?"

Nathan shrugged. "We both wanted to run my life. I wouldn't let him. He got mad when I tried to do it myself."

"That's it?" Lawson scoffed. "You let him cut you off from your entire family because of that?"

"I can't make them take me back. In my family, whatever Pa says, goes. The rest of us have little choice but to go along with him."

"When was the last time you tried to contact them?"

"I gave up a long time ago."

"Try again." Lawson leaned forward in his bed. "They're your family. You can't just let them walk away. You have to stop them. You have to get them back."

"I'll think about it, all right? Now, it's time to sleep. It will be an early morning for both of us." He leaned over and blew out the lantern.

Placing his hands beneath his head, he replayed Lawson's words in his mind. What was it about families that made them so hard to hold on to? He'd already lost two—the one he'd been born into and the one he'd chosen for himself. His heavy sigh turned into a silent prayer. He asked God to bless them all and maybe, if He thought it best, to let him hold on to at least one.

Chapter Six

Kate gave the pancake batter one more stir as she waited for the stove to warm up. She heard the front door fly open followed by the familiar sound of loud, clomping boots. Ellie appeared in the doorway breathless and grinning. "You have to see this."

Kate stared at her sister in amusement but shook her head. "I need to fix breakfast. Why don't you just tell me?"

Ellie's eyes widened in desperation, then she surged into the kitchen and grabbed Kate's sleeve. "Believe me, breakfast can wait."

Kate decided it was probably in her best interest to find out what Ellie was so excited about. Especially since she was out the door and being pulled toward the barn before she could protest. Sean was waiting by the door with a smile on his face. Kate frowned as she stepped inside. "What is going on?"

Ellie pointed toward the stalls. "Look." She pivoted toward the cows. "Look." She turned in a circle. "It's all done."

"What's done?"

“The chores,” Sean explained from his spot near the door.

“Every single one,” Ellie said as she stopped spinning and held her hands out to regain her balance.

“Almost every single one,” a deep voice said behind them. Kate turned to find Nathan entering the barn with a large bucket of water in his hand. Lawson followed with another. “We needed more water for the horses.”

“You did everything,” Kate said more for her own benefit than anyone else’s.

Sean chuckled then shot Nathan a smile. “She’s a little slow in the mornings.”

She flashed Sean a glare, then glanced around the barn with new eyes. She noticed the full grain bins, the fresh hay in the stalls, the curried horses, the full pails of milk covered in cheese cloth and she didn’t like it. She didn’t like it one bit. It gave her a strange feeling in the middle of her stomach. It felt like dependency.

Nathan handed the bucket to Lawson, then tilted his head to survey her face carefully. “You don’t look happy.”

Ellie bounced toward them doing a little jig. “I’m really happy. I hate chores. Thank you. Thank you.”

Sean stepped forward. “What do we do now?”

“I guess we eat breakfast,” Kate said, then led them all back into the kitchen. After everyone had a plate of pancakes she filled Sean’s and Ellie’s lunch pails. She set them aside and started pumping water into the sink. Maybe she could get a head start on the dishes.

“Kate.”

She was startled to find Nathan standing beside her. The kitchen was noisier than usual so she hadn’t heard him approach. “Did you need something?”

"We're waiting for you, to start eating. Where's your plate?"

She glanced over her shoulder to find the children's plates untouched. They didn't seem to care because Ellie was retelling a story of some mishap with Mrs. Greene, but Kate caught her breath. "Oh, you didn't have to do that. They need to eat. I'll eat—"

"A biscuit later?" he asked.

"How did you know?"

"It took me a while but I caught on." He sent her a knowing look. "Are you trying to save time or money by not eating breakfast? I guess it's probably a little of both, right?"

She narrowed her eyes at him. "I don't see how my eating habits are any of your business."

He smiled as though he wasn't intimidated by her bluster in the least, then he nodded toward the table. "Eat with your family, Kate. Sit down and say grace. Take my plate. I'll fix myself some more."

"Fine." She complied more for the time she'd save from not arguing than anything else. As she slid into the seat he'd vacated she said, "Please, bow your heads for grace."

Sean frowned at her. "Kate, we never say grace at breakfast."

She bit her lip but refused to allow her eyes to move guiltily toward Nathan. "I guess we'd better start then." She bowed her head. "Lord, thank You for providing this meal. We are truly grateful for another day. May this day be blessed as we live it in Your presence. Amen."

Everyone echoed her amen. The conversation lagged as they began to eat. Nathan slid into the seat across from her with a modest pile of perfectly round, perfectly golden pancakes on his plate. They almost looked better than the ones she'd made. She hid her frown by taking another bite.

Ellie slid closer to quietly say, "Kate, we're using all the chairs again."

It took a moment for Kate to realize what her sister meant. When she finally did, her entire being stilled and she glanced around the table. Ellie was right. They were using all the kitchen chairs again—even the two that had been vacant since their parents' deaths.

She swallowed a lump of pancakes, then glanced at the two men filling the seats. The one to her right could hardly be called a man. He wasn't much older than Sean but from what she had heard, he was just as much an orphan as they were. Her heart broke a little each time she saw the cautious world-weary look in his eyes. He hesitantly took a biscuit from the plate in the center of table, then glanced around to see if anyone minded. She caught his gaze and sent him an approving smile. He offered a cautious one in return before returning to his meal.

She glanced past him to the man sitting across from her. He was saying something that made the children laugh so hard they could hardly eat. Kate stared at her plate and had to bite her lip to keep from speaking out. She wanted to remind them that this situation wasn't going to last forever. They wouldn't always have someone to do their chores or teach them to lasso or give them rides on a half-wild horse.

Nathan was leaving and it would be best if they remembered that. In the meantime, she hoped he would live up to the hero worship he was receiving. They had already learned the hard way that not everyone could be trusted and villains easily masqueraded as heroes.

Nathan didn't have to look up from his plate to know Kate was seething. He could literally feel the heat of her glare from across the table. He rubbed the moisture from his forehead as he reminded himself that he was prepared for this and knew exactly what he was going to do about it. He used the last few minutes of breakfast to remind himself of what he needed to say. When Sean and Ellie grabbed their lunch pails and left for school, Nathan caught Lawson's gaze and cut his eyes toward the door. Lawson gave a short nod then murmured something about needing to do something in the barn before he slipped out.

They were alone. Kate refused to meet his gaze as she gathered the dishes and set them in the sink. He watched her pump the faucet with a bit too much force and realized it was now or never. He winced at the pain that raced across his back as he stood to carry his plate to the sink.

Oddly, the room seemed to sway so he gingerly leaned against the nearby counter. "Kate, I think we need to talk."

She whirled toward him and lifted her chin in defiance. "So do I."

"As your hired hand, I'd like to go over my job responsibilities with you. I figured it would be best for me to take over the bulk of the barn chores. I did them all today just to give everyone a nice surprise but I guess you'll probably want Sean and Ellie to retain some of their responsibilities there."

He'd managed to regain his equilibrium and he

waited with baited breath to see if he'd pulled the right bee from her bonnet. She began to speak then stopped. Her chin lowered just a tad. "Yes, that's exactly what I want."

He didn't dare give the sigh of relief he wanted to, but instead allowed himself a serious nod. "Good. Just let me know what to leave for them."

"I will," she said almost reluctantly, then turned to sprinkle soap on the dishes.

"I thought you'd also want me to take on most of the outside chores." He hid a smile at the suspicious gaze she leveled on him. "I may not know much about wheat but I'm a quick learner. I hope you won't mind teaching me."

She bit her lip. "I suppose I won't."

"While I'm here, I figure I might as well make repairs to whatever might need fixing. Why don't you make a list for me with the most important ones first? I'll take care of those, too."

She frowned and he sensed she wanted to resist but she gave him a short nod. "I'll have it ready for you tomorrow."

He swallowed, knowing that if she was going to balk it would be about this next part. "The Bible says if you don't work, you don't eat. I figured Lawson and I are working for our food."

He reached into his shirt pocket and pulled out a folded-up envelope. He handed it to her. She looked at it in confusion. "What's this?"

"That's for our rent," he said.

She frowned, then opened the flap of the envelope and looked inside. Her eyes widened. "Nathan, you don't have to do this. You're already paying by working for me."

"You didn't think I expected to stay here for free, did you?" He placed his hands in his pockets when she tried to give the envelope back. "Count it. Make sure it's enough for the first month."

"Nathan, you really don't have to do this."

"I already did. Now, why don't you tell me what's on your schedule today? Lawson and I will need to know what you want us to do."

He waited through the long moment of silence, then watched as Kate slipped the envelope into her apron pocket. "I've never had a hired hand before."

He smiled but tried not to show his relief as she went over the day's schedule and told him what she needed him to do. Keeping the farm was obviously important to her. All of her hard work was meant to take care of her siblings and preserve her parents' legacy. He might not have gotten the future he'd hoped for, but maybe he'd be able to help Kate get hers.

The next day, Kate stilled at the sound of someone shouting her name. She slipped the potato seedling into the ground and covered it with soil before shifting on her knees toward the sound. Lawson stood near the edge of the field waving at her. She waved back in confusion for a moment before she realized he wasn't really waving. He was beckoning her.

She set her garden trowel on the ground and wiped her hands on her apron as she stood and hurried toward him. "What's wrong?"

Fear etched across his features as he led her into the field. "Something is wrong with Nathan. We were working and he suddenly knelt down and now he can't seem to get back up. I think he must be sick."

Kate spotted Nathan a few yard ahead of them. He sat on his knees with one hand braced on the ground in front of him while the other rubbed his forehead. "Nathan."

He glanced up at her and grimaced. "I told Lawson I'd be fine in a minute. It's just a headache."

Lawson placed a hand on Nathan's shoulder. "Did you throw up like you said you might?"

Kate let out a frustrated breath. "Obviously it isn't just a headache." She knelt beside him. She was close enough to notice he was sweating profusely. Narrowing her eyes, she gently moved his hand out the way to feel his forehead. "You're burning up with fever."

He groaned. "I don't know what's wrong. I was fine earlier, but now I feel too weak to even stand up."

"We'll help you," she said then glanced over Nathan's bent head to Lawson. "We need to get him into the house. You take one side and I'll take the other."

He nodded then slipped his arm around Nathan's back. She did the same. On the count of three they helped Nathan to his feet. He immediately let out a cry of pain. Her worried eyes lifted to his pain-filled gaze. "Is it your head?"

"No, it's my back," he bit out as he walked between them. "Doc said it would heal on its own but it hurts."

"Wait. What's supposed to heal on its own? I thought you just had a concussion."

He grimaced guiltily. "I didn't tell you. When the horse reared…one of its hooves…hit my back. It cut the skin."

"Why didn't Doc tell me?"

"I was supposed to…but I didn't want to bother you. I thought I was leaving. I tried to clean it on my own." He swallowed harshly. "If I keep talking I might get sick."

She glanced at Lawson in time to see the boy's eyes widen. "Then don't talk."

They helped him into the house, then into Sean's bed. Lawson pulled off Nathan's shirt while Kate prepared a cool cloth for his head. When she stepped into the room again Nathan was under the covers but his back lay exposed. She took one look at the cut and grimaced before meeting Lawson's gaze. He frowned. "It's infected, isn't it? That's why he's sick."

She nodded then pulled a chair close to the head of Sean's bed. "I need you to go in to town and bring Doc. If you can't find him, bring Ms. Lettie."

"I think I know how to get to town but I don't know who those people are."

"Oh," she breathed. "You know who the sheriff is, right? Ask him to help you. Take one of the horses."

"You can take Delilah. She's faster," Nathan muttered, then passed his hand over his forehead again. "Tell her I sent you."

Kate and Lawson exchanged a confused glance before he hurried out the door. Kate laid the cool cloth over his head. She knew Doc would want to clean the wound so she decided not to mess with it. There was really nothing she could do but wait and try to make Nathan as comfortable as possible. He groaned. "I'm sorry, Kate."

"You don't have to apologize to me. Why don't you just close your eyes and rest until Doc gets here?" She watched as he smiled faintly then closed his eyes. She began to pray.

* * *

Nathan strained toward the voices edging in and out of his consciousness. Every so often they called to him but he could never reach them. The heat engulfing his body stood in stark contrast to the streaks of cool relief that intermittently traveled from his brow to his chest or back. He slowly slipped further away from the sweet familiar voices as the whisper of haunted memories filled his mind.

Nathan. Nathan.

Eli, he breathed then spun to face the desperate whisper.

Eli backed away. His were eyes filled with panic. His appearance was disheveled. His hand crept toward his holster. *Let me go, Nathan.*

You know I can't do that. Stay, Eli. Stay.

A struggle, then the room exploded in sound. He dropped to Eli's side but it was too late. Blood spilled on the floor and covered Nathan's hands. He couldn't get it off. It spread until it was everywhere. There were traces of it on his arm, streaks of it in his hair. The smell of it sickened him. *Get it off,* he demanded.

He heard a gasp and the heat increased. Pale faces stared back at him in disbelief, then condemnation. *You did this,* they whispered. *Murderer. Murderer.*

"No." They wouldn't listen. They were trying to restrain him. They were trying to lock him up. He had to get out. "Let me go. I didn't. I didn't do it."

"I believe you."

He stilled. He turned toward the voice. It was out of place. He knew this nightmare well. That wasn't what happened next.

He suddenly became aware of his labored breathing. He turned toward the cool hand on his cheek, then forced his eyes open. Deep blue eyes stared back at him from the prettiest face he'd ever seen.

"Say it again," a young voice whispered from behind him.

"I believe you," Kate said.

Calm enfolded him and he closed his eyes but braced himself. The nightmares would return. There was nothing he could do to stop them.

Chapter Seven

Kate watched as Nathan's face relaxed into more peaceful sleep. Her gaze lifted to the children who stood at attention on the other side of the bed. Lawson and Sean had tried to help restrain Nathan's wild thrashings but nothing had calmed him until she'd said those words. Sean watched Nathan soberly. "What do you think he didn't do?"

"When people are delirious they say a lot of things that don't make sense," she said. "I'm sure it's nothing to worry about."

They nodded as though they accepted that as fact. She wasn't so sure. He'd mentioned something about a man named Eli and muttered something about blood before she'd had to call for reinforcements. He might have just been having a random nightmare. He also might have been reliving some event in his past—but she couldn't tell the children that without scaring them.

Ellie leaned against Sean while tears of concern filled her eyes. "You should hold his hand. When I'm sick, I always feel better when you hold my hand."

Kate reluctantly covered Nathan's hand with hers to

make Ellie feel better. To her surprise, his hand tightened around hers. She looked at him more closely but he still seemed to be sleeping so she left her hand in his. "It must be after ten o'clock. Ellie and Sean, you need to go to sleep so you can be ready for school in the morning. Sean, you can bunk with Ellie. Lawson—"

"I'd like to stay in here with you, ma'am. I can help keep watch." He pulled a chair to the side of the bed and took his seat when she nodded her approval.

"I think he's starting to get better," Sean said as he guided Ellie toward the door.

Kate nodded. "He might be over the worst of it. You two try not to worry. Get some sleep."

Nathan turned his face away from the warm sunlight and opened his eyes. Ellie sat in a chair beside the bed, toying with her hair as she read the book in her lap. A sound from the other side of the room caught his attention and he turned to see Sean showing Lawson how to carve small figures out of wood. Sean met Nathan's gaze and his eyes widened. "Look. He's awake."

Nathan watched the three children crowd around the bed. "What happened?"

"You almost died," Ellie whispered cautiously as though saying the words might somehow change his fate.

Lawson leaned closer. "I rode to town and brought Doc back. He took a long time cleaning your wound. He gave you medicine, too."

"How long have I been lying here?" he asked groggily as he tried to sit up on his side.

Sean placed a restraining hand on his shoulder. "Since yesterday and Kate says you aren't allowed to get up. She and Lawson stayed with you all night so she's taking a nap right now. We're supposed to tell her if you wake up."

"I'll do it." Ellie set the book she'd been clinging to aside, then patted his cheek. "I know you'll do the right thing."

Nathan watched in confusion as she sent the boys a meaningful look then slipped out the door. "What's she talking about?"

"We think you should write to your family," Lawson said.

Nathan's head started to pound. He was trying to figure out what his family had to do with this but he couldn't. Unless… "You think I'm still going to die."

Sean looked startled. "No, that's not it at all."

"Kate mentioned that she wouldn't know how to notify your family if anything worse had happened," Lawson said. "Sean and I decided that when you woke up he should tell you something." He prodded Sean forward. "Go on."

Sean gave a nod then pulled in a deep breath before he began. "I don't talk about my parents much. I reckon you know they died in an accident when I was ten. One day they were here. The next day they were gone and there was nothing I could do to bring them back." He swallowed then gestured to the bed. "You still have a chance to make things better with your family but you never know when something like this will happen to take that chance away."

Sean ducked his head then lifted his gaze to Nathan's. "That's why I couldn't hold my peace until you got better. You ought to send a letter to them. It's important." His gaze slid from Nathan's to the doorway. "It's so important I risked Kate's wrath to say it."

Nathan followed Sean's gaze to where Kate stood in the doorway. She didn't look angry. Instead her eyes glittered with unshed tears. She lowered her gaze for a moment, then met his to see how he would respond to Sean's speech. He almost sighed but it turned into a cough. Ellie slid past Kate to hand him a cup of water. He thanked her with a smile, then pulled in a deep breath. "I guess if you can risk Kate's wrath, I can risk my pa's."

"You should do it because you want to, not because you feel pressured," Kate gently cautioned.

He shook his head. "No, they're right. There's no harm in trying again. Maybe this time will be different."

He wanted to believe it would be different. He didn't see how it could but glancing around at the children's young hope-filled smiles he knew he had to try. He prayed this time that it would be enough.

An eerie howl pierced the night and Kate almost shivered at the sound of it. It was a week after Nathan agreed to send the letter to his parents. During that time he'd managed to gain back most of his strength and grow closer to the children. So much so that Sean had begged to spend the night roughing it in the cabin with Nathan and Lawson.

Another howl split the night. If they didn't settle down soon she might just go out to the cabin and put a stop to their antics. *You have ten minutes, boys. Make the most of it.*

She pulled the bed covers closer to her chin and snuggled into the pillow as a satisfied smile curved her lips.

She was sure one of those howls belonged to Sean. It was good to hear him having fun and acting like the child he still was. The same went for Lawson. He'd told her a bit about what he'd been through before he'd shown up on her doorstep. Survival had been his aim and having fun probably hadn't been anywhere on his agenda.

She couldn't speculate about Nathan. He hadn't mentioned anything about the delusions he'd experienced during his fever. She'd be tempted to believe that the words he'd mumbled were meaningless if he hadn't seemed so shaken after his sickness. Every once in a while she'd catch a haunted look in his eyes that she hadn't noticed before. Maybe it had been there all along and she just hadn't been looking.

She sighed. Her original resolve to forget Nathan as soon as he left now seemed ridiculously naive. He'd only been at the farm for two weeks but he'd managed to become almost like family to her little brother and sister. It was obvious they were craving male attention. The same attention she'd tried so hard to avoid since her run-in with Andrew Stolvins.

Her fist clenched the edges of the pillowcase. That romance had ended in complete disaster, yet the whole time she'd been so sure she was following God's will. Either she had been mistaken the entire time or God had led her down the wrong path on purpose. She wasn't sure which it was but both options were frightening.

That was why she needed to be careful when it came to Nathan. She was attracted to him, she could admit that. She just couldn't allow her feelings to go any further. She didn't want to end up in the same mess she'd gotten out of with Andrew Stolvins.

Just then another howl sounded through the air. She pushed her troublesome thoughts from her mind. Maybe she couldn't howl at the moon, but she didn't want to lie in bed agonizing about the past when she should be sleeping. The mattress dipped on Ellie's side and Kate heard footsteps. She turned over to see Ellie walking quietly toward the stairs.

"Where do you think you're going, young lady?" she asked.

Her sister froze. The room was silent until another howl pierced the air. As if that released Ellie from her spell, the girl turned to face Kate. "It isn't fair. They're having all the fun."

Kate stared at her sister. "What do you suppose we do? Go trooping through the weeds at nearly ten at night?"

"Yes." Ellie's eyes grew larger and more pleading.

"Ellie, you know we can't do that. The cabin is too far away."

Ellie hung her head. "I knew you'd say that."

Kate felt guilt creep up and overtake her. Since her parents' deaths she'd been so focused on surviving that she hadn't really thought about fun. Was that why Ellie felt the need to create her own fun even at the expense of others like Mrs. Greene? She sat up, then slid to the side of the bed and met Ellie's gaze. "How did you know I'd say that?"

"You're really serious most of the time."

"What's wrong with that?"

"Nothing," Ellie said, then fiddled with the folds of her nightgown. "It's just that since Nathan came, we all laugh more. You know, like we did when Ma and Pa were here."

"I know," Kate admitted.

Ellie lifted her shoulders in a shrug. "I like that and I want to go howl but I'm supposed to mind you, so..."

Ellie stepped toward the bed but her gaze slid toward the stairs. Kate bit her lip for a moment, then glanced toward the moonlit window thoughtfully. "Oh, what would it hurt?"

Kate pushed the covers away and grabbed her sister's hand.

"Where are we going?" Ellie asked.

"Just follow me." After they made their way downstairs, Kate took a lantern and led Ellie outside. The two ran in the direction of the old cabin where Nathan, Sean and Lawson were, until Kate brought them to a panting stop about thirty yards away from the farmhouse.

Ellie was watching her suspiciously but Kate met her sister's look with a daring one of her own. Throwing her head back, she let out a strange howling yodel that carried well on the still night air. In the dim light of the lantern Kate saw her sister's mouth drop open then curve into a grin. Ellie let out a howl more convincing then Kate's. The two waited a moment. A chorus of answering howls filled the air just as Kate expected.

Ellie giggled. Kate howled again. When was the last time she'd done something just to be silly? When was the last time she'd tossed her cares aside and howled at the moon? It had been a while, at least the tossing cares aside part; she'd never howled at the moon before.

Ellie let out a mournful yipping sound so loud Kate had to cover her ears. The answering call was so real it was almost eerie. Somehow she knew it came from Nathan. Kate gave an answering *aroo* and the same yowl sounded in cadence. She took a breath and they all howled in unison, each one with its strange man-made sound except for one that sounded almost real.

There was silence for a breath, then one voice lifted in a kind of growling sound. She and Ellie spun to face the same direction. They exchanged glances.

"Nathan, is that you?" Kate asked.

The bushes moved just beyond the lantern's reach.

"Sean," Ellie called. "This isn't funny. Come out so I can see you."

Three howls sounded from the direction of the old cabin one after another, rising to a different key as if harmonizing. Then that strange sound lifted from a different direction.

"Kate?" Ellie moved closer to press against her side. "Something is in there."

Something definitely was. Kate swallowed. Placing an arm around Ellie, she lifted the lantern higher. "What was I thinking bringing you out here?"

"Oh, Kate, I had fun. I'm glad I laughed before I cross the river Jordan."

"Cross the river—Ellie don't talk like that. You aren't crossing any river. I won't let you. You're staying right here, do you understand? I don't want to think of losing you, too."

Ellie glanced up at her. "This is very sweet and I'm glad you care, but could we focus on the problem here?"

"I wish I had a gun."

"Howooool," Ellie called in the air.

"Now who isn't focusing on the problem?"

The animal let out its strange call again and Ellie looked up smugly. "Now we know where it is. It's right in that bush over there."

Kate stared at the bush that seemed to quiver from

the inside out. "Let's just walk back home slowly and calmly."

"What if it attacks us?"

"Don't you know you aren't supposed to ask questions like that?"

"Don't you know you're supposed to question something when it might kill you?"

Kate looked at her in exasperation. "I'll bash it with the lantern if it attacks us."

"Let me bash it."

"No. I'm stronger."

"I'm smarter."

"Ellie O'Brien, I've had more than enough sass from you for one night. Contain it. I'm trying to get us to safety."

Ellie grumbled something Kate couldn't quite understand. Ignoring her, Kate reasoned, "We have to pass it if we walk home. If we go to the cabin then we walk away from it but it's a much longer walk. Then again, the closer we get to the cabin, the easier Nathan can hear us if we call for help."

"What's your decision?"

"Thataway." Kate pointed toward the cabin. "Walk calmly. Do not run or it might chase you."

"Wonderful thoughts."

They walked calmly but lengthened their strides to cover more ground. Ellie kept looking behind them, so Kate figured she could watch ahead of them. Minutes later, Ellie asked, "You do know where you're going, don't you?"

"Yes, I do."

"I think it's following us."

"Why?"

"Just a feeling. Plus, when we're quiet I can sometimes hear panting."

She spotted the cabin and barely resisted the urge to run to its shelter. Kate banged on the door while watching furtively behind them. There was no response. She banged again. Suddenly the door flew open. She stared down the length of a rifle then up into Nathan's eyes.

"It's Kate," Nathan announced as they moved past him into the cabin. Kate closed the door firmly behind her then glanced up. She found herself in a room with two boys who seemed not the least bit drowsy and one overgrown boy who looked very sleepy.

Ellie sat on Nathan's vacated cot. "Something was following us. It was big and I heard it growl."

Kate was leveled with Nathan's questioning glance. She nodded. "Our howling must have attracted it. I came here because it seemed the safest route. I think it's still out there."

As if on cue, scratching sounded across the door followed by a whine. Sean and Lawson jumped from their cots. Ellie followed more sedately, then snuggled into Kate's side. As Nathan moved toward the door Kate put a restraining hand on his arm. "You aren't going to open it, are you?"

"How else will we know what's out there?" He went to the door then paused. "Do you know how to handle a gun?"

"I'll learn if I have to."

He handed Lawson the rifle. "I'll open the door enough to see what's out there. Sean and Kate, I want you to be ready in case I need your help to close it."

He put a hand on the door handle and braced himself, then pulled it open just a crack. He glanced at Kate with laughing eyes. A bad feeling settled in her stomach and she watched as he opened the door wider, then bent down. "Kate, here is your big scary monster."

He straightened and turned to her with a grin. She was distracted momentarily when she suddenly noticed his mussed hair and the twinkle in his eye. Shaking the thoughts from her head, she glanced down to the rather large bundle of fur cradled in Nathan's arms. It was anything but scary.

A brown short-haired puppy with all the fine qualities of a mutt took in the new surroundings and people intensely. His ears were alert, his eyes watchful. He looked about ten months old.

"It's a puppy!" Ellie squealed and carefully reached out to pet the dog causing its tail to rub happily against Nathan's stomach. "Oh, Kate, let me keep him. Oh, please."

"No."

"But we gave you Nathan, and Sean got Lawson and I don't have anybody."

"She has a point," Nathan commented.

Kate shook her head. "I'll just end up taking care of him."

Sean looked at her pleadingly. "He won't be any trouble. We can feed him table scraps and take him for a swim when he gets dirty. I'll help."

"Me, too," Lawson said.

"It might be someone else's dog," she reasoned.

"But if it isn't," Ellie pleaded.

Kate bit her lip. "I don't know."

"Please." The three children said, one by one.

She looked to Nathan to weigh his opinion but was confronted with his own version of puppy dog eyes that melted more inside of her than she wanted to admit. Finally, she looked at the dog that appeared to be smiling at her as he panted. "Well…"

She glanced at Ellie. The girl looked so hopeful that Kate couldn't disappoint her. "Oh, all right."

She waited until the whoops died down before saying, "Y'all better take care of this dog or I'll find someone else who will."

Nathan's chuckle reached her ear before he said, "There's just one thing left to say."

She refused to take the bait but Ellie eagerly asked, "What?"

He howled that eerie rendition causing the puppy to launch into his strange yowl. Ellie, Sean and then Lawson joined in to harmonize in some strange melody. Kate covered her ears then, glancing at Nathan, who grinned. She shook her head and laughingly let out a spontaneous howl.

It somehow felt good, not necessarily the howling because it hurt her throat a bit, but the freedom she felt to do it. As if, for a little while, she didn't need to carry the responsibility by herself. As if she could just be herself, Kate O'Brien. Her eyes caught Nathan's and her heart seemed to whisper—*Rutledge*.

Chapter Eight

Nathan carefully stretched his back and sent a silent prayer of thanks Heavenward. The pain was gone, his back was healing nicely and he was finally able to work again. He watched in anticipation as Kate uncovered the scythe. He stepped forward for a better view. The curved blade was impressive.

"May I see it?" Lawson asked, trying to peer around Kate.

Kate shifted, stepping back and to the side. Her heel landed right on the toe of Nathan's firm leather boots. He caught her around the waist to keep her from stumbling, then gently guided her heel off his boot onto the floor. She stilled then lifted her gaze to his apologetically. Their eyes held for a moment, then they both glanced away.

Nathan's gaze landed on Lawson who was looking back and forth between them with interest. Lawson turned back to the scythe and reached for it. "Do I get to use this?"

"Carefully," Nathan amended. "You get to use this carefully."

Kate leveled her serious blue eyes at him. "Nathan, have you ever used one of these?"

He frowned, then picked up the scythe to test its weight. It felt solid in his hand and the wooden handle fit nicely in his palm. "Absolutely not."

Under Kate's instruction, Nathan was soon wielding the scythe as though he'd been born a farmer instead of a rancher. He frowned as he thought about his family. He'd agreed to write a letter to them in a moment of weakness but he didn't regret sending it. They must have received it by now. He wondered if his pa would let the family read it, rather than burning it upon receipt.

He hadn't gone into detail about the events that had led him to answer Kate's advertisement. At the time, they'd been too fresh in his mind. Those nightmares had been more vivid than he'd had in a while. He had a vague memory of Kate soothing him during the worst of it but he hoped that was part of the dream. If not, that meant he'd been talking in his sleep. The images racing through his mind weren't meant to be shared.

He'd done his best to put them behind him but the image of one of his best friends dying right in front of him wasn't always easily shaken. The feeling of being cooped up in a jail cell and the accusations that sent him there weren't easily forgotten. Here with Kate and the children, that life felt an eternity away. He wouldn't ruin that by bringing it up or even thinking about it.

He knew that staying here would be difficult. He kept thinking if only. If only, things had worked out with Kate. If only, he had an entirely new life to make him forget his old one completely. If only, there was hope that something might change.

But there wasn't. He couldn't change the situation

and dared not want to. If he did, he was destined to find a new kind of heartache spelled *K-A-T-E* with an apostrophe Sean, Ellie and now Lawson.

It was thinking about Lawson not Kate that caused him to look over his shoulder. Kate was helping Lawson pull the wheat into neat sheaves. Having already paused, Nathan wiped his forehead on his sleeve then pushed it farther up his arm. The sun had already taunted him into unbuttoning his shirt yet, in consideration for Kate, he'd refrained from removing it completely. He turned to survey how far he'd made it down the row in the past hour and had to remind himself not to become discouraged.

He lifted the scythe again but paused when he spotted Kate making her way toward him. Her cheeks were tinged by the sun and her hair was a bit mussed from removing her bonnet, but she looked beautiful. She shaded her eyes to meet his gaze. "I've left you two some water. I'll need to go inside for a while to do my own chores."

"That sounds fine," he agreed.

He watched as she turned and headed toward the house. Then, drumming his fingers on the scythe, he picked it up and prepared to swing.

"You like her, don't ya?"

Nathan stopped the motion quickly. "You shouldn't sneak up on me when I have this thing, Lawson. It's plain dangerous."

Lawson frowned back, "What do you mean sneak up? I was talking to you the whole way here."

Nathan didn't reply, waiting impatiently to get back to work.

"You like her, don't ya?" Lawson asked for the second time.

"You like her, don't *you?*" Nathan corrected.

Lawson grinned knowingly. "Sure, she's very nice. What I mean to say is, I like her but you like her in a different way."

"Lawson," he warned.

"Well, it's true. I may not be ancient but I'm old enough to recognize when sparks fly, and you two could start one of them prairie fires."

Nathan stared at the young man whose freckled face squinted to peer up at him. "Sparks and fires?"

Lawson nodded.

He pulled off his Stetson to let the slight breeze cool his face before setting it back on his head. He shrugged nonchalantly. "It makes no difference one way or the other."

"Of course it does. If you two got married—"

"We're already married. I assumed Sean or Ellie told you."

Lawson looked thoroughly confused. "Did you two have a fight?"

"Not exactly." He paused, looking at the boy's expectant face. "Sean, Ellie and Ms. Lettie got together and decided Kate needed a husband. I wanted a wife and happened to see the ad in the paper. I wrote a letter. The person I thought was Kate answered. We got married without seeing each other. Kate didn't know until I got here, so when the judge comes back we're going to get him to…unmarry us."

"Oh." Lawson seemed thoughtful then shrugged casually. "I'm sorry she doesn't like you back."

Nathan froze for a second, then opened his mouth to

reply to the comment but Lawson had already turned and walked away. Nathan shook his head, muttering, "Yeah, well, so am I."

Kate placed her hands on Nathan's shoulders as his slid around her waist and he lifted her from the wagon. The warmth of his hold disappeared as soon as her feet touched the ground. She glanced over her shoulder and happened to catch sight of her sister. "Ellie, don't! You'll hurt yourself."

Ellie stopped just before attempting to hop out of the wagon. "The boys did it."

"Yes, but they weren't wearing a dress."

"I've got you," Nathan said as he lifted Ellie from the wagon.

Ellie thanked him then tugged at his hand. "Nathan, I want you to meet my friend. Come with me."

Nathan looked back at her to shrug his shoulders helplessly while Ellie led him away. Kate glanced around the crowded churchyard and a thin brunette caught her attention with a quick wave. The young woman hurried toward Kate, hesitating only a moment to eye Nathan as he passed. As she reached Kate's side she lifted her brows curiously. "Who was that?"

Kate rolled her eyes then gave her friend a wry smile. "Hello to you, too, Rachel."

"Sorry." Rachel laughed. "Hello, Kate. It feels as though I haven't seen you in two weeks."

"You haven't seen me in two weeks," she admitted.

"Part of that is my fault—my brothers and sisters started trading sickness so I had to stay home and help Ma last week," Rachel said as they slowly walked toward the church. "I came to church but you weren't here."

"Nathan was too sick for us to come," she said with a nonchalant shrug. This would be the first time they appeared together in public and she intended to make their relationship appear as innocent as it actually was. That way Nathan and Lawson could continue working at the farm while Kate's reputation stayed intact.

She wanted to keep the news of their marriage a secret from the town but she thought that her best friend deserved to know. "Rachel, I'm going to tell you something that you can't tell another soul. Do you promise?"

Rachel came to an abrupt stop then turned to Kate. "Of course I promise. What's going on?"

Kate quickly told her who Nathan really was. When Kate finished Rachel shook her head in astonishment. "At least something good came out of it. You have Nathan and Lawson to help with the farm for now. I've worried about you being out there all alone so much with your siblings in school. This is good."

"I don't think so."

"Why would it be bad?" Rachel stopped to look at her with new interest. "Does this have anything to do with the fact that he's married to you and happens to be one of the most attractive men in town?"

"No." Kate glanced past Rachel and smiled. "Besides, I thought you said Deputy Stone was the handsomest man in town."

Rachel's turned to watch the deputy walk toward the church. "He's all right, I guess."

Kate laughed. "Has he gotten the hint that you're in love with him yet?"

"Unfortunately, no." Rachel winked. "Here comes your hired hand."

Kate turned to find Nathan approaching. She introduced him to Rachel. It wasn't long before Rachel excused herself to join her family and Kate decided it was time to find hers. They started toward Ellie but only walked a few feet before Mrs. Greene suddenly appeared with her daughter in tow.

"It's wonderful to see you up and around, Mr. Rutledge," Mrs. Greene exclaimed while extending a hand to Nathan.

Nathan smiled charmingly. "Yes, well, it's good to be up and around."

Mrs. Greene twittered almost more than her daughter, and Kate could hardly keep from rolling her eyes. The golden-haired young woman smiled demurely. "Ma told me how you jumped in front of that runaway horse. It's quite thrilling. I meant your bravery and not your injury, of course."

Nathan nodded. "Thank you, Miss?"

"Greene. Emily Greene. Will you be in town long?"

Nathan glanced at Kate. "I don't think so. Probably only another month or so."

"Oh, I do wish you would stay longer," Emily protested with a smile. "Though this town is rather rustic, it can be very diverting if you give it half a chance."

Kate nearly choked at the blatant flirting but Nathan's smile grew and he looked as though he would say something else. Kate beat him to the punch with a gracious smile. "Emily is right. This is a very nice town, but speaking of leaving, I think it's time I rounded up Ellie and Sean. Mrs. Greene, Emily, it was nice talking to you."

Mrs. Greene stepped forward. “Mr. Rutledge, I don’t suppose you’ve been able to see the gazebo the town is building. My husband donated a large portion of the funds. I think Emily could show you now. It’s just around the corner of the church.”

Nathan’s eyes widened. “I don’t think we’ll have time. Perhaps after—”

“Nonsense. You have plenty of time.” Mrs. Greene nudged Emily forward causing the girl to blush becomingly. “Go ahead, Emily.”

Nathan met Kate’s gaze for a long moment as though waiting for her reaction. She started to make up an excuse for him but suddenly realized he might not want one. She pressed her lips together then glanced away. Nathan offered his arm to Emily. “A quick trip wouldn’t hurt.”

Emily took his arm then pointed him in the right direction. Kate chewed her lip as she watched the woman’s beribboned hat thread through the crowd. Mrs. Greene turned to give her a satisfied look. “I think they hit it off rather well, don’t you?”

Kate turned, her blue eyes flashing as she whispered, “He’s still a married man.”

“Not for long,” Mrs. Greene replied, then strolled away.

Kate took a steadying breath, inwardly warning herself to let the woman walk away and not say anything impulsive. She didn’t see Ellie with the other children so she decided to check inside the church. Stepping inside, Kate almost ran into Lawson who proudly held the church bell, which was actually a cowbell, in his hands. He muttered an excuse before hurrying out the door. Sean and a host of little boys of a variety of ages followed him out.

As Kate sank into the pew beside Rachel, the bell clanged loudly. A moment later the sound of Ellie's voice drew her attention. She glanced back to see her sister walk inside with Mrs. Greene and her husband. She groaned. What was Ellie telling Mrs. Greene now?

It had to be a humdinger because the woman's face had grown even redder than it usually did when Ellie was around. Mr. Greene seemed to listen in amusement. Kate grimaced as Ellie waited in anticipation. Mrs. Greene loudly snapped, "No, I do not want to learn how to howl."

Kate covered her warm cheeks with her hands. What could she do with the girl?

Ellie patted Mrs. Greene's arm comfortingly, then headed up the aisle to Kate and sidled in next to her. Before she could scold Ellie, the girl looked up at her innocently. "I know you told me not to talk to Mrs. Greene, but I was sure her face would turn purple. Too bad that whenever I have a good one Mr. Greene always has to be around. He calms her down too much."

"You better be glad he does," Kate scolded in a hushed voice. "I really mean it, Ellie. I want this behavior to stop. What does the Bible say about how you should treat people?"

"'Do unto others as you would have them do unto you,'" Ellie supplied.

"How would you feel if someone was constantly trying to make you angry about something?"

"All right, Kate." Ellie sighed as if her world was coming to an end, then looked up at Kate. "After all,

I don't think it's even possible for someone's face to turn purple. Is it?"

"I hardly know."

Ellie leaned toward Kate. "Wouldn't you like to?"

"No."

"Oh." Ellie sat back to stare sedately at the front of the church.

The first hymn started just as Sean and Lawson slipped into the pew. Ellie tugged at Kate's hand. She bent down and her sister's voice sounded just above the music. "Is he really going to sit with her?"

Confused for a moment, she followed Ellie's pointed gaze and found Nathan strolling down the aisle with Emily Greene still on his arm. A woman behind her spoke to someone in a low tone but one that Kate could hear over the singing. "It seems Emily has found a beau. Won't her mother be relieved?"

Kate, still watching Nathan, saw him glance toward the woman as he passed that row. His gaze then met Kate's. He sent her a panicked look as Emily made a big show of allowing him to precede her into the pew where her family sat.

Kate bit her lip. Short of reaching out and dragging him into the seat beside her there was really nothing she could do. She widened her eyes and lifted her shoulders in a minuscule shrug. She caught a glimpse of disappointment in his eyes before they dropped to the floor, then lifted to Emily. He guided her into the pew then settled on the end.

This might be a good thing, Kate realized. *By sitting with Emily, he's showing there is nothing between us, and Sean and Ellie see that he isn't really tied to our family.*

Ellie made a dissatisfied sound deep in her throat. It was loud enough to draw the attention of a few people nearby. Kate was sure others heard it but were too polite to acknowledge it.

Once everyone looked away, Kate sent her sister a reproving look, then gently poked her in the ribs which unfortunately caused the girl to gasp just as the music paused. Several more people turned to look at them but Ellie only seemed to notice Nathan. He looked back at them and winked. Ellie smiled in satisfaction, then leaned onto Kate's leg and stared up at her. "I think that means he still likes you better."

Warmth rose in her cheeks as the women from earlier began to murmur behind her. Ellie had just managed to undo all of Kate's efforts. She lifted a finger to her lips and whispered, "No more talking."

Ellie nodded, obviously satisfied that her work was done. Kate let out a frustrated breath. Lifting her voice with the rest of the congregation, she tried to shift her focus to God and ignore the tiny part of her that was relieved Ellie might be right.

Chapter Nine

Kate pulled the ties from her bonnet and glanced down the peaceful residential street as she waited for Ms. Lettie to respond to her knock. The door opened a moment later. Ms. Lettie stared at her in shock, then glanced past her. Realizing Kate was alone, Ms. Lettie's brow lowered in worry. "What's wrong? Is it the children? Did Nathan relapse?"

"Nothing is wrong. Everyone is fine. I just came to visit you." She lifted the small plate of tea cakes she'd baked for the occasion as proof.

Ms. Lettie watched her for a minute as though unconvinced. "I don't think you've ever just come for a visit, child. Are you sure nothing's wrong?"

Kate rolled her eyes. "Nathan and Lawson started harvesting last Friday. I tried to help them when I was done with my chores today, but they shooed me away like I was unnecessary. I believe Lawson's exact words were, 'Why don't you bake a cake and bring it to a friend or something. You do have friends, don't you?'"

"Oh," Ms. Lettie breathed, then a smile lit her face.

"In that case, come right in. I was about to have tea. You can tell me all about it."

The woman ushered Kate into the breakfast room, then bustled into the kitchen for another place setting. Ms. Lettie returned just as Kate set her tea cakes on the table. Ms. Lettie smiled as she poured Kate a cup of tea. "I am so delighted that you came. I can't remember the last time we were able to just sit and visit. You said Nathan and Lawson took over most of the chores?"

"Yes, they've been doing all of the outside chores and the heavy labor. I've been doing more sewing, mending, washing, cooking and cleaning type of things." She frowned as she stared into her teacup. "Honestly, I don't like it."

"I'm sure you don't," Ms. Lettie said as she gingerly sprinkled a teaspoon of sugar into her tea. "I bet it's been simply awful having them take control over your farm. You've managed on your own for over two years. How dare they act as if you're unnecessary? Why, it's practically an insult."

"Thank you!" Kate exclaimed. "I'm so glad that I'm not the only one who sees it that way. I…" She narrowed her eyes at Ms. Lettie who was obviously struggling to keep a straight face. "You're laughing at me, aren't you?"

Ms. Lettie nodded as she pressed her lips together to keep in her laughter. "I'm so sorry, dear. I didn't think you'd take the bait. You really are upset, aren't you?"

"Yes, I am," she admitted as she shoveled two spoons of sugar into her tea. "I know it doesn't make sense to be angry that Nathan and Lawson are doing what I've hired them to do, but I am."

Ms. Lettie tilted her head and shrugged. "At least you know it doesn't make sense."

Kate set her teacup on the table and leaned forward. "I think what bothers me is that I'm not really paying them. In fact, it's the opposite. Nathan is practically paying me to let him work for me."

"I don't think that's really bothering you, Kate." Ms. Lettie took a sip of her tea then met Kate's gaze knowingly. "What bothers you is that you're sitting here enjoying tea with me while someone else takes care of the farm, and you're actually enjoying it. What's bothering you is that you like not having to work until you're exhausted, then go to bed to get up and do it all over again. Am I right?"

Kate took a nice long sip of her tea so she wouldn't have to admit the truth. "I was fine on my own."

"I'm not questioning that." Ms. Lettie took one of the tea cakes from the plate and placed it on her own. "In fact, I doubt anyone in town questions the fact that you can take care of yourself and your siblings. We all know you to be a strong, determined woman. My only concern is that you might become too strong."

"How could I be too strong?" Kate asked.

Ms. Lettie swallowed a bite of her cookie before continuing. "Before Nathan came along you shunned help from anyone. You were in danger of believing you could get through life on your own. You can't. No one can. God didn't create us that way. We need to give help and receive help. I don't mind telling you that you hadn't been doing either."

"What do you mean?"

"After your parents died you accepted help for a while until that episode with Andrew Stolvins. You say he didn't break your heart but I don't think you can deny he broke your trust. You shut almost everyone out. Rachel and I managed to maintain our relationships with you simply because we wouldn't take no for an answer. You were grieving, vulnerable and hurting then. What about now?"

"I've recovered somewhat."

Ms. Lettie nodded decisively. "You have and it shows. You're accepting help from others by allowing Nathan to work for you. You're helping others by opening your home to an orphan who has no real hope for a better life outside of the opportunity you're giving him." Ms. Lettie reached across the table to touch Kate's arm. "These are good things, Kate. You shouldn't fight them."

She glanced away from Ms. Lettie's sincere gaze. "I don't want to get used to it. I know Nathan is going to leave. When he does, the burden will fall back on my shoulders." She bit her lip. "Do you think God may have allowed this to give me a reprieve?"

"It's possible," Ms. Lettie said. "Or, God could have allowed this to happen because he wants you to fall in love with Nathan and stay married."

"No, that's why you allowed it to happen." Kate sent the woman a pointed gaze, then tried one of the cookies.

"Why don't you trust God to reveal it to you? Find out what He wants you to do in this situation."

"You make it sound so easy."

Ms. Lettie looked at her with new interest. "You mean it isn't?"

"I tried that with Andrew. Look how that turned out."

"He put on an act, dear. He was one person with you, and another person with the rest of the town."

She smiled sympathetically. "You were so desperate for something good to happen after your parents' deaths that you ignored some of the more obvious signs. For instance, Sean and Ellie despised him. He talked about building that saloon whenever you weren't around." She shook her head. "Everyone in town knew he was wrong for you."

She set her cookie down and stared at Ms. Lettie. "So I really was just oblivious?"

"You were physically, emotionally and spiritually exhausted. It isn't surprising that you missed a few things." Ms. Lettie placed a comforting hand on her arm. "You made a mistake. That's all it was. It wasn't the end of the world."

"Why didn't God keep me from making it?"

"How would you ever learn?" Ms. Lettie laughed. "Besides, I think he kept you from making the greatest mistake of all."

Kate frowned. "What do you mean?"

"Your last name isn't Stolvins, is it?"

"No." She breathed a sigh of relief. "It's still O'Brien."

Ms. Lettie smiled as she raised her teacup toward her lips. "Actually, Kate, I believe it's Rutledge."

Nathan stopped outside the Post Office to stare at it, then removed his hat and fiddled with the brim. He nervously stepped inside the small building. A white-haired man peered up from the book he was reading. "Howdy. How can I help you?"

Nathan stepped up to the counter. "I wanted to see if you might have any mail for me. I'm Nathan Rutledge."

"I know they're here somewhere." The man grabbed

a pack of letters and sorted through them. "Here you are."

Nathan stared at the letters the man offered to him. He checked the return addresses on the envelopes. The first was from Davis Reynolds in response to his job inquiry. He didn't need a job immediately, so he was free to focus on the other one for now. It was from Mariah Rutledge of Rutledge, Oklahoma. His youngest sister had written back. He swallowed the emotion rising in his throat, then choked out his thanks to the postmaster before he hurried out the door.

He glanced around the busy street for a private place to read the letter. With none in sight, he ducked into the alley next to the Post Office and opened the letter. Several other envelopes were inside but a sheet of paper enclosed them. It was a letter from Mariah. He decided to read that first.

Dear Nathan,

I can't tell you how happy I am to hear that you are alive and well. We are all fine but we've all missed you. Pa has, too, even if he won't admit it. I was only fifteen when you left but even I knew Pa was too harsh with you.

Oh, Nathan, I wish you had contacted us earlier. Even a few months would have made a difference. You see, Pa found out about what happened when you lived in Noches. Your business partner, Jeremiah Fulton, wrote him a letter about his brother's death, your trial and escape from justice.

I'm sure it can't all be true, although Pa believed every word. He had softened where you were concerned but now I fear all of that has been lost.

Mr. Fulton has written several times to Pa to check if we've received any information about your location. Pa usually tosses them in the waste basket after he's read them so I've enclosed them....

His sister went on to talk about what had changed since Nathan left, but he stopped reading to look at Jeremiah's letters. He glanced at the postmarks on the envelopes. If Jeremiah was trying to find him, he was looking in the wrong part of the state. He frowned as he scanned the contents of the letters. They presented an account of what happened skewed by Jeremiah's anger and grief and his stubborn certainty that Eli's accidental death was actually murder. No wonder his pa was upset.

He leaned against the wall of the Post Office and took a deep breath. Mariah had written back. That's what he needed to focus on. It was a big step in the right direction. Now if he could just get the misunderstanding that Jeremiah had caused under control, then perhaps he could improve his relationship with his pa. He walked back into the Post Office and wrote a response immediately.

Dear Mariah,

Thank you for writing me. I will send another letter soon. In the meantime, please write to the sheriff of Noches, Texas, and ask for a full explanation of what happened. I'm sure Pa will be pleased to find out the truth.

Please refrain from giving Jeremiah my infor-

mation. He doesn't seem to want reconciliation and I'd prefer to leave the past in the past.
Love,
Nathan

He mailed the letter, then tucked the others safely into his saddlebag. It wasn't long before he reached the edge of town. He pulled his Stetson lower with a jerky movement, then gave Delilah her head. The horse set out at a gallop. The ground flew beneath her feet but no matter how fast he went, he couldn't seem to outrun the memory of his past.

With the Fulton brothers in Noches, he had been so focused on his dreams that they'd blinded him to everything around him. If nothing else, he'd learned there were no "take backs" in life. There were no "do overs." There was only the present and it was to be lived, protected and cherished.

He reined Delilah in to a smooth canter. The stakes were higher now. He realized he could lose something much more important than any ranch. He'd tried to ignore the attraction he felt for his wife but he couldn't. Worse, he was starting to care for her as more than just part of an ideal future. If he couldn't rein in the emotions he was beginning to feel for Kate, then he could very well lose his heart. And not just to her. It would be too easy to love Sean, Ellie, Lawson—even the puppy they'd named Lasso. It felt like they were building a family, and he wanted to keep it more than he'd ever wanted anything before.

Nathan was stunned at the thought and even more at the truth of it. He'd just have to remind himself that this family wasn't his to keep. He would leave soon and he was determined to leave nothing behind but good wishes and fond memories. He had a feeling that was all Kate expected from him anyway.

He reined in Delilah and settled her in her stall of the O'Briens' barn, then grabbed his saddlebag and went in search of Kate.

He found her kneeling in the loose dirt of her vegetable garden. The sound of his footsteps on the softly packed earth made her glance up and give him what could pass as a welcoming smile. He met her gaze with a determined nod. She tilted her head questioningly. His gaze shot around the barnyard. "Are the children around?"

She shrugged, brushing her hair from her face with dirt-streaked fingers. "They've been running wild the past few hours so I haven't the slightest idea. Did you get everything taken care of in town?"

He realized he was still wearing his Stetson so he quickly removed it. "Yes. I just wanted to send off a letter."

"Good." She rubbed the dirt from her hands and glanced up at him curiously. "Is everything all right, Nathan?"

"Yes." He tapped his Stetson on his leg then decided to get on with it. "I just want to get a few things straight between us."

Suddenly incessant barking erupted from the house, followed closely by Ellie's scream. Nathan's heart skipped a beat. Kate scrambled to her feet and ran toward the house and he hurried after her. He reached the door a moment behind Kate and burst through it into the sitting room. His heart pounding in his chest, he surveyed the scene in confusion.

"What is going on?" Kate asked.

Sean whirled to face them and over the painfully loud barking managed to say, "There is something furry under the settee. Lasso chased it in."

"Is that all?" Kate met Nathan's gaze with shared relief. "I'll get the broom."

He set his saddlebag by the door then said, "We need to quiet that dog."

Sean jumped to orders, calling the dog's name over the frenzied barking. Ellie was standing on the settee and seemed to be trying to dance. "I think it's a rat. I think it's a rat. Oh! Get me down."

Lawson was hunkered on the ground trying to get a view of the animal. "Ouch, Ellie, that was my finger you stepped on!"

Kate reappeared holding the broom like a sword with one hand and covering her ear with the other. "Everyone calm down. We'll deal with this in an orderly way."

"What? I can't hear you," Sean yelled.

Nathan walked over to the settee, picked Ellie up and set her down beside Kate. Then he firmly commanded, "Lasso, sit."

The dog looked over his shoulder at Nathan and let out a moaning sound. Then it obediently lay down to stare under the settee. With the noise under control, Nathan turned to Lawson who was peering beneath the settee. "Now, do you have any idea what's under there?"

"I think it's either a cat or a skunk."

"A skunk!" Kate exclaimed. Ellie resumed her dance. Lasso took that as a cue to start barking again. Sean tried to shush him. Lawson hunkered down for a better look. Nathan took in a deep breath, commanding, "Sit, Lasso."

The dog growled deep in his throat.

"Sit."

Lasso moaned but lay down.

"With this racket, a skunk would have let us know it was here." His words seemed to have a calming effect on everyone.

"It's a cat," Lawson said confidently, then added, "I think."

"Nathan, we need to get Lasso out of here before we can do anything else," Kate said. "He needs to go to the barn."

"Right," he agreed. "Sean, do you think you can help me with that?"

"Yes, sir."

Nathan scooped up the gangly pup and headed out the door that Sean held open. He didn't stop until he'd set the dog in the barn. He quickly closed the barn door behind him then hurried back inside with Sean trailing after him.

As he walked inside, Lawson said, "It's a cat. Either that or a snake with fur."

Ellie gave a pronounced shiver.

Lawson grinned, watching the effect of his words on Ellie until she glared at him, then he turned to look under the settee again. "Listen."

Everyone was quiet a moment and they heard a soft hissing sound.

Sean shifted his weight. "If that's a cat it isn't happy."

"The poor thing it's probably scared to death," Kate sympathized.

"I have an idea," Nathan said.

Soon Lawson and Sean stood at one end of the settee while Nathan stood at the opposite end with a sack.

He was ready to slip it over the cat upon its appearance. Kate stood beside Sean and Lawson just in case the cat went that way. Ellie had a sheet to throw over the poor animal in case it didn't go either way.

"On the count of three," Nathan commanded. "One. Two. Three."

The settee moved and Nathan saw the cat. He lunged for it but the cat was already moving his direction to get away from Sean and Lawson. It completely missed the sack and instead it ended up clinging to Nathan's shirt. He let out a startled yell then decided to catch it in the sack anyway. Just as he brought the sack up, the cat fell from its precarious position. It landed on its feet with a thump then took off running.

In a split second it was in Ellie's arms, its face hidden in the crook of her elbow. Everyone stared in astonished silence filled only by Lasso's faint bark from the barn. Ellie stared back at everyone for a moment before her large green eyes lifted to Kate. "May I keep it?"

Chapter Ten

Kate nearly groaned at the pleading look on Ellie's face. Instead, she shook her head. "No, Ellie. You have a dog. You do not need a cat, especially not that one. It can stay in the barn until we find another home for it, but that is it."

"But Nathan—"

"I'll not go against your sister, Ellie. We'll have to find another home for it."

Her little sister lifted her chin. "Fine, but at least I get to keep it until then. Come on, boys. Let's go play with it outside."

She flounced toward the door in her shirt and bloomers. Her pert little nose was in the air so high she tripped over Nathan's saddlebag. She would have fallen if Sean hadn't managed to catch her arm. Lawson knelt down to pick up the envelopes strewn across the floor. "Hey, what's this?"

Nathan hurried across the room to gather the letters. "It's a letter from my family."

Lawson stilled then glanced up at Nathan. "They wrote you back."

Nathan stacked the letters in his hands then nodded. Silence sounded throughout the room for a heartbeat then the children erupted in cheers. Kate smiled at their exuberance. Ellie shifted the cat in her arms to get a better look at the letters. "Those are a lot of letters. They must have had a lot to say."

He placed the letters in his bag and set it upright. "Just one was from my sister. The others were letters she forwarded about some business I need to take care of."

Sean leaned against the door frame. "What did she say? Do they want you back?"

"I haven't read all of it yet. She said Pa is still upset but she's going to try to help me."

Kate smiled as she sank onto the end of the misplaced settee. "That's wonderful, Nathan."

He sat back on his haunches to glance up at her and shrugged. "It's a start."

She held his gaze, wondering why he didn't seem as excited about the letter as the children were. Perhaps he didn't want to get his hopes up. *Did* he hope to go back to his family? Would he head to Oklahoma after the annulment? He was working hard on their crop, but she knew he wasn't really a farmer at heart. The children began asking question after question but Kate admonished them, ignoring the fact that she had some questions of her own. "Nathan hasn't even had time to read the whole letter yet. If he wants to tell you about it later, then fine, but give him some time to think about it first."

Nathan sent her a grateful look as the children reluctantly went outside to play with the cat. He helped her set the room to right. Once they were finished, he slid the settee back into place then collapsed onto it. Kate settled beside him with a sigh. "I don't know what I'm going to do with Ellie. She knows just what to say to get her way."

He laughed. "She'll turn out all right."

"I certainly hope so. I'm all she has so if she doesn't we'll know who to blame."

"You're doing a good job with them, Kate."

She met his gaze. "You think so?"

He nodded. "I really do."

Kate smiled ruefully then, leaning her head back against the settee, she let out a sigh. "Well, at least that makes one of us."

He was quiet for a long moment before he cleared his throat. "Kate, I was trying to tell you something earlier."

She opened her eyes and shifted on the settee to face him. "Yes, I remember. You were behaving rather oddly and then you said something needed to be set straight."

He met her gaze seriously. "You remember when I spoke to Mr. Potters about the annulment and he said it would either be one or two months or more until the judge was back?"

Kate nodded and waited for him to continue.

"Well, this will be the fourth week since the judge left so he could be back at any time."

"Oh," she breathed. "I see."

Why did that leave her feeling strangely bereft? After all, she'd only know Nathan for little more than a month. She suddenly realized she would be sorry to see him go. Though she tried to convince herself there was nothing romantic between them, she couldn't deny the friendship they'd managed to eek out.

This is silly. I should be overjoyed. This is exactly what I wanted. He's leaving and that's the way it should be, she sternly reminded herself.

"Or," Nathan continued, "he might not be back for another month or more."

Kate's gaze flew to his. *Did he say another month or longer? I barely made it through this one without weakening my resolve.*

His warm brown gaze searched hers. "We'll just have to wait and see how everything works out."

She set her pride aside to smile. "Either way, I'm glad you came. You've been a great help to me and my siblings. I wish I could offer to let you stay on as my hired hand once this is over but I doubt I could pay you a fair wage."

His gaze seemed to shutter before he glanced away. "No, I couldn't do that."

Uncomfortable with the silence between them, she stood up. "I'd better start supper. I don't suppose Ellie will be any help." She paused to turn back to him. "If you aren't busy, I wouldn't mind," she hesitated, "I mean, if you just wanted to..."

"Help?" he asked, then smiled. "Sure, I'd like to."

After supper Kate set the dress she was mending down to glance around the empty room. She frowned, wondering where everyone had gone. She'd sent Ellie outside to help with the chores since the girl couldn't seem to sit still long enough to complete a stitch, but that had been nearly half an hour ago. She set her sewing basket aside, accidentally sending a spool of thread rolling across the floor. The cat shot from the hallway into the kitchen to chase it.

"Who let you in here?" Kate asked. As she stepped forward the spool rolled from the cat's grasp and she quickly covered it with her boot. Scooping up the cat, she set her aside. The cat rushed toward her boot again but Kate managed to pick up the spool before the cat reached it. "You're a feisty little thing, aren't you?"

The cat meowed pitifully.

"Oh, don't try that act with me. I know what you're really like." She set the spool back in the sewing basket. "I ought to put you outside. I don't like animals in my kitchen."

The kitchen door opened and the cat streaked outside a moment before Nathan stepped inside. "What are you doing?"

She'd been talking to the cat but she didn't want to tell him that. She settled back into her chair, then picked up her needle. "I'm just getting a head start on the mending for tomorrow."

He straddled the chair next to her. "You should come outside with me," he said. "Sean and Ellie say they're just dying to 'watch the stars,' whatever that means."

Her needle stilled. "It's something we used to do with Ma and Pa. Every so often after our nightly Bible reading, they would let us stay up really late to watch the stars come out."

"Maybe you should continue their traditions," he advised thoughtfully. "Since the children are already outside, you could start with this one."

She glanced down at the mending in her hands and saw it for what it really was. It was busywork to keep her mind off… Her gaze lifted to Nathan's. She wanted to groan. So what if she was beginning to like him? That didn't mean she had to pursue those feelings. She'd simply choose not to. There. She wouldn't like him anymore. She couldn't trust that feeling anyway. Every time she thought about liking him, she'd just remind herself of the mistake she'd made with Andrew Stolvins and eventually those feelings would dissipate.

Before she had the chance to try, Nathan stood and tucked his chair back into place. He held out his hand, then with a gentle smile of entreaty, he asked, "Are you coming?"

"I'm coming." But she certainly wasn't going to take his hand. She stepped outside and immediately spotted the children sitting along the pasture fence. She ducked beneath the top railing of the fence while stepping over the bottom. Sean smiled at her from his perch on the fence as she went to stand between him and Ellie.

She turned her back to the fence and was trying to figure out how to hoist herself up without landing in a heap on the ground when Nathan appeared in front of her. He caught her waist then set her carefully onto the fence.

"Thank you," she said as he claimed a spot on the other side of Ellie.

"We're watching for the first star," Ellie said.

Sean nodded. "Nathan said the person who spots the first star gets to make a wish."

"I spotted the moon but that doesn't count." Lawson pointed to the right spot.

"I see it," she said after following his gaze to where the half moon hung in the slightly clouded sky.

Several minutes later Ellie was sitting safely between Sean and Lawson. Kate had Sean on one side and on the other, entirely too close, sat Nathan. For safety sake, he'd said. Trying to ignore the man beside her without making it painfully obvious, Kate focused on her siblings' conversation.

She felt a presence behind her. Before she could

react, Delilah's muzzle appeared over her shoulder. She gasped. The muzzle disappeared then pushed her forward. She would have fallen off the fence if Nathan hadn't caught her. She gasped then turned to stare at Delilah. The horse nudged Nathan's shoulder, only much more gently. Kate narrowed her eyes. "Do you think she did that on purpose?"

Nathan guided the horse's muzzle away from his shoulder then rubbed her nose. "No. I trained her better than that. She was just looking for attention. I'm sorry. Sometimes she doesn't know her own strength."

She wasn't convinced. "I don't think she likes me. She sneezed into my hand the first time I tried to pet her."

Nathan quirked an amused grin. "Maybe she's allergic to you."

"She seems fine now."

"I'll put her in her stall before she sneezes again." He jumped down from the fence and led Delilah away. When he returned he asked, "When did you say the combine and threshing machine would be coming through?"

"The day after tomorrow," she said then glanced around Sean to Lawson. "Did you hear that, Lawson? You won't have to work in the fields after that."

"I liked working in the fields."

Ellie leaned forward. "Don't you want to go to school, Lawson?"

He shrugged. "I've never had much use for it."

Ellie grinned. "Me, neither."

Once the sky was filled with stars the excitement was gone and the children jumped down from the fence. Sean and Ellie wanted to show Lawson how to catch fireflies in the fields. Kate glanced at the fields that were just beginning to sparkle. "Stay close enough that you'll hear when I call you in."

They waved in acknowledgment then scampered off. Silence hovered in their wake. Nathan moved his arm from behind her to brace himself more fully. His hand landed close to hers on the rough wooden fence. She bit her lip. Glancing upward, she stared at the millions of stars twinkling in a dark sky. It looked so immense it was almost frightening.

"It's amazing, isn't it," Nathan asked upon observing the same view.

"Yes," she agreed, as she glanced out at the fields. The fireflies danced across the fields in what appeared to be a reflection of the sky on a still lake. She pulled in a deep relaxing breath. She couldn't remember the last time she'd allowed herself to appreciate the beauty of the land she was working so hard to save.

Nathan's deep voice should have jarred her out of her calm reverie, but its warm tones just enhanced the spell. "It's enough to make you feel weak and powerful at the same time."

"I know exactly what you mean," she breathed, then her entire being stilled when she suddenly wondered if he was still talking about the stars. His words perfectly described the feelings she'd been trying so hard to ignore.

Did he share those feelings? Did she want him to? No, she reminded herself. Because he wasn't staying—and she didn't want him to…did she?

"I guess I should call the children." She carefully lowered herself from the fence. Then she walked away from him and the question she was too afraid to answer.

* * *

As Nathan and Lawson returned to the cabin, Lawson spoke up. "You know, even if your pa doesn't accept you back, at least you've got a sister who loves you."

Nathan didn't point out that his sister seemed to have some doubts about him, too. He hoped she followed his advice and wrote to the sheriff in Noches. If not, he doubted if he would ever have a chance to reconnect with his family. Lawson seemed to follow his line of thought, for he continued, "Even if you don't hear from them again, at least you, Kate, Ellie and Sean are all a family."

Nathan sent him a skeptical look. "If you consider me part of their family then you're family, too."

Lawson shook his head. "No, I'm not much like family to anyone."

"I disagree."

"Listen, I may be saying this all wrong but it all comes down to dreams."

"Dreams?" Nathan asked in low disbelief.

Lawson nodded. "Haven't you had dreams, Nathan? Things you hope for and keep close to you? Things you don't want to let go of?"

Nathan agreed slowly. "I've had a few of those."

Lawson took in a deep breath as he looked up at the stars. "Well, I've always wanted a ma and pa. Real ones."

Nathan silently waited for him to continue.

Lawson glanced at Nathan and the desperation he tried so often to hide would not be denied. "Nathan, I'm fourteen years old. I've never had a family. Not one that loved me enough to stick around. Being here, for the first time, I know what I missed out on and it makes the ache that much worse. Sometimes I just wish I was someone else. Someone good people might want to choose."

Nathan leaned toward him, resting a hand on the boy's shoulder. "Lawson, you are chosen. Not just by Kate, Sean, Ellie and me but by God. Do you understand?"

Lawson shook his head. "I don't think so."

"He loves you. He never wants to be separated from you. He gave up everything He knew and came to this earth so that he could have a relationship with you." Nathan allowed those words to sink in for a moment before continuing, "If you accept that, you become His son and can trust that He wants the best for you. If that's a ma and pa then that's what He'll give you. If that's living with me then that's where you'll stay."

"You mean that?" Lawson asked quietly. "You'd let me go with you even if you have to leave?"

Nathan smiled, amusement lighting his eyes. "I reckon."

Lawson quirked a smile and gave him a short nod. "Thanks, Nathan."

He sat up. "Now wait just a minute. What happened to wanting a real ma and pa?"

"Nothing. It's just good to have a backup plan even if it is pretty shoddy."

"Shoddy, huh?"

Lawson grinned.

"I'll try not to be offended," Nathan said.

There was silence for a long moment, then Lawson asked, "Want to know what I think you should do about Kate?"

"Not particularly."

Lawson shrugged. “All I’m saying is it doesn’t hurt to remind a girl she’s pretty.”

Nathan stared at him skeptically. “How would you know?”

“I have my ways.”

Nathan snorted.

“I’m also saying it doesn’t hurt to remind a girl you know she thinks you aren’t too bad looking, either.”

Nathan’s opened his mouth to speak then closed it. He considered the idea for a moment then said, “Lawson, do me a favor. Stop thinking whatever you’re thinking and go to bed.”

Lawson smiled. “Yes, sir.”

Chapter Eleven

A rough knock on the door prompted Kate to step away from the table where Nathan and Lawson sat eating lunch. Nathan moved to stand. She shook her head. "I'd better get it."

Today was the day the harvesters were coming. That meant it could only be one person at the door. She smoothed her stark white apron as she walked out of the kitchen, then paused in front of the door. Ready for the confrontation, she opened the door. Andrew Stolvins had wandered away from the door to stare at the field. She leaned into the door frame and placed one hand on her hip as he turned to frown at her.

"Kate, what happened to the field?" Andrew pulled his hat from his head to uncover his dark blond hair.

"I harvested part of it myself."

He looked mad enough to spit. "Why'd you go and do a fool thing like that? I told you we could negotiate some sort of payment."

She gave a dry laugh. "I don't even want to know what sort of payment you would have expected."

His innocent expression almost looked genuine. "I

was trying to help you just like I did after your parents died. I was here for you then, wasn't I?"

"Sure you were. Unfortunately it was the kind of help that pushes someone down when they're already falling." She lifted her chin as she gained control of her emotions. "We've gone over this before, Andrew. I don't want your help. I don't want to negotiate. I want you to treat me like you would any other farmer."

"Fine." He shifted in his fancy boots, then continued in a businesslike tone. "I insist you pay me the rate for the whole field since that was our agreement."

She narrowed her eyes. "Our agreement was that I would pay you eighteen percent of the wheat you harvest."

He smiled smugly. "No, it was eighteen percent of your total harvest. That includes what you've already done."

Kate gritted her teeth in frustration. It was his word against hers in their verbal agreement. He stepped closer. "I set up payment plans with a few farmers. If you'd like to do that, I'm sure we could come to some agreement."

Kate stepped aside as he tried to place a hand over on the door frame above her head. She watched him with suspicion. "What sort of payment plan?"

"That all depends on you. You could work three nights a week for a month and we could call it even or—"

"Is that the deal you set up with the other farmers?"

He looked her over appraisingly. "The other farmers weren't pretty enough to be a saloon girl."

Her fist clenched at her side.

He took note of her fist then raised an imperious

brow. "I'd pay you eight dollars a week and you'd earn commission off the drinks you sold. Take the offer. It isn't as though your reputation could get much worse now anyway."

Kate froze. "My reputation? What are you talking about?"

"Half the county is talking about how you have that man living here."

"Nathan? He doesn't live here. He works here. He lives in the cabin about half a mile away."

"It makes no difference. I still can't take the chance. The only job I have to offer you is the one at the saloon." He lowered his head to stare at her. "There your reputation certainly wouldn't be a problem."

"I've heard enough."

Paying no heed to her objections, he continued. "In fact, it might even prove profitable."

Her breath caught in her throat. "Get off my land."

He ducked his head, finally realizing he'd gone too far. "Kate, won't you listen to me for a minute? The truth is—"

"You heard the lady." Nathan's voice cut him off. Relief filled Kate as he stepped from the house to stand beside her.

Andrew stared at Nathan for a moment then sent him a mocking smile. "Ah, this must be the man all of Texas envies."

Nathan's jaw clenched with anger. "Leave now."

Andrew laughed. "I don't take orders from no-account drifters like you. You have a lot of gall standing there like you aren't after the same—"

Kate gasped as suddenly Andrew flew through the air and landed on his backside in the dirt.

* * *

"Lord," Nathan muttered as he rubbed his aching fist and watched the man struggling to sit up. "I believe you'd agree there is such a thing as righteous anger."

He heard a laugh escape from Kate's direction but he didn't look her way. He was too busy trying to see if the man was going to throw a punch of his own. That was the only trouble with defending a woman's honor. In doing so you might find yourself in an all-out brawl. Not that the pain wasn't worth it, of course. He waited while the man regained his equilibrium and tried to get to his feet.

"I'm sorry I had to do that, Stolvins," Nathan said. "You see, my pa didn't raise me to sit back and do nothing while a lady's honor was being wrongfully challenged. I think we both know you deserved it."

The man eyed Nathan as he stood to his feet. He drew his arm back as though ready to throw his own punch but then his hand relaxed and covered his stomach. "You sucker punched me."

"I did. Now, I'd appreciate it if you would be so kind as to remove yourself from the lady's presence. For your own good, you understand? I'd surely hate to have to do that again."

Stolvins stared at him in defiance then reached down to pick up his hat. Setting it on his head he said, "You remember what I said, Kate."

"I believe I've already forgotten."

"Then you can forget my help with your crop. Do it yourself. I'll be glad to see little Miss High and Mighty fail." Stolvins gave them both a dirty look which Nathan returned with a polite nod. Nathan didn't relax until the man galloped away.

Lawson tumbled from the doorway with a grin. "That was amazing. I saw the whole thing through the window."

Kate shook her head with a soft smile. "Thank you, Nathan."

He shrugged. "I only did what any decent man would."

"Do you suppose what he said about my reputation was true?" she asked. "Is that what people think of me?"

"I truly hope not, Kate. If so, it's my fault. I should have realized there would be talk. However, you have to realize the worst thing the townspeople could do is force us to get married."

Lawson's eyes widened. "You already are."

"Exactly," he agreed, then frowned. "Listen, Kate. Why don't I go into town and see how things stand?"

"What about the wheat?"

"We can start tomorrow. We'll need to buy a few more scythes and Sean may have to stay home to help."

She sighed. "I hoped it wouldn't come to that but I suppose there is no other choice. If you're going to town then I'm coming with you. What better way to find out what people think of me?"

Nathan didn't like the idea but knew he wouldn't be able to convince her otherwise. "I'll get the horses."

Kate frowned at the glass of lemonade in her hands as she sat in Ms. Lettie's parlor. "So there has been talk?"

The woman smiled kindly. "Barely snatches of it, Kate, and those people were quickly put to right."

"I see."

"As far as I know, it's only that horrible Mr. Stolvins

and his saloon people who speak of such nonsense. Everyone else respects what you've done with the farm and is happy that you have help. I wouldn't worry about it. Now, tell me. Have you any idea how you'll bring in the harvest?"

"Nathan suggested we keep Sean at home. Other than that, I suppose we'll be working dawn to dusk."

"And you'll be keeping more of your hard-earned money." The widow paused in thought. "Kate, I have an idea that will bring you more workers than you can manage."

Kate smiled but watched her in suspicion. "What are you thinking?"

"Just leave it to me." Ms. Lettie leaned forward. "Oh, Kate. I'm so glad you came to town. I have news of my own. Luke has finally proposed!"

"I'm not surprised," Kate teased. "I wondered when Doc Williams would get around to it. I'm so happy for you!"

"Yes, well, it seems I've found myself in desperate need of a maid of honor and seeing as you're like a daughter to me I was hoping…"

"Oh, I'd love to!" She squeezed Ms. Lettie's hand. "You were my mother's best friend, after all. You took me under your wing when she died. This is the least I could do."

Ms. Lettie smiled. "Wonderful. We'll need to pick out some fabric then. I was thinking blue for you but I'm not at all sure of what color I should wear. Nothing white, of course. You'll have to help me choose."

Kate followed Ms. Lettie into the kitchen to place her cup in the sink. "You don't have to buy a dress for me."

Ms. Lettie smiled. "My dear, you are getting a new

dress. I want you to have one so fancy and becoming you'll be half ashamed to wear it."

"Wait a minute—"

"It will be perfect," Ms. Lettie soothed. "There's no better time than the present. We'll go pick out the fabric then visit the seamstress."

The two were soon talking over the fabric and possible embellishments at the mercantile. Glancing up, Kate caught sight of a familiar set of shoulders. Nathan stood at the counter talking with Mr. Johansen. The two scythes that lay across the counter spoke of the nature of their business together.

"Should we ask Nathan's opinion about the dress?"

Kate's eyes widened. "No. Why should we? Men hardly know of such things."

"I've found that doesn't stop them from having an opinion," the woman quipped as she waved at Nathan.

"Ms. Lettie, I hate to say this, but you're embarrassing me."

"I'm sorry, dear. This has to happen every once in a while. It's hardly fair for you to miss out on this type of thing because your dear mother is gone." When Nathan arrived Ms. Lettie held up sample of the two cloths. "Nathan, we need your help to decide which shade of blue suits Kate best."

Kate sent him an apologetic look. "No, we don't."

"Do you think the lighter or the darker shade would be better?"

Nathan seemed all too amused as he considered the two fabrics. Finally, he pointed to the bolt of medium blue fabric. "I'd have to say this one matches her eyes almost exactly."

Kate looked at him in surprise. Her eyes? He hadn't

looked at her to compare, which meant he didn't need the reference. She tried not to let that thought flatter her but when her gaze met his she couldn't seem to look away. Mrs. Lenworth's voice broke the moment, allowing Kate to glance away though she still felt his eyes on her. "It's a beautiful color isn't it, Nathan?"

"Very beautiful," he replied then took a step back. "Was that all you needed?"

"Yes, thank you."

As soon as he was out of earshot Kate turned to Ms. Lettie with a tired sigh. "I wish you wouldn't waste your matchmaking on me."

"We must pick out my fabric. I'll take this dark blue one and I think this pretty cream ribbon would complement it nicely. We need buttons, of course. For you." She looked at the lighter blue fabric. "Let's go with white ribbons. I suppose you should purchase some white fabric now to be prepared," she muttered, then hurried toward the buttons.

It took a moment for the meaning of her parting comment to dawn. When it did Kate gave a sharp laugh that caused a nearby customer to look up. Grimacing, Kate followed Ms. Lettie.

Kate and Lawson waited in the wagon with the few supplies they'd gotten from the mercantile while Nathan stepped into the Post Office. He pulled the letter he was sending from his pocket and set it on the counter. The older gentleman with the white hair searched under the desk for the appropriate stamp. "Did that fellow find you?"

Nathan stilled. "Was someone looking for me?"

"Sure was." The man smoothed the stamp onto the

envelope carefully. “It was a man about your age. He wanted to know if you were around. I told him I’d seen you a while back. He wanted to know where you were living but I couldn’t remember and didn’t care to speculate.”

“Do you know if he stuck around?”

“He said he’d be back.” The man handed Nathan his change back. “He was a tall fellow but skinnier than you. He had real dark hair and light blue eyes. That caught me as strange or I never would have remembered him. Do you think he might have been a friend a yours?”

“Probably not,” Nathan said before he could catch himself. He didn’t like the idea of Jeremiah Fulton coming to Peppin. Eli’s death had changed a lot of things including Jeremiah’s friendship with Nathan. The man’s bitterness and anger didn’t belong in this place where Nathan had tried to make a fresh start. But judging from all those letters Jeremiah had sent his folks, Jeremiah wouldn’t stop tracking him.

Perhaps it was time for them to finally talk about what had happened. If he showed up, Nathan would try to reason with him. Maybe they could part as friends. Doubt pulled his mouth into a frown. Trying to talk rationally to his friend hadn’t worked at the time. He could almost hear Jeremiah’s screams after Eli fell dead.

“You’re going to pay.”

Nathan’s gaze flew to the postmaster. The man stared back at him. Surely, he’d misheard. “What did you say?”

“I said I can only mail the letter if you’re going to pay.” The man lowered his bushy white brows. “You were expecting to pay, weren’t you?”

Nathan ignored the chill that brushed over his skin,

and paid the man. "Do you have any mail for me or the O'Briens?"

The man shuffled through his stack of mail but came up empty. "There's nothing today."

Nathan thanked him then couldn't get outside fast enough. Kate glanced at him in concern when he climbed into the wagon. "Are you all right? You look so pale."

"I'm fine," he said brusquely then set the wagon in motion. "Everything will be fine."

Kate placed her hands on her lower back and leaned into them. It felt wonderful to stretch her aching muscles. She leaned farther back and felt a satisfying pop. She had just turned back to her work when Sean called. "Kate, look."

She followed her little brother's gaze to find her friend Rachel riding toward them on a small black horse. The young woman grinned and waved.

"Rachel!" Kate exclaimed in surprise before hurrying toward her. The petite brunette slipped off the horse to give Kate a hug.

"What are you doing here?"

"I'm with them."

"With who?" Kate asked but turned in distraction when Sean let out a whoop and hurried past her. It was then Kate noticed a group of ten or so men walking toward the field, scythes in hand.

"Ms. Lettie said you could use some help."

Kate frowned. "But I can't take you all away from your farms. You have your own harvests to worry about. We'll be fine."

"Of course you'll be fine—because you'll have our

help. There should be a few more men coming this afternoon. Ashley Walker, Cynthia Pikes and Erika Pikes should be waiting near the house. We all brought food, of course. Lena and John Talbot said they would come tomorrow since Mr. Stolvins is harvesting their fields today. This will be so much fun, Kate!"

"But I can't just accept your work for free," Kate protested.

"Naturally not," Rachel agreed. "There are two things we want as payment. First, you all have to come to the Harvest Dance. It's been two years since we've had O'Briens there, and we miss you." Rachel grinned. "It's just not the same without Ellie's antics."

"And second?" Kate pressed.

Her friend smirked. "One punch to Andrew Stolvins. That was paid in advance."

Kate couldn't help but smile at the recollection as the men approached. Jeffery Peters slapped Nathan on the back. "Sure wish I could have seen it."

Deputy Stone laughed. "Sure wish I could have done it."

"I've been aching to for years," said old Mr. Murphy. The kind eyes that always seemed to twinkle landed on her. "Miss Kate, we come offering our services. Do you accept?"

Her pride urged her to say no, but for once, she pushed it back. These were her friends and neighbors, come to help out of the kindness of their hearts. Just this once, she was going to let them. "How could I not? Thank you all for coming."

Her gratitude was waved off. Billy Joe said, "I don't see how we'll do you much good standing around here talking."

"Truer words were never spoken," Mr. Ives agreed.

As the group of men moved toward the field, she walked arm in arm with Rachel as they made the short trip to the house. Giving her friend a sly look, Kate said, "So tell me how things fare with the deputy."

Rachel laughed. "Only if you tell me how things fare with Nathan."

Kate rolled her eyes. "The two are hardly comparable."

"You're right. The absolute nothing happening between Deputy Stone and I hardly compares to what's happening with you and Nathan." She sent Kate an expectant look. "What *is* happening between you two, anyway?"

"What makes you think something has happened?"

Rachel shrugged. "He's been here for a while now. Your feelings have had time to change. Have they?"

"I don't think so," she said quietly as her gaze trailed back to the field.

"That isn't a firm no, so maybe there is hope after all."

"There's more hope for you than there is for me." Kate smiled teasingly. "Perhaps I'll be attending another wedding soon."

"Perhaps you will," Rachel agreed. "It may not be mine, but perhaps you will."

Nathan crept silently through the early morning darkness. He'd hoped the full day of harvesting would be enough to ensure a good night's sleep. Unfortunately, memories of Eli had been stirred up by the postmaster's mention of Jeremiah and kept rest at bay. He hoped a hard ride might do the trick. An owl hooted over his head, rivaling the low creaking of the barn door as it opened and closed. He made a note to himself that it was time to oil the hinges. The sound was loud enough to wake the dead. Walking toward Delilah's stall, his hand trailed to the reassuring weight of the holster belted low on his hips.

Delilah welcomed him with a soft neigh as he neared her. Nathan smiled. "That's right, girl. We're going for a ride before we both get stir crazy. It will be just the two of us like old times."

He opened the stall then moved to get the bridle. Draping it across his neck, he placed the saddle blanket on the saddle in order to carry them both. At the plodding sound of horse's hooves he spun just in time to see Delilah heading for the barn door.

"Delilah," he scolded but the sound of his voice sent the horse bolting through the door by widening the crack he'd unknowingly left there. He rolled his eyes. Maybe he'd made a mistake naming the horse. She should have been named something like "Sugar." Then maybe she'd act that way. Nathan snorted, knowing he would never allow a horse the disgrace of being named something like that.

He walked through the door, lugging the saddle with him. He was all prepared to whistle to Delilah, a sound she instinctively came to, when his gaze landed on a dark figure walking across the barnyard. He froze as apprehension shot through him.

His gaze flew to the dark house where Kate, Ellie and Sean lay sleeping. He had to protect them. Yet, as he watched, it became apparent that the figure seemed more interested in Delilah than anything else. *Yes, that's right, take the fool horse,* he thought, then immediately felt guilty.

A voice reached his ears, sounding clearly in the early morning stillness. "How did you get out here?"

He relaxed. *It's Kate. What is she doing out here alone at night?* he wondered.

Delilah moved toward Kate, blocking her from his view. He almost called out to her but before he could she said, "Well, no need to pretend. I don't like you, either."

Nathan smiled.

"Why don't you like me? Is it because of Nathan?"

Surely he had nothing to do with this.

"I understand that you might feel angry since you were taken from your life as a cowpony to get stuck on this farm. Technically, it was Nathan who made the decision so you and I were just innocent bystanders."

I wonder if Delilah really doesn't like Kate. She does seem a mite edgy the way her hooves are dancing around like that. Nathan swallowed a laugh knowing he should make his presence known but things were just getting interesting.

"Unless, of course, you're only jealous," Kate continued. "It's hardly my fault that he likes me better than you though I can see why. I am a sight prettier since my nose isn't half as big as yours. But then, you can run much faster than me, so I suppose we both have our good points. Perhaps you would temporarily agree to share him with me until the judge comes back."

He decided it was time to stop Kate before she said anything else she might not want him to hear. He heard Delilah snort loudly which probably covered the sound of his approach.

"What am I talking about?"

This time he answered. "I haven't the slightest idea."

There silence was penetrated only by the sound of his footsteps and Delilah's soft breathing.

"Nathan, is that you?" Kate asked. He walked around the horse and came face-to-face with Kate. Instead of trying to discern her expression, he shifted the saddle so that he could place the blanket on Delilah. He smoothed it down then placed the saddle over it. That bulky hindrance removed, he turned to Kate.

She stepped closer. "What are you doing out here?"

"I'm going for a ride." He tilted his Stetson up for a better view of her.

"In the middle of the night?"

"It's nearly morning now. The sun will be rising in a little less than an hour." He shrugged his broad shoulders. "I couldn't sleep, anyway."

"Why not?"

"Bad dreams," he admitted.

"Bad dreams about Eli?" she asked hesitantly.

He caught her arms. "How do you know that name?"

"You mentioned him when you were sick." She placed a hand over his. "I guess he's the business partner you said died. If you ever want to talk about it…"

He shook his head. "It only makes the dreams worse not better."

Besides, he'd been forced to tell his story so many times he'd resolved to never tell it again. He suddenly became aware of the cold metal touching his arm. He glanced down then lifted her hand in his. "Were you coming to do me in?"

She seemed flustered as she tugged her hand from his grasp and slipped the gun into her pocket. "No."

"Delilah, then?"

"Of course not."

"That's good," he said before turning to tighten the saddle's cinches and slip on the bit and halter. "It's hard to find a good cowpony."

She stiffened beside him.

Placing his hat on the saddle horn, he stepped closer. "Though I must admit your nose is twice as pretty as hers."

Chapter Twelve

Kate turned away from him to face the house. He'd heard every word she'd said. She was sure of it. Oh, what had made her go spouting off to a horse? Better yet, why had she deemed it necessary to get out of her safe bed to investigate the opening and closing groans of the barn door? Who would have guessed she would find Delilah standing in the middle of the barnyard unsaddled, unbridled and looking downright ornery?

She was pulled from her thoughts when Nathan's rich low voice reached her ear and skittered down her backbone. "I do like you better than Delilah."

She turned to face him. "You could have told me you were there."

"Well, I didn't know it was you at first."

She narrowed her eyes and took a step closer to challenge him. "Didn't you?"

"No, I didn't," he said with what sounded like a smile. "Besides, I'm glad I overheard you. How else would I know I was being shared?"

"Maybe I should let her have you."

"Maybe I don't want to be had."

"Good. Maybe she doesn't want you."

Nathan's eyes narrowed as he stepped so close she had to look up to meet his gaze. "Maybe she does and she won't admit it."

She scowled. "Maybe she doesn't and freely admits it."

His gaze trailed over her features in such a searching way she wanted to turn her face away. She didn't. She had nothing to hide, nothing at all.

"It could be," he said and she felt his warm fingers on her waist just inches above where her own were perched on her hips. "Or it could be she's too afraid to look past her pretty little nose to see what's right in front of her."

"What is in front of her?" she asked slowly.

"She has to find out for herself."

"How?" The question was out before she could stop it. "How does she find out?"

He reached down, cradled her cheek. His thumb brushed lightly across her cheekbone. He lowered his head to say lowly, "I reckon that would be up to her."

Kate searched his dark brown gaze. It seemed to hint at feelings mysterious to her yet amazingly familiar. A strange ache filled her heart, moving throughout her chest. Something inside her begged for the freedom to dare to throw caution to the wind and…do what? Trust that she was right this time? That Nathan was someone she could or perhaps even should love?

The thought startled her so much that she caught her breath. "I think I should go inside."

He gave a slow nod then released her just as slowly. She didn't move. She just watched him for a moment intrigued by the emotions that played across his features in the nearly nonexistent light. Finally, she took a step backward then turned to walk into the house.

Once inside, she closed the door behind her, leaned against it and closed her eyes. Was she right this time? Was God leading her down this path? More importantly, could she trust Him enough to believe it would end well?

She slowly shook her head. "I don't think I can, Lord. I'm sorry."

She pushed away from the door then locked it behind her before carefully making her way back to bed.

Nathan watched her until she closed the door to the house. He stepped into the saddle and immediately pulled his Stetson over his eyes as though he needed to block out the moonlight. With a soft nudge to Delilah's sides, he set off at a moderate pace to allow her muscles to warm up. Once they moved past the field, he let her run like she begged to. He needed the speed, too—needed to feel like he could outrun his problems and his doubts. If only it was that easy.

They raced across the open meadow before turning toward the woods. He reined her in as they entered the forest then allowed her to pick her way through the trees. When he could no longer bear the load on his shoulders, he dismounted and led the horse to ease her heaving sides. Eventually he released the reins and continued walking forward allowing Delilah to follow if she wished. He stopped to stare up at the sky as the stars did what little they could to fight the darkness.

He was in love with Kate. The knowledge came with enough power to pull the wind from his body, leaving him to take in a sharp breath.

He'd done his best to keep this from happening but it had been a lost cause from the start. He was in love with his wife, God help him, and there was nothing he could do to change that. He might as well stop trying. Nathan stilled. *Stop trying.*

None of this made sense. He'd been so sure God had given him this dream. He'd been equally sure God was taking it away. What if He wasn't?

Nathan had given up at the first sign of trouble. Yet it did not matter how many times he tried to do as Kate had asked and walk away, circumstances outside of his control always brought him back. It couldn't all be a coincidence. Perhaps God still had a plan in all of this. Perhaps this had been His plan all along.

"God, I don't want to do anything outside Your will so if I try, please warn me." He swallowed. "If, however, You have me here for a reason beyond what I have allowed myself to imagine…if You have me here for Kate and her family, then I'd like to follow You in that."

He shook his head then smiled wryly. "Since her father is no longer here, I guess what I'm really asking is for permission to court your daughter, Kate, my almost-wife."

He waited in the stillness of the morning just before dawn as the rest of nature seemed to hold its breath in wait of answer. He heard no audible voice, not even a small internal one. All he felt was a sudden and acute blossoming of hope in his chest.

Hope. It was something he'd been missing of late but it settled within his chest with nearly tangible warmth. It called him to believe and even to love. He put his hand over his chest then pulled in a long breath.

It wouldn't be easy, he realized. Achieving a dream

never was. He knew, because he'd tried before and failed. But this time things were different. This time hoping was worth the risk of disappointment and refusing to hope was not an option. He gave a short nod of appreciation toward the Heavens. "Thank You."

Kate took in a shallow breath since it was all that the formfitting bodice allowed. "It's a beautiful dress, Ms. Lettie, but are you sure it isn't too small?"

The bride eyed her laughingly. "No, Kate. It looks perfect. You look perfect. Stop worrying!"

Kate shook her head incredulously. "I hardly think this is worrying."

"Then what do you call it?"

"Fretting."

Ms. Lettie laughed.

"Oh, that's fine." Kate lifted her chin playfully. "Laugh at my expense. I don't mind. Just make sure someone is behind me should I faint dead away."

"Women have gotten by without breathing for centuries."

"That doesn't encourage me."

Ms. Lettie smiled mischievously as she handed Kate a bouquet. "Then be encouraged that if I even see you so much as sway I will alert Nathan in plenty of time for him to catch you in his arms."

Kate lifted her gaze from the flowers suspiciously. "How convenient."

Ms. Lettie's picked up her own bouquet of flowers, then glanced at Kate with dancing brown eyes. "Yes, it seems we've stumbled upon the reason women have gone without breathing for centuries."

Kate laughed as they moved to wait outside the double doors of the small chapel's inner sanctuary. She could hear the piano warming up as she took her place in front of Ms. Lettie. She glanced down at the bouquet in her hand as she tried to concentrate on pulling in short, frequent breaths and willing away the lightheadedness she felt.

Suddenly she was aware of being watched. She looked up to see pews full of people all staring at her expectantly. Quickly turning her grimace into a smile she hoped would take the focus from her burning cheeks, she took her first step down the aisle. The second was easier than the first. By the third she managed to look at something besides the plank floor. On the fourth her gaze lingered on Doc who looked very distinguished. The fifth step she looked behind him to Nathan.

She lost count. Her breath caught in her throat but didn't go very far into her lungs for lack of space. She managed to avoid his gaze as she continued down the aisle. Once she reached the spot where she'd been told to stand, she turned toward the entrance to watch Ms. Lettie walk down the aisle.

A moment later the couple held hands before the preacher and everyone waited while the two exchanged vows. Doc's voice sounded strong and clear and she found herself wondering what it must be like to have the man you loved pledging those words to you. She found herself watching Nathan as he pulled out the rings.

Their eyes met and he gave her a grin. Kate was suddenly reminded that Nathan had taken these very same vows toward her with every intention of keeping them. Of course he hadn't known her then—except for what the letters had told him—and certainly hadn't loved her. No. The words couldn't have been spoken with the same tenderness that Doc said them.

Kate pulled her attention back to the woman who spoke softly but firmly. "With this ring, I thee wed."

"Then by the power vested in me through God and this church, I now pronounce you husband and wife." The preacher nodded. "You may kiss your bride."

Nathan watched Kate as she laughed at something Ms. Lettie said, then forced himself to stop staring at the woman.

Hearing Doc's voice speak his vows had reminded him of when he'd said his own. He'd had no idea what he was getting into with that proxy wedding. If he had known, would he have gone through with it? He gave a short nod. Without a doubt.

Even if he never changed Kate's mind, at least he'd met her, Sean, Ellie and Lawson. At least he'd been able to help them. At least being a part of their family for a short time had inspired him to reach out to his own. But he wanted more. He wanted so much more.

He turned to search for the children. He'd only gone a step toward the door of the chapel when a man paused in front of him to buckle his shoe. Stopping short, Nathan glanced down. The man was wearing cowboy boots. His gut clenched in wary surprise as the man straightened. Hate-filled eyes met his and instead of saying "excuse me" the man muttered one word, "Graveyard."

Nathan gave a nod and kept moving in his original direction but he couldn't help glancing back to make sure what he'd just seen was real. Yes, the man was still there and he was also looking back, but not at Nathan. The man had his eye so locked on Kate that he nearly ran into the person in front of him. In a move similar to what had just happened, the man muttered something then moved around the person.

Nathan detoured to exit out the back of the church. When he stepped outside he found the man waiting for him.

"Good to see you again, Jeremiah." Nathan extended his hand in a gesture of hopeful reconciliation. The man eyed his extended hand with something so akin to contempt that it made Nathan's skin crawl. Even so, he managed to retain a polite air. "It's been quite a while since we've seen each other, hasn't it? How have you been?"

"This isn't a social call, Rutledge," the man warned tersely. Nathan was saddened at the change in his friend. A man who had once lived with enthusiasm, ever ready for a joke, now stared back with cold blue eyes.

"Well, then," Nathan drawled. "What brings you to this part of Texas?"

"I want justice for what you did to my brother." Jeremiah stepped closer. "You and I both know what happened in that barn and I don't care what any two-bit jury has to say about it."

Nathan gave a weary sigh. So much for his hopes that the passage of time would help Jeremiah see things more clearly. "Jeremiah, why do you still believe I'm guilty after the jury found me innocent?"

"You'll always be guilty in my book. I can't get back my brother but I aim to take back the money you stole from us."

"I can't give you what I don't have."

"You're lying," Fulton growled. "You think you have a great setup here, don't you? The people in this town don't even know who you are. Does your wife know you're living a lie?"

Nathan felt the blood drain from his face. "My wife?"

He smiled coldly. "Yes, I know all about her. The record of your marriage is what finally helped me track you down."

Anger rose in Nathan's gut causing him to step forward and grip the man's collar. "You listen to me and you listen good. If I even see you so much as look in her direction, I'll bring the law down on you quicker than you can blink."

The man tried to pull away. "I'm not afraid of the law."

"Then you'd better fear me on this one thing, Fulton." Nathan released him with a jerk. "I'll say it only once more. I don't have the money you're looking for. I never did. The sooner you realize that, the sooner you can get on with your life. I have nothing more to say to you." As he walked away, Nathan hoped that would be the last of it. Jeremiah was angry, but surely no amount of anger could turn his one-time friend into a violent man. Yet he couldn't shake the creeping sense of dread that told him his troubles were just beginning.

In seconds flat, Nathan pulled, cocked and shot the gun at one of the metal cans nailed loosely to the corral fence. Metal punctured metal with a satisfying bang. He was slow on the draw, slower than he'd been for a while. He couldn't allow himself to be lazy anymore. He hadn't seen nor heard from Jeremiah Fulton since the wedding nearly a week ago and he hoped more than anything that the man had moved on for good. But if Nathan was going to try to stay and become a permanent part of this family, he had to be sure he could protect it.

He frowned as he slipped the gun back into his holster, then tried again. The shot came off much quicker that time. *Better,* he acknowledged to himself, then continued shooting at the cans one after the other in a familiar rhythm until he ran out of bullets. He lowered the gun.

They'd finished with the harvest yesterday. Today he'd taken the children to school early to talk to the teacher about Lawson. As far as he could tell, the boy was seriously behind on his schooling. The teacher had promised to do his best to help him catch up. Once Nathan had returned to the farm, he'd decided to carve out a few minutes of target practice.

"Very impressive," Kate's voice lilted.

"Thanks." He turned to offer her a distracted grin as he reloaded the gun.

"Where did you learn to shoot like that?"

"I picked it up here and there," he said, slipping his Colt in the holster and walking toward her. Adjusting his Stetson, he propped his leg on the fence between them. He figured this was just as good at time as any to continue the courting he'd begun over the last few days. "How about I give you a shooting lesson?"

"I don't need a shooting lesson."

"You've already learned?"

"No," she said slowly.

"Don't tell me you're afraid of this little thing." Nathan pulled the gun from its holster and watched her blue eyes drift over it.

She lifted her chin. "I'm not."

"Prove it."

She bit her lip then met his challenging gaze with one of her own. "Fine. I will."

He waited while she slipped through the fence. Then reaching up, she knocked the Stetson from his head only to catch it and place it on her own. She paused to tug the gun from his hand and moved to where he'd been standing earlier.

She glanced over her shoulder impatiently. "Are you going to tell me how to do this or what?"

"No need to get testy." He took the gun from her and dropped it in his holster. "We're going through it without the gun. First, you have to find your stance." She was soon standing in the correct position. "Now, keep your wrist strong so the barrel stays level."

"What barrel?"

"Not the one that points at my feet. Focus up." He stepped in front of her, guiding her chin upward. Suddenly her liquid blue eyes focused on him and he knew he'd made a mistake. She stilled. His gaze trailed down to her lips.

"Pow." Kate jerked as if she'd shot something and Nathan realized that something was him.

He stared at her. "Of all the nerve—"

Kate's blue eyes filled with the laughter she barely kept from showing on her lips.

He chuckled then pushed her arms to the side and away from his chest. He kept a hand on her arm then slipped behind her. She froze. "What are you doing?"

"I'm teaching you to shoot," he said as he pulled the gun from his holster. He cocked the gun then showed her how to hold it. "Remember to keep your arms taut but not perfectly straight. Your wrists need to stay strong. Keep that right foot slightly back."

"Nathan, I can't remember all of this."

"Sure you can. Keep your finger off the trigger but go ahead and aim." He watched her adjust the gun while she gazed intently at the can. "You want the piece on the end to line up with your target. I'm going to stay where I am and all I want you to do is pull the trigger."

A bang followed as she fired. Unfortunately, a second tinnier sound did not. She stumbled back. He was there to steady her. She glanced up from under his Stetson and he smiled. "That was good. Try it a few more times."

Each time he had to remind her less about her form and keeping the target in her sights. "Try it by yourself. Mind the kickback."

Nathan crossed his arms as she shuffled back into place, aimed and fired. Nothing happened. He paused then said, "You didn't cock it."

A click announced the cock. Another bang sounded and the kickback caused them both to fall backward, which unfortunately for Nathan meant being sandwiched between the dusty corral and Kate. Somehow he managed to rise up on his elbows then brace himself with his hands. He took in a Kate-scented breath which surprisingly was like a mixture of cinnamon and gunpowder. "Kate, are you all right?"

She turned her face to the side giving him a very close-up look at her profile. "Yes. Are you?"

"Yes, I suppose that means we should get up."

"Right." She quickly leveraged herself to sit beside him, then scrambled to her feet. He slowly followed suit. Kate's pretty mouth grimaced. "I'm sorry."

"That's quite all right. I shouldn't have assumed I

would be safe that close to you," he said, wondering if she would realize how true those words were.

If she did she didn't acknowledge it because, though she huffed, she glanced at him with concern. "I didn't hurt you, did I?"

"Not too much." He picked his hat off the ground and shook his head to clear it. "Maybe we should stop for today."

She rubbed her elbow with her free hand. "I didn't hit the can."

He extended his hand for his gun. "You don't need to hit the can. I doubt you'd ever shoot at anything that small. Besides, you didn't even want to come anywhere near the gun when I first asked."

"You convinced me and now I want to hit the can."

Nathan shrugged. "Then hit the can for all I care."

Her blue eyes narrowed. "You needn't be rude."

"Who was being rude?"

"You were getting close."

He looked down at the Stetson in his hands. "I was about as close to being rude as you were to hitting that can."

They eyed each other. Challenges were issued and accepted. His arm gave a sweeping motion toward the target as he stepped back. Kate turned. She aimed then shot dead through the middle of the can. It actually came off the nail and tumbled from the fence to land in the dirt.

Kate smiled and turned to him triumphantly. "Well?"

He tilted his head. "Well, what?"

"I hit it, didn't I?" She narrowed her eyes at him. "Don't you have anything to say about that?"

He shrugged. "Congratulations?"

She pointed the gun at him. Nathan's fingers twitched near his gun belt before he stilled them and stepped out of the way. He stared at the gun until she presented him with the handle and not the smoking barrel. He reached for the gun but Kate didn't release it. He looked up questioningly.

"Thanks for the lesson, Nathan." A smile danced across her lips before she continued, "It was fun."

"Whoa. Let's not get carried away." He grinned slowly. "I'm just glad shooting me gave you so much pleasure."

"Oh, it did." Her eyes sparkled as she pressed the gun into his hand, forcing him to take it as she stepped past him. She suddenly spun toward him. "I almost forgot why I was looking for you in the first place. Since Andrew Stolvins didn't harvest our wheat, we'll have to take it to market ourselves. I need you to bring it to Colston. There are two mills close to the town."

He thought of his lingering concerns about Jeremiah and frowned. "Kate, now might not be the best time. I'm not entirely comfortable leaving you and the children here alone. You see—"

Kate narrowed her eyes at him. "Don't be silly. I ran this farm just fine on my own for two years. I think I know how to take care of myself and my siblings. Lawson will help out while you're gone."

He placed the gun in his holster. "Kate, really—"

"We have no choice, Nathan. We have to sell the wheat. Without selling, I won't be able to pay the mortgage and the farm will not survive." She blew out a heavy breath and glanced at the sky. "Nathan, I need you to go."

"To Colston, right? I actually have a friend who lives

there. Mr. Reynolds may help us out." He slowly nodded. "I'll go, but I'll ask Deputy Stone to keep his eye on the place."

"That is hardly necessary, but thank you," she said. "You can leave right after the Harvest Dance. That should leave you plenty of time to prepare."

He tipped his hat up as he watched her begin to walk away. He hesitated for half a second before he called after her. "Kate, wait! When we were in town for the wedding, I saw a man who..." Nathan didn't know what to say.

"Who what?" Kate asked.

He shook his head. There was no way to warn her without explaining the whole situation, and that dark part of his life wasn't exactly something he wanted to show to the woman he was trying to impress. Besides, he still couldn't bring himself to believe that Jeremiah was serious in his threats. "You'll be careful while I'm gone, won't you?"

She promised she would, and Nathan prayed that that would be enough.

Chapter Thirteen

Kate sat reading the large family Bible in the living room as she and her siblings waited for their parents to come home. It had been raining since early that afternoon but the strength of the early winter storm had only increased since nightfall. It raged outside, spewing sleet and sometimes even hail. The thunder bellowed like a madman and sent tremors through her little sister's body while putting a grimace on her little brother's face.

She placed the Bible in her lap and closed the covers. Obviously her attempts to cover the storm's ferocity had failed. Instead, silence filled the small room as they each sat lost in their own thoughts. Kate tried to speak over the storm. "I think we should go to bed."

Sean frowned. "But Ma and Pa aren't home yet."

"They probably decided to stay in town once they saw how bad the storm was getting," Kate reasoned. "I'm sure they'll leave first thing in the morning."

Quiet descended once more as they all sat still waiting for their parents to return. Finally, Kate stood and ushered everyone to bed. The dark loft she shared with

Ellie flashed bright in cadence with the storm. A small hand searched for hers on top of the covers. Suddenly she awakened to the sound of someone banging on the front door. She grabbed her housecoat and hurried down the stairs in time to see Sean stumble from his room. She opened the door, only to stare blankly at the man before her.

"Sheriff Hawkins," she said in surprise. "Is something wrong?"

The man glanced over her shoulder then stepped backward. "Perhaps it'd be better if we spoke outside, Ms. O'Brien."

She glanced behind her at Ellie and Sean then stepped out the door. The sheriff opened his mouth to speak but his lips moved silently. She struggled to hear. Finally his words whispered past her ear in small phrases filled with words like accident, dead, joint burials.

She couldn't breathe. She couldn't move. Then his voice grew strident, demanding her attention. He was asking if she wanted help with the children. She said she didn't know. There had been no time to think. Her breath caught as she'd spun toward the door. What would she say? How would she tell them?

Suddenly there was nothing around her but that wooden door. She tried to back away from it but her hand was already on the knob, turning it. She would have to tell them. She would have to tell them just as the sheriff had told her, quietly and calmly but with a firmness that left no room for doubt.

She lifted her chin and stepped through the door, closing it firmly behind her. She avoided looking into the eyes of her brother and sister, knowing she would have to tell them the unthinkable. She swallowed, then lifted her eyes as courage won out...

Kate gasped and forced her eyes open as she sat up in bed. Dim morning light spilled from the windows and painted the room in soft purples and blues. Ellie's slow steady breathing countered her accelerated gasps. She pushed her loose hair away from her face and turned to sit on her side of the bed. She forced herself to pull in deep, even breaths. It had been nearly a year since she'd relived that moment in her sleep. Perhaps it was the end of the harvesting that brought it on. The wagon was loaded, and Nathan would leave for Colston the next morning, after the dance that night. It had been a good harvest, and Kate no longer worried about the mortgage. But the knowledge that she'd saved her parents' farm was cold comfort when she thought of how much she still missed having them in her life.

Why can't I relive the good moments we had together? Why must it always be that night? She longed for her father. At a time like this, he would have pulled her into his arms and told her not to be afraid. He would have reminded her, in his subtle Irish brogue, to trust in the Lord so He could direct her paths.

Had God been directing her parents' path the day of the wagon accident that took their lives? If so, why hadn't He directed them to wait out the storm in town? She buried her face in her hands as she whispered, "I do love You, God. You know I do. It's just so hard for me to trust."

Ellie shifted in the bed. Kate froze then slowly opened her eyes. The girl continued sleeping so Kate pulled in a deep breath, then continued with one last request. "Lord, help me. I don't know how You can or will but I need You to do something. Prove Yourself. Let me know You're real. Let me know You care about my future. Right now, it's just a little too hard to believe."

That evening Kate stared at herself in the reflection of the only looking glass they owned. Her hair was piled high on her head. A frown painted her face and it was caused by more than just the new freckles that had appeared on her nose from spending so much time in the sun. The first month of her marriage had been over for two weeks and the judge had not made his appearance. She had given up all hope that he would return soon. It looked like she would be stuck with Nathan Rutledge for the long haul. She was frowning because right now that didn't seem like such a horrible thing.

Ellie peered over Kate's shoulder into the looking glass. "Your hair is a mess."

"I know." Kate released her hair from the fancy hairstyle she'd attempted. She met Ellie's gaze in the mirror as she fished the hairpins out of her curls. "Why aren't you dressed?"

"I can't reach the buttons."

"Turn around then." Kate turned from her task to help her sister.

"I don't understand why the buttons are in the back."

"I sew them that way to make things difficult. Didn't you know?" she asked.

"I would be perfectly happy wearing my day dress rather than this scratchy old thing."

Kate buttoned the last hole then turned around to survey her sister. "You look lovely."

Ellie couldn't seem to figure out whether to take that as a compliment or an insult. The girl smiled mischievously. "No one there will care a fig about what I wear except Mrs. Greene, but everyone will be watching you and you haven't done a thing to get ready."

"Yes, I have."

Ellie sent her a disbelieving look and plopped on the bed with her skirt inching up past her knees. She frowned and managed to pull her skirt down to the proper length.

Kate lifted her chin. "I'm nearly ready."

"You plan to go with your hair undone and your petticoats showing in the back?"

She glanced behind her and sure enough Ellie was right. "No."

"Then I suggest you hurry up."

Kate looked at her sister sitting so properly on the bed strewn with clothes. Before her eyes her ten-year-old sister was ever so slowly shedding her tomboyish ways and turning into a young lady. She still preferred her old bloomers to her new skirts but there was a beginning to be a perceivable softening to her sister's demeanor. Kate decided Ellie would turn into a proper young lady yet. She sensed it would probably happen gradually over time. She wouldn't rush the girl but vowed to enjoy the process.

Ellie frowned. "What?"

"Nothing," Kate responded with a smile. "Fix my dress back there, will you?"

Downstairs, Nathan leaned back onto the wall near the front door as he waited with two very impatient gentlemen.

"Aren't they ready yet?" Sean asked from his seat near the fireplace.

Nathan glanced toward the stairs and shook his head. "I don't think so."

Lawson frowned. "What takes them so long anyway?"

He shrugged. "They have more to put on, I suppose."

"What do you mean?" Sean asked.

Nathan glanced toward the two boys with the answer on his lips, then paused to take in their freshly scrubbed faces and pressed shirts. He shook his head. "Never mind."

Lawson shifted on the settee. "At this rate, the dance will be over before we get there."

"I don't think they'll let that happen." Nathan laughed. "Besides, if I know anything about women it's that the longer they take the more it's worth the wait."

Sean looked at him. "What is that suppose to—"

Lawson's low whistle cut him off.

Nathan followed Lawson's gaze then straightened from the wall. Kate moved toward the bottom of the stairs and paused to say something to Ellie as she pulled on her gloves. She looked so beautiful in her pale green dress with its rounded neckline and fitted waist.

Kate turned to find them all watching and met their stares with a curious look. "Shall we go?"

"Yes, please," Sean moaned and walked out the door.

Lawson turned to follow Sean but paused to hold the door open for Kate, then glanced back at Nathan with a laughing gaze. The boy's smirk plainly said, *you are in so much trouble.*

Ignoring him, Nathan caught the door to allow Lawson to precede him. Ellie hung back to frown at her shoes. Seeing the problem, Nathan knelt down to fix the button on her shoe. He paused to look up at her.

Tapping her nose gently, he grinned. "You look very pretty, Ellie."

She looked at him seriously for a moment before chancing a small smile. "It's not too fussy, is it?"

He shook his head. "Not at all."

"Good."

He stood and waited for her to exit the house before closing the door firmly behind them.

Kate pulled her skirts toward her as she slipped through the doorway of the crowded hallway leading to the hotel's small ballroom. Glancing to the right, her gaze faltered as it landed on Nathan. Ever since that night with Delilah he seemed to be behaving differently toward her.

He'd always been kind in the past but lately there seemed to be a bit more motivating his actions. She would catch it every now and then in the tone of his voice or the way he looked at her. Something seemed to have subtly shifted in their relationship and she wasn't entirely sure what to do about it. She had decided the safest thing was to avoid him whenever possible.

Their eyes held for a moment longer as she stepped past him. Moving away, her lashes drifted down and up, then biting her lip she glanced back in time to see Nathan shake hands with the sheriff. He met her gaze again and he pushed from the wall. Her eyes widened and she stepped into the main room that was crowded with dancers. She moved toward the punch bowl then felt Nathan's hand on her back. Steeling herself against his warm gaze, she turned to face him with a smile.

"Are you enjoying yourself?" he asked.

"Yes, thank you. Actually, I was looking for Rachel. Have you seen her?"

He turned to scan the room. She reached for a cup of punch and took a cooling drink as he faced her. "She's dancing with Deputy Stone."

She nodded and took another sip.

"Would you like to dance?"

"What?" she asked, using the excuse of the noise of the hoots and hollers coming from the dance floor to stall for time to think. Dancing with Nathan would be a very foolish thing to do. It would, however, be rude not to dance with him at least once, she reasoned.

Nathan leaned closer to say, "Would you like to dance?"

"Well," she began, then set her cup back on the table. "Yes, I would. Thank you."

He guided her through the crowded room to the dance floor. She felt as though everyone was watching to determine the familiarity of their relationship. She allowed him to take her hand. She placed her other hand lightly on his shoulder, then followed him as he led her into a fast waltz. She glanced up to find him frowning. "Relax."

"I am relaxed," she said, though she knew she was lying through her teeth. Rather than focus on her partner, she allowed her mind to wander. Although the waltz was still considered a controversial dance in other towns, Peppin had accepted it long ago. Town protocol demanded that the dance was never done slow enough for a person to do much more than move his or her feet, thereby avoiding any complications.

She grimaced as she stepped on Nathan's toe. When she glanced up apologetically his smile was so painfully polite that Kate vowed to redeem herself. She forced herself to relax and allowed Nathan to lead her carefully across the floor but a moment later the song came to an end. He stepped toward the punch bowl but she stayed where she was. "Let's dance another set."

The music began again. This time it was a quick two-step and she missed the first step. She tilted her head up to frown at him. "I do know how to dance, I promise."

He grinned. "Prove it."

She allowed herself a smile and placed her hand in his once more. This time they moved easily into the dance. Kate pushed all the doubts from her mind and allowed herself to truly relax in his arms. He led her through the steps simply and naturally obviously feeling at home on the dance floor. The longer they danced the easier it was to move in sync with each other. When she could no longer contain her curiosity she asked, "Where did you learn to dance like this?"

He laughed. "I have three sisters. Who do you think they practiced with?"

She would have responded but the music stopped for a split-second then began at a faster pace. They were caught off guard for an instant but quickly caught up. Suddenly Nathan angled his steps, causing her to step sharply to the left then right. Kate's eyes flew to his as she smiled in delight. He grinned then slowly turned her under his arm while they two-stepped. Once she faced him again she didn't falter but instead moved right back into the dance.

"Do you believe me now?" she asked with a triumphant smile.

"Maybe." He smiled and her heart skipped a beat. Wait, no. The music skipped a beat then continued even faster. This time they were ready for it and easily moved into the faster step. She twirled under his arm without missing a step. The music picked up its pace again.

Her eyes widened as she glanced over her shoulder at the ragtag group of musicians. She barely had time to place her feet before it was time to pick them up. She heard someone let out a whoop and looked over to find the deputy grinning ear to ear as he and Rachel danced. Kate's laughter blended with Nathan's low chuckle. Finally, the music made by a lone fiddle, harmonica, banjo, washboard and other makeshift instruments swirled to a halt.

"Enough?" Nathan asked.

She looked at him innocently. "Why? Are you tired?"

He began to speak but the caller's words sounded over his. "Fellers, grab your gals. It's time for the 'Courting Game.'"

Chapter Fourteen

Nathan looked at the man in surprise then transferred his gaze to Kate. "The 'Courting Game'?"

"Oh, that." She waved her hand as if dismissing the game completely. "It's a square dance. We don't have to play." She was already moving off the floor.

Nathan frowned. "Wait—"

He was cut off when the caller said, "Kate O'Brien, where are you going?"

Nathan's gaze flew to Kate, who was waving the man off.

"You send that young man up here so I can talk to him."

Her eyes widened and flew to his. Nathan made no attempt to hide his amusement as he shrugged. He walked over to the man who said, "Now, you just position yourself across from that gal and I'll make sure one of you gets a hat, you hear?"

"Yes, sir," Nathan said then did exactly that. Kate looked at him from across the circle and shook her head. He ignored that, hoping she wouldn't leave the two circles of dancers that were being formed with the men on the outside and the women on the inside.

They were suppose to thread through each other, he was told. Between the hats and the name the 'Courting Game,' Nathan was sure mischief was afoot. To clench it, the caller said, "Now in years past the parson demanded that the kiss be given on the cheek…"

Kiss? Nathan glanced across the circle at Kate who pointed to herself then away from the circle. He shook his head and pointed to the ground motioning that she should stay. However, the action was poorly timed for it was done just as the caller robustly exclaimed, "But he ain't here tonight!"

Kate frowned at him then turned to talk to the brunette beside her. He watched suspiciously as the lady responded to Kate then glanced around the circle to look at him. The woman laughed and whispered something to Kate. As the two giggled, the caller continued, "Seein' as we got ourselves a room full of gentlemen, I think tonight we'll allow the ladies their preference."

There was much laughter around the circle and not all of it came from the men. Nathan caught Kate's gaze. She gave him a satisfied smile. One of the men near Nathan called, "Start the music, already!"

The caller grinned and gave a nod to the rusty band of musicians who managed a pretty good semblance of "Turkey in the Straw." Nathan soon caught on, extending a hand to one woman. Passing her, he took the hand of the next lady. He knew from glancing across his shoulder that Kate stayed opposite him as the distance between them diminished.

The music stopped and so did the dancers. Everyone searched for the bearer of the hats and Nathan saw a man a few spaces in front of him collect a kiss on the cheek. The caller told everyone to pass the hats back three people. He wasn't surprised when a hat tied with a green handkerchief landed in his hands. He glanced at Kate, but she was looking at the hat that landed one person ahead of her.

The music started again and many women eyed the hat whether he extended that hand to them or not. He could no longer look across and see Kate. Then suddenly the music stopped and Kate was nowhere to be seen.

Kate laughingly watched as Nathan smiled wryly at Mrs. Redding. With infinite care to propriety, he leaned forward and placed a smacking kiss on the woman's cheek before glancing around in search of an irate husband. The music started up again and Nathan threaded through the line once more.

As he passed by she lifted her cup of punch in a silent salute and grinned at the feigned reproachful look he sent her. Draining the rest of her punch, she turned to look for Ms. Lettie but suddenly stopped short. "Mrs. Greene."

The woman glared at her, obviously annoyed about something.

Kate searched for any sign of Ellie but found her innocently talking to a few girls her age. "Is something wrong?"

"I should say so. Why, the way you're throwing yourself at that man is disgraceful. It's all over town."

"Ah, yes. The rumor industriously circulated by Andrew Stolvins," Kate acknowledged. "I wasn't under the impression that you frequented the Red Canteen, Mrs. Greene."

The woman bristled. "Sinful, that's what it is. All the while knowing the man is going to leave you. To think, I once imagined him suitable for my Emily!"

"Mrs. Greene—"

"Well, you've done your parents proud, haven't you? Your poor mother would roll over in her grave if she heard the words I did."

Kate lifted her chin. "My mother wasn't poor in any respect. She lived fully and completely with a compassion for others I doubt I'll see again on this earth. Unlike you, my mother would never have entertained malicious gossip much less spread it."

Silence stretched for a moment. Mrs. Greene seemed to tremble in silent anger. When she did speak it was in a very cool, almost icy tone. "Young lady, if I had any doubts about the truth of what I have heard about your reputation, they have just been destroyed. I have never met such a disrespectful young woman in all my life. Why, if I hadn't kept my mouth shut about this business in the first place—"

"You may say what you like but I'm long past the point of caring what you think about me, Mrs. Greene. Good evening," Kate said. Setting her cup down with a decisive thud, she turned and rushed quickly away.

Nathan looked past the colorful swirl of dancers in search of Kate and moved to where he'd last seen her at the punch bowl. He paused in his search when he nearly ran into Doc Williams.

"Nathan," Doc said reaching out a hand.

Nathan shook it firmly. "Hello, Doc. How's married life treating you?"

"Very well," he said, then grinned. "A better question is how's it treating you?"

Nathan smiled wryly. "It isn't."

"Kate is still adamant about you leaving then?"

"As near as I can tell."

"The children will be disappointed to see you go."

"Yes, so will I." Nathan's gaze tripped nonchalantly over the doctor's shoulder to survey the room.

Doc frowned. "What will happen to Lawson if you leave? Do you think Kate will take him in?"

"I'm not sure. When I spoke with the sheriff he said he was still looking for a home for the boy. I figured if he hasn't found one by the time I head out, I'll take him with me."

"I should think Lawson would be easy to place," Doc mused. "He's a good age to help around a farm."

Nathan glanced to the left and spotted Kate talking with Mrs. Greene. "Yes, but everyone knows he tried to steal from us and no one is willing to take the chance that he'll run off with their possessions."

"Even now that the boy has proven himself trustworthy?"

Nathan nodded. "The more I talk to him, the more I realize that he's really just a victim of poor circumstances. He's done the best that he can by himself. Unfortunately, that wasn't enough to keep his belly full. He resorted to stealing in order to survive."

"I'm sorry to hear that," Doc Williams said. "I'd like to see what he could make of himself given the right opportunity."

"Maybe you should give him a chance then," Nathan challenged.

"The thought has passed my mind." Doc Williams nodded thoughtfully. "I'll talk to Lettie about it. I won't keep you."

"Wonderful." Nathan grinned as he took the doctor's offered hand. "It's always a privilege, sir."

Doc moved away, giving Nathan a clear view of where Kate had been standing, only to find her missing. Frowning, he searched the crowd then glanced back at Mrs. Greene in time to see the woman glare at something to his left before she turned on her heel. Following a hunch, he glanced to his left then moved that direction.

Kate sat on the second step of the stairs spilling from the hotel's small yet well-constructed wooden porch onto the lawn of an overgrown garden. The winsome call of the fiddle carried through the air, melting into the sounds of cicadas and crickets calling to each other. A puddle of light slowly spilled from the doorway onto her dress, alerting her that she was not alone. She glanced behind her and smiled seeing it was Nathan. "You found me."

He left the door open behind him but stepped onto the porch. "You disappeared. I wanted to make sure you were all right."

"I'm fine." She paused then admitted, "I just had a horrible fight with Mrs. Greene."

"Who hasn't?"

She laughed. "You haven't. She wanted you to be her future son-in-law for a while."

"I assume I have since been disowned."

She gave an amused nod. "Quite viciously at that."

"Lucky me." He gestured toward the stairs and with her nod of approval he sat on the bottom step. He was quiet for a while before he asked, "What did you fight with Mrs. Greene about this time?"

She rolled her eyes. "My poor reputation. What else?"

He met her gaze sincerely. "I'm sorry, Kate."

"Don't be." She sat up proudly with a glimmer of laughter in her eyes. "I think I did very well for myself. Her face nearly turned purple. Ellie would be proud."

He laughed just as the fiddle wound down, leaving near silence. They were quiet for a moment, each content in their own thoughts. He looked toward the door. "I should go back inside. We don't want to fuel more gossip."

He began to rise but she quickly caught his hand. "Stay."

He glanced at her in surprise.

"The gossip ignited without any fuel so it hardly matters now." She shrugged. "Besides, you left the door open."

His gaze trailed to where her hand rested upon his. He stilled. She followed his gaze and quickly released her grasp just as he turned his hand over to tighten his. She knew if she tugged her hand once more he would have to release it. He knew it, too. They both waited in the breadth of the moment for her to make her decision.

She bit her lip then slowly relaxed her hand in his hold. The music started again as if it had been waiting for that cue. Nathan sat facing her then gently intertwined his fingers with hers. "I've been waiting for a month and a half to hear that word. It sure sounds good."

Her breath stilled in her throat. "Nathan…"

His gaze was gentle, undemanding yet seeking. She didn't know how to respond. For the first time in a long time she wanted to believe that she had correctly discerned God's will and it was this. It was him. She wanted it to be him so badly.

What if it was? Slowly, trepidation rose in the pit of her stomach, then turned into pure fear. She turned away and tugged her hand from his grasp. He immediately leaned back. His hand lifted toward her cheek then dropped once, twice, back to his side. "Kate."

She turned toward him.

His eyes spoke to her gently. "It's all right."

Tears suddenly pooled in her eyes, blurring her vision. She turned to face the garden and placing her elbow on her knee she buried her face in her hands.

"I might think it's something I did, but it's more than that, isn't it?"

She nodded.

He moved to sit on the same step as her with his shoulder touching hers, but kept his hands clasped and propped on his knees. He didn't try to talk about it. He was just there, waiting if she needed his shoulder to cry on.

How could she possibly explain that she was crying because she thought God might actually want them to be together? He wouldn't understand. He would be happy but all she felt was fear of what that might mean to her heart and the plans she'd made for her future. She leaned against the stair railing so she could look at him. "Nathan, you said God led you here, didn't you?"

He looked perplexed at the sudden change of subject but nodded. "Yes."

"Do you still believe that, after everything that has happened and hasn't happened?"

He smiled. "Yes, I still believe that."

She shook her head in confusion. "But, why? I mean, aren't you the least bit angry that God allowed you to believe he was leading you in one direction when you ended up arriving somewhere else entirely? Doesn't it feel like…" She bit her lip, almost afraid to go on.

He straightened with new interest. "Like what?"

She swallowed then met his gaze more fully. "Doesn't it feel like God lied? In Jeremiah, He says something about having thought of peace toward us and not evil. He says He wants us to have 'a future and a hope.' It doesn't seem like that's true. It seems like every time I let Him direct my path I just end up going through heartache. The same goes for my parents. They always prayed God would direct their paths but look what happened to them."

"You're right," he said quietly.

"I am?" she asked in surprise.

"God never promised that if we followed His will life would be easy or even make sense. He just promised that in the end it would all work together for our good. He promised that if we'd follow Him He'd take us to the best possible future, but He never said the journey would be easy. We're supposed to go through hardships knowing that we'll end up better for them in the end."

"You think I should stop focusing on the painful paths God has led me through and focus on where I'm going instead," she said thoughtfully. "What if I'm not sure that He's leading me to a good destination?"

"I guess that's where trust comes in. You have to trust that His word is true. You have to believe that despite how it seems now, He hasn't lied. At the very least, ask Him to prove His word is true."

She nodded thoughtfully.

"I think the same goes for love," he said quietly. "You have to be willing to trust the other person. You have to be willing to depend on them. You have to let yourself be weak enough to find strength in others."

Her gaze slowly lifted to his. "I'm not good at any of that."

"Maybe not yet, but I think you could be." His gaze seemed to say that he was counting on it. "We should go inside, but first—" He reached out and gently lifted her chin to its familiar defiant tilt, then winked. "That's much better."

The next morning, Kate bit her lip as she watched Nathan say goodbye to her siblings and Lawson. *Goodness, the way everyone was acting you'd think he was leaving permanently.* He'd be back in a week with the money that was supposed to keep her from needing him. Of course, by then the judge might be back and Nathan *would* be leaving permanently.

An awful feeling settled in her stomach at the thought. Perhaps it would be best to treat his departure now as a practice for the real thing. Maybe it would make things easier for her siblings when that day came. Perhaps, her heart seemed to whisper. But, would it make it easier for her?

She watched as Nathan gave a kind word and an affectionate gesture to each of the children. Ellie wouldn't settle for anything less than a hug, but was also rewarded with a grin and a tap on her pert nose. "Try to stay out of trouble, Ellie."

"Yes, sir," Ellie said as she slipped her hands behind her back and rocked from her heels to her toes and back again. "It probably won't do any good but I'll try."

Nathan clasped Sean on the shoulder. "You just keep taking care of your sisters. You're doing a fine job at it."

Sean nodded solemnly but Kate didn't miss the way his chest swelled at the praise. Nathan moved on to Lawson, who stood with his arms crossed in front of him. Nathan didn't try to penetrate that barrier. Instead, he surveyed his young friend carefully. "Remember what I said about keeping up with the chores and school. Don't run off before I get back."

Lawson shrugged. "I'll be here. It's not like I've got anywhere else to go."

Kate braced herself with a casual smile as Nathan stepped in front of her. He didn't say anything at first. The silence made her nervous. She spoke first. "I left a satchel with a few more provisions under the seat of the wagon. If you think you're going to stay more than a week, write a letter and let me know."

He tilted his head slightly as though to question her businesslike demeanor after what had passed between them last night. Her gaze strayed to where the children watched them with eyes that missed nothing. She didn't want to do or say anything that might get their hopes up about her relationship with Nathan. It wouldn't be fair to them.

"You'll be careful, won't you?" Nathan asked. "Be wary of strangers. Keep the pistol with you at all times."

She glared at him. "Really, Nathan, if you tell me to be careful one more time, I'll—"

"You'll what?"

She began to respond out of her bristled pride but

stopped herself before the words did anything more than form on her lips. He was only trying to keep them safe. She gave up with a minuscule shrug. "I'll be careful."

A disbelieving smile tilted his lips as he caught her arms and gently tugged her closer for a better look at her face. "Are you feeling all right?"

She lifted her chin threateningly but smiled reluctantly. In her peripheral vision, she saw Ellie hit Sean on the arm to make him pay attention to what was happening. Nathan's gaze slid from hers to the children then he casually released her. "It's probably best that I didn't hear the rest of that sentence, anyway."

"I'll be back." He squeezed her hand then stepped into the wagon. He placed his Stetson on his head and tipped it at them all before urging the horses onward. She crossed her arms as she watched him disappear around the curve in the road. For one week, life was going to go back to the way it had been before Nathan Rutledge had ever shown up. That was a good thing. Wasn't it?

Chapter Fifteen

Nathan squinted against the afternoon sun then finally pulled the brim of his Stetson down to block it. He pushed open the heavy wooden door in front of him and stepped into the lobby of the hotel. He glanced at the clock realizing he would make it to his appointment at the agreed-upon time. He hurried across the lobby to the restaurant and paused inside the door.

"Are you looking for someone, sir?" asked a young man dressed in the uniform of the hotel.

Nathan glanced up from searching the tables to meet the youth's gaze. "Yes. I was supposed to meet a gentleman here named Mr. Reynolds."

"Yes, sir. Right this way." The young man led the way through the tables, stopping at one near the large-paned windows.

"Nathan, my boy, it's good to see you," the older man exclaimed.

"Davis, it's been a long time." Nathan grinned, extending his hand for a hardy shake.

The large Nordic-looking man motioned to a chair.

"Sit down. Tell me how you're doing. I don't suppose you've had any contact with your family?"

"Actually, I have." He grinned at Davis's shocked look. "Mariah wrote to me. She says they're doing well."

"That's wonderful, Nathan. I always knew that girl had gumption."

"She sure does. It's nice to know that at least one member of my family is willing to risk Pa's wrath to contact me," he agreed. "How is your family, Davis?"

"Oh, we're just fine. Faith is just approaching her sixteenth birthday and of course Tyler is spending his days out on the range. He's a wanderer for sure. Just like you were, the last time I saw you."

Nathan smiled then shook his head. "Not anymore. I've been looking to settle down."

"That's good. I hope one of these days Tyler will do the same. The missus is doing as well as can be expected with both of her children nearly grown. I'm sure she hardly knows what to do with herself these days except to plan one function or another." He paused to take a drink of water then pointed to the lemonade in front of him to indicate it was for Nathan. "But you didn't come all the way over here just to hear an old man blather. We have business to discuss."

By the end of the conversation, Davis promised to personally introduce Nathan to a wheat buyer who was a good friend of his. "I'm sure he'd be willing to buy what you have. Since you're a friend of mine he'll definitely offer you a good price for it."

Nathan let out a smile in relief. "Thanks for your help, Davis. I appreciate it."

"You're welcome, Nathan." He pushed his plate away to show he was finished. "Farming is a hard market."

"I don't mind farming." He especially wouldn't mind if he was doing it for Kate.

"You're at the mercy of nature day in and day out. That's a hard way to live. It certainly wasn't what you came to Texas to do," he said as a waiter came to take the plate away. "Personally, I think you should go back to raising horses. You've always had an interest in it."

"It developed into more than an interest. When I was a partner at my old ranch it became my passion." Nathan smiled wryly. "Not that I'd do it again."

"Why not?"

"I already failed at it once."

"No. You were failed at it. Someday you might be ready to try again. When you are, let me know." The waiter extended the check. Davis grabbed it, then smiled. "I hope you know you're staying with us tonight. My wife would have my head if I didn't bring you home."

He smiled. "Yes, sir."

So this was what life was like without Nathan Rutledge, Kate thought to herself as she sat grimacing at the cow's udder. Funny she hadn't remembered it being so empty.

How pathetic. He's only been gone three days but I'm already waiting for his return, she thought.

Flick meowed loudly. The sound pulled Kate's gaze from the milk streaming into the bucket. She caught sight of Flick, then with an unpracticed twist, Kate shot a stream of milk toward the cat as she'd seen Nathan do. She missed. The small stream landed few feet from Flick rather than in her mouth.

She closed her eyes, tried to picture what she'd seen

Nathan do. She tried again. This time it flew over her own shoulder, barely grazing her hair. Giving up, she lifted her shoulder to wipe away the few droplets that clung to her cheek. Looking toward Flick she shrugged. "Sorry, pretty kitty, none today."

The cat let out a plaintive meow and slunk toward Kate to rub against the milking stool. Kate stood to stretch her arms. Flick jumped toward the bucket almost as if to submerge her entire body in the warm liquid. Kate gasped but managed to block the cat from reaching its goal.

"Flick!"

The cat continued to struggle toward the bucket.

"That is quite enough, young lady. I fed you this morning so you needn't act as though you're starved. Have some dignity." She moved her legs to guard around the bucket. It took only a few more minutes to get the rest of the milk. Standing, Kate gave the cow an appreciative pat and reached for the pail. "Thank you, ma'am."

She slowly yet carefully made her way toward the barn door then glanced up as Delilah gave a loud neigh. Kate smiled sympathetically. "I know you miss Nathan, but he really did have to take the wagon. He'll be back soon. Don't worry. You aren't stuck with me forever."

Delilah snorted.

Kate hurried across the barnyard lugging the heavy bucket. She paused to stare as she noticed a rider coming toward the house, then continued walking to keep the milk from sloshing onto her skirt. She looked in the direction of town with concern. Why would anyone be riding out this way? Hopefully nothing was wrong.

Her straining arm forced her to hurry to the kitchen

and leave the milk on the table before rushing back out the door. She stepped outside just as the man was dismounting. Remembering her promise to Nathan, she wondered for a moment if she should have grabbed a gun before hurrying out to meet a stranger while she was alone, but the friendly smile the man gave her quickly put her at ease.

"I'm looking for—" he glanced down at a paper "—Nathan Rutledge."

Nathan? This man knew Nathan? She bit her lip. "He's not here. Is there something I can help you with?"

He frowned. "That depends on who you are. You wouldn't happen to be his wife, would you?"

She tilted her head and met the man's gaze suspiciously. How could this stranger know she was Nathan's wife? Only a few people outside her family knew she was married. "How do you know him?"

The man laughed. "We're old friends. He's probably told you about me."

Her suspicion grew. If they were old friends he shouldn't have needed to check the paper for Nathan's name. Kate swallowed and stepped back toward the house. "Well, you should come back later. I'm sure he'd be glad to see you."

The man looked at her oddly but what did it matter? She stepped back inside and closed the door. She heard him moving toward it and hurriedly tried to lock it but her hands fumbled nervously. The door flew open making her stumble back. She grasped for something to hold on to but her hand knocked painfully against the rocker and she found herself on the ground.

She stared at the floor in disbelief while a shadow fell over her. Her head jerked up at the sound of a gun cocking. She stared at the barrel of a gun before her gaze followed the strong arm up to cold blue eyes. The man's voice was like steel. "Get up."

Kate swallowed the dread settling in her stomach. She stood, wincing when she placed weight on her injured wrist, to survey the man before her. His hair was a remarkable shade of raven black at odds with his threateningly cold blue eyes. His features were just far enough from plain that he might be considered attractive if not for the anger that radiated from him. His gaze found hers with the look in his eyes bordering on hostile.

She met his gaze evenly then lifted her chin as she tried to speak. He cut her off by sharply asking, "Where's the nearest table?"

"Table?" she asked in confusion. "It's in the kitchen."

The gun flicked in his hand. "Go."

She slowly turned and led the way into the kitchen.

"Sit down," he commanded and she had little choice but to obey.

Kate sank into the nearest chair. She tensed, feeling the tip of the gun barrel press between her shoulder blades as a piece of paper and a pencil were set in front of her. "You'll write exactly what I say, do you understand?"

She nodded then wrote mechanically as the man dictated that he was taking Kate hostage. He requested that a large sum of money be deposited at a bank in a larger town that she remembered was about fifteen miles to the east. When his diatribe came to an end, she stared at the paper for a long moment, slowly realizing what she'd written. He snatched the paper from beneath her fingers and stepped up beside her to read it.

How did I get caught up in all of this? She set her

lips in a grim line. She wasn't sure but one thing was certain. She was ready to get out of it.

She eyed the gun he'd extended too close to her nose for comfort. Pulling in a deep breath, she slowly leaned back. Once she was in position, she slammed the man's hand on the table as hard as she could. He cried out at the same time the gun discharged, sending a bullet into the wall.

She spun out of her seat and took off running. Her first fumbling steps sent her through the living room and out the door. She saw the man's mount waiting patiently and ran toward it.

Her foot connected with the stirrup as she swung into the saddle. She heard the man shout and knew he must be coming toward her. She turned the horse and urged it toward town. A shrill whistle rent the air and the horse turned sharply; moving back toward the house.

"No," she whispered, trying to control the horse. Her efforts almost worked until the man whistled again. The horse tossed its head in protest to her leading and trotted back to its owner. The man jumped on the horse behind her, grasped the reins from her hand and spurred the horse on.

Chapter Sixteen

She couldn't bear to ride another moment. Any minute now the children would walk into the house and find her missing. What would they do? What could she? Every step the horse took carried her farther away from them. "Can't we stop now? I'm so tired I can hardly see straight."

"We have a half a mile before another camping spot. We'll stop there."

Minutes later, he lifted her off the horse. Her legs were stiff from hours in the saddle so she carefully walked to a nearby tree and collapsed near its base. He glanced her way and threw her a strip of jerky. "Rest up, we need to travel a few more miles today."

She stared up at him. "I want to go back to my family. They need me."

His gaze traced her features before he nodded. "I plan to let you go, but not until Rutledge pays his due. He owes me that much—and more—after what he did."

She couldn't fathom what he was talking about. "There must be some mistake."

He laughed. "You think he's a good man, don't you?

He certainly has you fooled. He's nothing but a liar, a thief and a murderer."

"Impossible."

He knelt in front of her to grab her arm while his blue eyes sought hers in anguish. "You don't know. You don't know what he's done."

She winced. "You're hurting me."

He released his grip. "What did he tell you about his past? Did he tell you about his arrest? His jail time?"

She shook her head. "You're delusional."

"Delusional?" He stared at her for a long moment then strode to his saddlebag. He pulled out a rolled-up piece of paper and handed it to her. "I guess the wanted posters didn't make it this far upstate."

She pulled her gaze from his to unroll the poster. She stared in shock at the rendering of Nathan's face with the word *Wanted* above it and a reward offered under it.

"The courts may say he's served his time, but he owes me more than that—and I mean to see to it that he pays."

Shock and betrayal made her shake her head. "I don't understand."

He grabbed her arm more gently but with a decided urgency. "He killed my little brother, Kate. He shot him down like a dog. Eli was my best friend. When he died a part of me died with him. I haven't been the same since."

He released her and began to pace. "I can't stop thinking about him lying on the ground lifeless in the hands of the man who killed him." He lifted his tortured gaze to hers. "Rutledge's hands were covered in blood—my brother's blood. All to cover up his own dirty, rotten thieving. Since the money meant so much to him that he'd kill Eli to keep it, that same money is what I'm going to take in return. It won't bring Eli back, but maybe it will help his soul rest in peace."

Her thoughts flew back to Nathan's feverish mumblings about Eli. He'd mentioned blood, hadn't he? He'd also said he didn't do it, but he'd never said what "it" was. She should have asked him. Now all she could see was the anguish in Jeremiah's eyes. She'd felt that anguish before. It was awful.

"You haven't fully grieved for him," Kate recognized softly.

"I haven't had the chance. I've been too busy trying to bring him justice." He wiped a hand over his face to forestall tears. "If you knew what I'd been through, you'd want to help me."

Kate swallowed. "I do want to help you find some peace. My parents died two years ago. I know what it's like to lose a loved one."

"Then you won't fight me?"

Perhaps she could lull him into a false sense of security. "I don't want to fight you, Jeremiah, but why did you have to bring me into this? Why not just confront Nathan yourself?"

"I tried. He wouldn't listen. And the lawmen…" He shook his head. "They shouldn't have let him go. That's not justice. This is the only way I can make him pay for what he did." He took the wanted poster from her and stuffed it in his saddlebag. "We have to keep moving."

Kate opened her eyes slowly to find the sun streaming through the green canopy of trees. She'd watched her captor wander from camp through her lashes, then immediately began pulling at the knots that bound her feet. It had taken the whole night to free her hands. She'd succeeded at daybreak just as her captor began to stir. The knots binding her legs came free. She cautiously rose to her feet.

"Where are you going?" a voice demanded and she whirled to find her captor only feet from her.

"I have to use the necessary."

He surveyed her carefully. She tried to look tired even though her exhaustion was being replaced by adrenaline. She had to get away. Despite his promise not to hurt her, he was obviously unstable. She couldn't trust him. He frowned at her.

"You have three minutes then I'm coming after you."

"I'm afraid it's going to take more than three minutes," she warned.

He looked annoyed. "Five then."

Kate turned on her heel and moved toward the thickest part of the woods and just kept marching. When she was a good distance from the camp, she picked up her skirt and ran like she'd never run before. After all, she had a five-minute head start, maybe more. He would probably stew over whether she was really trying to escape or just taking a long time. Well, let him stew. She wouldn't go down without fighting every inch of the way.

Ten minutes passed and her legs screamed for mercy but she pushed even harder. She knew she would only have a few more minutes before unwelcome company would arrive. She needed a place to hide. Suddenly the trees stopped and so did the land. She skittered to a halt on an outcropping rock and looked down. There was water, a lot of it. And mist—a lot of that, too.

She glanced back the way she'd come, looking for

any sign that she was being pursued. Finding none, she stared down into the murky depths of the water. She took a deep breath, then jumped into the lake. Her skirts billowed out around her as she landed in water up to her chest. Her breath caught in her throat as the cold water soaked mercilessly through the layers of her dress and petticoats to her skin. Lying on her stomach, she pushed off from the dirt outcropping and swam beneath the water, only coming up for air when absolutely necessary.

The water grew deeper as she swam toward the center of the lake. She paused a few moments later to stare back toward the outcropping. Through the mist she thought she saw a horse and rider. Her heart sped in her chest. Had she been seen?

She slipped under the water and swam farther toward the center of the lake. A few minutes later she again looked toward shore and this time she was sure she heard a horse's neigh echo across the water. The rider turned his horse away from the outcropping and disappeared back the way she'd come.

She let out a relieved breath and allowed herself to float for a moment in the water to gain her bearings. She found herself in the middle of a lake covered with mist and dawning sunlight with a looming tree line surrounding it. It would have been beautiful had not she been running from danger.

She closed her eyes. *Lord, I know I haven't been the best at trusting You in the past but, please, I need Your help.*

Something scaly brushed across her right leg. She flinched to the left. That was sign enough for her. It wasn't long before she stumbled onto shore. She sat for a few moments to catch her breath before she finally began walking.

Suddenly a sense of foreboding gripped her. She stopped walking and looked into the woods around her. She took a step back. She sensed movement to her left. She impulsively dashed back into the water. She swam beneath the surface and came up on the other side of the lake. She staggered to shore dripping wet and gasping for breath but instantly felt peace.

She set out at a quick but steady pace. Glancing at the sky, she was thankful she had many hours to walk in the daylight. She wouldn't even think about the night. Not yet. She had to trust that the Lord would provide.

Nathan reluctantly slowed the wagon as he entered the outskirts of Peppin. He wanted to rush to the farm so he could show Kate the envelope in his saddlebag. He was sure the check was enough to cover her mortgage payment. In fact it was probably more than she'd ever yielded off a crop before since she'd planted more wheat and hadn't paid the harvesters.

"Nathan." He turned to see the deputy wave at him as he passed the sheriff's office. Nathan nodded in return but didn't stop to talk. The closer he got to the center of town the busier the streets became and the more often people began to wave at him. He returned their waves at first but soon became thoroughly confused. Why was everyone so happy to see him?

He slowed the wagon and stared more carefully at the next person who waved. He realized they weren't waving. They were trying to get his attention. He reined in the horses just as Ellie's voice cried out, "Nathan, stop!"

He turned to see her running after the wagon on the

raised wooden sidewalk. He set the brake and jumped down. He rounded the side of the wagon just as she nearly stumbled off the sidewalk. He caught her before she could fall, then guided her into a hug. Wrapping her arms around his waist, she immediately dissolved into tears. "Ellie, what's wrong?"

Sean and Lawson came to a panting stop in front of him. He glanced past them to search the gathering crowd. "Where's Kate?"

Sean straightened. "A man took her yesterday while we were at school. He left a note saying we can't get her back unless you pay him a lot of money."

Nathan felt the blood drain from his face. Thoughts and feelings rushed through him so quickly that he could hardly grasp any of them. Shock, fear and anger battled for dominance. They were superseded by guilt. He should have known. He should have protected her.

He'd known that Jeremiah was desperate yet the man he knew would never have stooped so low as to harm an innocent woman. That Jeremiah didn't exist anymore. A stranger had Kate. That stranger might try to hurt her or may have already have done so just to get even with him.

He felt like he was going to be sick. Sean, Ellie and Lawson were waiting for him to say something. He pulled himself together. Kneeling in the dirt in front of them, he set a firm hand on Sean's shoulder and looked him in the eye. "I'm going to find her, do you hear me?"

Sean nodded while his face turned red as he struggled to contain his emotions. Nathan met Lawson's worried gaze. "I'm going to bring her back." He turned to capture Ellie's tear-filled gaze. "I promise." She nodded causing a large tear to drip from her chin.

He stood to his feet. "I need to talk to Sheriff Hawkins. Do you guys want to ride with me?"

They immediately nodded. The crowd began to disperse. He turned the wagon around in the direction of the sheriff's office. Minutes later, children sat on top of the deputy's desk while Nathan sat in the chair across from the sheriff's. He barely held back a frustrated growl. "Sheriff, I understand you're just trying to do your job, but it sounds to me like you want me to sit here and twiddle my thumbs while Kate is in danger."

Sheriff Hawkins's calm demeanor leaned a little too close to disinterest for his taste. "Nathan, we all want to find Kate, but you must be reasonable." Nathan watched the sheriff point to the map stretched out on the desk between them. "Here is Peppin. Here is Colston."

He drew a large circle with his finger. "This is the area where they could be. Notice I said 'could be' because they might have taken an alternate route. Even assuming they stayed on one of the main trails, it would still be a guessing game. I can't authorize a search. There is just too much space to cover. It would be a waste of manpower and supplies. The ransom letter shows me the man won't harm Kate as long as she remains his bargaining tool."

The sheriff sat back as if his point had been made. "He gave us four days and that's plenty enough time to get an operation in the works. We'll catch him when he comes to town."

"I don't care about your operation. Kate needs help *now.*"

"I understand but—"

"Pardon me, but no, you don't understand. Your wife is safe at home."

"Well, yes—"

Nathan placed his Stetson on his head and stood. "I'm going after her."

"You're searching for a needle in a haystack."

"At least I'll be searching." Nathan glanced at the children's satisfied faces and tipped his head toward the door. "Let's go. I'll need to get a few thing squared away with Ms. Lettie before I head out."

"Sheriff, I'd like to apply for a leave of absence." Deputy Stone's voice made Nathan pause and turn. He met the deputy's eyes as the man said, "It seems a friend of mine could use some help."

The sheriff eyed both of them. "Very well, Deputy. Go if you must. I just don't think it'll do any good."

Nathan shrugged. "Then we'll make it our mission to prove you wrong, sir."

Sheriff Hawkins looked at him for a moment then gave a nod. "You do that, son. You do that."

Kate cupped her berry-stained fingers and brought them to her lips, allowing the cool water to caress her dry throat as she swallowed it. She lay back allowing the sun to beat down on her. Its heat continually stole her energy the way hungry children pilfered bread. She closed her eyes against its glare only to feel a slight burning sensation beneath her lids. She knew it must be from lack of sleep. Perhaps it would be best to rest during the heat of the day and travel when the heat tapered off in the afternoon.

"Lord, were You proving Yourself by letting me escape from Jeremiah?" she whispered though no one was around to hear her. "Or, did you allow me to be abducted to show me I shouldn't trust Nathan?"

She didn't want to believe that Jeremiah's accusations were accurate. Yet she had recognized within his words a disconcerting ring of truth.

Who was Nathan Rutledge? She had felt such an immediate connection with him. She had invited him into her home. She had shared so much of herself. Yet what did she truly know about him? What if the little she knew was really a lie? What if it was an act, covering up the fact that he really was a thief and a murderer?

She covered her face from the glare of the sun but she couldn't hide from her fears. She'd made mistakes before. What if this time wasn't any different? Questions roiled through her mind but other memories rose against them. The sound of his voice as he read their family Bible every evening. Nathan kneeling in the dirt to comfort Sean and Ellie. Nathan's hand on Lawson's shoulder, praising him for his hard work while the boy smiled bashfully in response. The laughter in his eyes when he twirled her during the Harvest Dance. She didn't know what he'd done in the past, but he wasn't the heartless killer Jeremiah had described. She was sure of that. As sure as she was that it was past time for her to get home.

She'd barely rested since she'd escaped. Yet even then, the hungry gnawing of her stomach refused to let her truly rest. Her feet ached, her legs were tired, and her mind was nearly numb from fatigue. Her every thought was directed toward home—to where her boots were hopefully carrying her.

She closed her eyes tightly and imagined herself there, surrounded by her family. She would make it home soon. She had to.

* * *

"The prints stop here." Nathan tipped his hat back as he frowned at the ground.

"She must have jumped into the lake," the deputy concluded.

Nathan's eyes scanned the lake. "She tried to escape and by the looks of the other prints she was chased."

"So did she escape only to be recaptured?" The deputy searched the woods around them with his gaze. "We'll follow the horse prints and see if we pick up Kate's."

Both men remounted and followed the trail running counterclockwise around the lake. A little more than a quarter of the way Nathan pulled Delilah up short and let out a whoop, then dismounted. He was almost too busy to notice the deputy's sharp halt and questioning look. Nathan pointed to the tracks heading away from the lake. "She's free. Look how the horse's tracks continue that way and hers head off in that direction."

Joshua dismounted before squatting for a closer look. "She stepped right on this print." Looking up, he grinned. "You're right. She is free, or was at this point."

Nathan nodded soberly but could not deny a relieved smile. "We'll need to follow the other tracks to be sure."

After following the tracks around the lake, Nathan found they headed back off into the woods.

Deputy Stone reined in his horse. "Sorry I have to leave like this, Rutledge, but if I go now I might have a chance at finding this man."

"Are you sure you want to take him without backup?"

Joshua shrugged nonchalantly. "I figure I can handle him about as well as you can handle Kate."

"I reckon I'll ignore that," he said to the laughing

man. Turning Delilah around, Nathan said, "You just worry about catching that outlaw and let me worry about Kate."

Joshua snorted causing Nathan to roll his eyes before tipping his Stetson toward the man. "Nice riding with you, Deputy. Do me a favor and don't get shot."

"Same to you, Rutledge." He tipped his Stetson. "On both counts."

Kate stepped quietly from the cover of trees into the moonlit clearing before her. The loud song of a katydid drowned out the sound of her footsteps and covered her approach. With each step she took, she prayed the Lord would forgive her for what she was going to do.

Her steps slowed cautiously as she neared the campsite. In the dim light Kate could see the still form of the man who would unwittingly provide her first real meal in days. Her gaze scanned the campsite. There must be food somewhere.

Perhaps it was in his saddlebag? Her gaze faltered. He was sleeping on it. She continued her search from the shadows. There. On the other side of him, partially hidden by the shadows, was a small jar.

She moved out of the fire's light and circled around toward the man. Kneeling in the dirt dangerously close to her sleeping benefactor she reached for the jar. Her fingers felt only the maddening brush of its cool glass. She scooted herself forward a little more then reached for it again.

Just as her fingers touched the jar a strong hand caught her wrist. She gasped, jerking her arm back and away. The hold on her wrist slipped for a split second allowing her to wrench free. Before she could pull away entirely a second hand clamped around it. Her free hand pushed at the ones that held her captive.

"Let go of me," she demanded.

She heard the dark figure's sharp intake of breath and immediately realized she'd made a mistake by speaking. Now he knew she was a woman. She braced her free hand behind her to pull with all her might. The grip on her wrist slackened enough for her to break free. The man called out but she scrambled to her feet.

Her worn boots crashed through the knee-high weeds as she ran toward the woods. Her heart galloped ahead of her as she realized the man was chasing her. Fear tangled her thoughts as the torn hem of her skirt tangled about her legs. Finally reaching the woods, Kate wound through the trees in a ragged fashion until she could no longer hear the running tread behind her.

She lifted a hand to brace herself against a nearby tree trunk. Her breath resounded heavily in the stillness of the woods around her. Her hand went to the stitch in her side and remained there as she turned to rest her back against the tree. Leaning her head back, she closed her eyes against the swaying branches above her and focused on pulling air into her lungs.

Tears burned her eyes as she murmured a scattered prayer so soft that she couldn't hear it over the sound of the gentle breeze. A twig snapped to her left. Her eyes flew open. She froze for a moment then whirled toward the sound.

Powerful arms came around her, catching her hands and pinning them behind her. She struggled to free herself but was forced backward until the tree's rough bark scraped against her knuckles. She couldn't move.

She opened her mouth to scream but the man covered it with his hand. “Hush, Kate. It’s me. It’s Nathan. I came to take you home.”

Chapter Seventeen

She froze. Slowly her eyes lifted to survey his shadowed features. Her breath caught in her throat. How could it possibly be him?

"Nathan?" she questioned in a whisper only realizing after she said it that he'd released her completely. It must be him. No one else would let her go so easily. A sob of relief hitched in her throat. Before she even thought to question the wisdom of it, she stepped into his embrace and let her cheek rest against his chest.

He placed a kiss in her hair then tilted her head back so that he could look at her in the dim light. "Did he hurt you?"

It took her a moment to realize who he was talking about. When she did, Jeremiah's accusations flit clumsily through her mind like an annoying light bug hitting the lantern glass. She searched his face. Pure regard, concern and compassion stared back at her and her heart warmed under his gaze.

Jeremiah's words faded away along with any lingering doubts as she faced the reality she'd been running from since the night she'd found Nathan outside with

Delilah. She loved him. Her hand reached up to trace the angle of his jawline. He caught her hand and pressed a kiss into it. “Answer me, Kate. Did he hurt you?”

“What?” she breathed, then forced herself to focus on his question. “No, he didn’t hurt me.”

He paused. “You’re sure?”

“Of course, I’m sure. I think I’d know if—” Her words stumbled to a halt when he leaned down to kiss her. Their lips barely brushed before his muscles tensed beneath her fingers. He pulled away to stare into the forest around them.

Then she heard it. A rustling just above the breeze announced the presence of yet another stranger. The slow nearly muffled sound of hoofbeats confirmed it. Her fists clenched against the tension.

“Kate,” Nathan whispered tersely. “Promise me you’ll run if I tell you to.”

“But—”

“Promise me.”

She nodded. His hand crept down to his holster. A steely voice spoke from the surrounding forest. “Pardon me, but I couldn’t help but wonder if that woman you’ve captured is Kate O’Brien.”

Nathan spun to face the man with his guns at the ready just as the man stepped into the clearing ready to do battle. Everyone seemed to freeze for a moment then Kate stepped out from behind Nathan. “Deputy Stone.”

“So it is you, Kate.” The man grinned then waved his Stetson. “I was just making sure.”

Nathan holstered his gun. “I suppose this means you couldn’t find Jeremiah Fulton.”

“I tracked him as long as I could but he took the main road toward Bensen. I figured I’d have better luck getting their local law enforcement on the case than if I went off alone. What do you think?"

"It makes sense to me." Nathan glanced back to her. "I'm sure Kate is tired. Why don't we go back to camp and we can start home first thing in the morning."

She nodded. "I admit I'm a little shaky and sleep sounds good but food sounds even better. I've lived on berries for the past few days."

Nathan grinned. "That's something we can fix."

"Then what are you two standing there for?" she asked. "Lead me to it!"

Nathan lifted Kate from the saddle and carried her sleeping body to the bedroll. She moaned as he set her down and lifted her tired blue eyes to his. "Food."

He lifted the blanket toward her chin. "In the morning."

"Promise," she murmured, her lashes drifting down.

"I promise."

She turned on her side and went to sleep. Nathan let out a deep breath in relief. She was safe. He rubbed a hand across an unshaven chin then squaring his shoulders he moved back toward the camp.

"Is she all right?" Deputy Stone asked as he moved toward the fire with his bedroll in hand.

"As far as I can tell," he said then glanced over to her sleeping form. He hated the fact that Jeremiah was still out there somewhere but the important thing was that Kate was safe. He planned to keep her that way for as long as she allowed him.

Nathan felt himself being watched. He glanced over to meet the deputy's gaze. During the time they'd spent searching for Kate, they'd created the beginnings of a friendship. Nathan hadn't had a friendship with a man his age in a while and the last ones obviously hadn't turned out well.

The man grinned knowingly. "You've got it bad, Rutledge."

"You think I don't know that?" he asked with a wry smile. "Keep it down, will you? I haven't told her yet."

"Sure you have." He smirked. "She just hasn't noticed."

The smell of coffee tantalized Kate's senses. It pulled her slowly from her scattered dreams and made her aware of the insistent beams of sunlight that spilled across her eyelids. She sat up abruptly to stare through her knotted hair at the scene before her.

Nathan knelt near the outskirts of the campfire as he added wood to maintain the hungry flames. The deputy stood across the fire from him and stirred something in a small round bowl. A pan sat in wait on a log that had been rolled close to the fire. She didn't know what was in that bowl but her stomach growled at the mere implication of food being made.

She pushed her hair away from her face, drawing the attention of the two men. They both wished her a good morning but it was Nathan's smile that made her gaze linger upon his. He pulled the tin coffee kettle from the fire and poured her a cup. He knelt beside her to hand her the mug. "How do you feel this morning?"

"Better than I felt last night." She took a small sip of the coffee and winced. "It's rather strong."

He smiled. "Good. You'll need the energy."

She turned to meet his gaze. "The children, are they—"

"They're fine. They've been staying with Doc and Ms. Lettie."

"Good," she said then glanced away from him to where Deputy Stone poured a circle of batter into the frying pan. "Are you making pancakes?" she asked hopefully.

The deputy looked up with a grin. "I sure am. Are you telling me you might want one?"

"I'm telling you I might want a few."

He nodded. "It will only be a few minutes."

"I can hardly wait," she said. In fact, she wasn't sure she could wait at all. A hole seemed to be developing in the middle of her stomach and she wasn't at all sure that she'd ever be able to fill it. She pulled in another sip of Nathan's wicked brew. Lowering her hand, she noticed a streak of dirt on her wrist. She rubbed it but it wouldn't come off.

"There's a small stream not far from here if you'd like to freshen up," Nathan said.

She met his gaze for a long moment, barely daring to hope. "Do you have soap?"

Nathan produced a bar of the precious substance and showed her the way to the stream. He left her alone for a few minutes promising that he wouldn't be far should she call for help. She scrubbed the dirt from her face and hands, then, since she'd lost her hairpins long ago, she combed through her hair the best she could before pulling it back into a long braid.

When she realized nothing more could be done at the present, she returned to the camp with Nathan and was delighted to find a large plate of pancakes waiting for her. She didn't care that they boasted no preserves to sweeten their taste but took the plate and sat down on the log near the fire. She picked up a nearby fork. It was making its descent toward the pancakes when the deputy turned from the skillet. "Wait, Kate. That was for all of us."

"Oh," she breathed. Her fork wavered then came to rest beside the pancakes rather than on top of them. "Where are the other plates?'

He nodded toward them then turned back to the fire. Nathan picked up the plates then held them out toward her. She frowned in concentration as she carefully transferred pancakes onto the other plates so that each held the same amount. She quickly cut into the golden cakes on her plate, then placed a large triangle of it into her mouth.

She closed her eyes. Ecstasy. She swallowed. Unsatisfying ecstasy. She continued to eat but the more she ate the hungrier she became. The fork moved the pancakes to her mouth in what seemed to be increasingly unbearable slowness. She was only halfway through when Nathan noticed her desperation. "Kate, slow down. You're going to choke yourself."

She glanced up in questioning innocence.

He narrowed his gaze. "You heard me. Slow down."

Kate gave him an unappreciative look. Yes, she'd heard him but she could not imagine obeying him.

"Nathan is right, Kate. If you eat too much too soon you won't be able to keep anything down," Deputy Stone chimed in.

"Is that right?" she asked after another swallow.

He nodded.

She smiled then cut a particularly big chunk off her pancake and crammed it into her mouth. *Let's see them try to make me slow down. Don't they know I've been starving for days? I had nothing to eat but berries. Berries. Berries. I don't think I'll eat another berry again in my life.*

She closed her eyes to concentrate on chewing and suddenly her plate was snatched from her hand. Her eyes flew open to connect with Nathan's determined gaze. She narrowed her eyes. "What are you doing? Give me back my plate."

"You're going to make yourself sick."

"I don't care."

"Well, I do."

"Nathan Rutledge," she warned as she watched him scrape the rest of her pancakes onto his plate. "What are you going to do with them?"

She gasped as he cut into them and began to eat them along with his own. "You're eating my pancakes."

"I'm keeping you from getting sick."

"I'd rather you didn't."

He leaned forward. "Kate, listen to me. This is very important. Your body has existed on barely anything for days on end. You can't shock it by putting in so much food at once. I am not saying that you can't eat. You must eat. However, you should eat small meals throughout the day. You've had enough for now but I promise there will be more food later."

She looked at him for a long moment then glanced to the deputy. At his supporting nod, she sighed. "Fine. Not that you've given me any choice."

Nathan held his plate out toward her. "It's yours if that's what you want. I only wanted you to know the truth."

She shook her head. "No. You are right. I'll do as you say."

He almost choked. “What did you say?”

She lifted her chin and met his gaze with an attempt at a threatening smile. “You heard me. Just don’t get used to it.”

The deputy laughed. “Well, I’m finished. Let’s get things packed up and take this young woman back home.”

It only took a few minutes to put out the fire and destroy the evidence of their campsite. She soon found herself staring up at Nathan as he waited for her to mount Delilah ahead of him. He looked completely disreputable with the shadowy three-day beard of his. He could almost pass for an outlaw if not for the warmth and caring in his eyes.

She glanced away. *I can’t believe I’ve fallen in love with a man who has tangled with the law. Maybe he didn’t kill someone but he definitely hasn’t told me the whole story of what happened before he answered that advertisement.*

She couldn’t allow herself to envision a future with a man with a questionable past. She owed it to herself and to her siblings to find out the truth. As soon as she got home she’d cull through the letters he’d sent to see if he’d offered some explanation that she’d missed. If not, she’d demand he explain himself. In the meantime, she didn’t even want to think about his problems until after she laid eyes on her brother and sister.

As she debated the wisdom of riding with him for several hours, with the weight of her unanswered questions and unresolved feelings bearing down on her, Delilah turned her head toward Kate and bared her teeth. Repeatedly. Kate caught her breath. “Did you see that?”

Nathan glanced at her questioningly.

Of course, not. Kate narrowed her eyes at Delilah. The horse would probably bolt the moment Kate put her weight in the stirrup. That clinched it. Kate shook her head and took a step back. "I think I'd rather ride with the deputy."

He tilted his head to survey her carefully. "You think so? Well, Deputy Stone has plans of his own so it appears you're stuck with me."

She glanced to where the deputy was tying his bedroll to his saddle. "What does he have to do?"

"He's going to scout around to make sure we don't get any unwelcome visitors on the way back."

"Oh," she breathed in frustration. Praying Delilah wouldn't bolt, she placed her muddy boot in the stirrup and swung onto the saddle. The horse must have remembered their truce, for though Kate braced herself, Delilah stood perfectly still. Nathan quickly settled into the saddle behind her.

She let out a breath of relief. The saddle was bigger than it appeared. There was plenty of room between her and Nathan. Then his arms came around to hold the reigns and she stilled as his chest brushed her back.

"There, that's not so bad, is it?" he asked.

No, it's worse, she thought but instead let out an affirming mumble. She didn't want to be distracted by him or the emotions he so easily raised in her until she had time to sort out the past few days of her life.

They soon parted ways with the deputy. A few hours passed and the early morning sun inched its way across the sky until it shone directly overhead.

"Aren't we going to stop for lunch?" she asked.

"We don't need to." Nathan presented her with a long

stand of beef jerky. "Here. You can eat this as quickly as you like."

Ignoring the sardonic grin in his voice, she took it from him and broke a piece off with her teeth. Chewing it, she glanced around at the landscape. It was pretty enough but still unfamiliar to her. "How far away are we now?"

"Probably a good four hours," Nathan replied from behind her in the saddle.

"Better than a bad four hours, wouldn't you say?"

"I would."

She felt her spirits rising. They were getting closer. She glanced around but the deputy's horse was nowhere in sight.

"Why don't you try to rest, Kate?" Nathan asked, pulling her from her thoughts. "Just lean back and close your eyes."

She narrowed her eyes. "Lean back and close my eyes, is that all?"

"I'll have you know my intentions are nothing but honorable, Mrs. Rutledge, so you needn't worry yourself." He paused thoughtfully. "Unless, of course, it isn't me you're worried about."

"Don't be ridiculous," she breathed, although his comment hit a little to close to the truth.

His drawl was nothing if not casual. "Well, you were the one to send for a husband."

She tensed. "You know very well that I did not send for a husband."

He shrugged a broad shoulder. "No, but you didn't exactly send me packing, did you? I reckon that must count for something."

She was not in the mood for his games. She turned

in the saddle so he could see that fact for himself. She lifted her chin and pinned him with her gaze. "Don't tempt me."

Their eyes caught and held. He read the fire in her eyes just fine but instead of backing down, he inclined his head questioningly. His brown eyes flashed with gold then trailed down to her mouth before meeting hers. His voice was low and serious. "I'd say that's a fair warning."

She caught her breath. Her gaze clung to his for a long moment before she turned to stare at the road before them. "Are you sure I can't ride with the deputy?"

"I'm sure," he said calmly. "Why don't you eat your lunch?"

An hour and a half later, the horse's gait had long since become a lulling rhythm. Her eyes were slowly but surely closing on her. Perhaps Nathan wouldn't mind if she dozed for a bit. She grimaced. The man had obviously reverted back to his cowboy days. For the past hour he'd done nothing but hum, whistle or even occasionally sing. Strangely enough, all of the songs were slow or lullabies.

She knew he was trying to get her to relax. It was working. Her eyes closed and she felt her head nod forward. She snapped it back up. She decided she didn't want to break her neck by falling from the horse.

Staring at the piece of road framed by Delilah's dark ears, she slowly began to lean back. Small bursts of yellow against the green indicated the spattering of flowers growing beside the road. She blinked sleepily then looked back at the road.

She waited one last moment, then steeled herself by taking in a breath. Finally, her back met the warm solid strength of his chest. She waited a moment and was not disappointed. Nathan's whistling came to a halt with one last down-spiraling note.

She bit her lip then waited for his whistling to start again. It took another moment but it started up again slowly. Kate firmly decided that she was wrong. Exasperating couldn't fully describe Nathan Rutledge. A reluctant smile tilted her lips as she drifted to sleep.

Chapter Eighteen

Nathan leaned against the wagon as he waited outside the schoolhouse for the children. He hadn't liked leaving Kate at the farm all by herself but she'd been desperate for some time alone to rid herself of the dirt she'd accumulated during her days in the wilderness. She and Deputy Stone both seemed convinced that Fulton would move on. Nathan wasn't entirely sure. He had fooled himself into a false sense of security by believing that same thing before, and each time he'd been wrong. It wasn't over. That much he knew.

He'd already been to see Doc and Ms. Lettie, both of whom had promised to drop by the farm as soon as Kate had a chance to rest. He'd also stopped by the Post Office and was surprised to find a letter from his family. He slipped it out of his pocket, wondering if he should give in to the temptation to read it or wait until he got back to the cabin.

He glanced at the schoolhouse door. Realizing the children would probably be another few minutes, he turned the letter over to break the seal. He began to read it and smiled in relief. Mariah had done as he'd asked and written to the sheriff in Noches for a full account of the incident Jeremiah had mentioned to them. She wrote that their parents were satisfied that he'd been found innocent of all charges.

Her letter was short so he moved to the next sheaf of paper included in the envelope. He glanced down at the signature and his heart began beating harder in his chest. This letter was from his pa.

Dear Nathan,

I've wanted to write you for a while now but I didn't know how to contact you. I guess that was my own doing. It looks like you've gotten yourself into a heap of trouble since you left but you've also gotten yourself out of it. I'm proud of you for that. I just wanted to let you know that I regret the way things have been between us. I know you must think I've been too hard on you and the truth is, I probably have been. The reason might surprise you. You may not have realized it but I'd been grooming you to take over the ranch those past few years before you left. I know it was supposed to go to your brother but you have a head for business that would have made the Rutledge holdings grow into an empire.

I never told you that. I didn't think I needed to until you decided to leave. Everything I'd envisioned for the future came crashing down around me. Perhaps it was selfish of me but I didn't want to share you with anyone else. I wanted you to stay and work with me. When you rejected my offer it felt like you were rejecting everything I'd worked to provide for you. Your last letter showed me that wasn't the case.

Mariah tells me that you got yourself hitched to a girl who may not let you stay around. If she doesn't, I want you to know that you're welcome here. The position of foreman is available for your taking. Just send word ahead to let me know you're coming.

Pa

Nathan stared at the sheaf of paper, his thoughts in an uproar. His pa not only wanted to reconcile but was also offering him a way out. *Is this from You, God?*

He'd wanted so much to believe that he could leave his broken dreams behind him to embark on a new future here in Peppin with Kate and her siblings. Now he was beginning to wonder if that was even possible. His past continued to haunt him through the specter of Fulton's anger and need for revenge. As for his relationship with Kate, he wasn't at all sure where he stood with her.

He could hardly hold her to the emotions that had almost led her to accept his kiss. She'd been out in the wilderness for days without adequate food, water or rest. Before he'd left with the wheat, he'd thought he was making progress. Her attempts to avoid him on the ride home had left him second-guessing that assumption.

The schoolhouse door flew open and he slipped the letter into his pocket. Children began to scurry out the door, with some hovering in the schoolyard while others immediately went their separate ways. It wasn't long before Nathan spotted Sean in the bustle of children.

The boy's eyes lit on his, then grew wide with cautious hope. He skirted the other children to hurry toward their wagon. Staring up with world-weary eyes too old for his age, Sean asked, "Did you find her?"

Nathan smiled. "She's waiting for you at home."

A smile grew across the boy's face until it exploded into a grin. "I'll get the others."

Kate was tucking the last hairpin into her damp chignon when the creak of wheels drew her gaze to the window. She dashed down the stairs, then opened the door just as the wagon came to a stop in front of the house. Ellie jumped down. The little girl's eyes found hers and began to fill with tears. Kate sank to her knees as Ellie traveled the few last steps into her arms.

"Ellie," Kate consoled as the girl wept in her arms.

"I was so scared. We couldn't find you." Ellie's shoulders gave a small shudder.

"I know, but God protected me and He was with you even when I wasn't. You know that, don't you?"

She nodded, which set free a few large tears that spilled over her cheek and off her chin. Kate wiped the tears from her sister's cheeks then smiled. "It's all right."

She waited until Ellie gave her a trembling smile in return before she released her and looked for her brother. Sean was just hopping down from the wagon. He smiled as his gaze caught hers, then he quickly walked toward her and pulled her into a strong hug. He stepped back to look at her in concern. "Are you sure you're all right?"

She nodded.

He shook his head seriously. "If he hurt you—"

"He didn't. I promise you."

His eyes filled with desperation. "I should have been

here. I should have protected you. Since Pa died, I'm the man of this family. It's my responsibility to keep us safe."

"No, Sean," she said. "If you had been here he would have tried to hurt you. What happened wasn't your fault. Don't ever believe that."

Kate glanced behind Sean to Lawson. He stood beside the wagon looking unsure of what to do. She realized he probably wasn't used to such open familial displays of emotion but she didn't let it stop her. She stepped forward and pulled him into a hug. It took him a stunned second to return it.

"I'm glad you're back," he said in her ear before he released her.

She smiled. "Thank you."

Nathan cleared his throat from where he stood near the wagon bed. "Now that everyone is finally home, we have a lot of things to get inside the house. Everyone is responsible for their own things. This looks like Sean's."

He began tossing the children their belongings, making a game out of it, and easing the moment for all of them. When all of the children had disappeared into the house Kate shaded her eyes to look up at Nathan. "Is there anything I can carry?"

Nathan grinned then jumped down from the back of the wagon. "As a matter of fact, there is. Ms. Lettie sent an entire meal with us. She didn't want you to have to cook on your first day back."

"Bless her for thinking of that," she said as she joined him.

"Doc is planning to visit you in the next few days."

She nearly rolled her eyes but instead turned to look at him. "I'll be fine. All I need is a little rest."

"I know that but people are concerned." He shrugged then began gathering as much food as he could. He met her gaze. "They can't help it. They love you."

The door to the house flew open and as the children hurried out Nathan gave her a parting smile before carrying the load of food inside.

Sean and Lawson took what remained into the house, leaving Kate alone with her sister. When the girl moved to follow them inside Kate called her back. "Ellie, do you remember where you put the letters?"

Ellie stared at her in confusion. "What letters?"

"The ones from Nathan, silly."

"Oh." The girl tilted her head to stare up with a curious look in her eye. "Why do you want them?"

"I just want to read them."

"I see," Ellie said while staring at Kate as though trying to discern all of her secrets.

She glanced surreptitiously at the door of the house then back at Ellie. "Where are they?"

Kate slipped toward the back of the empty barn where several small wooden crates stored some of their father's old tools. She lifted the cover off one of the crates and there, partially buried by broken halters and old tools, rested their father's tackle box. Kate pulled it out and placed it on her lap. The lid opened easily to display a small stack of letters.

She shook her head. The lengths that her family had gone to, to secure her a husband never ceased to amaze her. She reluctantly had to give them credit for their cleverness. She never would have stumbled upon the proof of their guilt unless she had been told where to look.

It had been hard to ignore Ellie's curious glances

throughout the evening. It had been equally difficult to disregard her own unanswered questions until the children had gone off to school and Nathan was distracted by his chores on another part of the farm. She pushed down the guilt she felt for leading Nathan to believe that she was content to spend the day resting when she was really planning to discover the truth about his past.

She pulled the letters from the tackle box, then settled beside the crates to open the first letter. She was surprised to find the missive wasn't from Nathan at all but rather a letter of inquiry from another suitor. She smiled as she read the letter written by an older gentleman looking more for a companion than a wife. She set it aside then continued to read through the others in the stack. It seemed the advertisement had elicited quite a response.

The stack of letters began to dwindle and Kate had yet to come across one of Nathan's letters. She leaned back against the barn wall with a reluctant smile. Based on the letters she'd read from other potential suitors, she had been fortunate to end up with Nathan. She realized she probably would have made the same choice that her family and Ms. Lettie had made.

She let out a sigh and let one more letter float to the haphazard pile around her on the floor. Nathan's letters had to be in the stack somewhere. She opened the next letter, then glanced down to the signature. She hesitated at the sight of his name scrawled across the bottom of the missive. He'd signed it, *faithfully yours*.

Suddenly a wave of guilt swept over her. She stared unseeingly at the letter, then realized she couldn't do it. She gently folded the letter closed. It might be the most foolish thing she would ever do but she decided that she was going to trust Nathan Rutledge to be the man he'd presented himself to be. At least until she asked him about Fulton's accusations face-to-face.

As far as she could tell, Nathan had not had an easy life before he'd married her. She might never be sure of all the details of that life but she did know he was not the person Fulton had portrayed him to be. Her experiences with him were proof of that. She would have discovered such outrageous flaws in his character, especially since she had been looking so desperately for some reason, any reason, not to love him.

They had been living and interacting so closely that she had been given the opportunity to observe his character in many different situations. As it was, she had discovered that though Nathan was far from perfect he still strove toward and displayed the characteristics of his Father.

She realized her legs were aching from her sitting on them and slid them out in front of her. She wondered just how long she had been here in the shadows of the barn between the feed sacks and the crates, trying to peruse the pages of Nathan's past. Sighing, she began to gather all of the letters around her and fold them neatly back into stacks.

She had just lifted the pile of letters back into the tackle box when the sound of the barn door opening caused her to freeze. Glancing up in dread, she watched Nathan walk in. She bit her lip. What would he think if he found her here with all of these letters? Maybe he'd just get what he needed and leave. She carefully put the letters down and attempted to back farther into the shadows of the barn.

* * *

Nathan grabbed the muckrake from its post near the back of the barn. He heard the door creak open behind him.

"I thought you were going to rest," he called over his shoulder as he reached for the broom. He heard a quiet gasp from his right and glanced that way only to see the flash of a familiar blue skirt disappear behind the feed bags. *Kate,* he noted in confusion. *If that's Kate, then who...?*

"Fulton," Nathan growled and spun to face his adversary just as the man stepped another pace toward him with his guns at the ready.

"Drop your weapons," the man commanded. "All of them."

He considered his options then set the tools aside and slowly unbelted his holster. He dropped it to the ground so that it would slide closer to where Kate hid. Fulton tilted his head to Nathan's left. "Move away from them. You and me, Rutledge, we're going to settle this once and for all."

Kate blew the floating dust from where it tickled her nose and shifted on her knees for a better view. Peering around the sacks of feed near the ladder to the loft, she watched as Nathan's brown gaze slid over Jeremiah Fulton's shoulder and met hers. His face gave away nothing, not even a flicker of recognition. He looked down and away from her. She followed his gaze to where his gun rested on the ground. She had to get it.

"Why are you here, Fulton?" Nathan's voice drew her attention even as it drew the interest of the gunman. "I don't understand. You could be free from the law some place farther west or across the border."

"You would still be here walking around free. As if you deserve that. As if you didn't kill my brother," Fulton said.

Kate swallowed and glanced at the gun then slowly made her way toward it. Her heart thumped in her chest. All he had to do was turn around and she would be spotted. She carefully reached for the gun. She wasn't close enough.

"I didn't kill your brother, Fulton."

"Liar."

She glanced up. If she went any farther she'd be in Fulton's line of sight but she knew she had to take the chance. She placed a stabilizing hand on the ground in front of her, then reached her right hand to grasp the barrel.

"Listen," Nathan said sharply, barely stopping Jeremiah from turning to pace and inevitably spotting Kate. "You need to face the fact that your brother took your land right from under you. He did the same to me. We were both dense enough to sit by and let it happen."

In the corner of his eye, he watched Kate begin her slow and careful trek back to her original spot.

"I don't believe you." The man combed his fingers through his hair.

Nathan spoke in calming tones. "I didn't want to believe it, either, but there comes a time when we have to face facts no matter how painful they are. Eli was my best friend. I never thought anything was wrong when he made such a fuss about handling the financial end of things. It freed me up to work with the horses. That was where I wanted to be and Eli wanted to be in the office so that worked out real nice.

"I went over the records after everything fell apart. It looks as if the ranch hit some rough times because of poor management. Not his fault, at first—the job was too big for one person. Instead of asking for help, Eli borrowed from other areas to balance the books. You and I were those areas but mainly you."

Fulton looked down, shaking his head and Nathan used that opportunity to look at Kate. *Leave now. Slip out the back.*

She sent back a message loud and clear though she didn't say a single word. *You have to be kidding. I'm not leaving you with this crazy person.*

Nathan nearly growled in frustration but managed to withhold the urge in order to protect her. Instead he pulled his gaze back to his former friend and business partner just as the man looked up. He continued speaking as he tried to think of some way to get them out of this. The truth was the only weapon he had.

"He was probably more comfortable borrowing from you, thinking he'd pay it back. When that didn't work he started gambling. He lost more than he won. He realized everything was going to crumble so he got desperate. He pinned what he could on me and was going to hightail it out of town."

Fulton began to appear more agitated. He turned to pace. Nathan had no choice but to continue, hoping that for once the man would listen to what the courts had already proclaimed. "I stumbled upon him leaving and confronted him. He didn't come after me. He turned the gun on himself and said he was going to kill himself. I tried to talk him out of it but he wouldn't listen. That's when I tried to wrestle the gun from him. Somehow in the scuffle he managed to get a shot off. He killed himself, Fulton."

"Lies!" Fulton shouted.

"No. It's true. As to the money you think I have, it doesn't exist." Nathan tilted his head toward the door hoping Kate would read the message he'd carefully disguised. It was time for her to go. Things weren't going to get any better. She needed to make a break for it.

Either Kate didn't catch his signal or she ignored it. He was leaning toward the latter. Her inaction forced Nathan to continue his efforts to make Fulton see the truth. "Check the receipts. I barely broke even on what I paid for my share of the land and what I sold it for. I even offered you the land at more than a fair price. You wouldn't consider the deal. In fact, you threatened me."

The man snorted. "Of course I did. You tried to sell me what was rightfully mine."

"Fulton—"

"I'm tired of listening to this," he said then stepped forward with his gun at the ready.

"Stop. It doesn't have to be this way."

A chill went down Nathan's back as Jeremiah cocked his gun. This was it. It was best to take it bravely. *Lord, if only Kate didn't have to witness this.*

Kate. As a last effort Nathan shot a glance toward her with only one word echoing in his gaze. *Shoot.*

Chapter Nineteen

Kate's eyes widened. She raised the gun and pulled the trigger. Instead of the loud bang she was expecting all she heard was a click. Her mind stopped working for a moment. Then she glanced down at the gun and pulled again. *Click.* She caught her breath. The hammer was still down. She pushed it up then pulled the trigger again. *Bam!*

She glanced up to find both men shying away from the blast only now they were both facing her. Jeremiah's expression was filled with rage while Nathan's showed a mix of impatience, exasperation and relief.

Minutes later Kate's wrist chafed at the rough rope as she found herself in an all-too-familiar situation. She tried to wriggle her wrist yet found she was unable to do so. She tried wiggling her arms then her feet. Nothing below her shoulders or ankles moved.

It looked as if Fulton had learned his lesson. Escape for her seemed impossible. She glanced at Nathan. A thought hit her and a laugh bubbled up in her throat.

She managed to turn her upper body so that she could lean her head against the wall. "I never really thought about it but when one must die tragically, dying next to a handsome man is definitely the best option."

Nathan looked at her as if she was insane. "Kate, aren't you the least bit concerned about this situation?"

"Not really," she confessed. "Somehow I can't see your friend killing us. He's had so many opportunities. Yet, the most he's ever done is tie us up and push us around. He could have killed you after my gun went off but he didn't do it then, either."

Nathan shook his head and looked away. "I don't find that comforting."

Delilah edged toward Kate, nickering softly. She watched the horse warily. "Nathan, if you let that horse step on me—"

"She's not going to step on you."

"You keep saying that but I'm not sure it's true."

"It's true. Besides, when have you ever been afraid of horses?"

Kate looked at him impatiently. "I'm not afraid of horses. It's just a well-established fact that Delilah has a grudge against me and I don't like my head being in kicking range!"

"Would you calm down?"

"I'm not excited!"

"Then stop arguing!"

"Who's arguing?"

Nathan growled and turned away.

Kate scooped up a handful of hay. She turned her back to Nathan, which took considerable effort, and weakly threw it at him.

"You missed." His tone was a maddening mix of amusement and indulgence.

She didn't bother to turn around but instead leaned

sideways into the wood of the stall. “I don’t care. According to you, we’re going to die anyway.”

Nathan snorted. “It’s not my fault you forgot to cock the gun.”

She bristled. “I wouldn’t have had to cock the gun if you’d done what you were supposed to do.”

“Which was?”

“How would I know? Whatever it is you failed to do.”

There was silence a moment, then Nathan asked, “Why don’t we pray?”

“What?” she asked, caught off guard. Throwing her weight, she rolled to face him.

“Let’s pray,” he repeated, his eyes dark and serious. His head bowed. “God, You know where we are and how to bring us out of this. We know it isn’t Your will for us to be murdered so we ask for Your protection, for Your mercy. We ask that You send Your angels to guard us lest we dash our foot against a stone. Be our shield from persecution. In Jesus’s name, amen.”

“Amen,” Kate echoed. She sat in thoughtful silence. “What’s that smell?”

Nathan comfortingly clucked his tongue at Delilah when the horse moved toward him. “Fire.”

Kate froze. “Fire?”

He glanced her way. “Yes, fire, as in burning wood, scorching flames and unbearable heat.”

“Then why are we still sitting here?”

Nathan’s voice was irritatingly patient. “Where would we go?”

She responded in kind. “Somewhere besides here.”

“How do we get there?”

“We move? I don’t know. How long have you known the barn was burning?”

"Why do you think we prayed?"

"Oh." It came out as a laugh yet nothing was actually funny.

Nathan used the wall to push himself toward her. "Scoot over here and try to untie me."

With a new sense of urgency, she turned and backed toward him.

"I just wish I had my knife. Why, today of all days, did I lend it to Sean?"

Kate paused. "You lent it to Sean? I can't believe that. Not after I made him give me his pocketknife just this morning. He convinced Ellie her dress was on backward again."

Nathan turned to look at her and licked his lips. "Kate, there is something I've been meaning to say."

His voice droned on but her mind stumbled to a halt. *Pocketknife.* Her gaze snapped up to look at Nathan. "Pocket."

"What?" he asked distractedly.

"His knife is still in my pocket."

She watched Nathan freeze then hope flared like gold in his brown eyes. "Scoot over and I'll get it."

"Scoot over," she said more to herself then anyone. She half rolled and half scooted toward him.

Finally, Nathan had the knife in his hand and had managed to flip it open. A moment later his hands were free and he was bending to cut his feet lose. He turned his attention to her and she was free in a matter of seconds. In that short span of time, the fire had spread so that most of the north wall of the barn had flames licking at its wooden walls.

"Go open the doors," Nathan commanded. "Then come back and help me get the animals out."

She broke into a run toward the door and tried to push it open. "Nathan, the lock is jammed!"

He barely paused in his flight toward the milking cows to pick up a gun lying on the floor. She stepped aside. He shot the lock. She pushed at it again. It barely budged. "It's stuck!"

Nathan rushed for the door. "Get the cows."

She hurried toward the north end of the barn and went to the cows closest to the fire first. Their pens opened without difficulty. She herded them in the direction of the door just in time for Nathan to exchange glances with her as he ran for the hatchet. She went back for the last two cows and found the fire was spreading even faster. The heat of the flames caused her hair to feel wet with sweat.

"God, please let those doors be open when I get there," she mumbled to herself. She reached the entrance of the barn just as the doors flew open letting in a rush of cooler air. She breathed a *thank You* as she and Nathan shooed the cows out, then ran toward the south side to get the horses. They opened the gates to the stalls as they went, then turned to shoo the horses out the door.

They were headed outside when Kate heard a pitiful meow. She gasped and stumbled to a halt. She coughed out the smoke she'd drawn into her lungs.

"Kate," Nathan's voice yelled over the confusion. "Let's go. This place is burning up."

She shook her head and moved deeper into the barn in the direction the sound had come from. "Flick is in here."

The meowing was louder and almost incessant as Kate moved closer to the south side of the barn. The fire was already making its way toward her yet Kate couldn't ignore the cat's desperate call for help. She came to the last stall yet saw nothing.

She glanced up. The cat was sitting on the ledge of the wall. The ledge was no more than a few inches wide but somehow Flick had managed to climb up there and get stuck. Kate looked around for some way to reach the cat. Dragging over the ladder, she managed to pull the reluctant cat into her arms. Kate was carefully climbing down the ladder when Flick let out a loud meow. With that battle cry, Flick sprung from her arms and shot out of the stall in the direction of the barn doors.

Kate stood in disbelief for a moment, then hopped from the ladder onto the floor. The smoke and fire were now making their way toward her. She had to get out. Now.

She hurried into the smoke making sure to keep her wits about her. There were four stalls before the door. One. Two. Three. Four. She turned to her right and walked through the open space to the barn door. But where was the air? Where was the sunlight? She froze. She'd miscounted the stalls. She glanced around and saw through the smoke barely enough to find that the stall around her was on fire.

Eyes wide, she turned and stumbled back the way she'd come. This time she went too far. She found herself at the stairs to the barn loft. She held on to the stairs and closed her eyes. Think. If she was at the stairs near the loft, it meant the door was directly behind her. She opened her eyes even as the smoke stung them. The heat was becoming unbearable.

Nathan couldn't believe Delilah had thrown him. He barely had time to notice that the roof was on fire before he was on his feet following the horse through the dense smoke. When he spotted Kate struggling to get on the horse Nathan felt a smile touch his lips. So Delilah had had a reason for knocking him flat on his back. He'd been leading her in the wrong direction. *Good girl,* he thought. Then slipping behind Kate, he lifted her onto Delilah's back and quickly swung up behind her.

The steel band of Nathan's arms was all that kept Kate from tumbling off the horse as it bolted into a strong canter toward the exit. With one hand on Nathan's arm and the other tangled in the horse's mane she searched for the rays of sunlight that pierced through the intoxicating smoke. Then she heard it, the moaning and groaning of a roof begging to cave in. Her breath caught in her throat and echoed in her ears as desperation clawed at her chest.

Nathan's weight was heavy against her back as Delilah moved into a gallop. They were almost there. Nathan muttered something unintelligible, then placed a heel into the horse's side. Delilah picked up speed. The barn was nothing more than a blur of smoke and fire. Kate felt her eyes close. The muscles under her tensed as Delilah leaped. Kate bit her lip. With a whoosh, hot air rushed by her ears and was replaced with cooler air.

Her eyes flew open. Her gaze took in the house, the chicken coop and the barn animals that were milling about where they shouldn't be. Clean air met her lungs and surprisingly caused her to choke. A stiff breeze fanned the flames behind them. The horse hardly came to a stop before Nathan slipped off. He lifted Kate from Delilah's back, then glanced toward the barn.

"We'll have to round up the animals and put them in

the pasture for now," he said over the roar of the flames. "First, I have to find Fulton."

"What about the barn?"

He shook his head. "There's no time."

She pulled her gaze from his to turn toward the flame-ridden building. She'd worked so hard to maintain everything. She'd spent two years trying to prove to the town that she was able to take care of her siblings and the farms alone. There was no way she would have the money to replace the barn.

What would they do come planting and harvest time? What would they do when winter set in and they had no place to keep the animals? How would she take care of her family? Visions of her working at the Red Canteen for Andrew Stolvins danced through her mind.

She shook her head. "No, we have to save it. Help me!"

"Kate," Nathan warned but she paid him no heed.

She ran toward the house and grasped the bucket she kept close to the door. She needed water. She hurried around the back of the house then stumbled into the kitchen. She pushed the lever for the sink up and down as quickly as she could. Precious water gushed into the bucket. She lifted it from the sink then turned toward the door—

—and came to an abrupt stop as she saw Jeremiah Fulton leaning in the doorway, blocking her way out. He looked ready to collapse. Blood dripped from his shoulder to the floor. He seemed to consider lifting the gun in his hand then dropped it to his side as he met her gaze.

She stiffened. "Why are you doing this?"

He shook his head. "The fire was an accident."

"I suppose bolting the door was an accident, too."

"My brother—"

She set the heavy bucket on the counter. "He has nothing to do with this anymore, does he? This is about revenge. Killing won't get rid of that anger you feel."

He stared at her for a long moment then dropped his head. "How do I stop?"

"Pray," she suggested.

He glanced up in surprise.

She smiled. "And give me your guns."

He stared at the gun, then turned it over in his hand to grasp the barrel. He lifted his arm to hand her the gun but it slipped from his grasp to the floor. Kate watched a world of pain flash across his face as he groaned from the strain the movement caused on his arm. The man would have collapsed onto the floor had not Nathan appeared in the doorway to keep him from going down. Surprise and agony painted Fulton's features in a grimace.

Kate watched him glance at Nathan. Fulton's other arm began to move. She erased the distance between them with one quick lunge. Her hand made it to the gun still in his holster a second before his did. She wrestled it from its spot at Fulton's hip then stepped back to point it at him.

His dazed blue eyes met hers and for the first time since she'd met the man, he smiled. It was a weak smile but a smile nonetheless. "I guess you figured out who to trust after all."

She nodded. "I guess I have, at that."

Nathan sent her a questioning glance.

Kate lifted the other gun from where it had fallen and pointed the pair toward Fulton. Both men flinched. Nathan shook his head slightly as if to warn her that she couldn't shoot two-handed no matter how hard she tried. Her eyes narrowed then she set the hammers of the guns in place. "There. Now, they're both cocked. Why don't you tie him up while I hold these on him?"

Nathan stared at her for a moment then seemed to curb a smile. He nodded toward her. "Hold those guns steady. This shouldn't take long."

Chapter Twenty

Nathan lifted his hands from the pail of water and splashed the cooling liquid on his face hoping it would rid his eyes of the burning caused by smoke. Wiping his face on the inside of his shirt, he glanced around the barnyard lit by the golden sunset. Everywhere he looked, people gathered in small groups watching the fading embers consume what was left of the barn's standing structure. Five men circled the fire, throwing buckets of water onto the debris to control what was left of the flames.

The rocking chair had been pulled onto the lawn of the house. Sean sat there with his arm around his little sister as the chair rocked slowly back and forth. Lawson sat on the ground on the other side of the chair. Doc and Ms. Lettie stood near them. Nathan glanced around for Kate and found her standing nearer to the barn. One arm was wrapped around her waist while the other hand supported her chin as she stared at the fire.

He was drawn to the sight of her solitary figure standing alone in the midst of all that movement. She glanced over her shoulder at his approach and her lips lifted into a small smile. He returned the smile with one of his own. "I'm glad to see you can still smile after a day like this."

Her gaze traveled back to the fire and she shrugged. "I've realized that no matter how hard you try, there are just some things you can't control. This fire was one of those things. You were right. I couldn't have saved the barn. I probably would have gotten hurt trying."

He shook his head. "I'm really sorry about that, Kate."

A glint of determination lit her eyes. "We'll just have to rebuild, that's all. I'm not sure how or when we'll be able to, but by God's grace we'll rebuild."

"At least the fire did one good thing by drawing the sheriff over here to check out the smoke. He showed up just in time to take Fulton into custody."

"He'll be going to jail for a long time."

"That's what I'd guess. We'll know for sure when the judge gets back," he said. "I still can't believe you were able to get Fulton to hand over his guns."

She met his gaze with a smile. "Neither can I. I'm glad you arrived when you did. I wouldn't have known what to do with them." Her smile turned rueful. "Obviously."

He tilted his head, considering. "You kept him from killing me. That counts for something."

She lifted her chin. "I suppose I did."

"I was wondering about that earlier. Why were you hiding in the barn? I thought you were inside resting. Had you already seen him?" He was surprised to watch her eyes widen and her cheeks turn an alluring shade of pink before she turned to stare at the fire again. He stepped closer. "Kate?"

She frowned at him and glanced around. “You shouldn’t be so close. People will talk.”

“Will they?” She was trying to distract him but he could play that game as well. He lifted his hand to brush away the black streaks that painted her face. She stilled beneath his touch. “You’re covered in soot.”

“Nathan,” she said warningly, though it came out a bit too breathless to carry a real threat.

“Kate.”

Kate rolled her eyes and stepped away from Nathan’s touch. Of course it would be too convenient for him to have forgotten the small fact that she had been hiding in the barn. She glanced up at his curious gaze. “You really want to know?”

He smiled. “I really do.”

“You’ll think it’s silly.”

“So what if I do?”

“I was looking for your letters.”

“My letters?” he asked in confusion.

“Yes, the ones you sent me before you came here.”

He took a moment to digest that, then nodded slowly. “Why?”

“I’d never read them before.” She shrugged innocently.

The man seemed to have developed an uncanny ability to read her mind, for he inclined his head toward her and searched her features carefully. “Was that the only reason?”

She couldn’t maintain her flippant attitude another moment. The tension dropped from her shoulders. “When I was with Fulton he made a few accusations about your past. I didn’t want to believe him. At the same time I discovered I hardly knew anything about you in that sense. I wanted to see if you had offered any information about what happened."

"So you read the letters to find out about my past," he said, his gaze intent on hers. "What did you discover?"

Kate allowed herself a smile. "Nothing. I didn't read them."

"Why not?"

"I didn't need to. It was probably very foolish of me not to read them but I decided that I trust you." She laughed. "Don't look so shocked. I still wanted to know. I just planned to ask you in person instead."

He grinned wryly. "I wouldn't have blamed you for asking. I should have known Fulton would have tried to make you believe his version of things. I'm sure he said some pretty awful things."

"Don't worry. He did."

He tilted his head. "Well, if you have any other questions about my past you just let me know."

"Actually, I still have a few and, since your letters are most likely gone forever, it seems you are my only source."

He grinned. "Ask away."

She bit her lip. "He showed me a wanted poster with your face on it and a pretty hefty award."

"That is an interesting story within itself. After everything happened with Eli, I went to the sheriff's office for questioning. Once he finished, I thought he was done with me. I had a lot of my mind so I wandered here and there for a few days until I ended up at the next town and saw the wanted posters. Apparently, the sheriff had called on me for more questioning. When I wasn't around, Fulton convinced him I'd run off to Mexico. It kind of shattered his story when I turned myself in."

He shook his head. "Things were a mess for a while. I was charged with murder, and there was a trial. But I was found not guilty. I wasn't sure that I'd ever be free again. When I was let go, I did the best I could to find a new life. It seemed like God was smiling on me again when I saw that advertisement in the paper for a husband."

She watched as he seemed to gather his thoughts then he faced her again, obviously in search of more questions. She pursed her lips. "How old are you?'

He smiled again. "Three years older than you."

She did the math. "Twenty-three."

He nodded. "You've been wondering that the whole time?"

"No. I just wondered off and on." She paused, debating whether she should continue. Seeing that he was waiting expectantly, she gathered her courage. "Have you ever been married?"

He grinned slowly. "Well, now. That depends on what you consider married."

She felt her cheeks warm. "Before me."

"Never."

"Betrothed?"

"Once."

"What happened?"

"We got married."

Her eyes narrowed. "Then what?"

"I don't know yet."

She sighed.

He leaned closer. "Mrs. Rutledge, don't look so exasperated."

"Don't call me Mrs. Rutledge."

He tilted his head. "Well, isn't that like the pot calling the kettle black?"

"What? How?"

"You just finished making sure I was as single and unattached as any slightly married man can be."

"I assure you, that isn't at all what I was doing."

"Than what were you doing?"

"I was only making sure that you are the man you've presented yourself to be." She realized how close they were and stepped back. "You are exactly who I thought you were."

"Yeah, and who is that?"

"A good, honest, Christian man and a very trustworthy friend," she said seriously then smiled at Nathan. Her smile faltered when she met his gaze. He looked completely flummoxed. She frowned. "That was a compliment."

He bit off a tight smile. "I understood that. Thank you."

She watched in confusion as he gave a brief nod and stalked off to speak to the men controlling the dying embers of the fire.

Nathan banged his Stetson against his leg in agitation as he strode down the wooden sidewalk of Peppin. He couldn't get Kate's words out of his head. Didn't that beat all? After courting the woman for weeks she still only saw him as a friend. He pulled in a calming breath. Being friends was definitely better than nothing but it was so far from what he wanted to be for her and her family.

He set his Stetson on his head and tugged it low. His

hand immediately strayed to the letter in his pocket—the one he'd reread a thousand times. His pa wanted him to come home. Kate seemed to want nothing but friendship. The children obviously wanted him to stay. What did he want?

He paused in front of the sheriff's office and stared at the building. One thing he wanted was to leave the anguish of the past behind him once and for all. To do that, he had to talk to the one man who probably never wanted to see him again. Maybe some sort of reconciliation would lead to a complete end to the nightmares that now visited his dreams less frequently. That's what he was hoping for, but these days he'd take whatever he could get. He removed his hat and stepped inside. Soon he met Jeremiah Fulton's glare through the harsh metal bars of the jail cell. The man frowned and stepped closer to the barrier between them. "Look, I don't know why you're here. I have nothing to say to you."

"I'm here because I have something to say to you."

"What then?"

Nathan took a moment to swallow then said, "I'm sorry."

Fulton froze. "You're sorry?"

He nodded. "I didn't kill your brother and I think you know that. All the same, I'm sorry for the way things turned out. I'm sorry if I said or did anything that caused you more pain than you were already feeling."

"Just leave me alone," he said, distrust apparent in his gaze.

Nathan lifted the book in his hands. "I brought this in case you get bored."

Fulton backed away from the bars. "Why are you

doing this? I am not your friend and you are certainly not mine."

"We were friends once."

"That was a long time ago." Fulton sat down on the bunk and wouldn't look at Nathan. "You should go."

"You're right." He slid the Bible he'd cleared with the sheriff through the slats between the bars. "I'll leave this."

Jeremiah frowned but otherwise didn't respond. Nathan left him to his solitude and turned toward the sheriff. The man stood from his desk. "I guess Kate probably hasn't had a chance to think about a barn raising, but you let me know when you're ready to put that new barn up. I'll be glad to hammer a few nails."

Nathan agreed and was ready to bid the sheriff farewell when a knowing expression shifted across the man's features. "By the way, Rutledge, I heard tell Judge Hendricks was looking for you."

He curbed his surprise. "Judge Hendricks? You don't say?"

"Sure enough." Sheriff Hawkins gave a twist of a smile. "He didn't seem all too happy, if you ask me, so if I was you I'd get over there real quick. He's like a rattlesnake—the longer you wait the madder he gets."

Nathan smiled though he didn't find the analogy amusing. Thanking the sheriff, he waved at Deputy Stone and stepped from the dim jail into the brightness of the early afternoon sun. Pulling the brim of his Stetson low over his face, he allowed his eyes to adjust then paused beside the dark form of his horse. Nathan felt his fondness grow for the dark beauty. She'd done exactly what he'd needed her to do during the fire, practically without his help. Delilah gave out a huff as if to express her annoyance.

He grinned at her and gave her nose a pat before he moved past her. "Just give me a minute more, girl."

The sound of horses' hooves near the front of the house piqued Kate's curiosity enough to set the soapy dishes into the sink. She dried her hands on her apron as she walked to the front door. Opening it, she was surprised to see a fancy black buggy and two beautiful matched horses waiting in front of the house.

She stepped cautiously around the buggy to find a tall older gentleman surveying the barn's destruction incredulously. It took her a moment to believe what she was seeing. When she did, her heart filled with dread even as her lungs let out a happy gasp. "Judge Hendricks!"

The dark-haired man who had been her father's closest friend stepped forward with a concerned smile and pulled her into a warm embrace. "Kathleen Grace O'Brien. I just arrived in town and heard what happened. I had to see for myself that you were all right."

She shook her head in amusement. "My, news travels fast in Peppin."

"You just have to have the right sources," he said then stepped back to survey her. "I heard no news of the children. Were they injured?"

"No, they were still at school when it happened."

"You must be exhausted. Perhaps we should sit down."

"Come inside. I have a lot to tell you." Kate led the way inside and sat in the rocking chair while the judge settled near her on the settee.

He removed his hat and met her gaze. “First of all, I want to assure you that I will see this matter through to the full extent of the law.”

“Without partiality, of course,” she teased as she removed her apron.

“Of course,” he agreed then shook his head. “I admit I’ve learned about the fire and your abduction from the sheriff but I’m still unclear on the details. I heard your abductor was the friend of a new man you hired.”

She folded the apron and sat it in her lap. “I doubt the two men involved would call each other friend and Nathan isn’t really a hired hand at all.”

“Who is he then?”

She bit her lip. “I’m afraid he’s my husband.”

“Your husband!” Judge Hendricks stared at her until he surmised she was serious then asked, “Since when?”

“We met a few days after you left.”

“Mr. Potters couldn’t approve a marriage license.”

“He didn’t.” She laughed. “Actually, neither did I.”

He shook his head in confusion. “Perhaps you’d better explain.”

I’d rather not, she thought. Then she looked into the judge’s brown eyes and suddenly couldn’t hold the story in. “I hardly understand it myself. It seems Ellie, Sean and Ms. Lettie decided I needed a husband so they found one for me. I didn’t find out they had married me to him until the poor man showed up at my door with our marriage license in hand.”

“That does not make sense. How did he get a marriage license if you didn’t know about it?”

“Well, I knew a little about it,” she admitted. “They told me they wanted to marry me off by proxy. I signed the silly affidavit in a moment of weakness but I never intended to send it."

He sat back and stared at her with a thoughtful look on his face. "So he's been living here since then?"

"Yes. Well, not exactly. He's lives out at the MacGregor cabin with a runaway boy we took in," she said.

"Runaway?"

She sent him a warning glance. "That's a whole other story."

He nodded.

She set the apron in the chair beside her, then stood to pace. "We've been waiting for you this entire time. You see, we decided that the only sensible thing was to get the marriage annulled. Or rather, I decided and he agreed."

Judge Hendricks looked at her thoughtfully. "How do you feel about that now?"

"Oh, I don't know." She turned away, wringing her hands. "I've just been so afraid."

"You've been afraid of what? Are you afraid of him?" he asked, no doubt desperately trying to keep up with the turns in the conversation.

"No! I was afraid I'd fall in love with him."

When she couldn't bear the silence between them any longer she turned to face the judge. He caught her hand and gently guided her back into the rocking chair. His voice was kind as he asked, "And have you, Kate? Have you fallen in love with this man?"

She buried her face in her hands.

His voice held tender amusement. "You have. You love him, don't you?"

She met his gaze and said with an air of desperation, "I'm afraid so. It took me a long time to admit it because of the mistakes I made with Andrew, but now I know. Nathan is God's will for me."

He laughed. "Then why are you so distraught?"

"I'm just not entirely sure I can trust God's will. I think a part of me is afraid that I'll end up..." She couldn't finish her statement.

"You're afraid you'll end up like your parents," the judge said knowingly. "Kate, it would be a wonderful thing if you did."

She stared at him in confused shock.

He smiled compassionately. "You've been focusing on your parents' deaths so much that you're allowing it to eclipse the way they had lived their lives. They were never afraid to love those around them or to act out that love. They were so intent on living each moment that their enthusiasm and joy for life infected those around them. Do you remember that, Kate?"

She nodded as tears filled her eyes.

"Think about how they lived. Let that be their legacy. Let that be what you carry with you, not the pain and sadness of their deaths." He took her hand and leaned forward earnestly. "They'd want you to move on, Kate. They'd want you to trust that they ultimately ended up right where they were supposed to be. They wouldn't want you to miss today for fear of tomorrow."

"You're right," she breathed, as she accepted the handkerchief he gave her. "I know you're right."

"Good." He smiled then shook his head in awe. "I must say, if this young man helped bring you to a place where you can move past that tragedy, then he is worth keeping around."

She gave him a watery smile then allowed him to pull her into a hug.

Chapter Twenty-One

Nathan leaned back in the courthouse's waiting room chair, bouncing his worn Stetson on his knee. He was more than willing to try his luck at charming the old snake the sheriff mentioned if he ever showed up. Nathan had been waiting for the judge for nearly an hour. Thirty minutes more and he just might have to give up this stakeout altogether.

When Nathan had arrived at the courthouse he'd been informed that Judge Hendricks had lit out of town only minutes earlier leaving no information regarding his return. For all Nathan knew, the judge could have set out on another one of his prolonged journeys. While he waited, he'd been able to get reacquainted with his old friend Mr. Potters. The man had offered his skilled assistance but Nathan had been more inclined to wait for the judge. At least, he had at the time.

He pulled the crisply folded letter from his pocket and reread his father's letter for the second time since he'd been at the courthouse. The offer was still there. He'd decided he was going to take it. He didn't have any other option. Now that the judge was back, all it would take was Kate's signature on a piece of paper to divorce him from her life forever.

He'd tried to have faith but it was time to face reality. Kate's decision had been made long ago. Despite his attempt to woo her, she'd given him no real indication that she felt anything more for him than friendship. She had declared him exactly that after the fire. "You are a good, honest Christian man and a very trustworthy friend," she'd said.

His jaw tightened. He would only be fooling himself by continuing to hope there could be anything more between them than what already existed. He swallowed against the sudden lump in his throat and carefully placed the letter back in his pocket. He bowed his head. *I tried, Lord. I really did. Now I'm giving it up to You. Do whatever You like with me.*

Suddenly a tall, dark-haired man breezed through the small courthouse's door. The man's boots rang confidently across the wooden floor as he strode toward the office door directly across from Nathan. Nathan grasped his Stetson and stood quickly to his feet, earning the appraising eye of the gentleman before him. "Sir, are you the judge?"

"That's what I've been told. Who are you?"

"Nathan Rutledge."

The man's eyes narrowed which couldn't be a good sign. "Nathan, you say? Well, come on in. There's no use jawing out here in the hallway. Does this have to do with that new criminal sitting in the town jail?"

Nathan followed him in but couldn't bring himself to sit down. "Not particularly."

The man set his hat on a wooden rack and settled

into his chair before bothering to ask, "Well, what else would you like to discuss?"

He set his shoulders and met Judge Hendricks's gaze directly. "I need an annulment, sir."

"You *need* one?" he asked, then read a paper on his desk before placing it into a drawer. "Why is that?"

Nathan finally took a seat. "The young woman I married doesn't want to stay that way. It was all a misunderstanding. She never really wanted to marry me. She doesn't want to try to make the marriage work, which is completely understandable. I probably would have made the same choice if I were in her shoes…probably."

Judge Hendricks still didn't look up. "Who is the young woman?"

"Kate Rut—" He caught himself. "Kate O'Brien, sir."

The judge shuffled through his papers and read over another. "I see."

Nathan frowned at the man's obvious disinterest. "Listen, I'd like to get this done as soon as possible. Is there some paperwork we need to fill out?"

Finally, Judge Hendricks looked up and met his gaze. "No."

"What do you mean 'no'? There is no paperwork?"

The judge tossed his papers aside. "I mean, no. I will not give you the annulment."

Nathan shook his head. "I don't think you understand. The marriage was never consummated. It was a mistake from the start. Kate never agreed to marry me. Her siblings devised a scheme to marry the two of us by proxy with the help of Ms. Lettie. It all happened without Kate's knowledge. This marriage probably isn't even legal."

The judge nodded in agreement. "It might not be at that."

Relief filtered through Nathan. "Then you'll give us an annulment."

"Absolutely not."

Nathan sat back and stared at the man. "You can't be serious."

The judge tilted his head as he surveyed Nathan. "Tell me, do you want to make this a problem? Because we can make this a problem."

They glared at each other for a long tension-filled moment. Nathan dropped his gaze then leaned back into his chair. He tried to appear calm but his thoughts were racing. The judge's expression turned contemplative for a moment, then he tossed his pen back onto the desk. "All right, Rutledge, I'll give you one last chance to persuade me."

Taking a deep breath, he straightened. He began to speak then thought better of it. *What is the use anyway?* He met the judge's gaze. "Nothing I say will change your mind so let's not play games."

Judge Hendricks gave a slow nod. "All right then, no more games. Agreed?"

"Agreed."

The judge leaned forward then waited for Nathan to do the same before he spoke. "I want you to understand that I'm not worried about what's best for you. I couldn't care less. Kate's father was my best friend. We served in the war together, came out alive, took this fledgling town and made something of it. If her parents had died but a few months earlier, I would have been her legal guardian.

"Marrying you would be the best thing for her and

those children. So the answer is no, Nathan. I will not authorize the annulment." Judge Hendricks leaned back and crossed his arms.

Nathan tapped his Stetson on his leg. "You're sure?"

"I'm sure."

"Then I reckon there's nothing I can do about it." Nathan stood, then placing his Stetson on his head, he moved toward the door.

"Nathan."

He turned toward the judge who gave him a wry look of amusement. "I expect you'll be making a visit to Reverend Sparks first thing."

Nathan grinned, realizing he hadn't fooled the man for a second. "Yes, sir, your judgeship," he said. Tipping his hat, he walked out the door.

Kate smiled as Doc snapped closed his black leather bag on the kitchen table and pronounced her healthy enough, considering the circumstances she'd been subjected to. She shot a glance toward where Ms. Lettie sat across the table. "I told you I was perfectly fine."

Doc frowned. "That is not entirely true, Kate. You are still dehydrated so you will need to drink plenty of fluids. I also want you to rest and give yourself time to recover."

"I understand your concern," she began, "but the barn—"

"The barn will wait until you are physically able to deal with it. Is that understood?"

Kate bristled at his tone. "Perfectly, Doctor."

Ms. Lettie sighed and exchanged a glance with her husband. "Now, Kate. Don't be upset. You have to take care of yourself. If you don't, you won't be able to take care of your family."

"I know that," she said. "There is just so much to catch up on. Now I have to decide how to move forward with the barn. Then I have to figure out something to tell the bank about all of this. We've just now caught up on the mortgage. I don't know how we'll get the money to rebuild."

Ms. Lettie caught her hand in hers. "Let us help you."

Kate glanced from Ms. Lettie to Doc. "How?"

"Leave that to me. In the meantime, Luke has some calls to make, but I would be more than happy to stay with you and prepare dinner."

"Then who will prepare yours?"

"We'll eat here."

"I don't know what we have in the pantry."

Doc smiled and with an uncustomary drawl proclaimed, "Well, now. It seems a certain woman we are all familiar with just happened to bring a few things in our buggy."

Kate laughed. "Then stay. You've worn out my resistance."

"That sounds like my constant state of mind," Doc said with a smile just for Ms. Lettie.

Kate watched in amusement as Ms. Lettie blushed then she teased, "Maybe you should attend to Ms. Lettie, Doc. She looks a little flushed. What medicine would you give her for that?"

Ms. Lettie frowned at her in exasperation and affection. "You are an impertinent young woman."

"Yes, I've been told that before," she said, then smiled at Doc. "I'm still waiting for your answer."

Doc met her smile with his own. "You've forgotten I don't want her to recover."

She laughed.

"Love can be both the affliction and the remedy." Doc met her gaze seriously. "You don't look surprised. Maybe you were already aware of that."

Kate held Doc's gaze though she felt her cheeks grow warm as she realized what he was implying.

"I wish she was," Ms. Lettie sighed then glanced at Kate. "My lands, I think she is. Don't worry, dear, it really is a wonderful affliction."

Nathan spent the afternoon at a workstation he'd created near the paddocks, that consisted of nothing more than an old table and a few borrowed tools. He figured he may as well try to do something productive while he waited for a chance to speak with Kate.

The day was beginning to try his patience. When he'd arrived home from town, he'd found Doc leaving and Ms. Lettie settling in for the day. There had been no chance for him to find a private moment with Kate.

The longer he waited, the longer he had to wonder about how things would end up. His initial relief at the judge giving him what amounted to a second chance had faded with the realization that he had to give Kate a choice. He wasn't going to go along with everyone else in her life by trying to decide her future for her. If she wanted him to stay, then he would be thrilled to do so. If not, he was resolved to leave and let her live her own life.

He'd managed to replace a few essential things the fire had taken and was just starting to build a new feeding trough for the horses when the children arrived home from school. They tied their horses to the paddock gate then rushed toward Nathan. Lawson made it to him first. "Nathan, the news is all over town. The judge is back."

Nathan didn't glance up from the groove he was trying to carve into the wood. "I know."

Ellie gasped. "You do?"

He glanced up to meet her panicked gaze. Sean placed a calming hand on Ellie's shoulder. "What are you going to do, Nathan?"

"The only thing I can do. I'm going to talk to Kate."

"You mean you haven't already?" Lawson asked.

Nathan smiled at the urgency in Lawson's voice that reflected his own. "She's been busy."

"She's not too busy for this," Ellie said. "I'll go get her."

Nathan caught her sleeve before she could get far. "Hold on, you three. This is something Kate and I have to figure out for ourselves. I'll talk to her when the time is right."

"When will that be?" Sean asked.

"Soon," he promised. "In the meantime—"

Ellie's eyes widened. "We won't say a word."

He grinned. "That wasn't what I was going to say, but that works, too."

She grimaced. "I'm sorry I interrupted."

"I was just going to remind you guys to take care of your horses." He let Sean and Ellie slip away but asked Lawson to stay for a moment. "How did you like staying with Doc and Ms. Lettie while I was gone?"

Lawson shrugged as his eyes became guarded. "It wasn't bad."

"Doc asked about you today."

"Why?"

"He wanted to know if you might consider settling with him and Ms. Lettie permanently."

Lawson stared at him as hopeful silence stretched between them like a thick blanket. "They did?"

He grinned. "They sure did."

"What did you tell them?"

"I told them they'd have to ask you about it," he said. "That isn't your only option. You can always stay with me. You know that."

"You say that now, but what if things don't work out with Kate? Where will you go then?" he asked.

"Oklahoma. I told you my pa offered me a job there. You would be more than welcome to come."

"Oklahoma," Lawson echoed.

"Just think about it."

Lawson nodded thoughtfully. He began to turn away, then paused to glance back at Nathan seriously. "Either way, I think you should know that we're brothers now."

"Thanks, Lawson. I—"

"No, I mean we're really brothers. I prayed after Kate came home. Now we have the same spirit or Father or whatever you said."

"Oh. In that case." Nathan grinned then held out his hand. "Welcome to the family."

Lawson shook his hand then smiled teasingly. "Thanks. Now if you've got half the sense the Lord gave you, you won't waste any time in getting your own. You fit, remember?"

He nodded. "I hope you're right."

Yes, he hoped. He hoped but he had surrendered the situation to God. It was up to Him now. Nathan could only pray His will would be done.

Chapter Twenty-Two

Kate let out a quiet sigh. Her blue eyes lifted toward Nathan as she shifted in the rocking chair until she faced him more fully. The rhythmic cadence of his voice had drawn her attention. "Therefore, behold, I will allure her, and bring her into the wilderness, and speak comfortably unto her."

I don't remember reading that particular verse in Isaiah before, she thought absently. She dragged her gaze from his distractingly handsome features to stare at the arms of the rocker her father had made. Her mother had rocked her here when she was little, shushing her fears while offering love to replace them. She missed their guiding lights even now. Or was it especially now?

She wished she could ask her mother's advice about Nathan but she knew what the judge told her earlier was true. Her parents would want her to put aside her fears and live as they did. She thought of the way she had been living for the past two and a half years and couldn't find a starker contrast.

She had been so focused on protecting her heart, on

being careful, on being sensible that she'd nearly forgotten everything they'd taught her about how to live. She'd even allowed the thing that least represented who they were—their death—to become a stumbling block between her and God. She wondered how her life would be different if she followed their example. How would she change if she really allowed herself to trust?

Her gaze lifted to trace the room and its inhabitants. A small kerosene lamp battled the dusk creeping in through the windows and touched the golden strands in Ellie's hair. The girl lay on her stomach close to the settee as she toyed absently with a piece of string. Flick lazed before her, halfheartedly lifting a dainty paw toward the twisting string, prompting a smile on Ellie's lips.

Lawson slumped in a wooden chair, his arms on the armrests while he stared in thoughtful consideration at the ceiling. Sean leaned against the cool brick of the fireplace with his brow knotted in deep concentration as he faithfully shaved at the chunk of wood in his hands.

More importantly, how would my family be different if I was able to restore some of what we lost when Ma and Pa died? She bit her lip, then glanced down at her rich green skirts. It would take a lot of courage for her to do so. The fears she'd allowed to distract her from God had become familiar and comfortable. She hadn't had to depend on anyone but herself—not a man and not even God.

Lord, I want to trust You with my heart. Free me from the distrust of You and this fear of the future. I want what You want for me.

She glanced up as the quiet timbre of Nathan's voice deepened. "I will betroth thee unto me forever."

He met her gaze. Her breath stilled as he continued, "Yea, I will betroth thee unto me in righteousness, and in judgment, and in loving kindness, and in mercies." A smile tugged at his lips as he regarded her. "I will even betroth thee unto me in faithfulness, and thou shalt know the Lord."

Their eyes held and Kate could not have looked away if she'd wanted to. The intimacy of the firelight played across his face, blurring the cozy scene surrounding them. Somewhere a snicker sounded. The world was suddenly in focus again. Kate's gaze flew toward the sound yet snagged as it drifted past Ellie. The girl lay perfectly still. A string dangled precariously from her fingers with her mouth slightly open as her gaze darted between Nathan and Kate.

Lawson was sitting up in his chair and, though his gaze rested on the floor, a smile pulled at his lips. Sean's green eyes watched them carefully. Feeling her cheeks warm, Kate turned toward Nathan and lifted her chin. "That was from Isaiah?"

He glanced down at the Bible. "Isaiah?"

"Yes, Isaiah forty-three, starting with verse two." She watched him suspiciously as he scanned the page.

His warm brown eyes met hers. "My mistake."

"Thank you, Nathan," Kate said over Ellie's giggles. "I think that's all for tonight."

Ellie sat up abruptly and placed her hands in her lap. "I have a wonderful idea. Why don't we go watch the stars?"

Kate stared at her sister in confusion. "The stars won't be out for another thirty minutes. Besides, it's a school night."

Sean set his carvings aside. "It won't take long this time."

"Yeah, just long enough," Lawson added with a sly half smile at Nathan.

Her gaze darted from Lawson to Nathan as she asked, "Long enough for what?"

"Long enough to catch a few fireflies before it gets completely dark," Nathan said as he closed the Bible and set it on the table. He turned toward Kate. "What do you say, Kate?"

"You want to catch fireflies with me?" she asked with a bemused smile. At his nod, she shifted her gaze to the children. Ellie widened her eyes then nodded adamantly. Sean and Lawson seemed to wait with baited breath. Kate finally understood.

"Oh." She bit her lip to keep from laughing then echoed Ellie's nod. "That sounds fine."

The children jumped up and rushed out the door with a few backward glances to make sure Kate and Nathan were following. Nathan held the door open then stepped back for her to precede him. The children dashed toward the corral fence. She and Nathan followed at a more sedate pace.

"I've wanted to talk to you all day," he admitted.

"You have?"

He glanced toward the corral fence and smiled. She followed his gaze to see Ellie waving them on toward the open land. Kate rolled her eyes then muttered, "Really, Ellie?"

Nathan laughed. "I can take a hint. Come on."

He caught her hand and led her toward the fields. The sun was sinking slowly behind the tree line to the west, leaving the meadow covered in deep blue dusk.

A few early fireflies began lighting up around them as Nathan cleared his throat nervously. "Kate, I talked to the judge today."

Kate glanced up at him as anxiety filled her stomach. Surely Judge Hendricks hadn't told Nathan about their conversation. She braced herself. "What did he tell you?"

"He said he wouldn't give us an annulment."

"Oh," she breathed, then waited for him to continue. He didn't.

She bit her lip and glanced away. So Judge Hendricks hadn't betrayed her feelings to Nathan. He'd just closed Nathan's only way out of their marriage and left her to do the rest. She didn't know whether to be amused or alarmed.

"Is that all you have to say?"

"What do you want me to say?" she asked softly as she lifted her gaze to his.

He tightened his hold on her hand slightly to pull her to a stop. "I want you to tell me the truth. Do you want me to stay or not?"

She glanced down at their joined hands and swallowed. "I want you to stay."

"Why, Kate? Why do you want me to stay?"

She finally lifted her gaze to his. "I need you."

He shook his head. "That isn't enough. Why do you need me? Do you need me to build your barn and milk your cows and keep the bank from foreclosing? If I've learned anything about you in the past two months, it's that you don't need me for any of that. You can do it all on your own, but it's the only reason you've ever let me stay around. I need to know if you need me for the same reasons I need you.

"I need you because the world is better when I'm with you. I'm better when I'm with you. I need you because I don't want to imagine my future without you living in it. I need you because I can't imagine God creating me for anyone else. Is that how you need me, Kate?"

"I—" she began but fear weighed her tongue down. She was tired of questioning. She desperately wanted to trust Nathan with her heart but it wasn't really about him at all. It was about surrendering to God's will—the very thing she'd prayed for just minutes earlier. But was she truly ready?

"I love you, Kate. I love you so much that I don't want to settle for anything else." He stepped back. "It's your decision now. I'm going to the cabin and I'm leaving in the morning. There's only one reason I'll let you stop me. You know what that is."

He began to walk away. She watched him in disbelief, then panic set in. That's when it hit her. This was life outside of His will. This was life figuring things out on her own. She was so paralyzed by fear that she couldn't stop the man she loved from walking away from her. It had to change and it had to change now—before it was too late.

She glanced up and saw Nathan had made it a good distance across the field. She bit her lip. Pulling in a deep breath, she yelled, "Wait!"

Her voice traveled quickly across the quiet field. Nathan slowly turned to face her. He didn't move toward her so she ended up picking her way toward him through the high grass of the meadow, dispelling fireflies in her wake.

"You can't just tell a woman you love her then in the

next sentence tell her you're leaving. It doesn't work that way," she said.

He stared at her in disbelief. "Do you have any idea how long you were silent after I said all of that?"

She stopped in front of him and lifted her chin. "I was thinking. Besides, it wasn't that long. You're exaggerating."

"I don't know, Kate. It felt like a pretty long time," he said then stared down at her cautiously. "Why'd you stop me?"

"Why do you think?"

He caught her arm and guided her across the distance that separated them until only a few inches remained between them. "You mean—"

"I mean I need you for the same reasons you need me. I love you, Nathan Rutledge. Completely, irrepressibly, desperately," she said then smiled ruefully. "Lord knows I tried to fight it, but the funny thing is I don't think I was ever supposed to. You came into my life and helped God change it completely. I'm so grateful for that and for you."

A slow grin spread across his lips. "I wondered how long it would take you to figure that out. I was really hoping I wouldn't have to leave tomorrow. I'm not even packed."

"Well, you're staying so don't even think about it."

"In that case," he said, stepping back and kneeling on one knee, he reached into his pocket to pull out the wedding ring Ellie had been so curious about months earlier. "Kate O'Brien, will you marry me?"

She responded with one word. "Rutledge."

His brow furrowed in confusion. "I'm sorry, what?"

"My name is Kate O'Brien Rutledge."

He grinned then asked, “And what, Kate O’Brien Rutledge, is your answer?”

“My answer is yes.” She smiled. “I would love to marry you.”

He slid the ring onto her finger, then stood and took a slow step that erased most of the distance between them. She caught her breath as his arm slid slowly into place around her waist. The corners of her mouth lifted into a gentle smile as she watched those dangerous gold flecks in his eyes warm to lustrous amber. She closed her eyes as his thumb trailed softly over her lips and he lifted her chin.

Her lashes flew open at the last moment. “What about the children?”

“I don’t think they’ll mind,” he murmured. Then softly, stirringly, sweetly his lips captured hers.

Epilogue

Kate sat patiently in a wooden chair in a small room in Peppin's church as Rachel and Ms. Lettie made a few last touches to her hair and endeavored to attach a veil to their wondrous creation. Ellie let out a less-than-patient sigh where she stared up at Kate from a nearby footstool with uneven legs.

The girl was so full of nervous energy that she rocked the footstool side to side at a nearly feverish pitch. After a moment of watching Ellie's ribbons quiver to and fro, Kate barely stopped herself from shaking her head and upsetting her curls. "Ellie, you're going to fall over if—"

She was scared speechless as the footstool tilted too far to one side sending Ellie perilously toward the floor. At the last moment Ellie shifted in the other direction to regain her balance and set the leg of the footstool down with a loud thump.

Ellie seemed to stop breathing for a second, then her wide green eyes lifted to Kate's. They stared at each other. Kate bit the inside of her cheek to keep from laughing. "Why don't you fetch Sean? It's nearly time to get started."

"Right." Ellie nodded and eagerly bounded from the room closing the door behind her a bit too loudly given the church service was going on just down the hall.

"Finished!" Rachel exclaimed. "Come, see yourself in the mirror."

Kate carefully stood and turned toward the mirror. Ms. Lettie smiled, then handed her a bouquet of wildflowers in a riot of different colors before stepping aside. Kate caught her breath at her reflection in the mirror.

Her hair was pulled back into an elaborate chignon but it was the dress that made her eyes fill with tears. The wedding gown was trimmed with the Irish lace Ellie had mentioned in her letter to Nathan, given to Kate by her mother, and had been altered only slightly to bring it into style. It had also been tailored to fit Kate's figure perfectly. She shook her head in wonder. "I look…"

"Beautiful?" Rachel questioned.

"Enchanting," Ms. Lettie stated.

Kate laughed. "I was going to say, I look like a bride."

Rachel grinned. "An enchantingly beautiful bride."

She turned to hug each of them. "I can't thank you two enough for everything you've done to help me plan this in just two weeks."

Ms. Lettie hugged her in return. "I believe you just did."

A rap on the door sounded. Butterflies began to flutter in Kate's stomach. She pulled in a deep breath. "That must be Sean."

"We'll make sure everyone is ready." Rachel picked up her smaller bouquet of flowers, then opened the door for Sean to enter before she and Ms. Lettie stepped out.

Sean caught sight of her and his expression shifted to one of awe. "Wow."

She laughed. "Thank you."

"You look wonderful, Kate." He swallowed. "So much like Ma."

She reached out her arms to her younger brother who always seemed mature beyond his years. His gangly arms pulled her into a tight hug. She sighed. "I miss them, especially today."

"I wish they were here. Pa would know just what to say at a time like this. Even so, I'll try my best to say what he'd want me to." He stepped back to clear his throat and met her gaze seriously. "I couldn't be prouder to have a sister like you. You kept us together when everything around us was falling apart. I am so grateful for that, and even more grateful that now you've found a love like Ma and Pa had. I know they are happy for you, too."

A smile blossomed across her face even as tears slipped from her eyes. She quickly wiped them away. "Oh, Sean, I couldn't have been more blessed than to have you for my brother. Thank you for stepping up in Pa's stead and giving me away."

He presented her with his arm. "We'd better hurry up if you still want me to do that."

"Of course," she said. Slipping her arm through his, she let him lead her out the door to the where Ellie and Rachel stood waiting.

"Doc and Ms. Lettie already took the seats on the

front row you designated for them next to Judge Hendricks," Rachel said.

She had asked them to sit in the front row to honor everything they'd done for her family both before and after her parents' deaths. "Good."

Rachel grinned at Sean. "Don't you look handsome?"

"Thanks," he said with a wry grin. "It isn't the most comfortable getup, but I guess it's all right."

Kate chuckled, then after receiving a curious look from the rest of the party she explained, "I just realized something. After me, Sean will probably be the next one in our family to get married."

The look on his face was a mix of confusion and horror that slowly faded into resignation. "I guess you're right."

Ellie giggled. Kate was going to question the mischief she read in her gaze but at that moment the music inside the chapel changed. "Get ready!"

They all stepped aside as Ellie took her position at the door with her basket of flowers in hand.

"Try to look the opposite of what you are. You know, sweet," Sean whispered.

Ellie shot him a glare. The door opened, signaling the beginning of the ceremony.

Nathan's heart beat rapidly in his throat as the doors to the chapel opened to reveal Ellie dressed in a spring green dress. The girl looked surprisingly innocent with her blond hair artfully arranged so that wisps of it purposely hung around her face. She glanced over the crowd then gave a demure smile. An "aw" escaped the crowd as one.

He knew Ellie too well not to notice the way her

lips curved a bit too smugly in response. She was up to something, no doubt about it. She gaily prepared the way for her sister by tossing brightly covered flowers onto the aisle. As she neared the end of the aisle she glanced up from her task. Nathan met her gaze and grinned. Delight sprang into Ellie's eyes. She nearly took an unplanned side trip toward him but Ms. Lettie caught her hand and guided her to her seat.

Rachel was the next down the aisle. Finally, the music changed and Kate appeared in the doorway. His heart, which had been pounding in his chest moments earlier, seemed to still along with his breath. She was stunningly beautiful in the Irish lace dress he'd read so much about.

Most of her cinnamon-colored locks were pulled away from her face in an elaborate knot with a few escaping tendrils. A filmy veil covered most of her face, maddeningly so, for he desperately wanted to see her expression.

Lawson discreetly leaned forward to whisper, "Breathe."

Nathan shot him a grateful glance.

"Dearly beloved, we are gathered here today in the sight of God and this congregation to join together this man and this woman in holy matrimony," Pastor began. "Who gives this woman to this man?"

"Her family and friends do," Sean said. At the minister's affirmation, he lifted Kate's veil and handed her to Nathan before he moved to sit beside Lawson on the other side of Doc and Ms. Lettie.

Hand in hand, they turned toward the minister but Nathan could not keep his eyes off Kate. Her blue eyes met his. She smiled and suddenly it was as if everything in his world was put to rights.

As the ceremony progressed, he repeated the words he had said once before but this time with a new understanding of their importance and the depth of their meaning. He'd certainly never dreamed that the pledge he had made then would lead him to this time and place with a woman he loved so deeply. He had to admit. This was better than any dream he could have imagined on his own.

Kate had never felt more at home than she did at Nathan's side as they accepted congratulations from the stream of well-wishers. Even Mrs. Greene managed a courteous, if mumbled, expression of congratulations. It was long before the streams of parishioners and guests dwindled to just their closest circle of friends.

Kate smiled in greeting as Judge Hendricks stepped forward. She accepted his kiss on the cheek, then watched as he shook Nathan's hand. "Congratulations to you both. I'll be heading out soon but I wanted to give you this."

Kate took the piece of paper the judge held out to her and studied it carefully before an amused smile lifted her lips. She handed it to Nathan. "It's our marriage license."

"Your official marriage license," the judge interjected.

Nathan grinned. "I'll be sure to keep this in a safe place. We might even frame it."

"You do that." Judge Hendricks laughed, then said his goodbyes.

For the first time all day, Kate found herself in a moment alone with Nathan. She glanced up toward him. He took a step closer. Suddenly Ms. Lettie appeared at her side.

"Sorry to interrupt but I thought you might be interested in taking care of the gifts now so you'll be free to slip off when you please later."

Kate frowned. "We didn't need any gifts."

Rachel stepped forward. "Don't be silly. Everyone receives gifts at their wedding. It's only proper."

Deputy Stone nodded. "In this case, it might even be timely."

"What are you talking about?" Nathan asked suspiciously.

Doc handed Kate a sealed envelope. "This was entrusted to me to give to you. Go ahead and open it."

Kate broke the seal. Opening the envelope, she gasped. She'd never seen so much paper money in all her life.

"Practically everyone in town who had something to give contributed. Life's been a bit rough for you lately. The town has wanted to do something to support you for years. When your barn burned down they saw that as an opportunity. There's enough in there to purchase the lumber you need not only to replace your barn but to build a bigger one for the future."

She felt Nathan tense beside her and knew he was wondering if she'd accept such a gift. A few months ago she certainly wouldn't have. She'd learned a lot since then. She'd learned to trust. She'd learned to love. She'd also learned to accept help. Kate smiled tremulously. "I don't know what else to say besides thank you."

Deputy Stone grinned. "That isn't the only gift."

"I'm not sure if I can accept anything more."

"This one isn't for you, Kate. It's mostly for Nathan. As much as I'd like to say I thought this up and carried it out, I can't. This one came from someone named Davis Reynolds."

Nathan caught Kate's questioning gaze but shrugged. He was just as confused as she seemed to be. The entire party followed Deputy Stone down the steps of the church to where the few remaining horses and buggies stood. "Davis contacted the sheriff, who put me in charge of the covert operation. There he is."

Nathan followed his friend's gesture toward one of the finest and largest stallions Nathan had ever seen. He heard Kate gasp and realized that even though she hadn't had much exposure to horses, she was able tell the quality of the animal. He stepped toward the horse haltingly, not entirely sure if he should believe what his eyes were seeing or where his brain was leading him.

"Was there any message with the horse?" he asked.

"He said you'd understand."

Kate stepped up beside Nathan. "Does the horse have a name?"

Nathan shook his head incredulously. "Samson. The horse's name is Samson."

The deputy frowned. "How did you know?"

"I guessed." Nathan turned to Kate to explain. "Davis is an old friend of mine. He always said I should raise horses again."

Understanding lit her blue eyes. "That sounds perfect."

"What about the wheat?"

"I have no particular affinity for it except that it puts food on the table," she said. "We can always try doing both until you become established in this."

Incredible, Nathan thought to himself as he strode forward to inspect the animal more closely. As impressed as he was by it, his gaze kept straying toward where Kate stood talking with her siblings. He felt someone nudge his ribs and turned to find the deputy's eyes twinkling meaningfully. "It's about time for you two to be heading out, isn't it? Why don't you attend to your bride, Nathan? I'll take care of the horse."

Nathan grinned. "Thanks. I owe you one."

"Good." The deputy's gaze strayed toward Rachel. "Who knows, I may actually collect on that."

Kate closed her eyes as a last sultry breeze of summer danced across her cheek like a warm touch. She pulled the ridiculous pins from her hair and tucked them in her skirt pocket before peeking inside the picnic basket Ms. Lettie had sent along with them. Her stomach growled. Ms. Lettie was right when she said no one actually ate at their own wedding.

She'd succumbed to the temptation of one of Ms. Lettie's cookies before the door opened behind her and Nathan stepped out of the house in his regular clothes. They'd both been uncomfortable in their wedding finery. Kate took a deep breath just because she could as they set out for the creek. It wasn't long before she slipped her hand into Nathan's strong yet gentle grasp.

He lifted her hand to kiss the tips of her fingers. She met his warm brown gaze and smiled at the love she saw echoed there. The corners of his mouth lifted into an answering smile as he tugged her slightly closer to his side. She sighed. "The ceremony was beautiful, wasn't it?"

His gaze turned teasing. “Best I’ve ever been to, that’s for sure.”

She laughed even as she sent him an exasperated look. “I’m serious. What was your favorite part?”

“My favorite part,” he echoed. He met her gaze seriously. “The wedding vows.”

She angled her steps sideways so she could see his face. “Really?”

He nodded. “Without a doubt.”

She turned to walk forward again, then hearing the gentle roar of the waterfall, she smiled. “Dearly beloved, we are gathered here today—”

“In the presence of God and these witnesses,” he interrupted. She laughed as he gestured to the empty woods around them before his deep voice continued. “To join—”

She placed a hand on his chest as she stepped in front of him, forcing him to stop. Lifting her gaze to his, she allowed her deepest feelings to show unrestrained as she said, “To join together this man…”

“And this woman,” Nathan said slipping an arm around her waist. “In holy matrimony.”

He would have kissed her but Kate shook her head and slipped out of his arms, teasing, “That doesn’t come until later.”

He grinned rakishly. “Well, I forgot what comes next so I thought we could just as well skip to the end.”

She laughed. “No. The next part is very important.”

“What’s that?” he asked as he took the basket from her and set it on the ground in a dry spot.

“If anyone knows of a reason the two should not be joined together, speak now or forever hold your peace,” she said over her shoulder as she slipped out of her boots. The water looked wonderful. She bet it was just the right temperature. She tiptoed through the mud near the bank of the creek to find out.

"You think that was an important part?" Nathan asked as he joined her to wade in the creek.

She lifted her chin to meet his gaze. "It's important because it leads to the most important question."

"What question would that be?" He reached out to slip his fingers through her cinnamon-colored curls.

"The question was, if you, Nathan Rutledge, would take me to be your lawfully wedded wife."

He stepped closer. "And I did."

A smile tilted her lips. "You do remember what came after that, don't you?"

Her lashes drifted closed as his lips covered hers in a loving kiss that was all the answer she needed.

* * * * *

WE HOPE YOU ENJOYED THIS BOOK!

Love Inspired® SUSPENSE

Uncover the truth in these thrilling stories of faith in the face of crime from Love Inspired Suspense.

Discover six new books available every month, wherever books are sold!

LoveInspired.com

LISHALO2019

SPECIAL EXCERPT FROM

Love Inspired®

Carolyn Wiebe will do anything to protect her late sister's children from their abusive father—even give up her Amish roots and pretend to be Mennonite. But when she starts falling for Amish bachelor Michael Miller, can they conquer their pasts—and her secrets—by Christmas to build a forever family?

Read on for a sneak preview of An Amish Christmas Promise *by Jo Ann Brown, available December 2019 from Love Inspired!*

"Are the *kinder* okay?"

"Yes, they'll be fine." Uncomfortable with his small intrusion into her family, she said, "Kevin had a bad dream and woke us up."

"Because of the rain?"

She wanted to say that was silly but, glad she could be honest with Michael, she said, "It's possible."

"Rebuilding a structure is easy. Rebuilding one's sense of security isn't."

"That sounds like the voice of experience."

"My parents died when I was young, and both my twin brother and I had to learn not to expect something horrible was going to happen without warning."

"I'm sorry. I should have asked more about you and the other volunteers. I've been wrapped up in my own tragedy."

LIEXP1119

"At times like this, nobody expects you to be thinking of anything but getting a roof over your *kinder*'s heads."

He didn't reach out to touch her, but she was aware of every inch of him so close to her. His quiet strength had awed her from the beginning. As she'd come to know him better, his fundamental decency had impressed her more. He was a man she believed she could trust.

She shoved that thought aside. Trusting any man would be the worst thing she could do after seeing what Mamm had endured during her marriage and then struggling to help her sister escape her abusive husband.

"I'm glad you understand why I must focus on rebuilding a life for the children." The simple statement left no room for misinterpretation. "The flood will always be a part of us, but I want to help them learn how to live with their memories."

"I can't imagine what it was like."

"I can't forget what it was like."

Normally she would have been bothered by someone having sympathy for her, but if pitying her kept Michael from looking at her with his brown puppy-dog eyes that urged her to trust him, she'd accept it. She couldn't trust any man, because she wouldn't let the children spend their lives witnessing what she had.

LIEXP1119

SPECIAL EXCERPT FROM

Can a mysterious Amish child bring two wounded souls together in Cedar Grove, Kansas?

Read on for a sneak preview of The Hope *by Patricia Davids available December 2019 from HQN Books!*

"You won't have to stay on our account, and we can look after Ernest's place, too. I can hire a man to help me. Someone I know I can…" Ruth's words trailed away.

Trust? Depend on? Was that what Ruth was going to say? She didn't want him around. She couldn't have made it any clearer. Maybe it had been a mistake to think he could patch things up between them, but he wasn't willing to give up after only one day. Ruth was nothing if not stubborn, but he could be stubborn, too.

Owen leaned back and chuckled.

"What's so funny?"

"I'm here until Ernest returns, Ruth. You can't get rid of me with a few well-placed insults."

She huffed and turned her back to him. "I didn't insult you."

"Ah, but you wanted to. I'd like to talk about my plans in the morning."

Ruth nodded. "You know my feelings, but I agree we both need to sleep on it."

Owen picked up his coat and hat, and left for his uncle's farm. The wind was blowing harder and the snow was piling up in growing drifts. It wasn't a fit night out for man nor beast. As if to prove his point, he found Meeka, Ernest's big guard dog, lying across the corner of the porch out of the wind. Instead of coming out to greet him, she whined repeatedly.

He opened the door of the house. "Come in for a bit." She didn't get up. Something was wrong. Was she hurt? He walked toward her. She sat up and growled low in her throat. She had never done that to him before. "Are you sick, girl?"

She looked back at something in the corner and whined softly. Over the wind he heard what sounded like a sobbing child. "What have you got there, Meeka? Let me see."

He came closer. There was a child in an Amish bonnet and bulky winter coat trying to bury herself beneath Meeka's thick fur. Where had she come from? Why was she here? He looked around. Where were her parents?